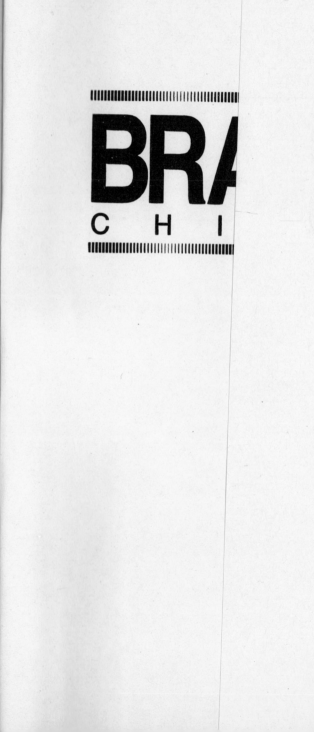

BRAIN CHILD

George Turner

WILLIAM MORROW AND COMPANY, INC. NEW YORK

Portions of Chapters 2, 4, and 5 appeared, in shorter form, in a short story, "On the Nursery Floor," in *Strange Attractors*, ed. Damien Broderick (Hale & Iremonger, Australia, 1985).

Recognizing the importance of preserving what has been written, it is the policy of William Morrow and Company, Inc., and its imprints and affiliates to have the books it publishes printed on acid-free paper, and we exert our best efforts to that end.

Library of Congress Cataloging-in-Publication Data

Turner, George.
   Brain Child / George Turner.
     p.   cm.
   ISBN 0-688-10595-5
   I. Title.
   PR9619.3.T868N87   1990
   823—dc20
                                  90-48541
                                  CIP

Printed in the United States of America

First Edition

1 2 3 4 5 6 7 8 9 10

BOOK DESIGN BY LISA STOKES

For
**The Nova Mob
(Melbourne Chapter)**

CONTENTS

"A character, to be acceptable as more than a chess piece, has to be ignorant of the future, unsure about the past, and not at all sure of what he's supposed to be doing."

—Anthony Burgess (*Times Literary Supplement,* reviewing Lucy Maddox's *Nabokov's Novels in English*)

He may be all of those things and yet remain a chess piece—a pawn—tactically useful but, in a pinch, expendable.

—G.T.

1 • POOR ORPHAN BOY

The trouble with an Orphanage up-bringing is that when the College discharges you at age eighteen you are burstingly healthy, educated to the edge of intellectual indigestion and as innocent of day-to-day reality as a blind dummy.

You read of orphanages (with a small o) in old novels and gain an impression of cruelty and exploitation visited upon children as punishment for their insolence in having been born, a picture of institutionalised revenge.

In this century, with the Population Control Laws hovering like the eye of God over the couplings even of the wedded, we children of the unwedded and the overenthusiastic are indeed born in sin but it is the parents who face fines and gaol sentences and occasionally chemical castration. Legal disapproval is at least not vented on the helpless issue by a social system that has raised contraception almost to the status of a competitive art form.

We orphans are treated very well by a State conscious of its humane obligations, but State arrangements (made, like the famous camel, by committees and ratified by point-scoring politicians) are subject to paradox, inconsistency and shortsightedness. Who, for instance, is being punished when the Illegal Issue is made a Ward of the State—the child or the parents or both? Allocation of blame tends to fall on the mother once the hypnotists and truth drug experts have extracted admissions of negligence, willful defiance of the law or unhealthy fixation on a desire to conceive. If you ask the right questions you can get any answer you require under those conditions but she is, by her answers, judged unfit to have charge of an infant.

Psychologists, nursing professionals and social workers may deride, argue and protest but the Control Laws have remained virtually unchanged since their inception in 2019, when the reality of overpopulation set the planet in a law-making frenzy. It was my luck to be born, without blessing of the State, in 2022. Hence the Orphanage.

Separated from my mother at birth, not knowing my father, I have few clear memories of childhood. Life begins at some stage of the Orphanage.

My feeling for the place where I spent my first eighteen years is without serious animus, but it was a dull place. We were schooled, we learned the elements of a variety of fairly useless manual trades ("preserving the skills" in a world gone past them), made "nature study" forays into the countryside (strictly controlled), visited the theatre ("cultural values," carefully selected) in tutorial parties, practised routine social graces on each other under the impression that people actually behaved like that and submitted to Intellectual Orientation checks twice a year. In his/her eighteenth year each of us was told, on the basis of these checks and tutorial persuasion, what profession we should desire to follow and sent into the world in a condition of smug intellectual satisfaction and total cultural ignorance.

It is hard, now, to credit the degree of innocence with which I entered the real world, harder still to realise how long it was before I took my life in hand instead of huddling timidly in a narrow circle of illusioned wimps like myself. Seven years, in fact.

The flexible outlook that the State did not give us, did not know how to give us, caused despairs and frustrations and withdrawals when we were decanted into an alien culture. One thing we did not learn in College (Orphanage was considered a disagreeable word on the outside) was who our parents were. Parentage and family were not subjects for discussion in the cloister; the College was an extended family, paternalistically guided and maternalistically cosseted. What more could a growing child need or want? The conception "parents" receded in our minds, then rushed forward in pain and anger when we joined a world where everybody had parents and a home and could produce them on demand.

Psychiatric guidance was available—at a price. Most of us had settled—or settled into—our traumas, inferiorities and alienations by the time we were earning salaries large enough to afford guidance. We floated as best we could on the tide of humanity, not so much unhappy as uncontent.

I entered journalism, more or less pushed into it by tutorial insistence, and believed that it was my free choice, the thing I wanted. Perhaps it was what I wanted. I began on the bottom rung of media cadetship, learning the uses of the multifarious hardware and software items of news-gathering equipment, learning what was news and what mere filler, learning the intricacies of "reporting" language, "slanted" language, "opinion-forming" language, "sub-libellous" language, the difference between the spoken word for the vidscreen, the written word for the print press and archival style for the accuracy of files, learning how to set traps for interviewees, how to slide beneath the guards of politicians and public personalities and how to put words into the mouths of hapless bystanders.

Three years passed in computer instruction and street technique before I was permitted to produce anything more publishable than the table of weekend football scores. Then, grudgingly, they let me loose as a police roundsman, where I could do little harm. For a while I was not very good even at that. My editor, normally a kindly man, once remarked that I must have had powerful friends to get me a job requiring an intact brain.

He was dead right, though neither of us knew it then.

I did eventually reach a reasonable level of competence and a feeling of actually earning my pay.

To the public, vidscreen reporters are a marvellous breed, sophisticated, articulate, always on top of the job. Fandom would writhe to see them putting on their personalities with their camera makeup and afterwards falling back into their commonplace selves with the sigh that goes with the removal of tight shoes. Most of them were pretty ordinary and I, who never attained the godhead of vidscreen anchorman, was more ordinary than most.

I did not plunge into the real world and achieve sophistication overnight; I plunged into a slugging round of newscub training by day and a brutal round of Degree study by night. I was ambitious, God help me. I took the full Basics Course for a General Bachelor degree—Comparative Political Systems, Major Religions and Philosophies, Scientific Literacy, Synoptic History, Psychological Systems, Citizen Law and a host of optionals—the Course that makes for a "well-rounded personality." So they say.

Somehow, in the cracks between learning and earning, I managed to dance badly, to be filled with dismay at a humanity not schooled in Orphanage perspectives and to discover, at the hands of three successive and exasperated idols of my heart, that there was much to be found out about sex as distinct from gender. I failed the day-by-day tests of life because my time was taken up with endless study and my social perceptions were embedded in the genuine but impractical morality of my Orphanage tutors. At twenty-five I remained a comparative innocent. As a newsman I knew the world's wickedness in terms of head-lines and scoopshots; as a citizen I was too busy with work and shy nervousness to observe wickedness in any sort of relationship with myself.

Then my father sent for me and the innocent past went away forever.

He sent for me a quarter of a century ago and I still do not know if I will ever be permitted to publish this account. I suspect not. The events took place in a period of a few weeks in 2047, when I was twenty-five years old, though their foundations were laid much earlier—to be precise, in 2002, when an experiment was launched. My father and I brought it to its disgraceful climax forty-five years later.

As a small child I dreamed secretly of my father's identity—a footballer or cricketer, depending on the season, always famous, popular and rich—until the gentle, irresistible pressures of College counselling closed him off along with all unproductive thinking.

So my first reaction on receiving his letter was chaotic. "Father" was an idea abandoned long ago and there were no ghosts for the letter to raise.

Mr. David Chance

Dear Son, David,
You are now sufficiently seasoned and professional to undertake the work for which you have been raised and trained.

Please present yourself at Workshop CAG 3 in the af-ternoon of Saturday next, to become acquainted with the project and with

Your loving father,
Arthur Hazard

PS: Regard this communication as inviolably confidential.

It had to be a joke and not a kindly one.

Inviolably confidential. A magisterial use of language, overblown and fake-dramatic.

Your loving father. After twenty-five years of non-existence? If not a joker, then mad.

And the signature, Arthur *Hazard.* Hazard, father of Chance? But what was the joke?

And what of this work for which I had been *raised and trained?* I had done what attracted me and done my own training.

I scratched for clues to the identity of the jester, resenting the mindless cruelty of the imposition—until a delayed impact surfaced and I toyed with the fantasy of having actually been claimed as a son by a genuine father.

Nor was Hazard a nobody. CAG 3 was an institution of note though little of its work in bio-electronics made noise in the news media and Hazard *was* the name of the equally quiet, low-profile sibling Group who operated it. The four Hazards—Arthur and Andrew, Astrid and Alice—formed a nebulous, unpublic, reserved entity of genius. (There were four other Hazards, a quartet of artists who, it was said, refused to speak to the CAG 4, professing themselves uninterested in the factory activities they referred to as "inhumanities." I knew little about them. They were not public personalities.)

Nursery Children.

We tended to forget (and, I know now, were meant to forget) that experiment in totally in vitro genetic manipulation of 2002 that ended in suicides and official double-talk winding down into silence. Now, one of the eight survivors was claiming me as a son.

Yet this was foolishness because it was known that none of the Nursery Children had ever become a parent. It was supposed by the few who thought about it at all (mainly journalists rooting through old files for some other information and lighting accidentally on these dead stories) that their genetic material was fraught with problematic genes whose transmission was banned under the Control Laws. If it should turn out not to be foolishness, I still did not care for the idea of carrying possibly monstrous genes bequeathed by an unnaturally propagated sire.

It was this pinprick of fear that prompted me to vid Public Documents and check the scanty information on my Birth Certificate.

Mother: Marion Mary Cockcroft
d. of
Charles Henry Cockcroft
and
Hazel Jane Cockcroft
Father: Unknown

Any man could claim me—if he had a reason.

I did the obvious, called CAG 3, to be answered by a hard computer voice, poorly humanised: "We do not accept unreserved calls. Please leave your name and vid number and state which Project Officer you wish to consult. Your call will be returned at the recipient's earliest convenience."

What happens to people like that if you are trying to tell them that a man with a gun is jimmying open their front door?

Thinking myself spry and cunning, I said, "I wish to speak to whoever claims to be the parent of David Chance," and for my trouble heard the irritated buzz of a vid-memory flipping through its files. It clacked back at me, "Mr. Arthur predicted your call and instructed that you be requested to confirm your appointment for Saturday next. Do you so confirm?"

Like a jerked puppet, I answered, "Yes," and the damned answering file cut the connection before I could think up a further protest.

At this stage intelligence should have dictated that I take the letter to the police for routine vetting but I was innocent and something of a romantic, conditions that do nothing for intelligence. In fact I was becoming belatedly taken with the possibility of having an in vitro monster for a father, and let the genes fall where they might.

On Saturday I caught the midday bus for the ninety-minute run to Westerton, the nearest town to CAG 3, and in that dusty, half-asleep farming centre hired its single taxi to carry me the dozen or so kilometres to the workshop.

It is not easy now to recover my feelings on that afternoon journey. Later events remain in sharp detail because they taxed my concentration and more than once threatened my life, but this was so far only a curious happening that might turn out to be a case of simple human error. I know I was no longer sure that I wanted a father, even as a biological showpiece; he might emerge as a fussy, demanding nuisance, though the few sketchy profiles I had been able to unearth painted the Hazards as grimly reclusive.

Hasty rummaging through old newspaper morgues and later computerised files had produced little more than could be called common knowledge. The Nursery Children had been created by genetic manipulation; they were born in 2002; some lived, some died; in 2022, with all of them just a score of years old, the most brilliant quartet committed suicide under circumstances never plumbed, at any rate for public consumption. There was more than that and much more to be discovered in time, but the detailed story is best told as I stumbled, fell and guessed my way through it. The bare bones suffice for the moment.

Of the entire experimental brood only two Groups still survived in 2047: the four artists who revolutionised twenty-first-century aesthetics and the four experimental scientists (one of them Arthur Hazard) who designed and exploited the discipline of bio-electronics.

An odd piece of information that surfaced was that CAG 3 was in fact the old Nursery in which the fabulous children had been created, a fact that had its place in happenings to come.

The building was nearly invisible from the road, set well back in a huge block I estimated at about ten hectares, surrounded by a three-metre hedge and guarded by sliding steel gates and cameras. My taxi driver was recognised by the gate robot as a regular arrival but I was not; I had to demonstrate my identity by documented ordeal of some exhaustive questioning before it admitted—grudgingly, I swear—that I was expected, and allowed our car into the vast, flat space surrounding the workshop.

Beyond the building itself there were only a few outlying sheds and in the distance a handful of sheep keeping the grass down. The whole area was repellently bare save where, huddling round the building itself, well-kept flower beds made a lonely human touch.

The Nursery—the Hazards still called it that—was an unlovable building, a single-storeyed structure of weathered concrete walls broken by windows at mathematically even distances along the wide facade. Given bars, they would have cried out gaol. A view from an angle of the drive showed the Nursery to be extremely deep, running back a good hundred metres into the surrounding grass.

I visualised workers by the hundred; there were in fact just four, the Hazards.

At the top of the front steps stood a tall man in a ragged and dirty dust coat. I saw, as the first hint of an exotic personality, that he stood perfectly still while I paid the driver and walked up the short path between the flower beds—carnations, I remember, and gladioli—and halted at the bottom step.

His stillness impressed me as total self-control, the unnatural immobility of a man who never made an unnecessary movement. I did not believe that by the wildest accident we could be father and son.

He was forty-five that year and as offbeat a human figure as might be assembled in a careless moment, a collector's item. He was taller than I and large-boned and thin, his wrists and knuckles were knobs and his face a tight mask—a peculiarly brown mask, not the slightly soiled mahogany of sunburn or the darkish brown of, say, an Indian with the tinge of melanin, but a dark, distinctly tan colour. A portrait painter would have mixed a hint of deep red-orange into the skin tone. Faintly negroid features framed green eyes—dauntingly, brilliantly green—under a frizz of African wool. But wherever did you see ripe-tomato-coloured African wool?

Against him I faded in ordinariness. Middle height, middle weight, blue eyes, nondescript brown hair and definitely Caucasian features made me the man unnoticed in a crowd, save for one unwelcome distinction—I was and am not albino but cursed with a very fair, tender skin that suffers in sunlight and itches intolerably with heavy perspiration.

We had each two arms, two legs and one head and scarcely another item in common. He stared down at me with those discomfiting eyes until I said, because sooner or later one of us had to speak, "I am David Chance."

He answered, moving only his lips, in a careful voice, as if not yet fully proficient in a second language, "I know that. I am Arthur Hazard."

It was like being addressed by a door robot and I made one of those uneasy jokes that try to cover nervousness, "Hazard and Chance! Is my luck holding?"

His face flickered briefly in what might have been a

smile, hastily sketched and discarded. "It probably is. Your surname is indeed a, er, frivolity of sorts; it was necessary to name you at a moment's notice." The green eyes registered my astonishment and his expression flickered again with what could have been an attempt, not quite managed, of ruefulness. "Not a very good jest, perhaps. Your uncle Andrew has studied that aspect of the culture more closely than I."

Whatever that might mean I left for later discovery. "You claim to be my father?"

His voice took on an edge of testiness. "You already know that."

"I have been told that. I need proof."

"Ah. Yes. Naturally so." The idea seemed not to have occurred to him until that moment. He moved very slightly, thrusting his narrow head minutely towards me. "Can you read a genetic match chart?"

"Roughly. I'm no expert."

"That will suffice." He seemed to realise that he was still peering down at me from four steps above. "Come up."

I marched up the steps and stopped before him. After a hesitation he put out his hand with a quick, stiff motion as though remembering that a social gesture was expected and getting on with it before the lapse became embarrassing. As if, also, he did not really care to touch me.

"Welcome home," he said. Not quite believing my ears, I took his hand. "Son," he added, and I was sure the word had just occurred to him. He had an extraordinarily strong grip for such a thin streak of a man but now seemed unsure what next was expected of him. He settled rather tentatively for "We should go inside."

I followed him through thick steel sliding doors, thinking that once I knew what this freak wanted of me I could vid the taxi and go home. Whatever Arthur Hazard might think, "home" was not CAG 3.

What plainly had once been a large reception area inside the front door was now a bare space without table, chair or sign that such civilised excesses had ever been there. In the middle of the floor stood the only decoration in that denuded cube of a hall, a large arrangement of flowers and ferns making a desperate glow in an impersonal void.

I said, if only to hear a voice affirming the existence of life beyond bare necessity, "The flowers are beautiful."

Arthur Hazard commented without slowing or turning round, "My sisters arrange them. They are your aunts, of course. They care for such activities."

I gathered that the female determinant gene presented in two of the quadruplet encouraged trivial, time-wasting fancies.

He led me into a huge room whose function I could not guess because its state of disorder disguised all intention. There were armchairs and straight-backed chairs, desks and small tables and one very large table set up with a drafting complex; there were racks and cupboards and a couple of structures whose purpose was unclear. Lying on all of these and piled on the floor as well were files, books, loose sheets, disks, tapes, recording apparatus, vid projectors and anonymous pieces of what looked like samplings from an electronics workshop. The three inside walls carried vidscreens, one of them the largest I had ever seen, about three metres by five and equipped with more special-function terminals than I had thought could exist.

One of the aunts had made her mark on the room with a tall crystal vase of gladioli on the mantelpiece over an old-fashioned fireplace. A more masculine touch was the clutter of dirty cleaning rags, yellow with chemicals, black with grease, tossed around it. The fireplace itself contained a self-heating coffee percolator and half a dozen cups, mostly used.

The man who called himself my father said, probably

thinking it an explanation, "I do most of my work here. Practical laboratory confirmation is most often the outcome of orderly thought and computation."

It was safest to say nothing; if his peculiar genius reached peak performance in chaos, so be it. (Not so. There was, I understood later, complete order here. He worked on half a dozen projects simultaneously and each was deployed in a self-contained sector of the room, with all relevant tools and references assembled conveniently to hand and eye. He knew where every item was and why it was in that particular place. It did not take long to find in him a mind so orderly as to be dismaying.)

"You shall have proof," he said. "Sit down." He indicated a chair opposite one of the smaller screens and perched himself on the edge of a desk that (like every other, I now noticed) sported a full console of remote controls, and punched Public Documents. At Selection he punched my name and National ID number.

I asked at once, "How did you get my personal number?"

"I asked for it."

"For Private Data? Asked who?"

He turned his green eyes on me, considering ... what? "In good time," he said. "The Hazards are not ciphers in the State. What we need, commonly we get."

He whipped through the Data File to the genetic diagram, the personal "fingerprint," and there I was, reduced to the ultimate simplicity, an assemblage of symbols on a screen. He said, "Check the diagram against your ID card."

"No need. I know who I am."

"But, do I?"

At the confession that he also needed confirmation I began to believe that this fantasy might be truth. I slipped my card into the Spot Check—and the two diagrams coincided exactly.

"Thank you. One must be careful when claiming sight unseen. Now, Marion Mary Cockcroft." As her data came up, he said, "She died within a day of your birth."

"Of what?"

He answered without looking at me, "Of, I think, an unwillingness to live."

"You were with her?"

"No." I waited for more but it seemed that the question had been answered and that was the end of it. He said, "Here is your proof."

The genetic diagram of Marion Mary Cockcroft occupied the right-hand side of the screen, major dominants and recessives coloured and tagged. Her eyes, I saw, had been blue and their colour had dominated in mine over the striking, uncanny but recessive (thank God), green of the Hazards.

Before he could bring up the third diagram I said, "My Birth Certificate says Father Unknown and Arthur Hazard is not listed in Public Access Files. Such privacy!"

"It is a necessary privilege. As young people we had enough of being treated as sideshows for idiots. Part of our contract with the State guarantees respect for our need of, uh, insulation."

Insulation seemed to mean something more than mere privacy. He was not a man to warm to.

He placed his ID card in Spot Check and his genetic diagram appeared with his name, birthdate and place of birth: *Arthur Hazard; 4th July, 2002; Victorian Institute of Advanced Genetic Manipulation.*

"For *advanced*," he said, though without real rancour, "read *hit or miss*. Now, can you match the diagrams?"

"Not very well; there's stuff in yours that I don't follow."

"Unnatural stuff?" A hint of mockery there?

"Unfamiliar."

"Of course. Induced hormone balances and gland secretions produced characteristics in the Nursery Children rarely seen in *Homo sapiens*. Nothing actually new, more like rarities that would normally breed out from normal populations as sports, unintended variations born of the operators having no certainty of what they were about—much less certainty than they thought they had—no sensible appreciation of the millions of side-effect combinations possible to even the smallest interference with multiple-gene expression, my very obvious hair and eye colours, for instance, or the excess melanin in my skin reverting strongly to the extreme pallor of yours. Superficially we are unlike but the cross-interactions tell the tale."

He wiped my diagram off the centre of the screen, leaving the two parental images at left and right, then built up my central assemblage again from the parental templates, explaining each match and variation. Some of the multiple-influence cross effects were hard to grasp but he carried me through the buildup of each characteristic until I understood it, right through to the point-for-point identification of myself.

I contemplated the indisputable evidence that this freak was my father, feeling like something poured out of a bottle from a laboratory shelf, not at all like anybody's son, more like the end product of a cheapjack manufacturing process.

"Enough," I said. He switched off the screen and we stared at each other—warily on my side, bleakly on his—until I asked, "What do you want?" and knew I sounded harsh and quarrelsome. One of the penalties of social insufficiency is an awareness of your lack, an insecurity that raises personality prickles where an ounce of wisdom would counsel a bland approach.

My father's own insufficiency—not innocence because there was nothing innocent in him—was in its essentials sheer ignorance. He just did not know what reactions were expected of him, but it took time for me to divine this; his hesitations now seemed simple dithering. At last he said, as if it were the best he could do in the way of a holding tactic, "You wanted to be sure."

"I'm sure. What then?" I was never an aggressive young man; my truculence covered a lack of direction as floundering as his.

At least he tried: "I thought that you would . . . that you would welcome a fa"— he balked at the word, strange to his tongue, and brought it out as —"a family connection."

He was at a loss because an expectation had failed. I had not cried *Daddy!* and leapt into his arms. "I was reared in a State Orphanage. Our thinking was gently but effectively directed away from family fantasies. You couldn't know that, but it was sensible."

"Sensible? Yes." Something flashed in the green eyes, perhaps a mild dislike.

"And now, after twenty-five years, you announce yourself and expect a sentimental reunion."

He thought about it; I could see him thinking over an aspect he had not considered in his planning. And when he had done thinking he had the situation rationalised. "Your growth was watched. Do you imagine that the son of a Nursery Child would be of no interest to—to scientists and—to ourselves?"

"The folklore says the Nursery Children had no offspring, in fact no sex lives because they didn't fancy close contact with common humanity."

"Folklore fostered by the State. Tales of mutant babies would have kept talk alive and media noses to the trail. You are the only one to have been born; some trouble was taken to have others aborted. But that is another tale. As your progress and abilities became apparent I was able to exert a discreet pressure on your training and to guide you into journalism. Yours was not entirely a free choice of profession."

I should have been angry but felt deflated, a pricked balloon shown that all its ego was hot air and its decision-making nonexistent, its free will bobbing at the end of a remote parental string. "But why?"

He had no hesitation over his answer and no realisation of it as another body blow to pride. "It was necessary that you be properly trained for the work required of you."

"Required by me?"

"Yes."

"And if I am not interested?"

He thought awhile on that in unruffled stillness. When he was ready he said, "I have been mistaken in thinking that a mutual affection was a natural concomitant between human parent and child. You must understand that we Hazards mix very little in human society—" (That iswhat he said: *human society,* as of some other, lesser breed.) "—and so we make observational errors. The literature also encourages the concept of innate family bonds. I imagined you would welcome me."

So I would have done . . . if he had been a working man, a clerk, a shopkeeper, somebody's gardener, even one of my hero footballers, but not this changeling curiosity.

Then he took me by surprise. He turned his face to look at me and his expression altered, not greatly but enough to suggest a hint of suffering, of helplessness in his inability to reach me. And I, like a cretin, felt a twinge of guilt at my rigidity in refusing to meet him halfway. I said, "For sweet sanity's sake, man! Do you expect to wipe off a lifetime's neglect in a few minutes?"

He nodded. "I have been clumsy and ignorant." His face did its unpractised best to accept blame and to plead— and to this day I do not know how much was genuine and how much a quick change of direction. My determination to concede nothing was weakened. I said, "Just tell me what you want of me."

And he did.

And I became enthralled. Taken. Hooked.

He began, "The Nursery Children are an incident that happened long ago, a failed experiment best ignored."

He had surprised me. "Failed?"

"What else?"

"The work of the Hazards makes a pretty daunting record of bio-electronic innovation for anyone who digs out the reports. They add up to genius."

He said sharply, "They do not! We are not a quartet of genius; we are four people with a practical cast of mind that enables us to work efficiently in empiric areas where accurate observation and clear thinking are required. It is an innate capacity, no more. Genius is something else. C Group had that but what it was or what it was good for I do not know. I don't think they understood it themselves."

That rang a bell in my scrappy research. "That's the Group that killed themselves."

"So you have done some poking in the files."

"Just that. Time was short."

"You need much more. The Nursery Project aimed to produce superior intellects; instead, it produced mutants with green eyes and strange hair colours and minds that were not superior to those of general humanity but different from them—and C Group, that *was* superior and monstrous in its fashion. We and the B Group Hazards, the four artists, are unable—if you like, unwilling—to accommodate ourselves to human cultural requirements. We think differently. We do not accept your values and cannot live by them." He fixed that bright green gaze on me. "Do you understand that?"

"No." In time I understood but not then; it sounded too much like a cult manifesto, a fringe vanity. Yet the work of these people earned staggering sums for the State and for industry each year ... I temporised, "You're strange to me. Give me time."

He agreed, with himself rather than with me. "I must observe more closely, make concessions."

"Why concessions?"

"If you cannot come to me I must try to move closer to you, to empathise with how you think and feel."

To him that was a plain statement of intention; to me it carried a hint of eeriness, as of blind men groping, each in his personal darkness.

He said strongly, "This is digression. To the point: The history of the Nursery Children has never been written, or at any rate never published, with the result that much of it is unknown even to those who lived it, spending our first eighteen years in this building. We were watched by physicians and psychiatrists by day and night, people who did not and still do not grasp the meaning of much of what they saw and recorded. There are questions: Why did Conrad of C Group spend years gaining the confidence and subservience of a Nursery gardener? Who started the grass fire that burned out the grounds and much of the local area? And why? What went on here after A and B Groups were freed into the world but C was kept behind? What was done to C Group? Why did they kill themselves? Those are unknowns."

On his own ground of knowledge he spoke rapidly and clearly, even with some expression; only our personal relationship broke him down to hesitation and blundering.

I suggested that after so long a time facts would have been dispersed, memories would have faded and answers would be hard to find.

"Facts do not vanish. What is not in data files is locked in heads. Old trails can be reopened when those concerned think them forgotten, when their sense of urgent secrecy has subsided."

"If, that is, you know who to ask."

"I know."

"So, why don't you ask?"

"I would not be answered. Being who I am, my motives would be questioned. But a biographer, a young man on his way to full professionalism, eager and researching a book . . ."

I think his glance was meant to be quizzical; the effect was of facial muscles creaking with disuse.

"Or a reporter," I said.

"Just so. People talk to media operatives; they hope for thirty seconds' fame on the newsvids. They say the little bit more than they should; they make mistakes, revealing the existence of the overgrown trail."

He was almost eager in his minimal way.

And I . . . I was more than interested. I was strongly attracted by the facet he had not mentioned, the newsman's thirst to be first with a secret. A mass suicide, a strange relationship, a suspicious fire—media souls have been sold for less. And he leaned forward to say, with just a touch of concern, "There may be an element of . . . um . . . resistance. Unwillingness."

It was the one thing needed to trap a media man's attention. Or, if you like, a young fool's attention. The project assumed challenge; it became desirable, mildly adventurous. But I asked only, "In what way?"

Playing it cool. We media types prided ourselves on playing it—everything—cool.

"There could be, if you are perceived as encroaching on secrets, a shutting off of confidence. Hostility. Perhaps violence."

"I have been thrown out of a house by a resentful union official. It hurt. But a week later he talked to me."

"No doubt you have techniques for such occasions."

If you call aggressive use of unwelcome publicity a

technique, so be it. It works. "Resistance means there's a secret; you look for alternative approaches."

"That is your expertise; I cannot advise."

"But you can advise me what I'm looking for."

"Answers to the questions I spoke of. Perhaps others also."

"And where should I start?"

You can see that I had walked myself headfirst into the job without so much as saying, *Yes, I'll do it.* My father was a persuasive man—meaning, he knew which buttons to press. I was to learn that all the Hazards had their peculiar modes of persuasiveness, but that was still in the future.

He said, "I suggest Samuel Armstrong."

That was a shocker. Armstrong had been intimately tied up with the Nursery Project but now tended to make himself out of bounds to newsmen. "The long lifer? The media can't get near him. It would be like trying to get a door-knock interview with the Pope. He talks to nobody."

"He will talk to you. We will offer him a bait he cannot refuse."

"Your name?"

For the first time he raised his voice. "Certainly not! Under no circumstances must our relationship as family or in business interest be mentioned. You must be a lone researcher, nothing more."

"Why?"

"Mention the Hazards' interest and nobody concerned with us will talk to you."

I asked again, "Why?"

"You will discover that for yourself."

"Tell me now."

"No. Your lack of special knowledge is your most disarming weapon. You will make simple errors of ignorance and people will fill you in; others will tell you lies and when you report the lies to me we will understand what they are hiding. Go armed with knowledge and everybody with a secret will suspect your motives. Go to them as an innocent with a quest. That must be genuine."

He was right; he had thought it through, even to the value of innocence. What a savage joke that was to be before we were done.

I said, "Perhaps I should even write the book," and was not prepared for him to agree.

"Yes; a work in progress will be proof of your bona fides."

Again he was right. The idea of nosing down trails eventually to hit the public with a book became part of the attraction of the job. The sucker bait.

I told him I would have to spend time researching background; a genuine biographer would have all the publicly available information at his fingertips. He told me to use the CAG terminals and that he could probably gain me access to a few genetic research files on the Restricted Index.

"I'll have to work from home. I have a job, remember."

He said simply, "Leave it."

"And live on what?"

"I am a rich man."

Yes, of course he must be. Nevertheless, "I need a job in order to keep my Media Accreditation. Without that I couldn't interview a kerbside busker."

He was taken aback; this was outside his isolated experience. He recovered quickly. "How are freelance journalists accommodated?"

"They have a separate union with special Cards, but I'm no specialist."

"Become one—a science journalist."

"I don't know enough."

He was patient. "I will provide you with information

at the cutting edge of Hazard disciplines. You will write it up."

(And that is how David Chance became, in a matter of weeks, the most sought after science journalist in Australia.)

There was more talk, of course, but I was committed and knew it. That night I posted in my resignation, losing a month's pay in lieu of notice.

A bed had been prepared for me in one of the disused offices, as though my acquiescence had never been in doubt, and in the morning I vidded the Westerton general store for changes of clothing to be sent to CAG 3, charged to my father's account.

Then I began the background research.

You burn your bridges, then regret having crossed them. My resignation was in the mail, my acceptance of the Hazard investigation was binding in all but a signature on a contract and my acceptance of Arthur Hazard as "family" (a word with uncomfortable, unexpected aspects) a settled fact—yet on the Sunday morning I had doubts. Behind them was an obscure suspicion, unjustifiable but strong, that I had been conned.

Perhaps I had (but to what end?) and perhaps I merely wanted an excuse to back out.

For one thing, I did not trust the man. His fleeting fits of human emotion did not sit well with his cool pragmatism or conceal a predetermined logic that emotional factors would not alter. (Or did I merely recoil from his green eyes and unnaturally red hair?) Nor did I enjoy the humiliation of having been treated as a useful item in an intellectual exercise, guided into a career, left to mature and lifted out when ready.

Above all, there was his assumption that he had only to declare himself my father and my natural affection would pop up from nowhere. Whether or not it existed on his side I could not make out; it seemed to be grasped at on necessary occasions, like a forgotten stage direction. He was who he said he was, no doubt of that, but did he give a damn for his son or did he merely observe a manipulator's right to skim the profits?

I was still in a haze of indecision when the parcel of clothing arrived from the store, conveying mutely that I had joined the game and must play it. (There was also, unacknowledged, the young man's welcoming of novelty for novelty's sake, as well as the engaging hint of intrigue and double-dealing in ferreting out information from unwilling or even hostile possessors.)

Perhaps Arthur Hazard was genuine in his fumbling unfamiliarity with common relationships and I was at fault in not meeting him halfway.

That was more easily thought than achieved because I had no way of knowing what a son should feel for his father. "Father" was an unfamiliar species, to be kept under observation until its powers and habits were understood.

Likewise, "Mother." She was another imponderable, a causative essential but unknown to me. On that first day she had edged into the conversation and edged out of it in a sentence or two. Who had Marion Mary Cockcroft been?

When I asked him he frowned as if trying to place her, perhaps wondering why the devil I should want to know, and eventually said, "I think the Cockcrofts were originally a Yorkshire family."

"That tells me nothing."

"What information do you need?"

"How you met, what she looked like, what was between you, why she died."

He seemed totally nonplussed, as though he was not sure of any of these things. He sounded vaguely experimental when he said, "As young folk, that is to say at eighteen, our A Group was very promiscuous. B Group seemed not at all interested in sexual adventure; indeed they recoiled from it." He stopped there, watching my face to see if that might be enough, saw that it was not and went on, "We were ignorant of some necessary cultural facts. Our watchdog scientists were so busy observing and collating that important areas of our education were neglected. For instance, we left the Nursery ignorant of the implications of the Control Laws and nebulous about contraception. There were certain awkwardnesses before administrative officers interfered and arranged more discreet contacts."

"You mean they made sure there were no children to complicate the experiment before all the results were in."

"That would have been part of their intention."

"But I am an exception."

"Yes."

"How? Why?"

"She carried you to term before acknowledging me as your father. Once you were born, even the judiciary balked at having you killed."

After which beneficence, I thought, my luck had run out. "And my mother? What was she like?"

He said with dumbfounding vagueness, "I recall her as a very good-natured girl, foolish but eager to please. I visited her on several occasions."

Such cool reportage would have angered a saint. "You make her sound like a prostitute or a casual pickup."

"Not a prostitute; she did not demand money. A pickup, perhaps. In a bar. And why not? At eighteen were your attachments more lasting?"

I did not confess that at eighteen I had been a vacillating virgin. I probably sounded surly as I answered, "I hoped it might have been a relationship with a little feeling in it."

"Unfortunately the feeling was wholly hers. She allowed herself to become pregnant when as a single woman she had no breeding right. Those early applications of the Laws were severe."

All this in his neutral voice—communication just a little livelier than computer-vox—without a definable expression on his tight, thin face.

"I offered her an abortion but she refused."

So he had made the sensible suggestion but she had persisted in foolishness. Not his fault, now, was it?

I said, "She wanted a child. Pregnant women often do. Even the Control Laws have had to recognise that."

"Not just a child. She wanted *my* child."

There was honesty for you! "The poor, luckless woman loved you!"

His expression did not change but he paused, searching for exact meaning, a stop-go habit that could madden conversation. Then he read me a little horror of a lecture. "Perhaps. People become sexually involved, highly emotional for a short period, then the . . . phase . . . passes. Is that love? Or is it a period of unbalanced stimulus? I think it is that. Love may sow its first seed in bed but an enduring emotion requires acquaintance in calmer temper, a time of knowing and adjusting."

Passion from the outside, looking in. I said, "*You* certainly weren't in love."

A little flash of surprise in him suggested that I had implied the impossible but all he said was, "It was hormonal, a passing thing, a relief."

Keeping the sap pressure at a comfortable level.

I thought I understood. The situation, in one form or another, has been commonplace since the caveman sorted it out no better than we—one loves and one is beloved and, lo, a bastard is born—but I could not adopt his practical standpoint. My mind responded too sharply to the terror of the unloved woman, menaced by the law and unwanted by the friends to whom her condition made her a discomfort and possibly a danger. That she was my mother did not impinge too greatly on my parentless void but I was struck deeply by the anguish of a woman sunk in useless love and hysterical defiance.

He said, "Her mental state was impenetrable."

To him, perhaps; only to him. "She thought the child in her belly would hold you a little longer."

He may not have been capable of such reasoning; that would not be his fault but for an irrational moment I hated him.

"So it did; she had to be cared for." Did he realise I had not meant that? After a silence he said, "It is a dreadful thing to be aware of another's overmastering desire and be unable to offer comfort."

My attitude somersaulted; he had not been passionless but trapped in another's passion. That, too, is an old human story. He had to spoil it by adding, "I was most careful after that experience."

A very practical mentality; his women must have known what it meant to be screwed by a robot. I said, "Go on."

"With abortion refused, there was nothing for it but to remove her to a public hospital. It was a troublesome birth. She died. I think she was allowed to die. In that way she was spared a prison sentence and population balance was preserved—one for one. You lived."

There is no pleasure in learning that your life is the price of another's death. "What did they do to you?"

"Nothing. The law restrained birth, not sexual congress, because contraception was simple and freely available, so . . . does that seem unfair?"

"In happy pragmatism, no. You could argue that my mother, by refusing abortion, created the circumstances of her death and was therefore responsible for it. Yet it was unfair."

He changed direction neatly. "Unfair to you also?

Reared in creches, educated in an Orphanage, never knowing who paid the bills, ejected at eighteen—with a useful education, admittedly—to make your way? Doesn't that seem unfair?"

"Not greatly." I had little feeling about it. They say that what you haven't had you don't miss; my life had seemed normal because I knew no other. Yet I wanted to evoke some feeling in him. "Perhaps a father to belong to, to run to, to be hugged by might have made a difference."

"I could not know such things then; I begin to understand now. Then you were a duty and I fulfilled it. We believe in meeting our obligations."

"Meaning you and the other three?" As yet they were unseen, hearsay. "They helped?"

"We conferred on consequences and possibilities, but you were otherwise no responsibility of theirs."

Quite a family, tarred together, it seemed, with the same pragmatic brush.

There is not much to tell about the events—more like nonevents—of my ten-day stay in CAG 3. The time passed in preparing print articles and vid treatments from the "cutting edge" information my father fed to me with the logical clarity of a coldly perfect instructor; the rest was spent in researching the background of the book whose compilation was to be my interviewer's calling card. There is no point in setting out here what I found out because it was only what anyone could have discovered, given the motive, and in any case all that is relevant will appear in its proper place in the narrative. My father's name opened a few Restricted files but the information in them was as obsolete as Restricted data usually is. I know now that other, more secret files existed but he said nothing about those.

A nonevent worth mentioning is my failure to see Uncle Andrew or Aunts Astrid and Alice. When I suggested that I should meet them my father asked, "Why?" and I recalled being "no responsibility of theirs."

"It just seems strange not to when we are in the same building."

"They are busy people. They have their own areas and establishments." It was the blank lack of comprehension of a man without a relevant culture.

"You don't meet socially, fraternise?"

"For what? There are occasional cross-disciplinary problems calling for meeting and attention."

I let the subject drop.

One day I saw a white-coated woman vanishing down a corridor, and that was all of my contact with the rest of the family at that time. It was not a family you became a member of; you merely added yourself to the current listing and from there on did your own thing, walled off by silence from a kin who would make themselves known if they happened to need you.

Nor did I see much of my father. If I needed him I could use the in-house vid, but soon learned that only urgency was excuse enough.

When, after five days, I asked to see his work area he asked (inevitably), "Why?"

"A man's workplace tells you something of him."

"Indeed? Some media technique of observation?"

"A human commonplace."

"Ah." I think he filed the answer for later processing, added it to his data on *Homo sapiens*. (Which raised the question: What species did he imagine he belonged to?)

He decided that I could look the place over so long as I kept out of his way, did not otherwise disturb him and touched nothing.

There were two work areas, a workshop of spotless maintenance and bloodlessly efficient layout leading into a biology lab glittering with glass, stainless steel, ceramics and a dozen or more fixtures I could not recognise. I looked, wondered, kept out of his way, touched nothing and went out as ignorant as I went in.

I was fed up of Arthur Hazard and CAG 3 when the time came to leave. Then, in contradiction of all his bland remoteness, his assurance faltered. "Perhaps it is too soon; we should rethink our preparations, double-check."

He appeared to register a hint of concern. For me? If so, he wasted time and words. I had my scripts for my journalistic assault on the science media, my head full of facts, figures and guesswork about the history of the Nursery and my curiosity fully roused about what I might turn up as I dug into the memories of others. I was sniffing the wind and panting to go. I did not have to pretend impatience.

"There's nothing left to add, to plan, to guard against. I'll begin tomorrow."

He looked down from his bony height, eyes not quite meeting mine though the brown face wore its usual tell-nothing mask, and said as if he hauled words from some internal abyss, "I will worry about you, Son."

That was the second time he had used the word, but I was not about to welter in belated sentiment. "For a quarter of a century you kept out of my way. It's too late to turn paternal now."

As usual, he selected what he chose to answer. "I watched your progress."

"At a safe distance."

"I would not have known how to treat you."

I could believe that. "You're getting what you wanted, in cold blood; be content with that. In any case, I'm committed. To pull back now would be to leave a gap; I would never know what might have been."

Thinking back on it, that must have satisfied him immensely. He shrugged, perhaps pleased to have the onus of decision removed from him, and said only, "Be careful," in a tone somewhere between a plea and an order.

He was impatient of emotional waste, yet there were dregs of feeling in his tepid veins and either he had developed some thin affection for me or had decided that I would react usefully to his sporadic attempts at what he thought rational sentiment. I still didn't trust him very far though I think I had begun to like him after a fashion, if scarcely after the fashion of a son.

"Of course," I said, cocksure, and then, curious to see what the effect might be, "I'll get in touch when I have something for you, Dad."

I had not used the word before. He looked hard at me, into me, deciding what might lie behind the flourish and probably concluding (rightly) that I was game playing. He twitched the midwinter smile on and off and said, "Better that I contact you, as arranged."

The Westerton taxi was at the door when I made the last attempt to surprise response from him. Probing was useless against his stonewall self-possession but I had to try.

"With me questioning and digging and pretending to want one thing while I listen for hints of another—what are you really after?"

What I got for my trouble sounded like nonsense. "It has taken you a long time to ask that. Please be more alert. I want Young Feller's legacy."

It took me a moment to sort that very wispy reference from the mass of Nursery data in my head. "You're joking!"

The "legacy" was a rumour, scarcely solid enough to be called even that, a whisper that had surfaced after C Group killed themselves. There had been some speculation on the more sensational vids that the brilliant children had left behind them some kind of testament of their "difference." It was the type of folklore outcropping that piles mystery on a mystery, elaborating the theme of *the Administration isn't telling all it knows—wheels within wheels—more there than meets the eye* . . . It had not caught the public fancy and had died for lack of a reasonable basis.

He said, "I am not joking."

"It was just a media yarn, a fairy tale."

"So?" I gathered that I was being mildly derided. "It may be better that you believe so, but be alert for any mention of it. However, do not ever raise the subject yourself."

"Why should I? Unless there is information you are not giving me?"

"Since you do not believe in the legacy, such information would be meaningless. Better so."

"But you believe that the Young Feller—Conrad—left something behind?"

"Having known him, as far as knowing him was possible, I cannot think otherwise."

At the time it seemed the most human statement I had heard from him, revealing an everyday weakness, the clutching at a dream because he wished to believe a reality existed.

He left me standing on the porch without so much as a good-bye, possibly unable to see that the word served any useful purpose.

I got into the taxi and started down the road of lost innocence where waited for me the frightened, the greedy, the mad, the corrupt and the dead.

2 • AN EX-MINISTER FOR SCIENCE AND DEVELOPMENT

1.

From the workshop/laboratory I went home to my Melbourne flat by roundabout ways. I spoke to such other tenants of the building as I met, establishing my return from a northern holiday whose actuality was attested by fresh filmpacks and could be, if necessary, proven by dated receipts and travel documents. (My father gave good service in the forgery department, whether by his own efforts or the talents of others I did not enquire. "When you set out to live a lie," he remarked at one point, "be aware only of the lie-as-reality and think only when necessary of the reality behind it. Believe what you say and do, if others are to believe it." A sound creed for a con man.)

Mail waited in the telebasket, most of its content predictable: A letter from my last editor damning my stupidity in cutting out too early from the safety of a regular wage packet, a standard acceptance letter from the Freelance News Media Association with a statement of fees and the required legal warning about responsibility for libel, a swag of letters from agents entreating first use of my irreplaceable talents (at 15 percent of the take) and the usual collection of junk. I sent a thank-you note to the editor, telling him not to fret because I had saleable work lined up (true), and despatched a membership fee to the FNMA. The rest, from vultures and timewasters, needed no answering.

There remained the one real letter—in an envelope, old style, sealed and addressed and engraved with the sender's Order of Australia emblem. It said that the Honourable Samuel Armstrong (an Order of Australia on his chest and a lifetime of dirty politics in his head) would be pleased to make an appointment. I should vid his secretary . . .

I had no idea what my move might have been if he had refused the appointment.

I had written from CAG at my father's insistence (but giving only my home address), citing my credentials, outlining my proposed book, stressing my interest in the lack of information amounting to mystery surrounding C Group and their unexplained end—and stressing very much the kind of ferreting possible to investigative journalism. My father had said that mention of the C Group babies would hook him infallibly and his certainty had infected me.

Away from him I had become less sure. Now it seemed that the hook had been better baited than I had allowed, though a full generation had grown up since the politician's connection with the babies had ceased.

With a sense of opening the game I keyed the Armstrong vid number, to be greeted by a blank screen with just the suggestion of colour telling that a connection had been made, that I was being identified by number backtrack and that my status did not warrant immediate visual contact, so it was no surprise when a cold female voice said, "Mr. Chance? Concerning your request for an interview with Mr. Armstrong?"

"That's so."

"He will see you on Friday morning at ten-fifteen in

the Private Office at his Toorak home. Please be prompt; Mr. Armstrong is a busy man."

At the Toorak home! Yes, he was interested. "Thank you."

She cut off at once. Nobody today would snub a caller with the blank-screen gambit but the mid-century saw a distinct rise in class consciousness as social mores shifted from the cash axis to the public honour axis and all sorts of "honoured" nonentities developed means of keeping the honourless—snooping journalists, for instance—in their places. It was a good period to live through, if only for the sigh of relief when it finally went down the drain of popular derision.

I had two days to fill and spent them writing up notes (dictated by my father for the purpose of providing me with a credible income while I did his work) into half a dozen articles on trends in technology, mostly in his own field of bio-electronics. Most of the material rode at the forefront of the art and would sell to the popular science media with no chance of refusal; with my father's knowledge on tap I might become a power in the technical writing area.

Looking back over what I have written so far—the chippy prose of a not quite arrogant but far from humble young man full of beans and snap judgments, with never a doubt of his ability to take on his mental weight in intelligent wildcats—I recall a first uncertainty.

It was not quite doubt that came to me that Friday morning so much as a realisation that I had so far put behind me—that this matter could turn dangerous. My father was sure that it would not while I played within his rules; after all, he had pointed out, he would hardly send his son out in risk and ignorance of what he might be called upon to face. I thought now that he would do just that if he had calculated the chances, decided that the risk was minimal and that nothing would be gained by alarm-

ing me in advance. I did not see him as a soulless manipulator who would sacrifice others at whim, but a little
uncomfortably as a man whose thought processes were not
like mine or yours and whose morality might have little to
do with everyday notions of right and wrong. He was no
monster; he simply saw things differently. Which made
him, as he said of my mother, impenetrable.

So to Toorak I went, telling myself that this was a
perfectly normal interview and that nobody could imagine
otherwise, and not quite believing it.

The year was 2047 and it was winter, a season usually
kind to my sensitive skin. The temperature that day was in
the twenties; it was one of the good winters before the full
force of the Greenhouse Effect hit us, so at least I did not
arrive at the house stinging with sweat.

In the last century Toorak was the suburb where Old
Money had its addresses and New Money still scrambled
for foothold, but fashions in settlement change with everything else and the Old Money had moved farther out
from the city. Not only New Money had taken over Toorak
but also the New Elite, with money and something more.

The New Elite referred jocularly to their suburb as
the Retirement Village; journalists and other iconoclasts
called it Rats' Retreat. Everybody else, spitting the envy of
the embittered, called it Toothless Town.

The bitterness had some justification, the "toothless"
none. The old retired Rats were anything but toothless;
they were among the healthiest people alive, kept so by the
bounty of a "grateful nation," the wonders of Metabolic
Balance Therapy and the expertise of bio-chemists. They
were the most honoured of Australia's children, the recip-
ients of Extended Span, that Victoria Cross among practical expressions of gratitude.

With the population crisis finally out of hand, even
our most obtuse of governments found it could not insult
a people denied children by reminding them of mortality

with the gift of long life to a selected few. The award was an idiot's error of judgment in the first place and soon became an honour demeaned and degraded by the intrigues of those desperate to win it. The offensive stupidity was soon withdrawn from the list of Honours.

The small group of legatees of this largesse could not in natural justice be cut off from the gift once given. They lived on, squatting forever, it seemed, on their plateau of preservation in Toorak. Sam Armstrong had been one of the first of them and, Honours aside, one of the most disliked by the contemporaries of his political career. Only Project IQ, which had in the end been his downfall, kept his name alive. That and the suspicion of his tentacles reaching behind scenes into the sources of dirty money as well as clean. It was suspicion only, but an open secret; his kind of influence is not easily overthrown by law or justice.

For a Toorakite his house was small—perhaps twenty rooms on two floors—and without the flaunting opulence of its neighbours. Foursquare, plain and set in the middle of about a hectare of lawn, with no trees or high shrubs to break the all-round view, it loomed like a small fortress. Perhaps it was a fortress. At one time these long livers had been the targets of bullets against which bio-chemistry offered no protection; public outrage had died down but the fear in the hearts of ageing Honourables, clinging to their gift, had not.

The gate scanner clicked discreetly at me, chattering to the porch scanner that I carried metal but no explosives. At the porch a human voice directed me to a square of grey tiles while the scanner assessed what I carried, paused for a flurry of clicks as it hesitated over the fashionable Lurex threads in my shirt, decided that it had seen their like before and that they were harmless. "Please remove your recording necklet and place it on the table by your right hand." The scanner decided that without it I was clear of metal of any significance.

The door opened, the owner of the voice appeared—an obvious guard wearing a servant's uniform—and expertly dismantled the necklet. "Seen some of these lately with a second circuit printed in a false wafer," he said. "You only take away what Mr. Armstrong says you take. No second record with all the deleted bits intact." He reassembled the necklet, returned it to me and called out, "He's clear, Kenny."

"Kenny" was a genuine servant, a butler. He led me through a small waiting room into a plain office with desk, chairs and bookshelves but no Armstrong. "Through here, sir."

The second door opened on to a wide, tiled verandah stretching the length of the house and shaded by two vast and spreading grapevines that must have been planted in the 1900s. The huge, empty back lawn, without even the conventional swimming pool, sloped gently down to a mesh fence that would certainly be electrified.

This was high ground; the verandah looked out across the river and suburbs, and the effect of distance and emptiness was of staring at a far land from the shore of a quiet sea. To the New Elite the city was no swarming organism, only a panorama.

On the verandah, as on the lip of the sea, Robinson Crusoe sat at a small table, waiting for Man Friday, solitary in his empire, marooned out of reach of the world, but his name was Armstrong and he did not lift his gaze from the data screen that brought the world to him as he said, with a sharpness probably habitual, "Sit down."

I pulled out the single chair that faced him across the table and learned a detail of Elite safety precaution; it ran in grooves and could not be lifted as a weapon. I waited while he studied the screen and was unreasonably irritated because its tilt prevented me from seeing the display that probably concerned me. Stillness and silence oppressed and diminished me for the great man to dominate the

interview. I lifted a hand to activate the necklet—and saw
that we were not in fact alone.

In the dappled shade of the vine, twenty metres away
at the end of the verandah, a man in camouflage dress
stood motionless and alert. There would, I thought, be
another at the other end, behind my back. The Honoured
ones must not have their gift of years beaten, burned, shot
or exploded from them. Nervously I dropped my hand.

Without looking up Armstrong saw or divined the
motion and said as if to himself, "Film if you like."

"Thank you, sir." Politeness with just a touch of servility. I shot the verandah with its statuesque observers and
the treeless lawn and the distant subservience of the city.
Stock shots.

In the heart of all this space I felt caged with tigers,
with one of them at table making a leisurely meal of information I might not share.

He was ninety-four years old and looked a healthy
sixty, the age at which "Honour" had descended on his
metabolism. He wore the sign of his kind, the too-radiant
glow of a hygiene advertisement, with a little too much of
the right colour in all the right places. Typically, for them,
he was the correct weight for his middle height and slender bones, with the right cover of fat for his build. He had
also the slight tenseness of his kind, not the alertness of a
sharp mind but the watchfulness of a mild paranoia like a
substrate to all else—an unsleeping suspicion of intent to
rob him of his stolen life.

He looked at me at last—

—and a small thing happened—or did not happen,
according to how you think of it.

His face changed, very slightly. That was all.

An interviewer learns to interpret fleeting expressions, those tiny giveaways meaning that the subject knows
of areas he must be very careful of, or that he means to
manage the interview his way and damn your guts, or that

he has you sized up as a cheap flack and can snow you with
his special brand of cant. This change was so faint, so
transient that I almost missed it in the push-pull of my own
tensions. It said that the sight of me reminded him of
something. A previous meeting? A face in a crowd? A
vague similarity? A nebulous connection with something
that did not at once spring to mind?

It was gone immediately, unexamined because all his
attention was on a matter more important to him than I as
yet dreamed of and his mind had no place for vagrant
detours while his wits were set to an exact handling of the
next half hour.

That, of course, is hindsight.

If he had followed up that moment of arrested attention . . . But he did not and it vanished from both our
minds, otherwise this account would never have been
written.

So, everything and nothing happened and he said
coarsely, "You have your interview; what do you want?"

He said it with a blunt authority that meant: *Show
yourself for my inspection—now!* This was display; he knew
why I was there.

His voice fitted the man who had risen from the shop
floor through union ranks to parliament and power—a
rasping, crowd-haranguing high tenor with the flat, open
vowels of the Australia of his youth—the voice of the dem-
agogue who spoke to his people (privately, "the rabble") in
a workingman's tone and idiom: *I'm one of you; would I sell
you short?*

He had another voice, learned and practised over the
years, the voice of the educated man who spoke on equal
terms with peers and presidents. I had heard recordings
of that essential hollowness and preferred the uncultured
version, though it was used on me now because the effort
of changing gear would be wasted on a scribbler. In either
voice he could make plain: *I matter; you don't.*

But once a journalist's foot is in the door the habitual rudeness of power becomes a stimulus. I said with all the hopefulness of simplicity, "I want to write a book about the Clone Babies." This was absolutely true; my research had found them fascinating. "The details are in my Request."

"I read it. What's your interest?"

Throw him the hook right away, my father had advised, and I dangled the line at once, though not obviously. "To cash in on a topical subject."

Cash in he understood; it chimed with cheap greed. But *topical?* His head shifted minutely; he was eyeing the bait though he did not know it. "That story's close to thirty years dead." *Don't feed me junk,* he was saying, but my ears were tuned to underlying wariness.

"By next year," I told him, "it won't be. The Chinese and the Egyptians are initiating research along the same lines, with some fresh clues of their own. I want to get a book out before the whole wordsmithery is on to it."

He was speculative, seeking the con, the hidden objective. "I've heard nothing of that."

"How should you, sir? You weren't looking out for it, but I'm a science journalist with good connections and both ears to the ground. That sort of news seeps through the bio-labs long before the general media hear of it."

With casual disinterest he said, "You aren't a science journalist, you're a police reporter. Or you were." He glanced at his data screen. "You threw your job and joined Freelance."

"And now I'm a science journalist. There will be a story of mine on *Science Roundup* on Sunday night and two more in the print media next week."

He said to the air, "Check that." I had to peer to see the thread mike hanging by his mouth. Inside the house somebody listened, took orders, fed the screen. Armstrong said, "Name your contacts for that story."

I gave him the names my father had given me; the

story was true and the names would back it. (And the
Chinese and the Egyptians would have a little more technical espionage to harass them.)

"Check," he said again to the mike, then to me, "Babe
in arms out to scoop his betters? A best-seller before you're
thirty, eh?"

"Why not?"

"Good for you—but give me a reason why I should
help you."

A little bland cheek was my only resource here. "The
press remembers and respects you, sir." (God forgive me.)
"Retirement from politics hasn't made you less of a man of
affairs. A new publicity angle never goes amiss."

Smarm. Or an expected tribute? His mind was already
made up to discover what I knew that he could use but he
said with snow in his voice, "If you write your book, what
it says of me will be what I decide it will say."

He expected no answer to that and I gave him none.
To the morning air he gave one of the earthy throwaways
that endear demagogues to the herd: "Journalists are the
shit of literature."

He probably meant it but in fact he was chattering
while he considered the gambits. Settling on one, he leaned
across the table, forearms resting flat and eyes alight with
aggression, the full picture of what he must have been in
battling union days. It was a tactic, a performance, but also
a genuine aspect of him.

"Think you might track down the legacy, do you?"
Voice rough as a rasp, heavy with contempt dredged up
for the occasion. "Scribbler's immortality in your own lifetime, eh? Scoop!"

Gently evasive action required: "I don't know any
good reason to believe in Young Feller's legacy."

"You don't?" Contempt again, laid on with a trowel.
He did most powerfully believe, therefore others must. My
father believed, too, and had no proof beyond his trust in

his ability to probe Young Feller's urges and intentions.

I said, uncertainly (after all, I had no useful opinion either way), "It may exist and pigs might fly, too. It's only biologist's folklore." He made a small, circular motion of his jaws, chewing me up for spitting out. I tried again: "I'd follow a clue if I saw one but a wild goose chase won't write me a book."

He stopped chewing my bones to say, "It exists." He said it morosely, like a man remembering an old pain. He tapped his chest, "I know it here," then knuckled his forehead, "but I can't prove it here." So his dream was a wish, no better than my father's will-o'-the-wisp. "A man will destroy himself but he'll preserve his work. Vanity will make him leave it to be found."

His conception of human motivation reflected only himself; his expertise amounted to no more than, *It exists because I will have it so.*

"Whatever Young Feller was up to," he continued, "was beyond any research group of the time. Maybe still is; his record of it might be impossible to make sense of, stuff you wouldn't recognise when you saw it, waiting for a genius like himself to stumble on and understand."

I waited because there had to be more. There was.

He took the barely visible thread mike and tugged it sharply, disconnecting it, and drew his finger across his throat in the signal we used at that time to mean, *Cut your recorders.*

I did so. He tapped the table, demanding. I removed the necklet and pushed it across to him; he did not touch it, only looked to be sure the switches were at Off. As far as I could tell, we were now really alone together, with the guards out of earshot.

He said very quietly, just a hint menacingly, "We'll make a deal, you and me. That means I'll make it and you'll take it—or we part company right now. Got it?"

This was bedrock, the gutter fighter without pretence.

It was also the man who knew how far he could go and how fast, and he had me summed as small stuff needing no finesse. It was time I showed a spat of personality. "If I don't, there are plenty who will, now that you know the research is being reopened in other countries." He nodded. "All right. You make and I take."

"Then that's settled."

"Not yet. What's the deal?"

He thought about it, smiled like a hungry dog and said, "You can follow the programme laid out in your Request, plus any other matter I may feed to you. You'll make a duplicate record, audio and visual, of every contact and pass it to me before you go to the next one."

"That's all?"

"For now, that's all. I'll see how you go. There could be more later."

"So I'm looking for the legacy?"

He called up sudden, blazing scorn. "You are looking for tittle-tattle. You look, I interpret. You get what you want if I get what I want."

"If what you want exists." He waved that away. "And if either of us is able to recognise it."

"There are those who can." Curiously, he corrected himself, in a private mutter: "Probably can."

"So, if I find it and if I recognize it and if you can get at it, what's in it for me?"

"Depends, doesn't it?" He showed me a big, expansive, warm smile. "Plenty, I'd say."

That smile was worth a challenge. "Like, perhaps, being fished out of the river—the man with one secret too many?"

He made a fine flurry of shock and anger, smashing his fist on the table and shouting, "No! No such thing! Where the hell do you get such ideas?" He sat back, playing at regaining his temper after outrage. When he had given it enough time he said with controlled patience, "If it works out well, really well, I'll need a confidant, someone as much involved as myself, and you'll be the only one with the answers—the science journalist, the specialist I'll need to stand between me and the questioning media. Secretary, technical adviser, whatever." His voice took on complaint as though he had only now realised how brutally I had accused him. "You don't actually think I'd have someone killed?"

He had missed his vocation of the drama. I said, "It could be a temptation."

At that point an honest man would have thrown me out. Armstrong retreated into stillness, watching my pleasant smile—I hoped it was pleasant. When he was ready he said, "Then you'll have to keep your mouth shut, watch your step and be very bloody useful, won't you?" With an expressionless face he extended his hand. "Shake on that."

I should have taken his hand; my role demanded it but some residual honesty (or plain dislike) weighed down my fingers. I had no intention of being more honest with this two-faced bastard than I had to but I wouldn't pretend mutual trust. It was only pretence on his side, anyway, making it all too cynical for my taste.

"Not yet," I said, playing the young tough. "See what we make of each other when we've worked together for a bit."

He sat back, deliberating, then decided, "I don't like you all that much, either, but at least I know where I stand with a self-seeking slob. We'll see how we go." He pointed to the necklet. "Ready?"

Here is the verbatim record of the interview with not too much of my personal reaction, though some of that is relevant to what happened in the days and weeks after.

Think of him speaking now with a third voice, one I had not yet heard, the snide voice of a man who could bend language to his pleasure and whose pleasure lay for the moment in telling tales out of school. He enjoyed telling truth to this easily bent media hack who was already caught in his web of threat and promise.

So:

2.

You're after truth, Davey-boy— Don't you like that? Too familiar? Get used to it, Davey-boy. Get used to the idea that you have to because it's too late to back out. You're mine. You agreed. It's on record.

So there's another mike, live, and I've been suckered as easily as that. So have you, Sammy-boy, if only you knew it. So you can call me pet names and I'll learn not to flinch.

You need facts because they're all that's useful between us two, but you want other stuff, too—the human-interest blarney you call investigative reporting, the tearing down of poor, harmless bastards because building them up doesn't interest the shithead reading rabble. After sixty years with sharks I know the hooks and the baits.

Tell you something! When I give you the words spoken you can take them as dead right. My memory is exact. I had a name for quoting verbatim, right down to the other twit's bad grammar, and I can still do it. I can repeat words that never saw print though I heard them half a century back. No slips of memory, Davey-boy; the treatments keep the brain as nippy as the balls.

He saw me as property and of no other account. With me he could be himself. It was obscene that his kind could persist in the world while Grade One couples fought and bribed for the right to a child.

If you want to go right back to the starting point you could say that Barry Jones made it possible. You never heard of him, did you? He was a Science Minister with some Labour government back in the eighties, last century, when I was still feeling my way among the shop stewards. Science wasn't a senior portfolio then but this Jones was vocal at a time when science was making itself felt—the Microchip Revolution, IVF and all that—but it was still hard to put across to a public reared on video, booze and football. Not that the MPs were much better. They all had their specialties that mostly didn't matter where policy was concerned but about science they knew bugger all and cared less until it started to stand up and bite them. With this Jones and a couple that came after him pushing at it, the job became more important.

When my time came in 2002 the portfolio was junior only to the PM, the Deputy and the Treasurer. If you think that means I knew any science, forget it. I wanted that job and I worked on the PM till I got it. I didn't need to know science, I had a Department full of brains to do the knowing; I was an administrator and a bloody good one and that was the Department with a big future.

Project IQ was already in the wind when we took government and I had my eye on it for long-term benefits—a big career, a name in the history books and a golden handshake hearty enough to last my life out. And who do you think was the organising mind behind the Extended Span Award? It turned as sour as I knew it would but that didn't harm me any, did it?

In the end I was wrong about Project IQ but we were out of office by then and other people took the blast. But I did all right when we got back into power and the Project fiasco had all blown over, didn't I? You've got to be a survivor, Davey! Anyway, at the start I pushed it for all it was worth and it was me that got it up and running.

It wasn't all that hard to do. I'd had this pack of geneticists and gene topologists snapping at my heels from the moment I took up the Science portfolio, claiming they had all the variants of the helix charted in the computers, that they'd sorted out the inert sections of the chain and mapped the most promising points of interlocation. They had a list of the microsurgeons they wanted and a design for the laboratory they wanted, all set to bounce if I could shake the money out of Treasury.

Science was news just then, with the Greenhouse Effect making headlines, and cloning big in the magazine sections, so the great silly public was in the mood for some sort of great leap forward, and what better than super-intelligence in the test tube? Australian test-tube biology had always been a special pride.

The scientific community was onside, except the astronomers, of all people. Did you know there's a high proportion of religious nuts among them, overwhelmed by the majesty of the universe, looking at their computer-enhanced pictures of the sky and thinking they're mapping the face of God? Some of them published an open letting quoting, "vaulting ambition that o'erleaps itself." I had a secretary who knew his Macbeth so I was able to answer that we'd learned a bit since the witches brewed. That got me a big response from the cartoonists and put the Bible bangers right back in the bag. It did better than that—it put me in the public eye as the big white father of the future. I was in the saddle.

The group I thought would back me by hitting the public in the entertainment field—and that's where the ratbag opinions are really formed—was the science fiction writers and fan clubs. Not a bit of it! They didn't *like* science! It was intrusive, obscure, boring and unimaginative—got in the way of real creativity! I tell you, Davey, in politics you learn something new and silly every day. It makes you wonder how we ever came out of the caves.

How did this vulgarian careerist con the electors into giving him a seat or the PM into handing him a min-

istry? He has intelligence but how did he hide the
grasping self-love that powers it? Perhaps he didn't
bother. Perhaps it is accepted as the norm in the
haunts of power. That would help explain the condition of the world.

I got the PM to back me. That was Rhys-Owen—
fourth-generation Australian and about as Welsh as a
wombat but the name sounded good—and he was never
truly happy about the Project because he didn't understand it, but I had the news media and the science lobby
behind me and he had both eyes on the next election, so I
got my way.

I can admit now that he had some reason not to like it
but I was on my way to power then and not admitting
anything. He felt we were going off half cocked. I knew
there were areas of doubt—always a useful phrase—but if
you wait for every hole to be plugged you'll never get the
job started.

The thing we had to gloss over was that giving a precise aim for the experiment just wasn't possible. The op-
erational teams had exact techniques but they couldn't
define intelligence. They still can't. Think of it like this:
They knew what genetic combinations influenced the development of intelligence and how to manipulate them to
produce what ought to be a super-intelligent mind—but
how super and in what way? The psychologists said there
might turn out to be different kinds of intelligence and
maybe some of them wouldn't be welcome, intellectual
monsters that didn't think like humans, or that a really
divergent intellect might go unrecognised for lack of anything to compare it with.

The answer was obvious: You've got 'em in the laboratory and you don't let go of 'em till they're under control. That was brought out by a news cartoon suggesting
that a proper super-genius would laugh himself sick at

humanity and start on some delousing research. It rattled a stupid biologist enough for him to comment publicly that undesirable laboratory animals could be relegated. His team tried to pretend that he was joking but it made bad PR. Then some fool of a journalist looking for a think-piece asked, "What if the super-brain turned out to be telepathic?" The same stupid biologist saved his skin and maybe mine by saying, "That's my point about relegation. Who'd want some genetic freak prying into his head?"

Telepathy is bullshit but you can count on a public reaction for two things—somersaults and self-regard. The public was happy to see that monsters would be nonhuman, experimental animals, disposable. Just as well, because Project IQ was already moving by then.

Next thing, Rhys-Owen started digging into the forecasts and got very unhappy. The thing wrong with him was his religion, Australian Basic Christian, something just short of creationist, and he heard a still small voice niggling about usurping the prerogatives of God. He was committed to the Project but he kept asking questions and being surprised by the answers. But then, he was an economist, no more a scientist than me.

He came running to me with one of the prelim presentations, bleating as if it were all my fault: "This says there can't be a definitive report for at least three years!"

He was worried because there would be an election in the meantime, with two hundred million of public money sunk in the Project and nothing to show. I told him that observations before age three would be only indications and that the Psychs were preparing IQ tests on new principles; it would all come right in the end.

"But what do I tell the electors?"

"Tell 'em fairy tales," I said. He didn't like blunt talk about the fundamental principles of politics but it always brought him down to earth. He started to bitch about the Opposition and Question Time and I said, "We'll get the speechwriters and the lab boys together and run up a snow job full of half-arsed conclusions in double-talk," and that's exactly what we did. And we pissed back into office with a fifty-four percent majority.

Then he wanted to know about these new IQ tests. To explain what I only half understood myself I had to talk a language borrowed from the Psychs and use the public-school accent to make it sound gold-plated. Always keep a locker full of quick changes, Davey, and know how to use the right one fast.

I told him, "They can't measure what only another super-genius could devise the tests for. They propose to measure a range of ability variables, physical as well as mental, to be plotted against statistical norms and combined to form a montage graph of the child's ability to use its capacities. Unexpected novel capacities must be assumed and these will be measured by their impact on the other, understood traits. They will then be able to postulate a descriptive value for logical parameters otherwise unassessable." That upset him because he only half followed it and I tried to cheer him up. "If it comes off we'll have the immense prestige of a world first, with your government taking the kudos."

"And if it doesn't," he said, "we'll have a party brawl on our hands and the public squalling moral outrage."

There was a thing he used to say when he was afraid other people's enthusiasm had persuaded him into actions he didn't understand as well as he should. He said it now: "Reassure me, Sam."

He was a solid party man, a fine public personality, a fine economist and a fine speaker once he had it all laid out for him—and behind the scenes he was as weak as piss. There were times when he made me sick and this was one time when I wasn't going to kiss his jitters to make them better. I asked, "How can I? Nobody can guarantee success in something done for the first time. They know what and how, but they can't prevent side effects or acts of God. Succeed or fail, there will be a huge advance in useful knowledge."

I could see his frightened thought: *A sop for eggheads— and a political failure with blood on its hands and mud in its eye.* And him out on his arse. But all he said, sounding like a girl seeing her first mouse, was, "Side effects?"

I said, "The surgeons know their work—which is done with chemicals and lasers, not scalpels—but some of them suspect that the mere fact of interfering might cause unpredictable results."

"How?" says he.

That was quite a question because the surgeons didn't know the answer so how could I? But for this man I had to try. He was capable of winding the whole thing down and out if he wasn't held to the job. I put on my technical expertise voice for him: "The simple presence of an observer effects the outcome of an experiment."

He didn't understand that any more than I did and I saw that in disgust with him I had led us into deep water. I tried to explain that in the microscopic world of genes what you think you see isn't necessarily what is there. It was all wrong, of course—the observer thing actually has something to do with quantum physics, if you want to look it up—but he had to think that I knew what I was about.

Then I thought I'd better keep a card or two in hand in case of accidents, and said, "But there's always the unexpected."

He answered like a man set to lose no matter which way the ball bounced, "A dollar each way on that." It's surprising how many religious men are betting men. It was the betting man who saw a straw for grabbing and said, "The unexpected could work in our favour, too—fifty-fifty."

I could have told him that in biology the odds are

stacked hundreds to one against successful accidents, but that wasn't the moment for truth. I agreed with him.

And right away he showed that he was preparing to shed the blame if things went wrong; he asked, "Are you confident?"

"I am!" And I sweet talked him until he went away happy.

Steady as a rock, me! I had to be. I had cased the odds in mathematical, biological and political terms and staked my career. But I can tell you now what I couldn't tell anyone then: I sweated in my sleep. I'll tell you more: I'd put so much work into it that the idea of Project IQ had taken over my head like a sort of grail to be chased after. I couldn't let Rhys-Owen or anybody put a stop to it.

For a moment there he had forgotten me, was talking to himself; I had an instant's glimpse of a part of him I wouldn't have believed existed. Fancy this animal struck with the sort of dream you associate with a Da Vinci or a Columbus and risking his career to bring it to life! Do we underestimate the slob dreamers? When you think about it, the great traitors to country and humanity have been the self-justifying intellectual dreamers. The selfish dreams of slobs, the what's-in-it-for-me types, have provided strong forces of cultural change.

We weathered the election and settled in for a second term. Early in 2006 came the first major report, three bloody huge volumes of gene-topology charts, tables, graphs, microphotographs and the language of creation, mostly gibberish. But there was a summary in something like English. The PM leafed through it and said, "Christ!"

I made a little joke: "A lot of labour goes into a virgin birth," but it didn't get a grin.

"You've read this?"

I certainly had, and with a bit of help understood most of it. I was getting an education along the way and had picked up some basic biology by then.

He asked, "Can you reduce it to what I need to face a media conference?"

I could and I started off in full public style—which is geared to directing attention away from where you don't want it. "With twenty clones—"

He butted in right away, to show his mastery of the subject, "Clones? All identical?"

"Not quite. The selected ovum was subjected to multiple cloning to create a control, a zero line for comparison of induced variations. Ten were left female but the others were given a Y chromosome to develop them as males."

"So," says Twitwit, "ten identical girls and ten identical boys."

He had that way of beating the gun, trying to be on top when in fact he was floundering. I had to explain that they were divided into five Groups, two males and two females in each, and that each Group was subjected to a different manipulation. "And you know that one entire Group ceased to develop after the fourth week and was discarded."

"Relegated," he said, remembering the dicey publicity days and looking unhappy.

"The other four Groups reached term and were born—or whatever you call being tipped out of total in vitro. Three Groups survived and are perfectly healthy."

"The fourth?"

"Died on the seventh day."

"Of what?"

"Some sort of hormone failure—leave the full technical explanation to the specialists—side effect if you like. Or call it experimental error."

"Christ!"

These churchmen! The name was forever on his tongue with no worship intended; you'd have thought he knew the man. I pointed out that the possible genetic permutations ran into billions, that the calculation of side effects was more art than science and that the team had done bloody well to get a 60 percent result.

What he said to that isn't on record but it can do him no harm now: "And we'll be doing bloody well if we can keep four dead kids out of the shock-horror news."

Any PM in his second term knows the odds are rising against him and every bad break looks like an electoral landslide, so I told him the good news: "Group A shows superior spatial awareness and number appreciation."

"Mathematicians?"

"Could be. Too early to say. Group B is body conscious, emotional and self-expressive."

"Artists?"

Gun jumper! "Who knows? It could be transitional to something else."

"And the third Group?"

"This is the interesting one. Groups A and B are well advanced with vocabularies of up to two thousand words but the C children don't talk at all."

"Christ! Retarded?" He was scared stiff. "A clutch of mongoloid idiots is all we need."

"Not idiots. They understand speech but won't talk and they don't seem interested in anything but each other. They won't play with A and B Groups, ignore them. They are physically retarded, about a year backward, completely healthy but taking longer to grow. They're the most promising."

"How's that?"

"As a general rule in the animal kingdom the greater the adult intelligence the slower the maturing period. It could be a good sign."

"What games do they play?"

That was a more perceptive question than I would have expected from him. "The same as ordinary nippers; lots of running and shoving and shouting, trying out the body and learning the controls—except that C Group plays alone and doesn't shout."

"No monsters," he said, with the sort of relief you give to escape from a firing squad.

I couldn't resist a drop of poison. "Too early to say. Lots of genetic complication only shows up in adolescence or maturity. This is only a preliminary report."

He frowned, then realised the gap of years. "I'll be out of politics by then." (And so he was: Ambassador to India. Not quite an insult but near enough.) He began to complain that the programme was costing too much, so I had to tell him that it would soon cost more.

"In a year or two there'll be a security problem; we'll need more guards for them and more technical gear. These kids are really bright. If they decide they want to get out . . ."

"Christ!" he said.

There's one good thing about religion—you have Jesus for a worry blanket.

3.

Except for the Rhys-Owen backroom portrait it contained little I could not have lifted from public records. I tried to get him reminiscing about the finagling that set up the Project so that the kudos flowed to him but he was too canny for an amateur approach. "You can have that stuff when I'm dead—if you think you can outlast me. While I'm alive I keep a clean nose. That means think what you like so long as you can't prove it."

He told me more anecdotes about Rhys-Owen, spiteful stuff showing up the man's public forcefulness and private dithering. "The official biographers'll chivvy you for printing it but I'll back you."

At length he said, "About this list of yours, the people you want to talk to . . ." His eyes were on the data screen that I supposed displayed the pages of my Request. ". . . these people are old, you know." I knew. "Scientists, administrators, top people. Their stuff's all on record. What do you expect from them that you can't find in data storage?"

"Names." For a second he seemed disconcerted that I should harbour a reason he hadn't thought of. "They can tell me the names of the nurses who had charge of the babies, the psych assistants who did the actual work of constant surveillance and note taking, the cleaners and cooks and gardeners who saw little things nobody else did and didn't put them on record. And the perimeter security men—I'd like some better firsthand accounts of that fire; they were under State orders at the time, so the media reports were censored, but now something fresh might slip off the tongue. It takes only one fact to open up new lines of sight."

He listened, if not with respect at least with some air of heeding an equal. I thought it worthwhile to show a little nous; the more he trusted my intelligence the more likely he would be to use me as something better than a fact-finding sniffer dog—and perhaps let me glimpse some shadowed areas.

He said, "There won't be many alive."

"There should be a few in their sixties and seventies."

He nodded and thought for a while before making the cutoff sign again. I switched off the necklet and he continued rapidly, "Forget the top men; concentrate on the little people. The scientists and overseers have been sucked dry, so go for the proles, the gossipmongers. I'll give you a name to start on; you can locate her through public info. She was in court a couple of months back—

illegal birthing racket." He produced a pencil and wrote on the tabletop. "Memorise it. Don't put hot stuff on paper until you've scrutinised it."

I memorised *Anne Constance Blaikie*. He wet the tip of his splayed, workingman's finger and rubbed out the pencil marks.

"We're in business," he said.

"Not quite."

It is not easy to pinpoint the change those two words worked in him. Think of a breeze passing over still water and leaving it unchanged but for a sudden recognition of the presence of forbidding depths. For an instant he suspected that he might not be wholly in control of the bargaining—his bargain and my submission. He smiled still—the same smile, unaltered—but now a wary game player was adjusting his impression of his tame scribbler.

"You want something, Davey? Something more?"

"Information." He said nothing, waited. "We agree on the gossipmongers but we haven't mentioned the fountainheads." He knew what I meant but played the game of looking mildly questioning. "I should interview clone Groups A and B. I can find no record of their ever being interviewed about their upbringing or about Group C. They must know something useful."

He said with a hard, abrupt finality, "There are no records because they are very private people."

I was supposed to shut up. I said, "It would be worth the try."

"It wouldn't."

I thought I might as well push the hand until it got slapped. "Surely other journalists have talked to them."

"Plenty tried. It wasn't worth their trouble." He looked me over with an air of deciding how much adult talk I could follow. Dumb journo! "How would you go about interviewing somebody with twice your intellect who isn't interested in the things you ask him and whose replies, if he replies, seem irrelevant, though they mean something to him? There's no contact. I tried it for myself. Never again! I felt as if I spoke a foreign language I didn't understand myself and listened to another one. They aren't interested in us. They don't pretend to be. They put up with us."

My thought was that he lied in his teeth or that he had not met my father. On the other hand, my father could easily produce the impenetrable impression if it suited him. "So I shouldn't try?"

He was blunt. "You won't be allowed to." It was not quite a threat but could easily become one. "Would you know how to find them?"

"Offhand, no. Their addresses are known but getting through the front door could be something else. And their vids are on silent numbers, I imagine. It could be difficult."

"For most people, including reporters, impossible."

A quick prod at his certainty was irresistible. "Media resources—"

"Don't try it. You'll only irritate them. And me." It was nearly an open threat; he added, almost as an afterthought, "The government has guaranteed their privacy to prevent their lives being made insupportable."

I gave in gracefully while wondering had I learned anything useful. My father would know. "All right, we're in business."

He nodded.

I waited for what might come next.

"Something else, Davey?"

I stood. "No, nothing."

He removed his attention. I might not have been there. He knew how to teach the slave his place. It made the fake playfulness of "Davey" doubly dirty.

3•TALKING TO MY FATHER

The persistent problem with robot detection systems has been with them from the first: They know what they have been told to look for and how to squawk when they find it but nothing else; the unforeseen is not their business.

My "unforeseen" was Lurex. Lurex is a fashion thread first marketed in the 1950s, a filament of anodised aluminium mixed with ordinary yarns to make glittering patterns in the cloth. It returns to current chic every so often when the designers run short of ideas, decorating shirts and dresses for a season and being again forgotten.

Lurex was "in" that year and, on my father's instruction, I had bought six shirts with the metal thread in different colours. What he had done with them I understood only vaguely (his bio-electronic systems were well beyond my store of working information) but when I wore them I became a walking recorder setup, powered by body heat.

Armstrong's gate and porch scanners had picked up the aluminium accurately and recognised it for what it was, decorative Lurex; they had not picked up my father's admixture of iron. The scanners looked for sensitised strip metal and miniature power packs, not for sensitive organic matter operating without a pack. The recording element was the film of colour, only a few molecules thick, an organic compound sensitised by quantities of iron so tiny as to be detectable only by microanalysis. Its photographic ability was poor but the results could be computer-clarified very well.

So I had a complete record of Armstrong's conversation in the blacked-out exchange—nothing to hang him with but revelatory for anyone needing an intimate portrait of a bastard. I did not want to hang him but possibly my father did, though he hadn't said so.

My father had his own key to my flat and when I arrived he was waiting for me, turned to the window, gazing out over the cityscape that I knew he despised as a clutter of ill-matched architectural ego symbols. I recognised him from the back, then came alert because this man's hair was brilliantly blond. He turned slowly and brown eyes instead of green gazed at me from the pale, freckled skin of a stranger, ten years too young, who placed a finger to his lips while he waved his other wrist at me with a faintly buzzing watch. As his arm approached me the buzzing became louder.

I was carrying a bug, probably planted by Armstrong's butler as he let me in or out.

The stranger found the pinhead instrument clinging to the cloth between my shoulders, as white as the main body of the shirt, difficult to see. He picked it out with a tiny magnet, automatically deactivating its chip, and said, "The flat is not bugged yet. You should assume that it will be."

It was my father's voice. Peering closely I could see no sign of makeup applied to face, neck or hands; the contours of his features were sufficiently thickened to take the leanness out of the bony structure but I could detect no cosmetic packing.

He bore inspection patiently before saying, "It is a

proto-flesh, electro-organically bonded and extremely uncomfortable." That was all he had to say about a workshop miracle. He asked, "May I have your shirt?" I stripped it off and gave it to him. "Was it an interesting colloquy?"

"Quite."

"So, not wasted." He surveyed the shirt almost lovingly. "When I have finished with this it will be returned to you from a public laundry. Laundering will sufficiently explain the silencing of the bug." He sat down facing the wall screen. "Would you play back your necklet for me? For a quick summation."

No hint of enquiry about his son's stretched nerves. Father, dear father!

I hooked the necklet to the wall screen and my familiar-unfamiliar father watched tranquilly the replay of my hour with that old snake. At first sight of the man he remarked, "Disgusting person," and said nothing more until the recital was over. Then he glanced impatiently at my rumpled shirt but I had no equipment that could replay its special content. "What did he say during the cutoff period?"

I could not match Armstrong's claim of total recall but a journalist learns to absorb and retain; I was able to give a pretty accurate account of what had passed.

My father was grimly unamused. "You tried to test yourself against him. It was too soon. You don't know his capacities—or your own." He seemed to think that comment enough because he asked, "Might I have a cup of tea?"

I reminded him sulkily that I had been threatened.

"If your report was accurate, you were not threatened. It was you who suggested to him that he might take reprisals. He capitalised on your apprehension by allowing you to feel that the threat is real."

"It is real."

"Of course. I was pointing out that you initiated the

gambit that he used against you. You must observe yourself accurately, not think you are making the moves when
in fact you are creating openings for your opponent."

I was trying to dredge up a pungent comment on the
philosophy of gamesmanship when he repeated hopefully,
"Tea?"

"In a moment. Armstrong is dangerous."

"He always has been. You now have a small advantage. You have enticed him into showing a basic malevolence he might otherwise have hidden until he needed to
take you by surprise. Had you done that deliberately it
would have been an excellent ploy but your shots in the
dark may not always be so fortunate."

Unsure whether I was being praised, reprimanded,
sympathised with or all three, I settled for the pot of tea.

He followed me into the kitchenette. "Never refer to
the threat. Train yourself to think of him as a business
partner."

"Smiling Serpents Incorporated?"

"Don't spend distaste on him; use him. He gave you
useful firsthand material on Rhys-Owen; get more, be en-
thusiastic. He has given you an excellent first chapter."

I asked furiously, as the water boiled, "Do you expect
me to write the damned book while all this is going on?"

He explained patiently to his idiot child, "It must be
written and seen to be written. Armstrong must believe in
it." Back in the lounge he sipped tea and suggested in his
irritatingly bland way that I seemed ruffled. "There is
some aspect of the affair that troubles you?"

"There is an aspect of yourself that troubles me."

He gave that silent thought before saying with his
usual infernal judiciousness, "That may always be so. Aspects of people trouble me, too; it is often difficult to understand that the planet's inhabitants do not see it as a
refuge for lunatics. No doubt my thought processes sometimes seem strange to you."

All that with bland placidity, not judging from on high, merely stating a point of view.

It occurred to me then that his careful speech was not so much a pursuit of accuracy as an effort to render his thinking in language I could not misinterpret. It was a brutal, demeaning recognition of intellectual incompetence. Knowing it is one thing; being forced to openly accept it is another.

It was the outraged guttersnipe in me that whined, "I'm sorry I'm not a bloody A Group genius but your cold-blooded screwing wasn't up to making the gene transfer. Still, I'm intelligent enough to do your legwork and play games against a man who'd think nothing of having me killed."

Something else occurred to me for the first time—that I had the power to hurt him. There was a limit to how well the pseudo-flesh could transmit the expression of the face beneath it but no doubt about the implied helplessness of the spread hands or the blink of stung eyes. I felt, ridiculously, that I had hit a child and now should stroke and soothe.

In fact I sat still, feeling inadequate and uncomfortable. Hurt or not, he followed his routine of working it all out before he spoke again, and then came at it from an unexpected angle.

"I am not a genius, as I understand the word. I have a more efficient brain than . . . normal . . . human beings but I am not creative in the inspirational sense; I see the logic of possibilities and follow them to a conclusion. That is not genius. There is no genius in A Group, only an ability to reason more accurately than . . . other people. There may be genius in B Group; they are inspirational, artists as Rhys-Owen rightly guessed, but my type of intelligence is not adapted for assessing them. I am only a reasoning machine."

Only. I said uneasily, "It seems like genius to me."

"Just as radio once seemed like magic to"—I'll swear he was about to say "savages" but switched it to—"those who had not seen it before. In Project IQ the clone Groups were each subjected to a different manipulation because the genetic surgeons had unproven theories of enhancement and some uncertainty as to what their enhancements might amount to. They thought imprecisely in terms of increased intelligence without defining the word. The psychologists who postulated varying forms of intelligence were right. B Group's mentalities became"—he searched, for once, for an effective word rather than an accurate one—"starbursts of associative and emotional inspiration. C Group became the intellectual giants their progenitors had in mind but nobody knows their potential; they were, finally, incomprehensible. A Group developed the plodding, rational intellection that made us inventors—that is, drudges who turn other people's visions into artefacts for the world's admiration."

These were, for him, long speeches. For the sake of saying something, almost anything, I murmured that in anonymity in a country workshop he did not receive the world's admiration, nor did his brother and two sisters so far as I or anyone knew.

He continued explaining in his cool, even, point-making voice: "We are retiring people, equipped for certain work; by popular standards we do it surpassingly well but we prefer privacy to plaudits. Privacy is our bargain with the authorities; we are not fitted for social contact. In genetic manipulation something may be gained at the expense of something lost; our loss is emotional rapport with the world. I am not saying that we lack emotion; our feelings are as powerful and as often overmastering as . . . as yours, perhaps . . . but we do not rationalise them in the same way. It may be a consequence of mechanically efficient mentation that we cannot share your . . . the world's ethical and moral outlooks, which seem to us emotional rather than rational. Unable to enter into a people's appreciation and interpretation of their mental life, we prefer to deal with them in pragmatic terms and at social arm's length. Otherwise we should become hated, and hatred is hurtful. You have called me cold-blooded. I am not."

In his inadequate fashion he was seeking contact and should have evoked my sympathy but I was full of my own concerns. I pointed out that his hauling me out of a promising career and sweet-talking me into a possibly dangerous pursuit smelt of very cold blood indeed.

It was not something that could be said without anger and he nodded with a sort of lonely bleakness, a hint of pleading he did not know how to humanise. "At first, perhaps. You were nothing to me. How could you be? You were a duty that I fulfilled until you could fend for yourself. Then you became potentially useful." He fixed on me a complex look I can describe only as combined of wariness and a shamefaced hope. "I trusted to your filial feelings to make you willing to assist me."

That took my breath away. It would have taken anyone's. My answering voice must have been at strangulation point. "What filial feelings? Why was I supposed to have what you hadn't?"

I had never before seen him unsure of himself. He muttered uncertainly, "I had observed that the child-parent relationship implied a bond of dependence and affection; it seemed possible that discovery of a father might incline you emotionally to ally yourself with my wish."

I should have bawled, *You soulless, scheming bastard!* but was stopped by the panic in his eyes.

"I will not pretend, David. You were to be useful, no more, and rewarded properly on completion of your assignment, but circumstances have changed. In my failure to understand the commonplace human assumptions as anything more than emotional confusion I created ignorance in myself. Of myself."

He paused, settled on his form of words and continued in his devastatingly unemphatic, rational way: "I have developed paternal affection for you to the extent that I have become afraid for you. Now that Armstrong is involved I cannot stop what has begun but I am impelled to protect you at every step of the way. Because you are my son."

There is nothing to be said to such a declaration, no precedent to fall back on. What I actually said, between vexation and incredulity, was, "You goddamned stupid rabbit of a man, you don't even know what your own feelings are for."

That should have angered him, but as usual his reaction was a model of intelligent civility: "I have never been called stupid before but from your standpoint you have reason."

Emotion, it seemed, had been put firmly back in the kennel after a short run to exercise stiff muscles, but it was nice to know that Old Coldblood had better than ice water in his veins. Less nice to know that he had more feeling for me than I for him. I liked him well enough as a sort of friendly curio but his was not a personality that I felt would grow on me. I felt, nonetheless, that little twinge of slightly shamed disquiet that comes when someone displays a regard we cannot return.

Still, there was the comfort of knowing that he meant well by me, a selfish care on both sides, but welcome. I trusted the workings of his engineered mind.

Typically, the confessional phase was closed off, put away with his mental baggage, for he asked suddenly, "Have you someone . . . a lover, girlfriend?"

"If you mean am I saddling up for marriage, not yet."

"But—women?"

"As and when, but heart-free. You will have noticed the double bed, made for romping."

The brown eyes held a peculiar look I could not read. "So, when the bugs go in, as they surely will—and once they are placed you must not disturb them, you must live with them—Mr. Armstrong will have some fine romping insights into your private life." It was a sour thought, but perhaps he was gently ribbing me, like a genuine human being, enjoying my discomfiture. But no, it was not a sense of humour at work, only his carefulness. "Beware of new faces, laid out to catch you in your romping. That man will never wholly trust you."

The return to business as usual was preferable to the secrets of the confessional and it made an opportunity for me to take up undiscussed matters. I referred to something Armstrong had said during the blacked-out period, about people who would be able to recognise Young Feller's legacy. "He said, 'There are those who can,' and corrected himself to, 'well, probably can.' Did he mean you clone Groups, or is there somebody else I should know about?"

"He meant us, probably B Group in particular for their ability to make intuitive connections."

"So he knows where all of you can be found?"

He was patient with me. "Naturally. We are in a sense his historical responsibility, his test-tube babies, as he would put it. He has never lost interest in us; we are always aware of discreet surveillance."

"Why? Does he think you will lead him to the legacy?"

"Possibly." He retired into one of his moments of sorting complexity into segments his legman could assimilate. "He wastes nothing, especially information and the flux of opportunity. The highly publicised deaths of C Group killed Project IQ; we other Groups did not offer the spectacular returns of transcendent intellect, so the taxpayers' interest in an expensive failure turned politically acrid, but he is not a man to close any account without profit. It is our opinion—A Group's opinion—that he hopes even yet to find a use for us. In a sense he already has; much of his income derives from our workshops."

I said, "I've checked his personal resources; if he lived to be a thousand he couldn't spend what he has. Or is he just personified greed?"

"He is, but not for money." He continued as though he said something quite ordinary, obvious to anyone who thought it through, nothing to make a song and dance about, "He would like to harness our minds but does not know how to do it. He would like to use us to set himself in an unassailable position of power. He would like to run the country."

While I tried to perceive the enormity of this, blanketed by his casual tone, he made one of his rare value judgments: "A delusion of some grandeur but not totally impossible of accomplishment. In his mind is the inchoate feeling that if he could use us properly, control us wholly, he could achieve anything he desired. He is, basically, an idiot." From a man who thought little of human standards this was a swipe of some power—but it was a description I would not have used and I said so.

He corrected me with the barest trace of impatience. "Any man is an idiot who thinks he can control minds intrinsically more competent than his own."

I asked, "Does B Group agree with you?"

"That I don't know. We do not communicate. We have no common interest. As you might express it, David, we operate on different wavelengths."

I supposed I might so express it, but one thought was leading to another. "The folklore says the legacy is a book of theoretical notes. What do you think?"

"Notes would be unintelligible. It will be seen to be a statement—a full analysis of the genetic manipulation required to produce any type or quality of intelligence in the human species, to produce it exactly, with full knowledge of the outcome and no divagations. It will be a series of biological theorems reducing the millions of possible genetic permutations to a predictable topology."

"Are you sure that he achieved all that?"

His hesitation was minimal but I caught it. "Yes."

So there was doubt; the thing might not have happened after all. Yet while the possibility existed it should be run to earth.

"Genius on demand!" That was my tongue wagging the obvious because the implications—for the future of the race and the planet and everything on it—were too great to take in. My deeper reaction was something like: *We don't want it; it would bring the end of everything we have and are.*

My father smiled thinly. "Genius might be easy enough but there are other, more immediate dangers to be considered. It would be a matter of recognising the limits of folly."

So he was before me, recognising the dangers and ready to confront them. Nevertheless it was to be a long time before I realised fully what he meant. He gave me no time to think about it then but, having said all he felt it necessary to say, changed the subject to what he held more important.

He touched the pseudo-flesh of his cheek with a falsely white finger. "Disguise is uncomfortable but essential. You must never allow Armstrong to connect you with me."

It is also uncomfortably essential, I thought, that if Young Feller's legacy exists, Armstrong should not get his megalomaniac hands on it. A more sobering thought was that my father might, from his intellectual height, call Armstrong a fool and be justified, but that though I might be the man's equal in intelligence (unproven), I was surely his junior in experience, cynicism and guile.

"You have shown him a sign of independence and will pay for it; assume surveillance every moment of the day because his kind believes that all men seek secret advantage." The brown eyes gave their frosty twinkle of whatever passed for humour in his emotive lexicon. "Wise of him, don't you think?"

"I'll only be conducting interviews and sending him the results. He'll have little to watch."

"Sending them to me also. Do not come yourself unless something goes desperately wrong. Then use diversion and disguise." He unstrapped his watch and gave it to me. "It will be worth knowing where and when you are not being listened to. Now I must go."

He stood indecisively moving his hands. I had an uneasy feeling that he thought to stroke my hair but instead he extended his hand to be shaken, doing it as though he had never made the gesture before. "Goodbye, David."

I felt pretty awkward taking it. "Good-bye, Dad."

The last word came out with a reluctance I could not suppress and he noticed it. But, dammit, I had to call him something.

Before I slept that night I switched on the watch's bugging alarm. It was silent. By morning it was purring to itself.

Two bugs had been installed while I slept, one at each end of the flat. Armstrong's buggers—pun intended—had drilled into the outer wall and placed their instruments in the bores. Since I had no one to talk to it hardly mattered at the moment.

I sat on the edge of the bed, thinking over what my father had said about diversion and disguise, so casually, as though every journalist learned such elementary tricks as part of the trade. My thinking was that any useful disguise must be devised long before it is needed, the method settled and the materials on hand ready for use.

Any cosmetic was out of the question; no art of application can survive even a passing scrutiny. On the other hand, close-up surveillance was unlikely; the legman trailing behind, relaying information of where I went and to whom I spoke, was a more likely operative.

"Behind" was the clue. We recognise people readily from the rear by the shape of the head, the set of the ears, the swing of the shoulders and, most of all, by the walk. You can disguise a walk by taking short, quick steps or long, slow ones or by faking a limp, any of which is swiftly exhausting and needs concentration if the body is not to fall back into its normal gait.

After breakfast I went to a shopping centre, careful not to look to see if I was followed (not that my inexperience could have flushed a competent tail), bought a pair of shoes with fashionable high wedge heels and ordered them to be delivered to the flat. I went then to a sporting goods store and picked up several lead sinkers, a harmless purchase needing no camouflage; I could happily treat myself to a couple of days in the trout streams to establish my angling credentials.

Next I used a public vid booth to order clothes from a display catalogue—snappy stompcat stuff suitable to my freewheeling age group, fine nylon reversibles with different colours inside and out, trousers with side zips that would allow them to flop loosely or pull in across the behind, jackets with removable shoulder pads. Some very quick changes would be possible. I paid by credit-print and arranged that the stuff be delivered. My ghostly tail, if any, would not know what I had bought.

Then it occurred to me that there was one cosmetic I could use, a macho sunburn dye popular with sedentary office types to dispense with the routine of ray lamps or skin-cancerous sunbathing. I gave the chemist a list of stuff to be packed and forwarded; no one but she would know that a sunburn dye was buried in it.

About my hair I could think of nothing to be done. Wigs require careful fitting, in itself enough to attract the attention of a tail.

I returned to the flat. When the shoes arrived I fixed the sinkers under the insteps and with my angler's gutting knife cut a slanting slice from the outside edges of the heels until they were set at a sharp angle of wear. The result was satisfactory; my knees took a slight outward bow that turned my walk into an amble while the weights shortened my stride and give it a slight clumping deliberacy. It was the walk of a stranger and required no concentration.

Lastly I glued the cutaway sections of the heels back on and removed the sinkers. These with the gutting knife, a small tube of glue and the sunburn dye would travel with me from now on and I would always be in clothes capable of providing a range of silhouettes with a few simple switches.

Thought of the gutting knife reminded me of the loose-brimmed nylon hat I wore for fishing; it could fold small and be carried in a hip pocket and would when necessary hide my hair and alter the shape of my head.

In some crowded public place—say, the lavatory of a hotel bar, where a stranger is unnoticed—David Chance would be able to vanish in moments.

I felt pretty satisfied with myself until, with an instinct too long delayed, I switched on the detector.

While I was out, my wall screen had been bugged. With the newest techniques it was not impossible that I could be watched when the thing was off.

It was sheer luck that I kept my tools in a cupboard in the kitchenette, which the screen could not see, and that I had doctored the shoes on the workbench. My heart skipped a panicky beat because I had not anticipated the obvious.

A little less self-assured, and thoughtful now of appearances, I set the screen to Process, brought out my workshop notes and began to rough out an article on my father's ideas about organoplastic adhesion theory. Let my observer soak that up and like it!

4•NURSE ANNE BLAIKIE AND HER SLY, SLY BABIES

1.

Armstrong had given me a name, a woman to locate. Had he decided to set me at once on a warm trail in the interest of saving time? It was natural and safer to suspect some deeper reason in him but for the life of me I could not imagine one.

To test his reaction to an independent approach on my part, I keyed Public Files for lists of the staff who had worked on Project IQ during its life of about twenty-one years. Searching archival data banks is easier than wearing your patience to tatters in a library, though in some ways libraries are more useful, but it takes time. It took, in fact, a day and a half to locate eleven surviving nurses, cleaners, cooks, clerks and groundsmen and their addresses, including Anne Blaikie's.

Ignoring her, I set out to interview some of the others, wearing my stompcat gear with the blue faces out and the zips pulled tight over a Lurex shirt and the wedge-heeled shoes. My tail, if he existed, would become accustomed to a particular, unchanging picture of me. I saw the picture myself, in a shop window, looking like a refugee from the Street Arts movement, and shuddered.

In this dreadful getup I interviewed three ageing, bored, unimaginative, self-contradicting people who told me little a researcher would find useful beyond the daily routines of the Project, filling in some background. After each empty, dithering round of question and garrulous answer I sent a copy of the interview to Armstrong by public mail, which is, short of personal delivery, as close as you can get to private communication this day and age.

I wasted a week that way and after the third pointless copy had gone to him he protested. He made his protest brazenly as a means of letting me know that nothing I did was hidden from him. *Remember, God sees you!* He simply spoke to me from my screen when it was not in operation from my end.

"Chance!"

Hard, sharp and businesslike. I was eating breakfast and it made me jump, which was what he intended. The voice was unmistakable and I said as calmly as I could manage, "Hullo there, Mr. Armstrong!"

See, boss? I'm not hastily covering up any incriminating evidence of double-dealing.

"Why are you wasting time?"

After the first involuntary glance I did not look at the screen. "I'm wasting nothing."

"These reports are useless."

"Not to me. Background material. I'm writing a book, remember."

He disregarded that. "See Blaikie."

Surly, very surly.

"I will. And what she tells me I will be able to set against an established background. It will have more meaning."

He had to accept that because the book would be his cover as well as mine if bad luck put the media on our trail.

"Then get on with it," he said and, I suppose, cut off at his end, because he said no more.

I had begun to wonder what to do with the growing number of information-loaded Lurex shirts that must be passed on, however useless their content. My father was supposed to collect them, but the days passed while they amassed talk and distorted pictures (because of the rumpling and creasing due to body movements) and sweat in the armpits. Then he solved the problem in his own fashion.

On the morning I was to call Anne Blaikie the caretaker of the flats rang me on the house intercom to say that my taxi was waiting.

"I haven't ordered a taxi."

"Very well; I'll tell him it's a mistake."

Two minutes later an infuriated driver banged on my outer door. I opened it to my father in his false face and a taxi company uniform, complaining to the world that this was the address and the number he had been given . . .

I played along with the game, deciding that I had an appointment and could after all use his car; he went downstairs to wait while I made up a parcel of laundry, including the shirts, picked up my recording necklet and raced after him.

He said as we pulled out from the kerb that we could talk freely. "I have installed a distortion field against directional microphones."

"Is that necessary? I don't even know that I'm being tailed."

"You are. I followed him for a while yesterday."

It was pleasant to feel cared for, still—"Why did you do that?"

He said with his usual practicality, "You are valuable; you must be looked after."

Valuable. Why couldn't he say, *Because I don't want to lose my son?* Or give me the chance to feel for him as a human being rather than a companionable data bank? But I had had that opportunity and rejected it for a passing selfishness. My fault. And now I could not guess what approach might work to unlock the humanity in him.

I took the three soiled shirts from the parcel of laundry and laid them on the seat. He nodded.

"Anything useful in them?"

"I doubt it. Today might be more productive." I told him of Armstrong's insistence on Blaikie.

"Is she still alive? Bitch of a girl. She was one of Young Feller's special nurses." Oh, good! He added an afterthought: "My guess is that she is a Retiree—of a kind."

That seemed unlikely in a person of no public importance. Anyway, I had other things on my mind.

I complained, "My screen is bugged."

"Of course. You were warned." A detail of no interest.

He drove, I noticed, with the sedate, unhurried, law-abiding accuracy of a dowager's chauffeur; he had acquired a taxi somewhere but he was no taxi driver. He asked, "Is there anything more you should tell me?"

"Nothing new."

"Then I'll let you out." He pulled into the kerb. "Be careful, won't you?"

It was well meant but the tone would have done for, *Looks like rain.* "Yes, Dad."

He smiled briefly. "I'm not your father." While I froze with shock and fright he said, "There were two male clones, remember? I'm your uncle Andrew."

I grinned at him in relief and, for lack of an adequate response, picked up my depleted parcel of laundry, stepped onto the footpath and waved good-bye to him. Promptly he stuck his head out of the cab window and bellowed at me, "Hey, mister, you forgot to pay me!"

What's more, he took the money, smirking about realism and attention to details. Only his leering wink assured me that it was all a joke, with me paying for it.

He was a better actor than my father. Perhaps he had practised it. I had an eerie vision of the cloned quartet allocating duties amongst themselves, with Andrew detailed to imitate human beings.

As he vanished in the traffic I wondered where he had got the taxi as an elaborate cover for meeting. Not that it mattered; I had games enough of my own to play without puzzling over his.

My mind was on the surprising piece of information Andrew had sandwiched between other matters. I had trained myself to catch statements on the wing, so to speak, for later consideration, and now, too late, I wished I had asked him to expand on his remark that Anne Blaikie was a Retiree—of a kind. What kind? The term has gone out of use with the circumstances that produced it; a generation ago it meant someone who, as a reward for meritorious service, had been granted a retiring pension over and above the universal pension. In these straitened days of mass unemployment and crashing financial empires few extras are granted to anyone; to the workingman, the man lucky enough to work, "a generation ago" sounds like paradise.

So Nurse Anne Blaikie had done well for herself—but what had she done to earn it?

And why did the information not appear in her Public Data Record?

Also, why had she, if a Retiree and in consequence comparatively well provided for, involved herself in the illegal birthing activities that had landed her in court two or three months back, and not for the first time?

Lastly, having been convicted, why was she not in gaol?

Provisional answers were possible:

One: Some activity in connection with the Clone Babies had earned her the Benefit.

Two: The activity was politically sensitive, even politically scandalous or criminal. Therefore the payment—

payoff—came from "funds" and was not on public record.

Three: She was involved in illegal birthings, (a) because she had spent her Benefit or (b) for simple greed.

Last: She was not in gaol because somebody—Armstrong, for instance—found it worthwhile to keep on the right side of her store of uncomfortable knowledge. Somebody with influence.

Other answers were possible, even harmless answers, but at least she sounded more interesting than the smoke-screen dummies I had so far followed up.

I wasted an hour, probably amateurishly, in trying to identify my tail but nobody seemed to loiter in elaborate disinterest, nobody turned to study a shop window if I swung suddenly about, nobody turned up repeatedly in places where I lingered. I concluded that he/she had been unable to pick me up again after Andrew's kidnap diversion.

Andrew told me, later on, that there had in fact been two, one a woman taxi driver who never lost sight of us, the other a private detective who did. They worked, he thought, in tandem but he had not mentioned them because my business was to act as though such things as tails did not exist.

I think the "need to know" principle has its limits.

The inner areas of great cities crumble into slums as the prosperous move out to the marginal countryside. Nurse Blaikie's address in Auburn, one of the older parts of Melbourne, should have prepared me but I had given it no thought; standing outside her ancient, single-fronted terrace dwelling with its mended fence, broken ironwork "lace," cracked verandah tiles and vanishing paintwork, I wondered why a Retiree should live in a house well into its second century of habitation.

There was a Dickensian taint to the idea of a midwife operating from a slum; I began to expect something of a

Sairey Gamp as I reached for a bellpush, found none and hammered on an antique iron knocker. Then a young girl's voice called unintelligibly inside and in a moment or two the door was answered by a greying, fiftyish, vaguely grubby man who stood defensively in the half-opened space, peering in suspicious silence.

"I'm looking for Nurse Anne Blaikie."

His eyes fixed themselves on my necklet. "What for?"

"I'm a journalist."

"I see that. What for?"

After a while on the rounds you react to defensiveness with fair accuracy; this one's mulishness smelt of frustration and distrust of a pitiless world. I lied, "I have an appointment to interview her."

"Interview? Her?" He was incredulous. "You mean for the screens?" The moment of glamour dropped into resentful pettishness. "She never said anything about it."

Behind the door the girl's voice cried excitedly, "It's right, Dad; she told me."

Did she, indeed? I had made no appointment. I had wanted her cold, not warned. Armstrong? Why?

The man's resentment gave way to the helplessness of a life spent running on the spot. His age group had been automated out of their undemanding, skilless jobs years before. He said over his shoulder, "Then you go and tell her," and to me, defeatedly, "Tells me nothing, she doesn't."

The girl's head appeared under his raised arm as he held the door; she would have been no more than sixteen. I said, "It's Nurse Blaikie I want; she's an elderly lady."

The girl sniggered and her father snorted, "Try telling her that! Mrs. Grant's my wife and Nurse Blaikie is her maiden name she uses for jobs." He batted gently at the girl's head. "I said go and tell her." Her footsteps receded. "What's it about?"

"I want to get her story of the Clone Babies."

His dull glance registered nothing. "Who're they? Some kids in the news? Did she middy them?"

So much for yesterday's fame.

The girl's voice called, "She says to come in."

Grant made one of those aimless gestures that cry aloud the failed marriage: *It's her business, none of mine.*

The interior was clean enough but showed the dreary signs of the amateur maintenance of those who cannot afford tradesmen or paint and plaster, that working-class refusal to admit despair. It was not a good age to live in. Perhaps no age ever was.

I was more preoccupied with the question of Nurse Blaikie's age. She should be about seventy, at least twenty years older than Grant and surely not the mother of a teenager.

The room Grant showed me into was what I supposed they called the lounge, cluttered with ancient furniture, lit by a single window looking out on a narrow backyard and flourishing the house's distant origins with an actual fireplace, unused save as a showcase for a vast basket of artificial flowers. The smart new wall screen with its up-to-date terminal array mocked yesterday's fustiness. A product of illegal birthing, no doubt putting her one up on the neighbours.

Mrs. Grant—not yet certainly my Nurse Blaikie—lay with her feet up on a sofa and did not stir to greet me. She was a big, lazy-looking woman, jolly enough except for her cool eyes, plainly bursting with health and no more than forty years old. I introduced myself and said tentatively, "I was expecting a rather older lady."

She said without surprise or even much interest, "Were you, now?" and in the same breath, to her daughter hovering in the doorway, "Bring me my purse, Elsie."

The daughter vanished. Grant sidled into the room and was half settled into a chair before she said, "This is private, Jim."

Her tone was neither contemptuous nor hectoring; it held only the flat lack of emphasis of one who habitually had her way. Grant went silently out. She called after him, "Go down to the pub for a couple of hours." Almost it sounded like an order. To me, now that it was my turn for attention, "Please sit down."

I sat in an antique armchair whose leather had at some time been replaced with plastic and, since it sometimes pays to open an interview with an unexpected impertinence, asked, "Why do you shame him?"

Unprepared, nonplussed, she covered confusion with activity, swinging her feet to the floor and sitting bolt upright. But she did not pretend to be insulted. "Do you think I do?" It was a woman momentarily shaken out of her poise who murmured, "I suppose I do. We've got used to it and don't notice."

"He notices."

Her eyes hardened. "I'm the earner in this house and I have it the way I want. And that's not what you've come to talk about."

Elsie came with the purse and received a note from it. "You can go out somewhere but be back for your tea."

The girl went regretfully, eyes on my necklet and head full of wall-screen excitements. But she went without argument; Mum was boss here.

Nurse Blaikie said, "That's them out of the way. Now what?"

I pressed the stud on the watch case but it did not purr. No bugs. She saw the movement and understood it and said with something like gaiety, "Clean, dearie, clean! Sammy wants me to tell you everything I can. I've gone over it with him time and again but he thinks a fresh head may spot a new angle."

"Sammy? Armstrong?"

She smiled with not enough mockery to spoil the impishness. "That's his daughter you just saw." She let that sink in before adding the snapper. "Jim doesn't know that and you'd gain nothing by telling him. Except two enemies."

At least the parameters of frankness were established along with the implication that I was in no position to make capital of anything I discovered. I said, "That's none of my business. I want to talk about the Clone Babies."

"So talk."

"But they were born nearly fifty years ago, while you can't be much over forty."

This time there was only mockery without the impishness. "Sixty-five, dearie."

The obvious fell into place, explaining Andrew's "Retiree—of a kind" and the Grants' poor style of living. Her payoff had not been in cash; she had demanded preservative treatment and Armstrong had obtained it for her. Her demand must have been backed by something close to blackmail, very persuasive blackmail to have made Armstrong accede to it.

"Does Jim know?"

" 'Course not! He just thinks how well preserved I am for a girl only his own age."

Poor bloody Jim.

She continued with a smug, schoolgirlish satisfaction, "People haven't started to notice yet. They will soon but it won't matter. When they notice I'll think what to do. Time enough then."

I began to see her not as intrinsically interesting but as a bitch—Andrew's word—who had struck it lucky. She had a common, slothful mind; she had grabbed for life and taken for cover a husband whose reward was a selfish woman's ill treatment because he was only a means to an end; now she cruised, resting on her luck, aware of problems waiting and refusing to think about them.

I asked her bluntly, "What do you know that was worth longevity treatment to keep it quiet?"

"Conrad's last message, of course." I must have looked

stupefied because she laughed at me. "It won't mean a thing to you and you won't be allowed to use it in your book. You are writing a book, aren't you?"

"Yes."

"So it's true. You never know with Sammy."

Plainly you did not. "So this will be time wasted."

"I think so, dearie, unless you are clever enough to outthink the old bastard." She was having a good time with her mockery but now she got to her feet. "Do you like tea or coffee? Or maybe beer? It's too early for spirits."

"Coffee, thank you." As she went to the dispenser in the kitchen nook I called after her, "Don't you mind wasting time?"

"Sammy wants it done."

"And what Sammy wants, Sammy gets?"

She popped her head round the corner of the nook. "You want to remember that, dearie."

"And do you believe I'll find something in your account that he couldn't?"

"No."

"So?"

"Sammy wants it."

The instant brewer squeaked and rattled a cup up to its nozzle. "He must want it bloody badly."

She brought the coffee and left me to balance it on the wide arm of the old chair. "Bloody badly," she agreed.

At a venture I asked, "Does the legacy exist?"

She took time sugaring her coffee. "Maybe."

"Why does he want it?"

"You ask him, Snoopy. Myself I wouldn't risk it; he likes his privacy. Can't we just get on with the recording? Do you think I'm not bored clear to the tits with going over and over it?"

I could imagine that. Here was a woman who had snared the prize of anyone's dreams and found nothing to do with it but live in a slum and use her training to make

a living on the wrong side of the law. She had life but
nothing to give to it.

I switched on the necklet.

At my nod she began talking, reciting her piece
learned through endless repetition while Armstrong
poked at it for hidden clues. Yet, in half a dozen sentences
her voice came to life. Her body, too, made tiny movements sketching the things she had seen and done. Nearly
half a century ago she had been on the edge of adventure,
all life waiting for her to suck and drain. Recital it may
have been, but she remembered with spirit and a quick-
ening of the blood.

She had been happier then.

2.

Those years in the Nursery were the best in my life though
I didn't think so then. I mean, it was right away from
everywhere and everyone and there was I, twenty-one and
pretty lively—not hard to look at, either—with nowhere to
go except home once a month. We had everything, of
course, books and screens and staff dances and all that, but
at twenty-one you want to go out even if it's only down to
the corner shop. I think now that it wasn't the restrictions
so much as the high security. You were always aware of it.
It didn't do much harm but it was *there*—perimeter guards
you couldn't see, satellite surveillance up there out of sight,
alarms and telltales and hidden microphones to catch every sound the babies made. Nobody interfered with our
private goings on—and believe me there was plenty of
that—but they always knew what you did and you found
yourself wondering what they thought about what you
were up to last night, even though you weren't sure just
which ones were "they."

If only the town had been in bounds, though it was

fifteen kilometres away . . . But it wasn't and we might as well have been on the moon.

There was a farmhouse a half hour's walk distant but we couldn't see it; all we saw was the perimeter hedge and the hills on the horizon. I'm a city girl at heart; I belong with noise and pubs, but the babies made up for a lot. Those kids were an experience nothing could match; even the Nursery couldn't spoil them.

The thing that made it different from ordinary child care was that nobody knew exactly what was best to do with them or for them, except feed them and keep them clean. The doctors didn't know but they made suggestions; then the Psychs would try to lay down rules and the rows would start. Can you imagine professional men shouting at each other the kind of words you hear in gutter brawls?

In the end we did what was plainly necessary and tried to learn what the babies needed from us, while the Meds and Psychs watched us to find out what was right and wrong.

Once, we got a lecture telling us to regard the babies as children of an alien culture, one that didn't exist yet and whose maturity could not be guessed. We weren't supposed to teach them anything; the poor little things had to find their own way of growing up. It may have been the right idea but it wasn't possible. How can you stay detached when a baby hurts itself through not knowing any better? It was hard on us and some of the girls didn't last out the first month. I stuck it for the twenty years, with just the one break, till the tragedy finished the Project. It was partly the good money and partly that I just got used to it; I suppose that after you make allowance for a girl kicking up her heels in the bedroom I was really a pretty sedate type. You know, when I came to live in Melbourne after the Project fell apart, I actually missed the Nursery! Now I wouldn't go back to it for a fortune. It was one of those experiences worth having, but only once.

I was with C Group; Sammy would have told you that. My babies loved me. At least, I think they did—in the early years at any rate. Later on it was hard to tell what they thought. But at first, well . . . I like to think they loved me. They made me feel life was beautiful.

At first all the four Groups were kept together. Then, after seven days, one whole Group died and the autopsies showed nothing that made sense. There was talk about hormonal imbalance but some of us were present when it happened and we didn't know we were seeing it happen. The four of them went to sleep—and stopped breathing. Just like that. I'll swear there was no physiological reason, no matter what the reports said. That was the first hint that we were dealing with things none of us understood and the whole staff was terrified that it might happen again and that we might be blamed because we couldn't find a reason for it. It was eighteen years before there was another fright like that—the fire, I mean, and I wasn't there then.

We weren't allowed to talk about the place when we went on leave, not anything to anyone. That's what the big wages were for, to keep us quiet, and with jobs harder and harder to get and every second person out of work, keeping quiet was easy.

I met Sammy quite early on. He was Science Minister then and he came with a party investigating the deaths, though most of what they did in the finish was to hush the whole thing up. Sammy and I got on from the start, if you see what I mean, and if you don't you're more innocent than you look. After a while I used to stay with him sometimes on my leave and he'd ask me about every little thing that happened in the Nursery. He wanted me to keep a notebook but with all the watching and bugging I didn't dare.

I held him for twenty years, even after his wife found out. I was useful, you see, and soon I got the idea of what he was after.

She stopped dead, leaning forward a little to hold me with her eyes, challenging me to the unasked question. So I told her: "He was after power, more and more political power. Your Nursery was his ladder to the top and every bit of information he could discover was analysed to see if it might yield advantage. Take it as read that he had other informants besides you. Project IQ had taken hold of his imagination and he was out to ride it clear to heaven. He picked up useless data like a hen picking grain, hoping one bit might be a diamond. How's that, Nurse?"

A good start, but don't flatter yourself you've got brains enough to understand him completely. If you do, he'll know and he'll deal with you. Be a good boy; take the money and ask no questions.

What, no money? Just your book? Dearie, aren't you the bright-eyed beginner!

Well, now . . . C Group. We couldn't tell them apart except that two were boys and two were girls. Tiny differences of attitude showed up later but knowing which was which was only possible when we put tattoos behind their ears. Before that it was they who identified themselves by choosing us, and Conrad chose me right at the start. I was his Special Day Nurse though he didn't seem to care who had him at night.

The C Group babies were tiny things, only two and a half kilos at birth and slow to develop, but they grew fast in other ways. From the beginning we knew these were clever ones. They didn't cry much and they used to kick and throw their arms about, all four of them, and always together; they'd do it like a set of exercises for a couple of minutes, then rest and later on do it again. We were sure they were exercises; they knew what they were doing, teaching their bodies to work properly. They would make noises, not squalling or yelling but quiet little noises like calling for each other's attention, and then they would do their flailing and kicking. And this was when they were only a few weeks old! We were sure they were communicating. It was eerie!

What made it worse was their expressions. You know that blank, reserved look you see on babies before they learn to laugh? Well, these four never had that; right from the beginning they had proper expressions that meant something if only we could have told what. My Conrad worried me when I'd talk baby talk to give him sounds to imitate and he'd watch me very gravely like a little old man, and after a while his face would change and an absolutely sly look would come over him and he would turn his head away. I felt that he was putting up with me because I fed him and petted him and that when he'd had enough he would just remove his attention, telling me in his way that he knew it was all nonsense. It was the same with the other C nurses and quite nerve-wracking until we got used to it. We told the Psychs and they looked wise but didn't have a clue to the kids. The other two Groups were normal by comparison.

Now, here's a really strange thing: A and B Groups began to talk at about seven months, not very much but definite sounds with meaning. That was surprising, but C Group who seemed so much brighter didn't talk for years, and that was worrying. It was when A and B began to talk that the Groups split up. They did it themselves and nothing could make C Group pay any heed to the other two. A and B got on all right together but turned away from each other later, when they were half-grown. But C set itself apart and stayed that way. A and B said they were snotty and who'd want them anyway, but you know what kids are like. It was as if Conrad's four thought the others didn't matter, that they weren't interesting enough to pay attention to.

As for not speaking, they didn't use words but they

did communicate with each other. They had a whole language of little signs between themselves, so little that for a long time we didn't catch on to them and we never did work out what they meant: the barest flick of a gesture, a shift of the eyes, a change of breathing rhythm, things like that. That was only between themselves; with us nurses they would use big, extravagant gestures to tell us what they wanted. They'd throw their little arms around us and nuzzle, tug the way they wanted us to go, mimic drinking a glass of milk or playing with a toy. The Psychs said they were effectively bilingual, using theatrical signs for us and a more subtle system for their private meanings.

Talking down to us! Well, it was true.

And their toys! They started on jigsaws before they were one and soon lost interest. Too easy. As they got older their favourite toys were just *things*—blocks and cutouts and lengths of string or wire, bits of almost anything lying around. They would push them about to make patterns, or sometimes deliberately not patterns, or pile them up and watch how they fell. The Psychs said they were learning geometry and physics, but they were only guessing. Still, there were brains at work and we were all very uncomfortable because we didn't understand.

Then you'd see them asleep, beautiful as flowers, and you knew they were only babies after all. But at other times you'd catch them watching you with that peculiar expression, rapt, intent, as though you were a study that had to be mastered. The look would go as soon as you caught it; they would laugh and want to play and you would wonder if you actually had seen anything strange.

She was garrulous when she got going, wallowing in a past more satisfactory than her unageing present; her face took on youth as she remembered. I saw what Armstrong had seen in her.

Her material was of little interest; that stuff was

all on record. I could only wait while the necklet soaked it up—until she said something, only a small thing, that was not on record. I nearly missed it, though my father would have picked it up later. She caught my nodding notice when she said, with the conscious virtue of the "lady" who would never, never swear in front of a gentleman:

I wouldn't use such language ordinarily but you'll have to excuse me this once so I can tell you about Conrad starting to speak. It was terribly funny.

He was just four and one day he was alone on the verandah, watching Derek, the new gardener. He didn't turn round when I came from behind though he certainly heard me because their senses were very sharp, but the hunch of his shoulders told me he was concentrating and his eyes would have that look as if his mind was taking Derek to pieces and putting him together again, *learning* him. That look could be creepy.

But it was mealtime and it had been one of those mornings and I suppose I was a bit sharp with him. Anyway, I said, "Come on, Conrad—upsy!"

He didn't let on that he heard me but kept on watching Derek, though all the man was doing was weeding the patch outside the playroom verandah. Usually the kids did at once what we told them; they were never naughty. "Keeping on the right side of us," the Psychs said, as if it were a conspiracy. It turned out there was something in that. But I'm getting ahead; that was years later.

Anyway, on this day I was in no mood for holdups and I snapped a bit, "Come on now, Conrad! Dinnertime!" And I took him under the armpits and tossed him a time or two as I always did because he liked it, but this time I found a little animal on my hands, squirming in black rage and screaming at me the first words he had ever spoken.

And what words! "Fuck off, Blaikie! Can't you tell by now when I'm busy?"

I don't know whether it was shock or what, but I put him down on the floor and my hands over my mouth and absolutely squealed with laughter. It seemed the funniest, wickedest thing I had ever heard.

Conrad calmed down and saw the joke, too, but he saw it like an adult who knew the laugh was on himself for losing his temper and his self-control. The sly look came onto his face and made him as old as sin, as if now we shared a secret.

But we didn't and he knew I'd have to tell the Supervisor, so he made a sort of flourish of making the best of it. He toddled across to one of the bugged pillars we thought the kids didn't know anything about and said right into the microphone spot, "Now I suppose we'll have to waste time answering all your silly bloody questions."

And so they did, but it seems that all the Psychs learned was C Group's ability to hear no question they did not feel like answering and to reduce logic to nonsense by deliberately floundering among the ambiguities of language. There must have been some temptation to reprisal among the psychologists but they were loath to risk coercion on unknown mental makeups; they could not be sure that the reactions would be those of normal children. For much the same reason they eschewed electronic probes; they did not know what they were dealing with or what the resulting charts and graphs might mean in reference to an "alien" mentality. So they were reduced to watching and learning what the brats allowed them to learn.

At the end of a weary recital of the growth of the C kids into an increasingly sullen adolescence—mostly a gawking wonder at their ability to absorb and retain

information and regurgitate it in unexpected juxta-
positions, all of which was fully documented in endless data files—she returned suddenly to the gardener,
Derek.

I've talked with Sammy about this and we can't make sense
of it, but Derek was the only member of the staff who
Conrad ever made a friend of. Oh, he was all right with
me, but I was a sort of mother surrogate to be made use of
and buttered up for favours and made a whipping post for
tantrums; that was a normal relationship with a child. But
he went and got Derek for himself. It was the only time I
knew him—or any of them—to initiate friendship with a
human being. I say that because in the finish they weren't
human, not really.

He used to watch Derek a lot, just stand and watch,
and one day I asked why and he said, "Because he's beautiful."

Well, that was a facer because Derek had a real Irish
potato phiz with big ears to make it worse and a permanent grin, and there he was with a garden fork turning
over topsoil and sweating like a pig under the sun and
looking about as beautiful as a bag of spuds.

But Conrad said, "See how he moves! I'll learn to
move like that."

So I looked, trying to see what the child saw, and there
was something in the way Derek moved, something absolutely loose as though he flowed without using his muscles.
If there was anything beautiful about him it was those
muscles—very nice, too, but the face put me right off.
After all, it takes more than muscles, doesn't it?

I told Conrad that was because Derek was an athlete
who used his body a lot and he was supposed to be very
good at some kind of combined sport, the pentathlon or
whatever it was. He just nodded and kept on watching
with the look you learn to recognise in a child's eyes—the

one that says, *Buy me that, Mummie*. He wanted a human all to himself! At four years old, mind you.

I told Derek about it and he spread his daft grin a bit farther and said Conrad was the best of that Group.

I asked how he knew, because outside staff had no contact with the babies, and he said he watched through the window.

"But how can you tell Conrad from Carlo? They're identical."

"Till they look at you they are," he told me, "then Conrad's different. He'd like to come out and play."

I should have told the Psychs but it didn't seem important at the time. Then again it seemed not to matter when Derek disappeared from the job, except that Conrad was as furious as if his property had been stolen. I had to explain that Derek had gone off to some international sports meeting—he was in his early twenties then—and might not ever come back because the Department would give us a new gardener in his place and Derek would be pushed off somewhere else.

The replacement was a tubby little redheaded girl who hated the babies on sight. She was a good gardener but when I caught them glaring and making faces through the glass I had her moved on. And Conrad kept looking for Derek to come back.

In the end he did, ten years later. He was finished as a top athlete by then but still as lively as a boy and by that time the kids had the freedom of the grounds and talked to whom they pleased. Not that they often pleased. They couldn't go out, of course, and the surveillance was as strong as inside, but at least they had space to move around in.

The day Derek came back Conrad made a beeline for him—after ten years, mind you—and Derek told me the first thing the boy said to him was, "Teach me to move like you."

And that is just what happened. The two of them would be out on the lawn before breakfast, with Derek showing Conrad proper exercises and how to do back flips and standing jumps and I don't know what. Conrad was terribly good at it. Derek said he was a natural athlete and he had to show him a thing only once. The Psychs were fascinated, seemed to think it opened up a whole new area of speculation.

I asked Carlo one day why he didn't join in and he said, "Because Derek is Conrad's."

That wasn't jealousy. He was just telling me that they didn't interfere with each other's affairs.

I used to watch from the verandah, seeing how Derek was as fascinated as Conrad, and that was peculiar because the rest of the staff found C Group a bit off-putting. I saw the way Conrad was always wanting to touch Derek and how Derek would give him a quick hug and I wondered about teenage crushes and the homo leanings of many sportsmen, but Derek was spreading himself around the female staff after dark in no uncertain manner and was rumoured to be doing some sort of carrying on with the daughter of that farmer whose house was hidden from us by the perimeter hedge. He must have had some arrangement with the guards to sneak out at night. So I had to admit that his behaviour was wholly hetero even if I didn't fancy him myself. Besides, I had Sammy, and why spoil a good thing?

I was watching them one day when one of the Psychs— Dr. Bates it was—came and stood beside me. They had done some acrobatics and Derek was lying on his back on the lawn while Conrad bent over him and tousled his hair. It wasn't an intimate gesture; it reminded me of something I couldn't place until Dr. Bates said, "Conrad's got himself a pet."

That's exactly what I was seeing—Conrad ruffling the puppy's hair in recognition of a job well done. It was revolting when I saw it for what it was and I said, "We'll have to stop it."

"Stop what, Nurse?"

"Them! It's humiliating. One day Derek will realise it and he'll hate the boy."

Dr. Bates looked sideways at me and asked, "Do you think the man doesn't know? Look at him. He loves it. Theirs is the only true intimacy in the place between the subjects and normal people—and how revealing it is of the capabilities of those remote, unloving children."

I turned away, not wanting to watch, and there was Carlo and one of his sisters, observing us with tight little smiles as wicked as witch spells, laughing at us for thinking we had discovered something.

I said to Bates, "I feel we aren't studying them as much as they are studying us."

"Of course," said he. "That's one point of the exercise, isn't it?"

After that I never felt quite the same about Project IQ or about Derek or Conrad. It had become grubby and nasty, but I had grown up with it and didn't know anything else to do.

So I stayed and it was borne in on me more and more that we meant nothing to these C Group children, nothing to their hearts I mean, and we had been fooling ourselves with loving and caring because they kept us fooled. They were intelligent, all right, much brainier than we were; they knew by the time they were teenagers how to keep us at arm's length while they conducted all sorts of secret talk among themselves in signs and looks and phrases that meant something to them and nothing to us. They laughed at us the way we laugh at babies trying out their first few steps and their first few words. But we laugh with delight and encouragement. They just laughed.

In the eighteenth year it got too much for me. I asked for a transfer and was sent to Melbourne for ward training. Sammy was furious with me for applying without telling him because I was his best pipeline into what went on in the Nursery, and for a year he wouldn't have anything to do with me. I didn't care all that much because I was nearly middle-aged and suddenly I had all the things a city can give you that I had missed in the godforsaken Nursery.

So I wasn't there when A and B Groups were introduced to life in the big world outside but I heard and read what everybody else heard and read until publicity made their lives impossible and they removed themselves from view. Or were removed; it was a bit of both, to tell the truth, and Sammy had his little hand right in there, looking after them and taking his profit. Compared with Conrad and his sibs they were dunces but they were still far enough ahead of the average . . . I'm not sure that's right. Perhaps they were so different from the average that their way of thinking made them seem more advanced than they were. Anyway, these eight eighteen-year-old kids started doing things that revolutionised the art scene and some aspects of engineering and bio-technology. But you know all about that, don't you? It's all on file.

C Group weren't allowed out of the Nursery. The Psychs were afraid of them and that's the truth. I don't care what they wrote afterwards or what excuses they made, they were afraid of C Group because they couldn't understand them. They had no idea what went on in the kids' minds and they didn't dare let them loose in public; they couldn't begin to imagine what they might get up to or what sort of trouble they might cause. They hadn't a clue to the kids' mental capacities; their evaluation system was probably as good as they could construct but the kids made it useless with inconsistencies and paradoxes and statements that became more and more ambiguous or just plain silly as the Psychs tried to probe them.

The staff knew they were clever enough to escape if

they wanted to but it seemed they didn't want to. My guess is that if we couldn't understand them, on their side they couldn't understand how such disorderly minds as ours could have created an orderly world; they probably suspected there were more advanced types outside. That's the way I see it.

In the end they sent Young Feller—by then that was what Conrad liked to be called because that was what Derek called him—to spy out the real world and report back. I wasn't there so I can't tell you any more than you can read for yourself about how the Nursery caught fire but Sam knows and I know that Conrad broke out under cover of the uproar.

He disappeared for over a year. That never came out publicly because nobody dared admit they'd lost a—a what? An experimental animal? If anybody ever found out what Conrad did while he was free, or where he lived, it didn't get into the news. Somebody must have known or guessed but we never learned.

Then one day he strolled back into the Nursery, as bold as brass, and the Psychs couldn't get a word out of him.

I wouldn't have known this if Sammy hadn't stretched out his arm to pluck me out of the clinic where I worked and said he wanted me back in the Nursery because he didn't have a properly trained observer there any longer.

I objected but I didn't have a chance. I'd done a couple of silly things at the clinic—I was into illegal birthing if you must know, and much good it'll do you if you try to talk about it—and he had found out, so I had to do as I was told.

That's when I made my little bargain with him and I must say he kept his word, but it gave him another hold on me because he can cancel the treatments anytime he feels like it.

So I was there on the last day.

I was in the room when they died, the only one with

them as it happened. I saw what there was to see, which was almost nothing, and I heard what Conrad said to me.

The four of them were sitting on the floor as they usually did, four ordinary-looking teenagers doing something communal that had meaning for them but not for us. They sat there, saying a word now and then. It was like a conference where one word had to do the work of a whole speech with maybe the flick of a finger or the twitch of an eyelid to help out. It was creepy when you first saw it but in the end it was boring.

I was there because it was routine to have somebody supervising. We called it that—present but ignored, more like it. I was in a deck chair, reading a book. I don't mean a print book but a strip novel. I never could be bothered with all that description and philosophising in the print books but the picture strips hold your interest because there's always something happening.

I tell you that because it seemed to have some connection with what Conrad said to me.

He called out, "I left something for you, Blaikie, something a good comic stripper should be able to read."

It was a curious way to speak even for those curious kids and we were always alert for the worst from them. I asked, "What do you mean, left? Are you going somewhere?"

He said, "Yes, we're going away. For good."

That frightened me because I didn't know what it meant and I started to struggle up out of the deck chair, but he laughed because the alarm switch was on the opposite wall and they were between me and it.

He said with a sort of giggle, "I've left a strip story, for you and anyone who can read it. All about how to create gods from dogs."

I ran for the alarm, scared out of my wits by words I couldn't make sense of, circling around them because they were as quick as cats, but they only sat there, unmoving, while the bell rang and rang.

I was still pushing at it when the nurses and doctors came rushing in but I was wasting my time because they were dead. I couldn't tell when it happened. There was no jerk, no collapse, no symptom. We were never able to work out how they did it, or why. They sat in a circle and died because they wanted to, and that was the end of it. Conrad gave me a message and went away for good.

And I didn't tell the Meds and Psychs because I suspected that this was the sort of thing Sammy had been waiting for all these years. In a way it was—and it has just about driven him round the bend.

She rambled on with commentary and anecdote that illuminated nothing—until something nagging at the back of my mind prompted me to ask what became of the gardener Derek. There had been no Derek Anybody among the names I had recovered from files.

Him? Why him? I don't know. I did hear that he finished up in the looney bin. Lost without his lovely Young Feller, you think?

That was not what I thought.

3.

"Now," she said, "what does it all add up to?"

"Nothing—yet. Don't expect me to spot in two minutes what has bamboozled you and Armstrong for a quarter of a century." While her mind was set in that direction I changed the subject with the interviewer's eternal hope of surprising at least a half truth before caution took over.

"How long will you continue to get antigeriatric treatment?"

She was too old a hand for such simplicities. Sammy would have been a stiff training course. The girl who had enjoyed life was banished with a flip of the mind and I was back with the calculating old bitch who had passed beyond such small kindnesses as generosity to a conned husband. She thought the question over and decided she could safely answer it. Was I not Sammy's tame ferret?

"Sammy can stop it anytime; he owns the doctor. Perhaps I'll keep going as long as he does."

"Not long," I said, not greatly caring whether or not this was a cruelty. "His metabolism should reach response-failure pretty soon now. They go fast after that."

She said, so carelessly that I believed her, "What of it?" She was shallow and selfish but somewhere in her was awareness that all her opportunities had petered out in dead ends of unfulfillment. And so—what of it? "He likes a girl his own age," she said, and corrected herself, "his apparent age. He calls me up now and then. That's all there is to it."

I left her soon after that, thinking that Armstrong's nastiness was outstanding in the records of petty bastardy. He kept his sex object—one among others if I understood her correctly—in reasonable trim because she suited him and because his obsessed mind suspected that she held a clue that she did not understand (perhaps it was so) but refused to maintain her financially. She had to seek illegal income to avoid poverty and his hold on her was his ability to pull strings when she got caught. His gift shackled her to his requirement. She had life, and no way to live it.

Instead of hailing a cab I walked to the nearest park and sat on the lawn, fixed my earplug and played back the interview, wishing there had been some way of finding out

Derek's surname. I had not dared to probe and so turn her attention, and thereby Armstrong's, to the gardener.

How to find him?

In the end I erased the final question that had led to her mention of a lunatic asylum; it might have raised a suspicious query as to why I had asked it. I didn't want him looking for the man who was, so far, my perquisite, but I left the question on the Lurex for my father to consider, along with Young Feller's final message.

I also took out the reminder of metabolic response-failure; Sammy would not appreciate that.

5•THE FARMER'S DAUGHTER

1.

At home I made a duplicate of my necklet record and sent it off to Armstrong by Courier Service. Then I sat down to think about the Derek who had been so matey with Young Feller in so bizarre a fashion and to wonder whether his spell in an asylum had had any connection with the happenings at the Nursery.

I checked my record of the still extant staff who had worked there during the Nursery's two decades and found that memory had not played me false. Very few of the large outside complement were on my list.

Well, now ... The perimeter guard—the watchers who, Blaikie had said, were never seen—had been soldiers; that much was common knowledge. I reasoned that they would not have been considered sufficient security as the capacities of C group became evident; the broad span of the Nursery grounds would have demanded more than an outer circle of surveillance to keep those kids in if they had decided to break out. The true problem would have been to prevent them crossing the couple of hectares of open lawn between the building and the perimeter hedge.

That was what the outside staff were for, surveillance and a closeness from which they could spring into action. They would be highly trained men and women, athletes like Derek, for instance. Special Services? Police Intelligence? Even a branch of the "secret service," whatever that might be?

Foraging for names in those areas would ring so many bells in so many quarters that Armstrong would be forced to do something serious to prevent my being questioned—for me, perhaps terminally serious. There was no problem, however, in locating Derek Farnham in Sporting Data as a prominent pentathlon competitor in the early years of the century. "Retired from competition, 2015; occupation: seasonal worker." I did not believe that last. Prominent athletes do not work at peripatetic, skilless jobs; they are looked after, eased into work that keeps them comfortably off while the glory lasts and they squirrel away their tranquil futures. It is so now and it was so then.

Derek Farnham of, say, Special Services? (A wrong guess, but not far wrong.) I had no intention of asking foolish questions of SS but I badly wanted some answers. It was a job for my father's logical intelligence.

I wrapped my Lurex shirt in a parcel, marked it Urgent Delivery and sent it off to my father, again by Courier Service. I saw no way that a tail could know of that or that Armstrong gained anything at all by having me tailed. (But, as they say, we live and learn.)

In the morning Armstrong summoned me and dutifully I hurried to pay my respects, having nothing else I was willing to offer.

The verandah setting was as before: camouflaged guardians, table, chairs, electronic hardware seen and unseen and himself pinkly healthy while anciently still and unamused. He had vidded the necklet replay and gained nothing from a recital he had heard a dozen times, so he saw me only as a household appliance that ate up money in paranoid surveillance and had so far produced no dividend.

He asked with the liveliness he might have shown in the divorce rate in Malagasy, "What do you think of Annie?"

Since the interview I had scarcely though of her at all. I said at random, "She must have been a dish in her day."

"She still is. From time to time." He did not bother to ape middle-aged lechery; she had long ago dwindled into a business proposition to be strung along in case her memory should disgorge a late, mislaid clue. "But is her story true? Is she hiding anything? Is there more to be winkled out?" He scowled at me. "A practised interviewer should sense these things."

That made it my fault that nothing had emerged. I said, "I'm not psychic or particularly sensitive. I think she has told the tale so often that she has lost the power to alter it. Say a thing times enough and in your mind it becomes the definitive version. Hers is probably the truth because I can't see that she has anything to gain by concealing or distorting. She can hope for profit if you get what you want but nothing if you don't."

He dropped that line; he must long ago have concluded as much for himself. "Young Feller's last message," he said, plunking down the words like counters.

"Means nothing to me. Has she ever varied the words in repeating it?"

"No."

"Then I need more background information. For instance, did the boy have any interest in comic strips? Could he draw? Did he leave any scribbles behind? Did the other three ever do or say anything worth looking at? To find all that you would have to winnow the whole record of twenty years of bugging and watching and questioning. It's a bigger job than I can take on."

He said irritably, "It's been done; I don't miss the

obvious. The whole lot has been computerised and examined with a glossary of key words designed to trigger relevant information. Nothing. I'll send you a list of the key words; you may be able to add more."

"I'll try, but it seems a roundabout way when there may be someone who knows what he meant. There must have been someone who knew he was preparing such a complex picture puzzle."

"Must there? Are you thinking of some such simplicity as a rebus? It would have to be the length of a city block to say anything useful."

"Biological equations?"

"More likely theorems, to be of any value."

So my father did not have that conclusion all to himself. "Did he study biology in the Nursery?"

"Study? We weren't that stupid. They studied nothing in depth. No advanced texts were permitted in the place and there were no terminals for technical data retrieval. Even the scientists had to live sealed off from the immediate world. Those kids were too damned good. The Psychs were frightened of them."

Those six words from him jolted my thinking more than the same from Blaikie had done. I had held a soggy, amorphous impression of them as vaguely "superbright," in the fashion of those repulsive brats who dominate the intellectual quiz shows and skewer their elders with shafts of erudition delivered from a patronising height, little monsters with computerised minds devoted to mischief. But now—what sort of mind frightens a psychologist? The answer: One so different from all of his professional experience that he does not know what it can do, how it operates, what it knows or wants to know or what might be the outcome of less than eternal vigilance.

The mind uses metaphor where conception fails. The metaphor that came unbidden was of myself peering into the dark maw of an intellect that could swallow mine without tasting its passage or being aware of the infinitesimal addition to its store.

With something more than a frisson, with the crawling flesh of waking from a dreamed terror, I was glad that the four of them were dead. God knows our human kind are a race of monsters, but we haven't earned such an inconceivable setback as the unleashing of C Group upon us.

"But he must have learned biology," Armstrong was saying. "How else could he have set himself up to create gods from dogs? He learned it in those eighteen months when he roamed free of the Nursery. We don't know where he was or what he did but you can be sure that he studied the life sciences. Do you imagine that in all these years I haven't thought of your mysterious stranger who must have known?"

"He would have needed a teacher," I suggested. "He or she might have glimpsed what he was after."

"Perhaps, perhaps not. Elementary texts to begin with, then the swallowing of whole libraries at photographic speed. Why a teacher?"

Swallowing. The black maw opened, frightening because it could not be understood. "What did the Psychs make of his last words?"

"Nothing, because they didn't hear them. The kids had developed means of beating the bugging systems; how, we don't know, but they had done it. Young Feller's message went to Annie and to no one else." He added a comment that shone a bright light on his mean soul: "His idea of a joke, perhaps, bequeathing wisdom to an idiot."

"And Blaikie kept it to herself?"

He smiled with vast self-satisfaction. "She was mine then as she is now. She told things only to me and not to any other unless I allowed it. Why else should I have paid her the highest price her imagination could encompass?"

"She doesn't seem to have taken any happiness from it."

"Her own fault. She wanted like a child and like a child she got. The rest was up to her." His smile became questioning and mocking. "How about you, Davey-boy? Are you too stupid to make the most of opportunity?"

"I haven't seen the opportunity yet."

"And you won't until you earn it. What's your next move towards earning?"

"To think. For a week or a fortnight if necessary."

That was sufficiently unexpected to interest him. "Think about what?"

"Who Young Feller might have talked to while he was free ranging, where he stayed, who fed him and taught him the mores of a big city. I assume the city for a start."

He said with something like petulance, "I've thought about that for years. He could have been anonymous in a tramps' flophouse."

"Even so, nobody in this century can move without leaving a clue. Nobody. Not even superbrain Young Feller."

"I know it. I've scraped my mind dry of speculation."

I threw him a bone. "You've thought like a man with power and resources, wondering what he would do if he wanted to hide. I'll think like a grabby kid from an orphanage who learns to snatch at whatever offers. A different angle gives a different picture."

It was extraordinary how small a thing could revive his interest. It was a measure of his hope and his obsession. Poor old Armstrong, who didn't miss the obvious.

I had an idea where Conrad might have gone. Who would have hidden him more willingly, served him more unquestioningly than faithful Fido who would roll on his back to have his tummy tickled by a teenage boy and shiver with delight at having his hair ruffled?

But to find Fido I would have to talk to my father, a problem in communication that needed planning.

Armstrong was suddenly done with me, as if one hopeful suggestion closed the meeting and I should at once put it into action. "Get on with it. I want a result while I can still use it. These damned treatments will begin to lose their bite soon."

So he was no better off than Anne Blaikie, no nearer to contentment through the gift of life because misuse had shrunk it to a mere desperation of desire.

In an access of the silly spite that leaps to the tongue before sense can stifle it, I said, "No matter what we do, we advance on death from the moment we're born."

He said, "Get out of here," with a tonelessness more menacing than black fury.

It struck me that his final desire was to live forever; his dream was that eternity would be part of Young Feller's golden hoard. Anne Blaikie had more than hinted that I had not probed all of this. I did not, for instance, suspect how greatly he had, by indirection, lied—and lied and lied—about the total of how much he knew.

"Your tails," said my uncle Andrew, "will by now have noted the number of this taxi, so we should not use it a third time but, now that we have it, where would you like to go"—he flashed me a smile marvellously combining mockery, hypocrisy and servility—"sir?"

"You called me; I didn't want to go anywhere."

"Driving without aim will alert our follower. She is a private detective, hired for this job and likely to be more professional than any Armstrong household hanger-on. He has sense enough to buy talent. I suggest the Bus Terminal."

"Anywhere." Then I remembered that I dealt with people who did nothing without purpose. "Why there?"

He was driving with a calculated ineptness that missed

crossing lights and snarled us in minor traffic confusions, a careful clumsiness that would stretch a shortish ride to the Terminal long enough for whatever communication he designed.

He answered, "It may turn out to be appropriate," which I took to be a warning for action. Then he got down to business. "We looked at the Blaikie recording last night and I came to town at once."

"She said something of importance?"

"Don't you think so?"

"Derek Farnham?"

"That is one thing. What about him?"

"Exciting, but he may be dead."

"Ah."

"I congratulated myself on spotting something Armstrong had missed but now I feel otherwise." Andrew nodded approval, as to a youngster who was coming along nicely. "With all Blaikie's repetitions over the years he surely must have considered him as a lead, but he didn't mention him. He may have tried to follow up but found him dead. Lunatics don't commonly live long lives."

"But you still think him important?"

"Somebody knew him when he was alive, somebody who knows about him and Young Feller. My guess is that he was in one of the confidential services, that in fact all of the outside staff were. It opens up a big field, one tough enough to preserve its secrets from a devious politician."

"I remember Derek well. He was a fine athlete, a lecher, a man whose eyes and ears were everywhere and who tried, without much success as far as we children were concerned, to seem poorly educated and interested only in his body and his bed wrestling. And in Young Feller. He was surely an agent for one of the confidentials."

I played my proud trump. "My guess is that he hid Young Feller when the kid escaped from the Nursery."

He was not bemused by my brilliance. "Possible."

"So find out if he is alive. If he isn't, find out who is still around who knew him. I can't do it but I think you can."

He asked in a very dry tone, "How?"

"You're the electronics man of the team, aren't you?"

"So?"

"If you're as good on your side as my father is on his, you'd be the best hacker alive."

"Possibly." It was, apparently, no compliment. "You want me to raid the files of the various security services?"

"Can you?"

"I can but I will not."

"For Christ's sake, why not? Do you think you'd be caught?"

"I would not be caught but you do not know much about security devices in the storage networks. Nobody, and I mean absolutely nobody, can invade a protectively coded file without tripping a backtrack. There are methods of diverting the tracker but no way, so far, of disguising the fact of invasion or what the invader took except by destroying the whole area of information—and I am not one to devastate the work of others simply to cover up a smash-and-grab ineptitude."

I gathered that I had come up against a quirk of A Group morality, one where the social conscience operated in a less than wholly pragmatic way. "Why destroy, if the tracker can be evaded?"

"We do not want the services asking why, after so many years, somebody is stealing information about the Nursery folk."

We did not. I had enough to handle without the eye of State guardianship turning towards me.

"Besides," he said, "it isn't necessary." His tone became avuncular, not quite patronising, only gentle about my shortcomings. "You saw the possible importance of the sporting gardener but you missed the mention of the farmer's daughter."

"The one Blaikie thought he was doing a line with?"

"Blaikie thought correctly. He was able to leave the grounds, which is another reason for thinking he had a second persona, and he made no secret of his chasing after the girl." He cocked a sardonic eye at me. "You might find him lacking in sexual morality." Remembering my father's attitudes, and that I was talking to his clone, I stayed quiet. "The girl's name is Adelaide Cormick and she lives in the homestead still."

The name was new to me; it did not feature in my ancillary checklist of people interviewed by media or otherwise associated with the Nursery. I could not recall all the hundreds involved but I could spot one that was not listed, as you spot an irregularity in a design. "Might she know something?"

"They were lovers before our Group left the Nursery, and probably after. He made casual use of the Nursery women but Adelaide seems to have achieved some—what? Continuity?"

I did not stop then to probe the nature of his emotional understanding. "She might know about the mental asylum, which one and where and why. What about Armstrong? Won't he have been at her?"

"Probably not. Her name did not appear in any reports."

So the Group had been doing some ferreting of its own; they could be relied on for homework.

"You should talk to her," he said, "without Armstrong being aware. Then, if a new trail opens up you will have it to yourself. You should be able to get to her undetected."

Should I, indeed? Any small cloak-and-dagger manoeuvre could be safely left to Lamebrain, wise as he was in the ways of his uncivilised environs. Too annoyed for good sense, I snapped, "I think so," and was committed.

He nodded satisfaction and stopped his fooling with the traffic; within two minutes he drew in at the Terminal. "Westerton is the nearest town to the Nursery; book yourself a seat. Will you be able to find the homestead from there?"

I could evade Armstrong but might not have the brain to locate a large property. "It will show on Military Survey maps. Any public library has those."

"Good luck." He began to pull out from the kerb, then stopped to put his head out of the window. I thought, He's going to encore his joke about the bloody fare, but I was wrong. "Arthur said I was to give you his love." Perhaps I looked confused or unconvinced or plain flustered because he added, "He means it."

His expression said that he merely passed on the message but made little sense of it. He was capable of a genial, human humour but that was most likely the outcome of practise rather than understanding. I nodded and waved him away.

I bought a ticket, not to Westerton but to Eildon, for the following morning, wondering the while if my tail was still with me, preparing some professional dodge to discover what destination I had booked for. No one was present in Taxi Service uniform but there was supposed to be a man on the job also, for the footwork; I had no way of spotting him.

I stopped worrying about them and spent some time in various sections of the State Library, though the only thing that interested me was the survey map that showed the homestead's name as Cormick and that its dimensions were huge, like a miniature empire. The other enquiries were smokescreen.

I had said, "I think so," committing myself to adventuring my untested disguise. Now I sweated through an hour of checking each point of the method in an agony of uncertainty, seeking the forgotten something that would betray me instantly. With pencil and paper I listed the elements, pretending that I made dispassionate assessment, doing it over and over until spurious calm faded in the admission that I was scared witless of the consequences of being caught out. Talking my way out of an Armstrong inquisition would not be possible.

Once I had admitted truth I was able to return to common sense. To be scared was rational; to let the scare dominate me was not; apprehensions must take their proper places as pitfalls to be observed and skirted.

Only then did I light on the unconsidered item, the necklet. An interviewer's necklet is a three-quarter circle of sprung metal about six inches across, sprung because the continuous circuitry does not permit of hinges for folding. You force it round your neck from the front, with the gap at the nape; the camera component is hooked on like a small medallion just below the chin. The camera could be detached and dropped into a pocket but the six-inch circlet was too wide to fit into the narrow pockets of my all-too-fashionable stompcat suiting.

It is a measure of my desperate nervousness that it took me an hour to think of simply resting the thing on the top of my head with the fishing hat covering it and holding it in place. I was not thinking well.

I found myself wishing for my father with his bright green eyes and his still, carven face, stumbling out stiff declarations of affection like a badly rehearsed recording, trying to bring comfort.

Next morning I went directly to the Terminal, timing myself to arrive twenty minutes before the Eildon Fisherman's Special departed. I did not carry rod or reel because an inquisitive tail would soon discover that I kept a personal locker at the Lake Club; he was not to know that it contained only a change of clothing.

On the Terminal concourse I suspected that I might at last be seeing my male stalker in the flesh. Leaning against the back wall in a position from which he could, if he looked up, see anyone moving through the departure gates, was a man I knew I had seen before. I recognised him as you recognise a stranger who has crossed your path a time or two; you have paid him no attention but something of him has registered. He was middle-aged, dark, taller and heavier and certainly much stronger than I but otherwise unremarkable save for deep creases at the corners of his mouth, the ruts cut in the flesh by wasting illness—or by too much of the wrong sort of experience. It was those I remembered. He seemed engrossed in a tear-off sporting printout, and did not appear to be observing over the edge of the sheet. But then, if he was competent I shouldn't be able to catch him at it.

Feeling that I had already stared a second too long, I walked into the Gents while a shadow memory—perhaps true, perhaps false—placed him in the ticket queue on the previous day.

If so, this was my test run.

In a cubicle I made the changeover, trousers and jacket turned inside out first, changing the colour to pale brown, then the heels and weights, then the suntan—and came to a simple trap for learners: An even application of the dye required the use of a mirror, and all the mirrors were outside the cubicle, on the washroom wall. And at this hour there were plenty of potential observers in the room.

I experimented on my forearms and found that by smearing the stuff on with the palms and then rubbing I could achieve a fairly even colour; this would do well enough for the neck also, but the face with its lines and corners and shadows would be a more delicate problem, requiring a mirror.

I could not hesitate. The Eildon bus was due to leave

in minutes and I did not want my tail invading the washroom, if he was not already there, to see what detained me.
I reversed the jacket, using the pads to square the shoulders in the aggressive stompcat fashion, hid the necklet
under my fishing hat and folded the brim to make peaks
fore and aft. A stompcat could wear almost any damned
thing, even a fishing hat with a flash suit. Then I went
outside into the washroom, shaking in my weighted shoes.

The mirror told me my face was more evenly tanned
than I had dared hope, but repairs were still necessary and
I went at them with more will than confidence, pretending
not to notice the smiles and glances around me. The whole
business had too much of the look of a gay makeup job.
With only a minute to spare I left the Gents.

My printout reader was troubled; he frowned, glanced
at his watch and folded his sheet but did not glance at me.
I had no time to watch him but as I moved away from the
departure gates I saw that he made up his mind and
headed for the Gents.

I went straight to the ticket queue, cancelled my Eildon ticket, booked for Westerton, boarded the bus without
seeing my tail again and arrived at the town in the early
afternoon.

Westerton was, and still is, a one-pub town with three
streets and a handful of small shops. I booked into the
hotel under a name I no longer recall, buzzed the local
directory for the number of the Cormick homestead and
in minutes was speaking with the farmer's daughter.

After all this time she was Miss Adelaide Cormick still
and she lived in luxury. Her screen looked out on to a
room that seemed enormous, profligately long and wide
by my inexperienced standards of the good life. Its windows were tall and narrow in the fashion of an earlier day
and through them I caught glimpses of verandah and
lawn. The ceiling was high, in the same older style (I
guessed five metres), and its light fixtures nestled in ornate

plaster mouldings. The walls curved into the ceiling in their upper joins, leaving no square corners, and more plaster moulding ran completely round the room whose walls were covered with a repeated design in pale blue and gold that did not look like paint. I looked and marvelled and forgot Miss Cormick while I guessed that the design was an antique wallpaper, something half a century unknown, that this room had possibly been a ballroom long ago, that it formed part of a house that might be two centuries old and that here was Very Old Money indeed.

Miss Cormick may have been accustomed to Very Small Money taking a moment of shock at such squandering of space in a private home (the room would have housed an extended family in a city tenement) for she waited without fidgeting until I came to some sense of fitness and held up my ID.

"Press, Miss Cormick."

She sat at the far end of the room; screen controls were built into the arm of her huge stuffed chair. She held down a switch while watching the screen and I assumed she was using an enlarger—a pretty expensive accessory—on my ID card.

Daylight through the windows was strong enough for me to judge her about fifty, which would have made her twenty-something when the fire and breakout occurred, and if she was now a touch too matronly to recall the figure Derek Farnham had fondled for a few years, she yet possessed form and dignity and the remains of more than common good looks. Her hair was the very pale blond that holds off greying long after its time.

Satisfied that I was who I said I was, she asked, brusquely but short of rudeness, "What do you want? I have no more tales to tell of the Cormick dynasty and the Western District."

Dynasty! Oh, dear God, a feature magazine staple and I had never heard of her. . . . Now, if I had covered the social columns . . . "I'm after a different sort of tale, Miss Cormick. I'm interested in a young feller who was around here just on thirty years ago."

Distance did not hide the startled reaction, immediately stilled. She said, coolly enough, "He died. That's common knowledge; I can't add to it."

"Not Conrad, Miss Cormick, but that other young feller, his friend, the pentathlon athlete."

She was taken thoroughly by surprise and showed it; her stiff lips formed a series of responses and repressed them. I guessed at: Who can you mean? Or: How did you hear of him? Or: What are you after? Or: I have nothing to say to you. What she chose to say, without friendliness, was, "That's an old and dusty matter. He was known in the district. Any of the older residents . . ." She let it trail off into unimportance.

I said, "The dust is stirring; there's a haze of conjecture."

She smiled incredulity with only a small sign of effort. "Concerning me? I find that hard to credit."

"Conjecture, Miss Cormick, not scandal." I fancied that her face softened a little. "It is he I am interested in. Few seem to have known him at all intimately."

The last word would make or break.

She sat perfectly still. I had to try again.

"There are few punishments worse than the conjectures floated when the press can't get at the facts. I'm trying to find Derek Farnham."

If she had stalled I would not have had the hard gall to make the open threat. Many would have, but that kind of hounding is not my weapon. What she thought I can only assume from what happened later; at the time I saw only that she turned over in her mind matters I could not guess at. When she was ready she asked, "Where are you?"

"In Westerton, at the hotel."

"Do me the favour of talking to no one there. You can

come out here and explain yourself. Please don't be long."

Imperious! She blanked the screen before I could get another word out. In the last glimpse I fancied thoughtfulness rather than alarm or annoyance. What had been at best a ranging shot had hit some kind of target.

Her lounge room, sitting room, salon—whatever they call it in circles where money creates its own dialect—must have been fifteen metres by half that width; the expanse of blue and grey carpet, like a lake, would alone have been worth a year of my income; the ceiling-to-floor drapes smouldered with the overblown richness of a period vidplay. Furniture dotted the room in little island clots of tables and chairs and sofas whose designs were as antique as their structural woods, timbers so old that I could not name them but only recognise rarities in a progressively deforested world that offers little to the joiner and cabinet maker. Pottery, crystal, pictures and brocades I took in sweepingly, not daring more than that because I might have been left staring like an idiot over my dropped jaw.

I had seen nothing like this before; I had never quite believed the photographs in the "stately home" books, suspecting their sumptuousness to be collated for the occasion and dispersed when the photographer had gone, and now I had difficulty in accepting the idea that real people lived in such unreal places. The flaunting expensiveness of Armstrong's Toorak fortress was vulgarity beside the assuredness of a room that had seen generations come and go.

I had never conceived of myself as poor; now I knew that I was, and not only poor but working poor with no excuse for my presence but impertinence and a job to be done.

Miss Cormick was where I had last seen her, as though she had not moved. I was halfway down the room before she said, "You took your time."

She did not get up or ask me to sit and her colourless tone gave me no clue to the conduct expected of me.

"I had trouble finding the taxi; there's only one in the town."

"A newsman without a car?" The lilt could have been mockery or suspicion.

"You mustn't believe in the super-journos of the vid-plays, Miss Cormick. The reality is different. Do you know what it costs to buy a private car these days, let alone run it?"

"Offhand, no." I had heard somewhere that the truly rich never think about money, they just accept its availability. "So you are not a super-journo, just a strug-gling . . . entrepreneur?"

"If you're asking am I in business for myself, I am. I'm a freelance and not struggling. On the other hand, if I chose to use publicity as a weapon I might be able to afford a car, buying it with the blood of others. For now I can do without one."

She watched me, not moving in her huge old chair, keeping me standing where I had stopped about three metres from her, revolving in her mind, I supposed, what I might know and how best to deal with me. That I was there, in the room with her, meant at least that I was worth consideration. She had the gift of silence, of communicat-ing the sense that I should remain still until she came to a decision; she left me nothing to do but stand, nowhere to look but at her, and at this closer distance she seemed more formidable than a mere one-time beauty, as though years and experience and some harshness had overtaken Derek Farnham's country love.

She said, "Tell me what you want and why. Tell it briefly but leave nothing out."

I thought she and Armstrong would make a fine pair of toughs. Then I saw the difference between them: Arm-strong operated from a base of power but was driven by devils of uncertainty and the fear of defeat while she was simply accustomed to authority and oblivious to the possibility of not having her way. She was doing no more than, rightly, demanding why a journalist's curiosity should be satisfied, in itself a hint that a proper answer could expect a proper reward.

I had only a second in which to decide to risk unforeseen consequences and tell the truth. Well, as much truth as touched her.

I switched on the necklet and her eyes widened. "I need a record of question and answer, Miss Cormick, so that later there can be no disagreement. As in a libel action, for instance. I'm not a muckraker."

(In God's name, then, what was I?)

She nodded and touched the console in her chair's arm. "So you will not mind my recording you."

Not a question, a statement. Nor did I mind. "What I want I don't quite know. I'm searching in the dark. I am writing a book on the Nursery babies and I am up against the same problem that stops every account dead: Why did the Group kill themselves? I've dug up some information that is not common knowledge, that the Young Feller, Conrad, escaped from the Nursery for a long period and nobody knows where he went or what he did. There is reason to suspect that during that period he studied biology and, perhaps as a consequence, returned to the Nursery, where he and his siblings killed themselves soon after. The clues to why they did this must lie in that period of absence, about a year and a half, and the person who holds these clues is the person who sheltered him. My guess is Derek Farnham."

It was the place to pause for a reaction.

She said, "No, not Derek. He remained at the Nursery during Young Feller's absence and did not finish his tour of duty until after the suicides."

It was the right answer but told me something of first

importance. "The public never knew that Young Feller was away, but you knew."

A faint smile came and went. "I knew. I had reason to know. I was present at his going."

"Yet you told no one?"

"Nobody asked me. Nobody had reason to ask me. Only Derek knew that I knew and he was in no position to tell. I seriously doubt that he told the truth even to his superiors. And now, young man!" She leaned forward, meaning to have some honesty from me. "How were you able to link Derek's name with mine?"

"By way of a garrulous old woman who remembered that he courted you."

"Courted? Did she actually say 'courted'?"

There was anger there. "Well, no."

"Chased after? Rolled in the hay with? Took for his floozie?"

"None of those. She mentioned, only in passing, that you were his girlfriend."

"Who was she?"

"A nurse on Project IQ. Anne Blaikie."

"None of us knew those people. The place was as closed as a convent." Now the edge of vengefulness showed clearly. "She'd have been another piece of his nightwork."

"She said not."

What the dynastic Miss Cormick said to that was without dignity. "Was she cross-eyed, bowlegged and bald? Nothing less would have stopped him."

"She said he did not attract her and that she was in any case otherwise engaged."

She laughed. "That must have riled him; he had no patience with virtue. So he talked in the Nursery, my kiss-and-tell man! I wish *I* had been otherwise engaged."

I waited for her to continue (never interfere when they're running) but quite suddenly she removed herself from the exchange. As if I had not been there she re-

treated from contact, into some other place and time. I
held my peace until impatience urged a small interrogative
cough. Without disturbing her stillness she returned from
her far place and said a most extraordinary thing, not in its
content but in the manner of her saying it, in the rough,
practical tone of the farmer's daughter discussing a promising stud bull: "If you could ignore his bland face he was
the most beautiful animal I have ever seen."

So Blaikie had not exaggerated. Adelaide Cormick
eyed my necklet with distaste. "Can you please wipe out
that last sentence?" But when I nodded she changed her
mind. "No, it no longer matters. I was in love and got what
an idiot deserved."

I said, trying to be gentle, "I am writing the babies'
history, not the tale of your secrets."

"For that, thank you. Perhaps you should sit down."

My mission was accepted. I chose a hard-backed chair
with brocaded seat and panel; the plush armchairs were
invitations to drowsiness.

In another swift change of manner Miss Cormick became hostess, offering a drink that I declined, then order-
ing tea through a microphone I could not see. She talked
trivialities while a uniformed maid fetched and carried,
giving me a feeling of being adrift in some dated comedy
of manners. Personal servants, by God! One read of them
in books.

When she was ready she took me by surprise, moving
without warning into her recital, cutting off my leading
questions with a raised finger.

I find it endlessly amazing how the most debilitating
memories can, in recounting, be caressed and fondled like
treasures, as if the act of recollection softened and beau-
tified the brutal facts. The careful, hardened personality
of Adelaide Cormick dissolved in the liquid flow of time
and speech; sentences formed in her clear voice as she
entered the young girl she told of, rummaging in the

young mind, making discoveries and stringing them on the narrative thread, speaking to herself as often as not and every now and then recalling my presence with a start of temporal displacement.

She said:

2.

I have never told anyone. You will see why. Only Derek knew and Young Feller and myself, and so nobody could ask questions. If someone had guessed I would have lied, disclaimed all knowledge, buried my head in forgetful sand and pretended none of it had happened.

I see now that it did not matter except in my furious mind. Young Feller is beyond revenge and I don't see why I should forever protect Derek's reputation, if he still lives, and there is no reason beyond conventional gossip-fear to protect my own. And I don't fear gossip. But in those days it was shame that stopped me bawling my anger and pain all over the countryside and to my family, who would have been horror-struck. Today I am the family, the last of them, the owner of Cormick, the wealthiest woman in a region of wealthy farmers—and it has never until today crossed my mind that I can tell what I please and let the disapproving be damned.

This happened in 2021. My parents and my two brothers were still alive. Then my father died fighting a grass fire, as you will hear, and my mother died, I think, of an inability to live without him. One brother became a policeman and was shot by a fool, the other died on the moon before that particular stupidity ceased for lack of money and a sane objective.

I became the Homestead Queen, the owner, the businesswoman, the guardian of nearly two centuries of relics and the welfare of those who depended on the spread for a living. It meant growing up quickly and that was not easy. Do you read social history? Do you know what we were like in the twenties? You should read it—the record of mankind as an object of self-derision.

In the twenties this country was passing through one of its moral cycles when prostitution went underground, women were decently covered in public, parents were wary of what they discussed before the children, sex was a private act between married adults and a subject of ignorant sniggering for the young. It was, I suppose, a reaction against the superficial liberation philosophies of the previous seventy years. Now the pendulum is swinging and we hear again all the dreary four-letter words used by the half articulate to drum up emphasis on the vacuous.

The pendulum swing disturbs only surfaces. We do the same things in one period as in another and talk about them or don't talk about them as the swing decrees, but we do them. So, Derek and I had been lovers, very physical lovers, for two years when the Nursery grounds were burned out. Nobody knew about us; the fact that it was a physical relationship made sure that I kept the secret though it now seems that he chattered in the Nursery of his conquest. My one good fortune was that the Nursery staff were quarantined from contact with the locals.

Have you ever been in love?

The sudden question stumped me. I had by then worshipped at the usual shrines of the flesh magnetic and delicious, had sworn the heartfelt I Love You to a dozen images of desire—and wondered in the next week where desire had gone and why the image had lost its power. How often I had assured myself: This time, this one, at last, at last—and fallen out of passion as fast as I had fallen in.

The problem of the itching crotch.

And now Adelaide Cormick demanded truth in my field of special ignorance. I thought of my battle-scarred old editor's dictum, that if two people are still friends when passion begins to wane there's a chance for them, if they keep their heads, to fall in love. I opened my mouth to repeat this as my own sophisticated experience, saw her glance turn quizzical and said, "No. In passion but never yet in love."

In passion. I was in passion and for all of that time thought myself in love. Think of me not long out of school, reared in the decades of oppressive morality, shepherded and protected from predatory males—and presented, out of the blue, with something so wonderful that every little repression leapt up and screamed its need.

Derek the gardener was a front; he belonged to Police Special Intelligence and was second in charge of security for the whole Nursery area; that is how he could leave the grounds whenever it suited him. We met one day in Westerton—by his contrivance, he told me later. It was the seduction sequence of a bad novel: The man's eye lights on the hapless maiden, he engineers a small accident leading to an exchange of words and a greeting at the next encounter—and so to a tryst, a declaration and all the tears, sweat and soothing that go with the conquest of a virgin who loves every minute of it.

How releasing it is to speak of it at last, even with the cynicism of hindsight; at the time it was unthinkable, a crime in a family that stank of money, arrogance and righteousness.

I was literally a schoolgirl in love. I suspected early that I was not his only love; odd reticences and evasions suggested that he was ploughing furrows through the Nursery girls. He swore not, of course, and I didn't believe him but I comforted myself as only a hungry libido can that they were stray attractions while I was the fulfillment to which he returned again and again. The delusions we can weave when sex is spinning!

I know now that Derek was a wholly self-centered man, that any easy woman was for the taking so why not take her? He loved his body and I can't blame him for that. He was so damned beautiful and he moved like water flowing. I'm sure he loved nothing else. Yet I had two years of him while the others got only the odd attention when Nursery boredom became too dire. His feeling for me must have been greedier. Can you, a man, understand a man like that?

> Lady, it amounted to no more than sexual convenience in a man who liked much and often. You were the best and easiest lay. I said, "No, not really."

With the men away all day in the far paddocks and my mother fussing with her visitings and fashionable charities, it was easy to carry on a liaison. We were never caught. Never, that is, until the day of the fire.

Of all people, it was Young Feller who caught us, Young Feller on the run to the big wide world.

Our meeting place was what the locals call The Willows, part of a picnic spot the townspeople use for carnival days. It is still there, still used, at a bend in the creek at the bottom of Long Paddock. The big old willows are there yet, weeping to the ground; in the heart of them you can't be seen from the farther bank and it was there we met and played at the world being well lost for love. Well, that's what I played at; God knows what went on in Derek's head, possibly no more than *Yippee!*

The fire was in the first year of the Long Drought, when the Greenhouse Effect began to turn the weather patterns to agricultural bedlam. Crops wilted, cattle had to be hand fed, what grass there was stood in tinder-dry sticks, our creeks were trickles, only a few springs feeding them from the water table, but the willows were green and sturdy and there we met.

We were to meet on the day of the fire but once the blaze started every man in the district was on the fire front. I don't know how it started but it swept through the Nursery grounds and leapt the road into our West Paddock. Have you ever seen a grass fire? With the slightest breeze it runs like a red river, so hot that the dry grass catches ahead of the breeze. On a bad day it can outrun a horse.

It came through in a rush, eating the paddocks. The homestead was safe with its big firebreaks and modern equipment and bore-water pumps, but the fire whipped round it and into our eastern sector and we lost six hundred hectares before the helicopters could arrive with foam bombs. Dozens of the poor cattle were burned and in the Nursery men were burned to death, a handyman and a soldier on the perimeter.

My father died also, out in the paddocks, but we did not know that until much later.

By midafternoon the helicopters were there and it was all over. The devastation had run its course in two hours. In the evening I went to The Willows, sure that Derek would come now to see that I was safe and to comfort me. There's the arrogance of passion for you! I saw myself the most important thing in his world, taking precedence of the aftermath of fire and tragedy.

The extraordinary thing is that he did come.

When I reached The Willows it needed yet an hour to dark. I had run stumbling across a kilometre of burnt stubble, trying not to look at it or to waste more tears over the ruin of the land; there had been enough of that through the day. I only wanted to see Derek alive and whole, saved for me unharmed. I told myself I could love him scarred and blackened but that not the greatest passion could love him dead.

Where the bank sloped down to the creek the fire had raced along the ridge; the edges by the water were still green. Our lovely willows were yellowed at their curving crests but had not caught fire; the shape of the ground had saved them and perhaps some prank of the wind.

I entered from the water's edge where the fronds overlapped in a curtain, hoping that Derek might be already there to catch and hold me . . .

Not Derek. I think I knew at once who waited there, though I had never seen him; Derek's occasional descriptions were those of a man trained to create images from significant details. I was not at once afraid, only resentful because this was the wrong man.

Say, the wrong male, because Young Feller was not human in the everyday sense. He may have been the next kind of human, the kind we may evolve into . . . or just a one-off mutation . . . I don't know enough to guess usefully. He was eighteen or nineteen then but Derek had told me that his Group lagged behind the others physically, so that he looked about fifteen. That is, his face looked fifteen but his body looked quite strong although he was not big.

He was dark, with green eyes. Have you ever seen really green eyes in anyone, like bright emeralds? His dark skin was mostly sunburn from the half-naked acrobatics Derek taught him on the Nursery lawns. He half lay, half sat against the trunk of the big central willow, at ease, resting under the dome of fronds, and he looked at me without any expression at all.

Derek had a rather bland face but that means nothing once you have seen Young Feller; the word doesn't mean anything until you have seen that incurious, unmoving mask. The inhuman absence of anyone behind the face shattered all my little reactions because I felt I was seeing something utterly wrong. I know I made some sort of frightened noise and stood still, panicking. Then I turned to run with some hazy need to call Derek or the police or anyone who might hear, though there was nobody between me and the homestead a kilometre away.

I didn't take two paces before he was on me like a snake. From reclining he crossed three metres while I was turning to run, spun me by an arm and threw me down at the foot of the tree. He seemed tremendously strong. He sat beside me and gripped my wrist and hit me with his other hand, not very hard but hard enough to stop my struggling and warn me of how hard he *could* hit.

I must have whimpered because he said—and I'll never forget him saying it, like a remark about the weather—"Be quiet or I will kill you. I have no inhibition against killing." Then he seemed to forget me, withdrawing into his thoughts, holding my wrist but paying no attention to the holding. He might have been a mechanism primed to say and do exactly this or that—and stop.

So we sat there, my lungs taking in air in short, horrified gasps while he breathed slowly but heavily.

You know how in fright your mind seems to split away from the emotions, how the surface continues to work on trivia while the heart of you is terrified? I was thinking how clever of me it was to grasp why he breathed so. Derek had told me that the children of his Group could control their autonomic systems to some extent and so could move with terrific speed and power for a short time, but then had to phase themselves back to normal metabolic rate, and that is what Young Feller was doing.

Then I thought of how Derek always carried a gun because in theory he was on duty twenty-four hours of the day. A gun nullifies strength and speed. Derek would hold the boy up and march him back home.

Young Feller said very softly in my ear, "Don't depend on Derek," and my face must have been a study in idiocy because his mask cracked in an imitation of amusement.

"What else would you be thinking of? We are both waiting for him."

He meant, this monster, that Derek had told him of our meetings here! He can have had no trouble guessing the outrage of my thoughts because he said, "He tells me what I want to know."

All I could think of was the betrayal, but I had a lot to learn. I told him, sulkily but in the same low tone as his, that we had no arrangement for tonight, that Derek might not come. He answered abstractedly, informing without actually thinking about it, "If not tonight, tomorrow. We can wait."

Then he ignored me. Derek had not, after all, succeeded in showing me the true nature of these children; I had thought of them as extensions of my own idea of cleverness, as cunning brats, lightning calculators, quick-off-the-mark super-exam swots. Now I saw that Young Feller was so different as to be impenetrable. No, that is not right. I did not see him at all because he was beyond my comprehension; what I saw was myself as a thing dealt with and shelved, not regarded as a fellow human. Someone ignoring you at least knows you exist; this was like being a piece taken off the board and forgotten.

In spite of fright I whispered at him, "Derek loves me. He will kill you! You can't escape with that State Project logo all over your clothes."

With a minimum of attention he squeezed my wrist and said out of that dreamy withdrawal, "Noise! Your fault if I kill you."

Too confused with fear and rage to be sensible, I wept, "I'm a person, not a thing."

"Then remember that cowardice is a survival trait." He hit me across the mouth with loose fingers like whips, hard enough to cut my lip, and removed the bit of his mind again. It penetrated to me that I could die here and I did not want to.

Eternity passed before I heard Derek coming, whistling under his breath as he always did. I recognised the scuffle of his feet as he slithered on the sloping track. I opened my mouth to cry out to him and Young Feller looked at me, no longer withdrawn but all present and laughing. He found my desperation amusing. I could not utter a sound then because being laughed at was somehow more dreadful than being in danger. Then, when Derek was precisely where he wanted him to be, he snapped my wrist back so sharply that I screamed with pain and Derek called out and came crashing through the wall of willow fronds.

He was a martial arts expert and very strong but he stood no chance against the boy's speed; he did not so much as clearly see who attacked him. Young Feller crossed the space between them like a stone from a catapult, at full speed in the instant of moving. He kicked Derek in the knee and struck his neck as he fell forward, and that was the end of my rescue—Derek stretched on his face, unconscious.

I kept on screaming but it did not matter where there was no one to hear.

Young Feller took the few deep breaths he needed to adjust his body and his face wrinkled at my useless noise. He said offhandedly, "Shut up," and I did.

Some fraction of him would have monitored my presence but he paid no overt attention to me as he turned Derek on his back and stripped him naked. That was not easy because Derek was dressed in the gear he had worn while fighting the fire, a filthy one-piece overall. Getting the thing off him entailed a deal of propping and rolling over and holding with one hand while the other worked, but Young Feller went at it as efficiently as though he had practised it. Perhaps he had. Or, perhaps, his kind of brain didn't need to fumble and make mistakes.

Stripping off the overall revealed the gun in its holster; he examined it, tested the mechanism, hesitated for the space of a blink and threw it aside. He had no use for it.

He stood and smiled then, contemplating my naked lover, for an instant more nearly human than I had yet seen him. He seemed regretful, appreciative and mildly affectionate. Then he did something quite abominable, squatted on his heels beside Derek and stroked his hair and said with a ruefulness I could only call loving, "There, there, Derry-lad; you'll be all right when you wake up."

He smiled at me with the familiar tolerance of one who shared an interest. "A beautiful specimen, isn't he? A fine breeding strain." He stood and nudged Derek with his toe the way you caress a dog's belly with your foot. "I'd like to keep him but he will be in the way eventually. There's comfort of a kind in unquestioning love that asks no more than food and a game and a pat of approval."

I split in two at that point. An old understanding of the world ended and a new one began. I watched, contemplating wreckage and regrowth, while Young Feller threw off his Nursery uniform and put on Derek's overall. It was a private garment without logo or markings. Young Feller was thin but wide in the shoulders and not so tall as Derek, but an overall is a shapeless thing and it did well enough when he turned up the cuffs. The boots were a size too large but he pulled Derek's thick, sweaty work socks on over his own and seemed satisfied.

Then, without a word or a glance, he left and I heard him whistle under his breath as he went up the bank. It was the same little tune that I suppose he had learned from Derek: "Will Ye No' Come Back Again."

On that same night he mugged and robbed two men in Westerton and took the clothes from one of them. Neither saw his attacker but I knew who it must be. Derek and the Nursery staff must have known but the public never found out that one of its most expensive toys was loose and predatory in the common domain.

I don't know when he returned to the Nursery, but the suicides could not be hidden, however much they were wrapped up and forgotten, but how long he ran free or what he did I have no idea.

She was quiet for so long that I had to remind her that news of Derek was what I needed. Her portrait of Young Feller was valuable but Derek was the link to greater knowledge. I needed to know when he went from the Nursery and where.

She asked, "Do you really want to know the end of that evening? Do you?"

I said earnestly that I wanted every detail that might lead me further. She laughed at my nose pressed so hard to the trail and I had to mutter about not wanting to invade privacy. She laughed at that, too, knowing that I would have dissected her with a psycho-probe had that been possible.

Mr. Chance, I have treated myself to thirty years of privacy and you have encouraged me to take the covers off memory; I am going to enjoy telling it all. Why shouldn't I have a moment's pleasure looking back on young silliness and fright? I'll tell you how our love affair ended and then I'll tell you the one tiny thing that might help you.

So—here was I with Derek naked and abandoned by his master. By the conventions I should have fetched water, cosseted and watched over him and tried to bring him round, but there are pivotal moments in growing up when illusion clears away and instead of collapsing in transports of grief you look at truth and say to yourself, Well, there went I . . .

While I waited for him to come round I searched

his face for love and found it empty of everything but self-satisfaction. That was unfair but there's always a touch of rancour in the ending of besottedness. When at last he sat up he faced me without any pretence of feeling, looked at Young Feller's clothes and at his own nakedness, picked up the gun and put it down and asked, "Which one?"

"He didn't tell me. I think it was the one you call Young Feller, your especial pet." I loved the irony of that.

He nodded and the movement must have given him a twinge because he fingered the back of his neck where the boy had struck him and said—and he was complaining, complaining—"He didn't need to do that; I would have helped him."

I gave him a full service of my awakening spite. "Your lover didn't need your help. He has deserted you."

"Deserted?" He stared not at me but at the ground, the clothes, the willow fronds, seeking something gone forever, his face drawing in to a slow dismay. Then he understood what else I had said and peered at me. "Lover?"

I related, in savage detail, Young Feller's farewell to his beautiful specimen of humanity. My upbringing had never taught me the word *homosexual* but I knew love when I saw it, and we girls had our secret jokes about it just as the boys did. He smiled a little crookedly and said it had not been like that at all. He muttered, more to himself than to me, "It was a bond. A sort of love, but not physical."

He stepped into Young Feller's discarded trousers, which were too short and too narrow in the hips, and had to pull his flat stomach farther in to fasten the waist while he said without deference to what I might think or understand, "If he had wanted that . . ." and let it die into private vision.

"You would have consented!"

He said out of his bland face, "He was persuasive

when he wanted something." He tried to pull the shirt on but his shoulders were too big, so he tied the sleeves round his waist.

I repeated—evilly because I felt evil—"You would have, you would!"

But he no longer gave a damn about me; he was bound up in the boy's desertion of him. I yelled at him, trying to hurt, "To think I've given two years of my love to a thing like you!"

He looked at me with puzzled patience and said flatly, "It was only fun. There were others."

That should have destroyed me, but a covert depth in me had known it all along and I still wanted to pierce his absorption, to wound. "To think I dreamed of marrying a half man!"

It was a random insult; I really had little knowledge of the implication of the words. They meant nothing to him— save for one. "I never said anything about marrying." In truth, he never had. "I've got a wife and two youngsters in Melbourne."

They were just a small something he had omitted to mention, knowing the straitlaced principles of country nitwits. But with *two* permitted children my dream lover was a man of mettle. Breeding stock. I wondered aloud what sort of life was lived by the poor bitch who had borne them for him but he was not listening to me; he was thinking of Young Feller, dreaming of loss while tears erupted slowly between his closed lids.

I left him there and went home in the fading light to pretend to take part in the desperate cleaning of the smoke-stained, water-spoiled house. About midnight they brought my father home, draped over his saddle. Not burned to death—heart failure. Then I had an excuse for tears but I had hidden them too long and they had all dried up.

It was time, as the Book suggests, for me to put away childish things.

3.

She fell silent as though a stress had been faced and released. Perhaps it had; twenty-seven years is a long spell of bottled quiet.

For my projected book all this was tremendous stuff, mint new, marvellous material, but it took me no further forward. Casting about for a fresh trigger, I suggested a little timidly that her inexperience at that time prompted the thought that it was as well she had not become pregnant.

She flushed, faintly, as if she still held inside her the girl in love. "I would not have known how to obtain contraceptives. Derek took pills. That was care for himself rather than for me; he was afraid of the legal repercussions of an unauthorised pregnancy."

(Quite so. At about that time my father was conducting his cool-hearted rompings in the city hay.)

I said, "Not a nice man."

"A beautiful man. Not the same thing."

"You never saw him again?"

"Oh, I saw him often when I shopped in Westerton and occasionally as a guest in other people's houses. He was usually hot after a skirt and we confined ourselves to the politenesses of strangers. He was around for another two years, until the Nursery was evacuated and turned into a mental hospital."

My pulses jumped. "And that was the end of that?"

"Not quite. I saw him once more." I must have put on my nose-to-the-trail aspect again, for she told me, "Now you get your reward for listening to me massaging my self-esteem. Before my brothers died and I was left to manage the estate I had little to do and I joined all the harmless clubs and associations of unbusy women; I think we did a little good but our reasons for joining were often no more than boredom. We have a small district hospital here, only a dozen beds, and we used to visit every week and play at angels of mercy between times by throwing picnics and bridge parties to raise funds for the wards. On one visit I saw a face I knew, Derek's.

"He lay on his back like an unconscious man though in fact he was awake, after a fashion. His arms lay straight at his sides, his feet together and making a little tent at the toes under the sheet, and he stared at something a long way off, not moving. He was in one of the two private wards and the only person present was a younger, rather fat man who rocked on the bedside chair and seemed about to cry. I stood at the foot of the bed and Derek's eyes went through me. He was white and drawn and marked with age like a man who has overnight accumulated a whole generation of years, and at the top of the sheet I could see the edge of a throat bandage. The fat man said angrily, 'He doesn't see you, lady.'

"I said, 'I knew him once,' and the little shift of his face told me what he made of a woman who had known Derek. 'What happened to him?'

"He said, looking for my reaction, 'He tried to cut his throat.'

" 'But why?' And it was shocking how little I cared. I was curious.

"I thought he really would cry then but he gave me as much answer as he could manage: 'People kill themselves when they don't want to live. People with disturbed minds often don't want to live.' He meant: *What's it to you, go away.*

"On the way out I asked Matron how Derek came to be there and that is how I learned that in the mental hospital that had once been the Nursery there was a ward maintained by the combined security services. They had rushed Derek into town for emergency surgery the night before, with his throat held together by clips, and had barely saved his life. The fat man was his brother, a security staff warder. No wonder he wanted to cry."

She sat up very straight, her typical faint smile opening into brightness. "There, now!"

Finding him might be possible, I thought, if I could manage to consult the hospital records, which was unlikely, but Adelaide Cormick had a sense of effect—she had saved the best for last. "One of the gambits I considered while you were on your way here was to refuse to speak to you but to give you the Farnham family address and suggest that you seek them out. So I vidded Matron and got the information she certainly would have refused you. There are advantages to being a chattering clubwoman." She laid a piece of paper on my knee. "That is the address of his next of kin, his wife, twenty-five years ago. It is at least somewhere for a bloodhound to start."

Bless Adelaide Cormick and the need for an audience that had changed her mind.

The confessional was over; it was time to go—save that I had one last question to ask, a piece of impertinent curiosity to be left to the last possible moment because it would be better to walk out than be thrown out.

On the verandah she wished me well, hoped the material would be helpful, said the meaningless things needed to fill in time until her chauffeur brought the car she was providing for me to the front steps. As it arrived and the chauffeur's ears were close enough to ensure that she would not erupt in loud anger, I asked softly, "Why did you never marry?"

In a low voice she answered, "I think that is not in your brief." She was not angry, only thoughtful, and in a moment she told me, "With my parents dead and my brothers gone, I had my kingdom. I ruled Cormick. A husband might have wanted a share in the power I would not have given him; another kind might have been content to be the queen's consort. Neither would have done. Power corrupts, Mr. Chance."

Neatly done, Miss Cormick!

Not quite. As I turned away she said, too quietly to reach the chauffeur, "When you've had the best, no matter how mean a bastard, second-best gentlemen do not attract."

She was on her way inside before I entered the car.

My day was not over. The most unexpected event waited for me outside the hotel, leaning against the wall, nondescript, unremarkable save for heavy creases at the corners of his mouth, the deep ruts cut by too much experience of irritations like myself.

He winked at me. It was like being recognised by a hungry wolf.

I tried to behave as though my heart had not plummeted to my bowels, but I was confused and frightened and needed to get inside, behind a closed door where I could think. I refused to look at him, tried to walk past him as if unaware, but he said very gently, my friendly wolf, "Hi, stompcat! Shall we dance?"

I dared not think of what would happen when he exposed my double-dealing to Armstrong. The only present move I could see was so drastic that my father would be forced to move at once to protect me. He was only a few kilometres away in the old Nursery complex; with quick action I might make contact with him before disaster struck. The tail, after all, could not attack me in public. The street was not quite deserted; he would not risk witnesses.

I said, making it defiant, and for a wonder my voice did not crack, "Tell Armstrong I'm dropping out. I don't like his ideas and I don't like him."

The gentle wolf nodded appreciatively. "I like a man

who thinks on his feet. The quick-change disguise was good, too, but you need more experience. So you figure to drop Armstrong and continue on your own, eh?"

I figured nothing of the sort; I did not fancy my chances as a free agent, and I have no doubt it was all print-clear in my face. My nondescript tail came away from the wall, stood straight, took on personality and became someone else, not at all one to be anonymous in a crowd and one who, though twenty years my senior, would handle physical resistance from me with precision and despatch.

"Bugger Armstrong," he said in that same friendly tone that sounded to me like the snapping of fangs, "There are bigger people in the game than that preserved pig. You haven't done badly for an amateur and you might even get thanked for it if you can stay long enough out of Piggy's way, but it's time we got together to decide how to make professional treachery produce results."

6 • JONESEY

It filtered through a welter of dismay that warning my father would be of no use until I knew what this leech wanted of me, that I must play along until his lunatic statement became clear. There was at the same time an urge to run, anywhere at all . . . which would only have given my wolf the trouble of catching up with me, and soon. His new manifestation appeared physically very able.

As well, I felt as great an idiot as ever dreamed that a bright amateur could outsmart a professional.

The professional, solidly efficient in his business grey against my flaunting trendiness, gently shook my arm with a bricklayer's spread of fingers. "Couple of deep breaths," he said. "Always helps when you've had a shock."

I was rattled enough to take him at his word, and it did help, but he gave me no time to start my own thinking. He pushed under my nose a business card that announced simply:

JONES
Confidential Enquiries

*   *   *

There was a vid number, followed by two hieroglyphs recognisable by any vidplay addict, affirming that his licences—investigator and gun—were current. I had never actually seen a gun in a man's hand and I did not wish to see his.

He said without haste, "Everybody calls me Jonesey because my given name is for friends only and my real name is no business of others, meaning you." He shook my arm again, a concerned elder offering advice to a favoured youngster. "But we will get to be mates, you and me; it will be necessary if we are to get anywhere. But mates and friends aren't the same thing, so to you it's Jonesey. Now, we have to have some understandings."

He stopped there, dropping my arm and raising his eyebrows, making it my turn to talk. Feeling utterly inadequate, I asked, "What do you want?"

"Lots, lots, David, but not here on the public street. I'm pretty sure nobody is interested in us but in a devious world pretty sure isn't enough, so we'll go for a drive."

He urged me towards a fairly old four-seater that needed some panel beating and a colour dip, but the tyres were new and the hydrogen line had a second feed sneaking under the chassis. I could only speculate on the engine under the decrepitude; a double feed was not for cruising. Just like the vidplays—no expense spared under the shabby bonnet.

He headed us out of town and up the arterial highway towards Mildura but soon turned off onto a dirt road servicing the local farms, one that headed towards the low hills a few kilometres away.

I must have sounded as aggrieved as I felt when I said, "I thought you were working for Armstrong."

"So I am, David. To him I report your daily doings, where you go, how long you stay there, who you talk to and sometimes as much as I can gather of what you talk about. Then, like you, I decide how much I will report to whom and, like you, make a second report to another party as well." He risked a glance away from the treacherous, pitted dirt road to show his sad, dangerous eyes alight with crocodile sympathy. "You've been sucked into the twilight world, lad, all lies and wickedness and double cross. Full of surprises."

I tried for insouciance, the young agent who took everything in his stride. "Your boss is bigger than Armstrong, is he? What Department?"

"Slowly, slowly, lad; you have to earn your answers. Be content that there are five intelligence-gathering agencies—that I know of—and that I work for one of them under my perfectly genuine public face of private enquiry flatfoot. That puts me, and you as well now, under the protection of what newscasts and vid addicts call the secret service. That's no comfortable spot for an amateur, so please don't do any foolish, courageous things without telling me first—so that I can stop you. I don't want you dying bravely for no good reason."

Nor did I, but I suspected that in a pinch professional need might override humane concern and that his chatter was mostly a lullaby. My mind ran in sullen circles as we bumped along between the clumps of shade trees sheltering cows chomping the short grass that was now growing poorly in the onset of the Greenhouse fluctuations.

Jonesey said, "You'll be wondering this and that. You mightn't always get an answer but you won't be shot for asking."

"All right: How did you find me?"

"Vanity hurt? Forget it, man; I'm a pro. Fast work and good communications is the trademark. When I heard the company in the Gents making jokes about the kind of bloke who applies his suntan makeup in public I thought that a man who changes his appearance could be about to disappear, couldn't he? So I called my missus, who is also my partner and drives a taxi for quick tailing"—he pulled back a sleeve to show me a very neat radio, wafer-thin and curved to fit an unpleasantly muscular forearm—"and told her to get to the booking queue fast and see who cancelled an Eildon seat and booked elsewhere. You see, David, freelance writers with middle income flats but no pay cheques due before the first of next month don't roll in ready cash, so I banked on you cancelling one trip to pay for the other. And so you did."

"Luck. I might have been flush."

"So you might, but never underestimate luck. I acted on the off chance—and off it came. If you were not such an amateur, young David, you would have put the bite on Armstrong for expense money. He'd have paid it."

He was teaching, not crowing. I felt no better for that. I began, "But how—"

"The wife? Oh, she flashed her ID and went behind in the ticket office and waited for you to show up and change your ticket for Westerton. She said your disguise is excellent, and so it is."

I felt stupidly warmed by his word of praise. "That would need to be a special sort of ID."

" 'Deed it would. Next question."

"What makes you think I report to a second party?"

The car rattled and bounced over ruts worn by tractors moving between paddocks and our heads came close to hitting the roof too often for comfort. Jonesey said, "I'm ninety-nine percent sure and you're a bloody fool if you're working a double cross on your own. Why should you? If you find what you're after you mightn't recognise it, let alone understand it or have a use for it. So you're almost certainly moonlighting a second job. Which is risky, lad, risky. I don't think much of Armstrong but he can be very vengeful."

"So what do you think I'm after?"

He sighed offensively. "Don't disappoint me, David.

We've known of Piggy's legacy dream for years. You aren't the first he has employed on the off chance, only the most unlikely."

I said sulkily, "It's only a fable, anyway."

" 'Deed so? There are other opinions about that and the fable had to start somewhere for some reason. Meanwhile, listen to what I tell you if you want to keep your skin intact. We can look after you so long as you don't get overconfident—or overfearful, which is just as bad and leads to standing still when common sense says jump. Armstrong's a mass of obsessions; he's had his nose in the public feedbag for half a lifetime and he's lost all sense of his limitations, but he has powerful friends and he's stupid enough to be dangerous. That's what obsession does to you. Be wary of him but remember that now you also have powerful friends."

I needed badly to assert myself. "Have I? I haven't agreed to anything."

"I haven't asked you to agree to anything," Jonesey said. "I'm telling you where you stand."

He said it in the good-humoured tone that frightened and soothed in the same breath and flashed me a sympathetic grin as we bounced over a crossroad where tractors had made chaos of the surface. "You'll start by feeding me all sorts of lies until you see I know better, then we'll get down to the business of working as a team."

"We will?"

My heavy irony was a whistle in the dark and I didn't believe a note of it.

" 'Deed we will because we need each other."

I certainly needed the goodwill, however temporary, of anyone who knew I was dishonest with Armstrong.

We emerged onto a better road, second grade but metalled, a tourist road leading into the hills, and began to climb. I asked suspiciously, "What's up here?"

"A view for viewing and a place for talking."

I took that to mean that the question was pointless, and he asked one of his own, "Is that necklet recording?"

I had in fact forgotten to switch off when leaving Miss Cormick. "Yes."

"Then each of us is in a position to betray the other to Armstrong; that's a first-class reason for cooperation. Treason requires trust in order to betray effectively. I like paradoxes; they assure you that nothing is as simple as it looks."

We rose a few hundred feet and cruised past a couple of picnic stops, unused in this wetter part of the year, past signposted lookout points from which I glimpsed the farming plains unrolling below and finally to a place where trees overhung the narrow road and shrubbery made a hedge on the downhill side.

"This'll do," Jonesey said. "Let's get out and stretch."

"Stretch what?" I got out, just the same.

"Your talent for lying. Over here's a spot."

He stepped off the road onto the descending slope and slithered down to a small flat space with a heavy tree trunk felled across it. With branches overhead and shrubbery in front it made a natural cubbyhole in the bush. Seated on a log with Jonesey relaxed comfortably beside me I could see over the shrubs, and what I saw made my skin crawl. This lookout could have been designed for the express purpose of framing the view of the little town of Westerton on the left and the lonely, sprawling, highly visible Nursery complex on the right.

I refused to look at it. I was frightened of friendly, protective Jonesey and his view for viewing.

He said, "This is ideal. A gyro roaming overhead could not see us, a car could not approach without our hearing it and at this distance anybody on the plain below would need a very powerful glass to try lipreading. Bend the head a little and even the directional mike is in trouble. This is as near to privacy as one can get in an unprivate world."

"Are you serious?"

"Not altogether, but people who want to know what you are doing will go to great lengths to find out. I don't think we have been followed but that's a mistake I have made before in a career of small disasters. And am lucky to be alive to regret it. Recognise the Nursery?"

"I've seen photographs, but it hasn't been the Nursery in my lifetime."

"True. What is it now?"

I shrugged. "Some government enclave, I suppose. Doesn't your Department know?"

"It does. So do you."

"I could look it up but why should I?"

"Why, indeed? I said you would lie to me. At first."

"Is that a technique? Whatever I say, you claim it's a lie, until I'm ready to say anything at all just to shut you up?"

"David, David, don't waste worn gambits on a patient old bastard like me. I'm not saying I won't shake the truth out of you if I have to but I'd rather have it gently. Now, you know perfectly well that the old Nursery complex is where the Vitro kids work."

"Who?" The word was startled out of me, the name was so totally strange.

"Surprise, surprise, eh? I can understand their not liking it, but the A Group kids were registered under that name. Arthur and Andrew, Alice and Astrid. A pretty lousy joke but that's what they got for christening." He watched me closely with a quizzical grin that hid nothing of his determination. "I think you genuinely didn't know. They weren't in love with the name, either. They complained, and a benevolent Authority relented and re-registered them as Hazard. Don't ask why. Who knows how Authority works? But it suggests chance, doesn't it, given a parent with a sly sense of humour?"

"You're joking."

"David, you'll never make a liar. Here you are in high tension, stiff as a board where a good liar should be relaxed into believing what he is saying. Whose boy are you—Arthur's or Andrew's, Alice's or Astrid's?"

"Why the hell should you imagine—?"

He held up a schoolmasterish finger in mock despair. "Let me explain how impossible it is to hide in an educated, documented society. If Armstrong had the scientific education of a trained giraffe he'd have been on to you within hours, but he was only a Minister for Science with a gaggle of experts to do his knowing and thinking for him. When he hired me to tail you and I got my first good look at you, sitting beside you in a tram—the sort of close look you can risk only once—I got a crawly feeling at the back of my neck because at a distance I had taken you for an albino but now I saw that you were something else. No weak, pinkish eyes for a start and not a properly melanin-free skin, either. Very white, freakishly white, but not albino white—and since it is my business to have a head full of trivia and since the Nursery kids were uppermost in my mind after talking with Armstrong and since we know all about his obsession, I was able to make a maybe-maybe sort of connection.

"It goes like this: All the A Groupers had strong sex drives and they did a fair bit of fornicating in a sort of up-and-at-'em fashion with not too much emotion in it, and though most of the kids were aborted because of the birthing laws, the foetuses were gene-mapped. All of them were melanin deficient. Now, that's enough to shine like a searchlight in an ID genetic match. So I winkled out your genetic sequence description in the birth records and your mother's and one of the Vitros—among clones it didn't matter which—and got a geneticist to read them. And, lo, David Chance who has sold himself to Armstrong as an investigative journalist—a good move on Armstrong's part because a journo gets answers where others get a scared silence—David is the son of one of the Vitro kids! Which one, workmate?"

There was no point in holding out. "Arthur."

"He's the bio-electronicist. Or is it electro-biologist? Whatever. Now start at the beginning."

I did. What else could I have done?

When I had finished he said, "Christ, what a mess! Everybody holding their breaths while you poke your amateur head in where the experts have got nowhere. And you actually have got a little way."

"Yet we don't really know that the legacy exists."

Jonesey hesitated before he said, "I think we know now. It's hard to make anything else out of the Blaikie woman's story of the suicide. The Department had always reckoned that Armstrong's maggot was just that, a maggot, but now we know that the old long lifer isn't just chasing a figment. And he mustn't get it."

We were agreed on that. "It must go to my father."

"Oh, filial loyalty! What's Daddy's claim?"

"He and his Group might be the only people who can make sense of it."

"That doesn't establish a right, only an interest."

"So what else? Destroy it?"

"It's an option." He stared hard over the farmland to where the Nursery shone white in the afternoon sun. "Do you trust your father?"

The question was so unexpected that my "Yes" was reflex, so I probably believed in it.

Jonesey's eyes came back to me and for once his face was perfectly blank. He asked, "You feel like a son with him? Affectionate?"

That, it seemed to me, was another matter altogether, needing thought. Unwillingly, I had to say, "I don't think so. He's strange, remote; it's hard to find the man to feel for. But I trust him."

Jonesey's blankness eased as though he had been holding his breath. "You feel what you are able to feel but not what you imagine a son should feel. How could you know about that, anyway? Some psychs will tell you father and son are natural enemies. They're probably half-right; you'll have to find out for yourself."

That I did not like; the situation was cloudy enough without my having to deal with undermined loyalties. I decided that what professional Jones said was not necessarily what human Real-Name Jones believed and that I would assuredly do the finding out for myself.

He only strengthened my attitude when he continued, "The Vitro Group are not like us. We don't know what they are like; we know only what they tell us about themselves—and that's nearly sweet bugger-all. Trust and truth and loyalty may not have our meanings for them. Be careful, David, very careful where you put your trust. Even with me. I am not always my own master."

It had not been necessary for him to add that final warning; it was, in its way, a kindness, and it was in that paradoxical moment that I began to put trust in him.

He stood up. "I must meet your father."

"I suppose I can arrange it."

"You will arrange it," he said with his wolf grin returning at full strength, "at the Nursery gate. Come on; we're on our way."

He started up to the road with me calling after him, "What if he isn't willing?"

"His willingness doesn't count when I wear my other hat, the one pulled down over menacing brow, standard issue for confidential agents."

A standup comic.

On the run downhill I thought hard about Jonesey, with only one conclusion: He was disconcerting, he held all the cards, he carried a gun and he used crude but effective methods. I asked, "Did you take me up there just to have the Nursery in sight?"

"Worked well, didn't it? You thought right away that I must know it all when I knew only bits of it."

He was not subtle and devious, merely well trained and good at what he did. He was probably an ordinary sort of man whose leisure loves were watching football and playing snooker. (Not far wrong, as it happens.)

A little later, when we were driving by the kilometre of high Nursery front hedge, he said, "This place has been under watch since I spotted you as a Vitro boy, but they won't stop us. They know my car."

If there were watchers, I saw none.

The outer appearance of the complex of workshops and laboratories was little changed from Nursery days; only the interior had been completely remodelled. The estate with all its hectares of summer grass surrounded by a three-metre hedge and the clumps of eucalypts spaced like sentries was much as it had been when the fire gave Young Feller his chance to inspect the world. The most recent feature, denying the past and brandishing money, was the sign over the entrance gate:

CAG LABORATORY 3

Smaller print confided:

Cooper-Armstrong-Gigliotti Pty Ltd

In the lower right-hand corner, in very small print as though it were nobody's business, was the really important information: Under Federal Licence.

The combined declarations meant that, technically, my father and his sibs were servants of the Federal Government, operating under the instruction of a go-between firm that marketed such products as the various interested Ministers did not sequester under the Secrecy Acts for handing over to other interests, such as the armed services. (There seems to be literally nothing that the armed services cannot find an unpleasant use for.) Superficially it seemed a reasonable marriage of confidential research and marketing expertise but it was open to all manner of corrupt practise; Armstrong and his associates fed well under a canopy of cover-ups and minor scandals.

The barrier robot recognised me, clucked to itself, consulted its instructions and announced in its melancholy monotone that it would notify Dr. Hazard. In a matter of seconds my father's voice blared from the grille with more life than I had credited as lurking in him. He was furious and I was not welcome.

"Why are you here? What do you want? You must stay away from this place unless I call you! Go away!"

No economy of words there; he was spitting the first that came to his tongue.

I said, "I have no choice and it is urgent."

"Urgent? Has something happened to scare you out of your common sense?"

I said impatiently, "Nobody will know; I'm in disguise."

He must have switched in vision because the lens at the top of the gatepost extended downwards for close-up and my father was a little appeased. "Effective," he said, but still grumbling. Then, "Who the devil is that?" The lens moved to cover Jonesey. "Are you insane, boy? That is the private detective who has been tailing you for Armstrong!"

"I know that," I said, and felt immeasurably better for the sound of Jonesey cursing himself for underestimating amateurs.

"Caught you out, has he? What does he want? Blackmail?" His voice changed, dropped to its normal remoteness. "Bring him to the workshop. If he refuses, the gate robot will shoot him."

The lens retreated to its perch.

"Nasty, nasty," said Jonesey.

The barrier retracted and we drove through.

*   *   *

I had to explain quickly to Jonesey that when my father said "workshop" he did not mean a shed full of machinery, gadgets and overalled assistants but a suite of rooms forming a living apartment and two large halls, the main feature of one hall being a high-performance computer dominating a scatter of workbenches equipped with small power tools and usually littered with models in various stages of completion. The biology component was a smallish but extremely sophisticated laboratory, antiseptic and white. To my father the living quarters were only a necessary annex; the work space was the area in which he existed. There were no assistants; the Group were essentially problem solvers, each working alone in a self-contained unit and making his or her own experimental models.

"Don't they socialise, talk, eat together?"

"I was here for two weeks and didn't see any of the others."

"Yet they can be involved. Your uncle Andrew, for instance, plays his little comedies with a taxi."

"You have to accept that they aren't like us in a social sense; they see things differently." I heard myself, not happily, echoing Jonesey. "They don't understand us very well, either; my father is often naive about simple relationships."

Jonesey muttered that what worried him was how they did in fact see us and themselves.

I said, "They're not like Young Feller."

"How do you know that?"

I did not know and the question brought a moment of chill.

No one waited for us on the steps of the porch or in the empty, soulless entrance hall. I led Jonesey through to my father's quarters, where the windows looked out on flat grassland where a handful of sheep saved CAG the price of mowing, and took him into the controlled chaos my father called his "lounge."

In the midst of this, my father. My father, indeed, twice. I had to look closely to detect a faint scar on the left cheek of one of them; it had been covered by pseudo-flesh the last time I had seen Uncle Andrew.

We speak of identical twins but see small differences when they are side by side; these clonal twins, exactly matched in vitro and not subject to the chance influences of placental dominance, were identical in all things but the scar. Even their voices were indistinguishable. Jonesey was fascinated and made no bones about examining them closely. Impassively, they scrutinised him as minutely. After an initial welcomeless glare I might as well have been elsewhere.

I said, "Hello, Father," but he ignored me and said to Andrew, "This is the man."

Andrew agreed. "He and a woman have trailed David each day, all day, until relieved at seven in the evening."

My father asked Jonesey, "Do you propose to explain yourself?"

Admittedly, Jonesey was the logical centre of their interest but I felt as though I had strayed into a private discussion.

" 'Deed I do," Jonesey said and sat down without being asked, settled himself comfortably and continued, "I am a confidential enquiry agent at present employed by ex-Minister Armstrong to tail your boy during the daylight hours and report on his comings, goings, contacts and conversations. I am also an agent of a Government Department that I don't propose to identify and to whom I report on Armstrong as well as on David. It seems that from now on I will have to report also on you and your siblings unless the Department is willing to provide someone to live here with you. You are becoming expensive of manpower."

The brothers exchanged glances that meant nothing I

could follow and Andrew asked, "Why did Armstrong hire you? Is he insane or merely paranoid about trust and betrayal?"

Jonesey thought it over. "Unbalanced, certainly, but consider the facts: Here's a man who has double-crossed and cheated his way through life and considers venality the normal human mode. To him, no man is trustworthy save under compulsion—and there are times when I agree with him. For instance, he sets me to trail David to keep him straight and each of us betrays him to a different third party. So, is he paranoid?"

My father said shortly, "Yes," having no patience with word play. "What do you want?"

"The same thing you want. It may be also that I don't want you to have it, but that isn't for me to act on without orders."

The warning did not seem to disconcert them; they may have foreseen the possibility.

"And David?"

"Is doing unexpectedly well." The approving tone was the equivalent of a friendly pat. Fuckwit makes good! "He pulled off a small introductory coup today and we should let him run with it. Always follow the luck while it lasts—with somebody guarding your back. I will guard his back."

The twins communed, with no detectable signal. My father said, "That could save us unnecessary waste of time in the city. We are busy here." A nicely practical response: *It gets the kid off our hands.* He stared hard at Jonesey. "On the other hand, what do we know of you who suggest that our search may finally go for nothing?"

"Only what your boy can tell you. Your turn, David."

Nobody interrupted my relation of the day's work. When I had done, my father gestured for the necklet, hooked it to one of his screens and ran the Cormick interview. Then he and Andrew played their little pause for sorting words and priorities before Andrew homed in on

Jonesey rather than on the interview. "There was always a long chance that someone would make the connection between David and Arthur. Statistically—"

Jonesey broke in on him. "Chance buggers statistics. There's always somebody with the odd bit of knowledge. My profession rides fifty percent on chance and other people's blighted luck. My luck is that I know what to do with Chance."

Nobody applauded and I was becoming impatient with his variations on the theme of luck. "The connection was made, how doesn't matter. What matters is what comes of it."

"What comes of it," said my father, "is that you look for Farnham and his brother, or his wife, hoping they are alive still."

"But you said Young Feller could not have lived with Derek Farnham."

"Nor could he. You play with your dog but you don't kennel with it."

Jonesey asked, "Is it true, then, that he used the man like a pet?"

"From our observation, yes."

"You approved?"

"What was it to us? We were all in our late teens, self-absorbed, discovering directions. Conrad's needs were his, not ours. We were, effectively, three groups of aliens with little contact. The scientists had created three totally unlike types of mentality with neither goals nor comprehension in common; no Group cared what the other two did. If Conrad wanted a pet, that was his private psychological mystery."

"So you didn't care?"

"Why should we?"

I was surprised that Jonesey forced that issue. "Can you imagine David, your son, in that position?"

"Yes, or any man. No ordinary human could withstand Conrad's seduction." He seemed faintly puzzled, as if a subtext to the question eluded him. Then a small tic of distress twitched his mouth and eyes, as though he had had to decide on the correct response before producing it. "We would not have known how to interfere. We think that Conrad and his sibs were groping towards techniques and psychological insights ungrasped by us. They would have been very dangerous to the world."

I had to remind myself that my father was floundering on unaccustomed emotional ground, to make allowance against the suspicion that he had been caught out in a deficiency in his role playing. Jonesey seemed to have got what he wanted, because he chose to follow my father's deflecting lead.

"Couldn't they have used these manipulative abilities to con their way out of the Nursery?"

"I think not. Conrad's success with Farnham was a pointer but they were still not adult and they were badly retarded by lack of practical experience as well as by the staff's watching policy, which precluded help or encouragement in uncharted areas. They did not yet understand their emerging strengths. It is probably as well that they died in ignorance of their power."

Declaring the subject closed, he switched to a mild jocularity that sat badly on him. "David, we have no name for your—what is your word for him? Companion? Captor? Gadfly?"

I wished he wouldn't try to be jokey (Andrew was better at that) and said stiffly, "Dad, Andrew, this is Jonesey. Jonesey, my father and my uncle Andrew."

Andrew queried, "Jonesey?"

Jonesey mimicked him, not very well, "The Brothers Vitro?"

Andrew was not pleased. "A laboratory whimsy."

Jonesey presented his business card. "A personal whimsy."

"The creation of an offhand personality to disguise the soul of a sneak?" I could have told Andrew that such unsubtle prodding would get him nowhere.

"Just so," said Jonesey cheerfully. "It gets the suckers in—and poor old David has been got in by just about everybody, present company included, hasn't he? Yet he has nosed out a trail nobody else sniffed at."

Andrew said, "There were no doubt indications that we missed at the time through lack of interest; Derek was highly promiscuous."

"As were both of you."

The deliberate reminder that he had done some background-hunting seemed not to concern them. They said, in a perfect twinship of disinterest, "Yes," leaving nothing for discussion.

Jonesey insisted, "David did well to spot the possible line."

My father considered me briefly. "Yes."

"You agree that he should follow it through?"

"Yes."

"To what end? What gain?"

If he was hoping for great originality he did not get it.

"We must assume that Conrad visited Derek in Melbourne during the man's monthly leave periods. He would have had no trouble smoothing over his act of violence. His need would have been for information on the simplest level, mainly behaviour patterns, conventional attitudes, idiomatic usages, social mores and the techniques for remaining inconspicuous in an information-based society. Remember that he was reduced to homelessness and robbery, with no reliable knowledge of the capacities of the police or even of the private citizen. Derek was his obvious and valuable contact."

"And then?"

My father said with uncharacteristic vagueness, "One contact leads to another. David must follow his nose."

"And see what turns up?"

"Yes."

Jonesey was playing bloodhound. "What should turn up?"

My father, who was not given to gesture, spread his hands. Pure theatre.

Jonesey complained, "Because I'm a flatfooted private snoop with a middling IQ and the outlook of a hungry rat, must I be also the village idiot? We want to know where the bastard studied biology, because *that's* what he queried Farnham about between survival courses and bouts of mugging. Mugging became a hazardous way of earning a living with the rise of the electronic watch system, but my bosses noticed a long time back that it increased markedly while Young Feller was loose in the city and eased off when he went back to the Nursery. He didn't get public mention because officially he had never broken out, but somebody with a very expert touch for neutralising electronic systems specialised in indoor muggings for about eighteen months and was never caught. He couldn't waste time amassing a bankroll so he picked up money as he needed it. He needed plenty because the kind of study he was after doesn't come cheap."

Perhaps they had been assessing Jonesey's brains. My father nodded. "So far, so good, but the standard of biology to be learned in a lifetime of practise cannot be taught in any school, no matter what the fee offered."

Jonesey turned vulgar. "Don't shit me, mister; you know he wouldn't put up with a teacher any more than a teacher would put up with him after day one. Departmental info says his Group had photographic reading skill and total recall—a textbook in ten minutes of page turning. What he needed was library access and Special Student Licences for restricted terminals. How to get those was the gen he needed from Farnham. Whoever actually got them for him is the next in line for David."

There was a silence of the brothers in stonefaced eye-ball consultation, but Jonesey felt pleased with himself and in need of applause; he asked, "Well, do I pass?"

My father clapped politely. "Cum laude. A question remains."

"Where did he live? I don't know."

"Nor do we, but we can suggest to you the manner of place he needed. Our sisters are biologists and we have discussed it with them. So: To learn advanced biology and bio-chemistry plus genetic surgery, gene topology and a dozen other ancillary systems would require much more than mere absorptive ability. It would require an array of screens and laboratory equipment beyond the range of any but a funded school or a private person of very great wealth and a willingness to lay it out. It would require also access to current research files in laboratories all over the world and to material buried in patent files. That would have necessitated the services of a full-time hacker of transcendent ability. On second thought, an intelligent operator with Conrad's mind to guide him might have sufficed."

Andrew said loudly, "No!" and nodded at me. "David?"

I had learned my lesson. "Could be, but only if he was prepared to destroy whole data systems to prevent tracker analysis of the search."

"Such wholesale destruction," Andrew said, "would not only have been noticed by the tracker system but also by the thousands of research workers and students using the deleted areas. It would have been publicly unhideable, grist to the media mills. And such a news story would be on file."

Jonesey looked glum. "The Department would have picked it up at the time but would have had no reason to hang it on Young Feller. Still, I'll have to check."

"You will find nothing; he would not destroy knowledge. He would kill individuals if he thought it needful, seeing them as infinitely replaceable, but he would not wipe out a part of the collective experience of the race."

That sounded impressive until Jonesey asked, "How would you know that? Aren't you transferring your own morality to him?"

They held silent, instant conference. Andrew conceded, "Perhaps. I was presenting a necessary aspect of a pragmatic morality."

"But that's your version, isn't it? A morality with no silly ideas about the sacredness of human life."

"The ideas for and against are not silly per se but the application of them often is. The euthanasia laws, for instance."

That particular tangle of ferocious argument, now into its eighth decade, was example enough for anyone.

Jonesey grunted, "He'd have to get the access and the gear somehow. Accept that for a start and our first problem becomes, Who was the provider, because Young Feller would not have had time to put together such resources. Maybe his intellect was formidable but cultural obstacles can't be brushed aside by a flick of the mind."

I had been thinking in terms of the hunted fugitive stealing for sustenance and studying furtively in his huddling place . . . and suddenly we were among the millionaires.

I blurted, "Armstrong! That bloody Armstrong! He had him and lost him."

Jonesey seemed stunned by the obvious but Andrew brought us back to earth. "We considered that and decided against it. At that time, twenty-seven years ago, Armstrong owned neither the wealth, the suitable housing nor the essentially private property needed for such sheltering. Conrad hid himself elsewhere." He smiled with the sad benignity of the cynic. "No doubt he found pet animals to stroke and dominate and bleed white."

So my burst of insight flickered and went out.

My father said, "With Mr. Jones guarding your back

you should proceed quickly. His professional expertise will be of great assistance."

That was all the thanks Jonesey got and it was, effectively, our farewell. All had been said that needed saying and the CAG laboratory staff was anxious to return to the more interesting pursuits of the life intellectual. We scavenging element could be left to our squalid devices. I was delivered into Jonesey's care, and that was that.

For a moment I felt like an abandoned child, but when I thought it through I saw that they must consider Jonesey a godsend. His assertion that he might have to dispossess them in the end would have been noted and filed but they were not likely to concede that they could be outwitted at the last. Privately I thought that he should have kept that to himself but already I realised that he gave nothing away without reason.

They did think of one other thing before we left. Andrew chased after us as we went to the car. "David's reports! Could you arrange to have them forwarded confidentially to us, perhaps through your nameless Department? Those Courier Services are expensive."

Jonesey had met a bland nerve to match his own; he stuttered slightly as he agreed that it could be done.

"Please don't doctor them," Andrew said. "We are much better equipped to detect interference than your people are to delete sections and reorder meanings."

Jonesey answered through rising blood pressure, "It will be in our interest to see that you receive them complete." He brought his wolf grin to bear for a parting snap. "After all, you are working for us now."

Andrew punched him lightly on the arm and cried, "Oh, good man!" for all the world like a tenth-rate actor— and added his own exit line, "We will be able to demand suitable payment, won't we?"

I wasn't sure that he hadn't the best of the exchange.

*　　*　　*

We headed for Westerton, Jonesey driving slowly in thoughtful silence until at last he asked, "Why are those vitro-decanted types so placidly content to have you carry on as though no such thing as an intelligence agent had interfered? Why, why, when I have told them that the snatched prize may never be theirs?"

"It will," I said, "because you have nobody else with the brains to handle it."

"Depends on the clarity of Young Feller's instructions."

"Probably theorems," I said, "perhaps diagrams and certainly a lot of mathematical language. My father thinks the problem is basically one of topology."

"Like maps, land surfaces?"

"That's topography. Topology is the math of connectivity. It describes how shapes interconnect and what the connections do to spatial relationships. Leave it to the decanted intellects."

He stopped the car with a jerk of irritation and plain bad driving, half turned to me and said without any geniality at all, "Those intellects are the other half of the investigation. Surely you must have asked yourself why they want the legacy!"

In fact I had not. They were scientists in a field where Young Feller's formulations could represent an enormous advance in knowledge and technique, especially to the biologist sisters who would presumably fall on it in intellectual gluttony simply because it existed.

I mumbled some of this and Jonesey asked sadly, "You don't see any of them as having selfish desires, plans they don't see fit to confide to the pawns in the game?"

"Evil genius seeks to rule the world? No."

"Sure?"

"Quite sure."

"Why?"

All I had was a feeling, a certainty that whatever

Arthur and Andrew wanted, power and influence were no part of it; they were remote from the common spectrum of human ambition. How do you explain a gut feeling? I tried and was relieved not to be laughed at.

"You mean," Jonesey said, "that they are not as you and I, that they neither like nor dislike people, just can't be bothered with them and therefore won't interfere with them. Their knowledge is pure knowledge, sacred by reason of its existence, eh? You could be right. And you could be wrong."

"You haven't had my experience of them."

"Don't get self-righteous about this, but what does your experience add up to? Fuck all! Tell me, David, do you really like that green-eyed pair?"

I had to think about that. "In a way, yes, but it's hard to imagine ever getting close to them."

"Even your father?"

"What's the difference? If I can't see Andrew's scar I don't know which one I'm supposed to be feeling for. My father does his best to show affection and I feel guilty because I can't respond."

"Do you now?" That seemed to interest him a good deal. He asked, "How did you feel when you found you had a real-live Dad who wanted you around?"

Such feelings are not easily defined. I remembered being at first disappointed because he was not a man I would have chosen for a father, then warming a little—only a little—to his clumsy attempts at affection and finally being pleased about a sort of inner solidity, as though I had at last a provenance, a footing in the world.

"I had always felt separate, not lonely but unanchored. A family is a sort of huddling place, and I had always felt like someone floating free, as if when the alarms rang I would be the only one with no burrow to dash into."

"And now you have your psychological burrow, even if the hearts in it beat without much warmth."

"Something like that."

"And for that small comfort you aren't prepared to think evil of your green-eyed dad."

He made me feel a fool, a resentful fool not prepared to endure needling. Yet I had nothing to say to the doubt he sowed so bluntly.

He put a tentative hand on my shoulder. "David, we may be running a pretty queer gauntlet before we're done and we can't afford illusions. I don't trust the Vitro brood. Maybe that's my illusion and you're entitled to reject it, but you have to know that's how I think. Then you won't place mistaken trust in a wrong expectation."

I said, "It was a kind of adventure; you make it dirty."

"It always was. Before you were born, Armstrong put his paw print on it and it won't wash off."

"I almost wish I could back out of it."

He said sharply, "You can't!"

"There must be a way out. Your Department—"

"No! You're in, to the end." His mood changed as he put the car in gear and headed us off again, for he started to recite some verse, peculiar stuff, hard to reconcile with my idea of him:

". . . after a pace or two,
Then, pausing to throw backward a last view
O'er the safe road—'twas gone! Grey plain all
   round:
Nothing but plain to the horizon's bound.
I might go on; naught else remained to do."

"What's that?"

"That's you, babe among the bastards, with nowhere to go but on. Don't you know Browning? Christ, what do they teach the kids these days?"

"How to live today. There's plenty of time later to discover Browning and Shakespeare."

He seemed struck dumb; there was an old-fashioned side to him. I said, "I've discovered them—a bit."

"Quote!"

" 'If it were done when 'tis done, then 'twere well it were done quickly.' "

"Yes! We've no time to waste. Too many people are playing too many double games; the thing must soon collapse of its own complexity."

By then we were entering the township. He dropped me off at the hotel, saying, "I can't take you to the city; we mustn't be seen together."

"For God's sake, he can't have watchers watching both of us."

"I wouldn't think it, but put nothing past a man obsessed. Just remember that it's chance that upsets plans, like the chance of one of his regular staff accidentally seeing us in the street. We have to put controls on chance. So what's your next move?"

"Pass the Cormick tape to Armstrong. This trip will have been a last-minute change of mind; I can't have been trying to outsmart you because I don't know that you exist. Then I'll start looking for the Farnhams."

"You'll have to try if only for the look of it but I don't think you'll get much from that lot. The next step after them is the tricky one. Think about it."

I did not absorb that at once but, as he prepared to move off, asked, "How can I contact you?"

"Why should you? You've never heard of me! Go on as though I don't clutter your landscape."

He took pity on my inexperience, even to the extent of a friendly smile. "As they say in the other illusion business: Don't call me, I'll call you."

7●FARNHAM

1.

Nightfall and I came to the city together. All my desire was
to reach the flat, stretch on the bed and let tension drain
away. I needed time to assess the day's debits and credits in
comforting darkness.

However, common sense insisted that this must wait
until I had despatched the necklet transcript to Armstrong;
too long a wait between Jonesey's report and mine might
start that infinitely suspicious mind pecking and peering. I
made the transcript, removing all trace of Jonesey from the
record, and sent the Cormick recording to Toorak by Courier Service under coded seal. He would have had it by nine-
thirty.

Then I felt free to lie on my back and consider my
approach to the Farnhams. There would be Derek and
wife and perhaps the brother; the children would be
grown-up by now and gone from the home. And there my
projection faltered under the nasty weight of Jonesey's
speculations about my father and his kin.

He had hit me harder than I had let him see or myself
admit, particularly in that blow beneath the belt of my

self-satisfaction when he had judged my experience of the Group worth exactly nothing. He was right, of course. What had I seen of my father and Andrew? Two masks playing roles unfamiliar to them and using their unfamiliarity to lead me into thinking that Arthur's clumsiness was an unaccustomed attempt at goodwill and Andrew's jokiness an effort to build a social bridge. But, perhaps the clumsiness and the jokiness were stiff-jointed essays at crossing the intellectual and perceptual barrier . . .

I fell asleep at some such intractable point and woke with the nightmare sensation of huge sound and a waking dream of my name called by demons.

One demon only; he called again in Armstrong's voice, and he was not in a gentle mood.

When I felt steady, I asked, "What do you want?"

"You visited Westerton!" The tone was thin, hard, furious.

"Yes; I sent you the tape."

The screen breathed heavily. "You did not inform me first!

He was reprimanding a neglectful servant. Remembering that he could probably see me, I tried to seem irritated rather than abashed as I asked, "Why should I? It was a spur-of-the-moment idea that paid off. Be glad of it. What difference does it make whether or not you knew in advance?"

More breathing. Bottled anger or shortness of breath? Was it time, perhaps, for another antigeriatric treatment? "I know where you are at all times, Chance! You can't duck out of sight on a whim; you are never out of my reach. You told me you needed time for planning and at once took off on an unscheduled interview without my sanction!"

"I get an idea, I work on it. What does it matter—"

"*I say it matters.* There must be coordination. You are not my only agent."

Liar. I am the current clutched-at straw, the only one. Jonesey's breezy dismissal of him had given me some mental armour against the Armstrong threat.

Winding down, he changed his tactic, assuming the persona of the cool mastermind projecting the condescension of power. "Don't ever alter our syllabus, Davey. I can reach out and take you at any time, anywhere."

Not when the taking hand is guarding my back, you can't. "If you always know, where's the need—"

He bellowed out of the screen so loudly that the sound dampers slid across my windows, "Don't be cocky with me, scribbler!"

I tried for contrition. "I've had a long day; I'm tired."

"You'll have a longer one tomorrow if you go looking for the Farnhams at that address the Cormick woman gave you. I've had it traced. That house was pulled down years ago to make way for a workers' tenement."

I said, "Hell!" and meant it. "Did you have to wake me for that? Wouldn't the morning—"

"It's bloody near morning and I'll talk to you when it suits me!" Then, quietly again, "My people will find the Farnhams and give you the address, then you'll discuss the approach with me. Understood?"

"Got it."

He was one of those mannerless types who cut off as soon as their piece is spoken. I checked the time—4:37 A.M. He must have been up all night, fuming. Jonesey had shrunk him to a paranoid spider whose web was smaller than he thought, whose power to strike was as much braggartry as reality and who was himself a watched piece on the Departmental board. He was worth a private smile.

But Jonesey had also said that he was an obsessed man, unpredictable and vengeful. In anger he might thresh dangerously at the nearest victim. Myself, as likely as not. I quenched the private smile.

* * *

Armstrong's finding of the Farnhams would have been by way of the Census Master File (some old political contact would have smoothed that access for him), then of sorting the wanted one from the names, addresses, birthdates and movement histories in Data Storage. For interest's sake I counted the Farnham vid numbers on the current display and found forty-eight in Melbourne alone; extrapolation suggested between four and five hundred in Australia, and they could be anywhere on the continent in a score of different Storages. His secretarial moles were welcome to that burrowing.

They located them, not at the far ends of the country but two hours drive away.

Then, with his messenger boy properly chastened, Armstrong made a mistake born of his suspicions and of his ignorance of his true position in the play. It was also a fairly reasonable consequence of the tangle of loyalties and private ends we had constructed between the lot of us.

He shouted at me out of the screen on Sunday morning.

"Yes, Mr. Armstrong." I was properly respectful.

"I have found the Farnhams." With some help from friends, contacts and flunkeys. "They are at Gunnamatta."

"Never heard of it." It sounded like a two-hut hamlet on the edge of the desert.

"Look it up. Household of three—Derek Farnham, Petra Farnham and brother Evan. The wife and brother are both trained psychiatric nurses; he's probably as mad as a hatter."

"Lovely! What then?"

"After thirty years the other two should know all he knows. Decide your approach and vid me back."

"Hold on! Is this Gunnamatta a town or just a map reference? Are they out on their own or in the town? It makes a difference. And what is their financial position?"

"Outside the village. What has finance to do with it?"

"If Derek's round the bend they mightn't want to talk. People have neighbours and feelings."

"But journalists haven't. I'll call you back."

He did so, two hours later. I wondered how many approaches were made, how many debts of gratitude were called in, how many moles set digging during that time.

"They live on their pensions."

"Peanuts. Barely enough and nothing to spare."

"What of it?"

He was unable to grasp what pensioned poverty could mean; it was a pointer to his isolation from the real world. I had found Gunnamatta on the map, a tiny place on the south coast, a hundred kilometres or so out of the city, and now had a crystallising vision of unhappy people on the wrong side of middle age seeing out their time with a destroyed man and bitter memories.

"The beaten don't always open up their miseries for prying publicists. I may have to touch their unhappiness with money."

"Huh!" He said grudgingly, "Not too much of it. Don't offer unless you must, then keep it low. I'm not made of the stuff."

Thousands for surveillance (JONES, Confidential Enquiries, did not come cheaply) but scrimping for necessary expense . . . the mark of the parvenu, so they say.

"I'll try."

He was silent for so long that I peered to be sure my hijacked screen still showed a faint flicker, but at last he said, "You'll need a car."

Surprise! I had looked up the bus route with its maze of changes and minor line connections and was happy to have the run made easy, though caution suspected a reason for generosity. A reason there was.

"You will be called for in the morning at nine o'clock. The driver will stay with you throughout the interview and at all other times." No more running off at whim, Davey-boy; my hand is at your shoulder, always. "Call him your assistant and invent suitable duties for him; he has brains enough for routine. You can address him as Mr. Jones. It is not his name but it will serve."

I scarcely believed I had heard correctly. I repeated like an idiot, "Jones."

"I will expect your report tomorrow night—" and now the reminder that only strict honesty was acceptable "—and his."

I did not notice when the screen gave up its faint flicker; I was counting unsolicited blessings.

In the morning, on the stroke of nine, the caretaker's desk called me. It *had* to be Jonesey, and by the grace of unholy good fortune, it was.

To tone with his conservative taste and to prevent our being instantly typed as clown and straight man, I wore a darkish grey sports jacket and trousers and a shirt with deep green Lurex threads. It was the best I could do; Jonesey would look as much like a newsman's assistant (whatever that might be) as he would like a French head-waiter, but I would have to manage with what I had.

I think he was relieved that I had discarded the trendy gear but all he said was, "The wife will be glad to be off the job now that I've got you to myself. She hasn't been getting enough time with the kids."

"Kids?" Did people like Jonesey have families and a home life?

Edging into the traffic, he said, "A boy and a girl. Beautiful kids."

For the space of seven words another Jonesey peeped out and immediately hid again, a proud parent with the simple values of an adoring moron. Then I thought: State approval for *two* kids! and wondered just where he stood in the hierarchy of his shadowy profession. He would be no flatfoot operative slumming round the streets for a weekly wage; somewhere in the corridors of suspicion Armstrong's obsession was being taken very seriously indeed.

"How did you work this job, and why?"

"Why? Well, now, to get the missus back home as much as anything. The extra money doesn't come into it."

Bloody rubbish! "You still don't do badly, paid by two bosses for the same job."

"David, you're an innocent. Do you think the Department lets me keep Armstrong's bit of pin money? I have to surrender every cent of it. You can't moonlight in the microchip culture."

"I'm laughing. Now, really why?"

He answered with spiteful savagery, "Because you need looking after. You think yourself sophisticated and cunning and everything you are not, when in fact you are being used by at least three sets of unscrupulous bastards who won't wipe an eye if you finish with a bullet in your brain—as you bloody well may if I don't make a better watchdog than your fish-blooded father. You babe in the woods of dirty tricks! I trust no one and I want you out of this alive."

I let that simmer for a while before I asked (and I like to think I was a bit humble by then, but I doubt it), "Why should you take special interest?"

He snapped at me like one driven to the limits of his temper, "I'm sentimental!"

That struck me, oddly and comfortingly, as somewhere near the truth. He was a strange man. For a while I did not know how to approach his mood but eventually had to ask again how he had managed this "closer surveillance."

Pleased with his own deviousness, he reverted to good humour. "With lowdown subtlety and stealth. I make my reports to Armstrong verbally, so I was able to hint—never saying it outright, you understand—that you might be holding out on him, that it was pretty suggestive that you had demanded time to work out your approach and then pissed straight off into the blue to chase a mark you had kept to yourself. I told him I had trailed you but not that I had bailed you up. I let him work out for himself that close-contact minding would keep you in line because you would feel his eye permanently on you. One false move and down comes the chopper. And, with me present at interviews there won't be any doctoring of tapes, will there? No hiding of facts your employer should possess. Very satisfactory, David. He gets added security and you get me, which you don't appreciate as you should. More importantly, I get *you* right where I want you and, if we're careful, access to the ideas of the A Group comedy quartet."

After the self-congratulation, questions remained. "Who takes over when you go off duty?"

"Nobody. You aren't going to like this but from now on you move out of the flat only in my company. Please don't protest; I'm all for it. It lets us operate under his nose with no surveillance at all. He'll have his own people watching the building when I'm not around, so it looks like good books and recorded music for you through the long empty nights. Do you good. You'll find your instructions waiting when you get home, together with the concealed threat he wouldn't include in front of me."

"Jesus!"

"Be good and I'll take you out twice a week. Do you like opera?"

That was a question to be expected from a man who quoted Browning. "No."

"You can learn."

This nonsense bothered me less than some other implications. "Why should Armstrong trust you when he suspects me so easily?"

He said without banter, "Because I'm bought. I'm a

professional with a record of probity and attention to a client's orders, and he pays me for that. You can always buy the loyalty of the disinterested."

"Dangerous. They may become interested."

"Just so."

"And what are you supposed to think of all the talk about the legacy and whatever else may come up as we dig?"

He smiled with monstrous enjoyment. "Nothing at all. The legacy is known for a fable that died out years ago. The rest will slay you: Armstrong is seeking information for his book on the Nursery babies, which you are researching under his direction and for which you, as a science writer, will provide relevant technical detail when he comes to write it. So, to me the interviews will be only uncoordinated scraps of data, all over my simple, honest head. I'm the dumb gumshoe saying, 'Yes, sir,' and asking no questions."

"I wouldn't put it past him to pinch my book, too."

"Grow up, lad! Snare the legacy and then waste time on a book? It's just window dressing to snow Jonesey."

By then we were on the freeway, heading for the Mornington Peninsula, out of the city and shooting through the middle-executive suburbs. North of the road and a couple of kilometres from it the huge tenement blocks of one of the slum suburbs of the city's dispossessed—unemployed, unwanted and assuredly despairing in a State-supported charity I could not properly imagine—lowered against the sky. Sight of them roused a sense of guilt, a feeling that only luck and a scheming father had stood between me and the dole life. Most people felt like that about the tenements and looked away from them, as I did, but most people did not have the nagging conviction that in some sense they belonged in them. My father could have ignored my existence, and then . . .

But, if he had supported me through all those years, even if only with absentee, disinterested money—could he have been so disinterested in fact? And could he now be using me as coldly as Jonesey insisted? I would have said as much if Jonesey had not just then nodded at the skyline and said, "I was born over there. Residential Eleven, Floor Twelve, Apartment Thirty-one. It was one of the first blocks built when the full meaning of unemployment hit the State."

That sounded exactly right. Casual, chatty, blunt, rough and probably self-educated Jonesey (he wouldn't have learned that old poetry in any modern school), whose brain worked in its own secret channels, was what I imagined a battler out of those ferocious slums would be. That he worked for a Department could only mean that he was one of those top-percentage intellects for which the State's agents ceaselessly combed every level of society, and that this man "guarding my back" was sharper and more dedicated (and harder and more pragmatic) than I had guessed.

I suffered one of the periodic accessions of fright that took me as new ramifications of this business opened out, seeing myself as a maze-running rat scuttling under the cold eyes of powers that could end the experiment—and me—with a cool nod to the killer in the shadows. Even Jonesey made sure that I stayed alive only until my usefulness ran out.

He asked, as if bored by my silence, "What do you think Piggy really wants from the legacy? More and better age treatments that don't turn sour after a few decades? Power? Leverage on the State?"

The question lifted me, gratefully, out of the rat maze. "Immortality."

He digested that slowly, frowning. "Are you serious?"

"I spotted his fear of death early on."

"But it's just a guess?"

"Call it that."

As we turned south and the tenements wheeled out of sight he said, "I'm no science buff. Is it genetically possible?"

"I think so. It would require halting growth at maturity, I imagine, and preventing the processes of decline before they set in. Perhaps decline could be arrested or reversed; I don't know. Either way it's governed by hormone and enzyme activity and those are genetically dictated. If a total gene topology could be mapped, the means of controlling growth and maturity could be traced."

"As easy as that?"

"Easy! With a total gene-interactive topology laid out—and so far biology has only superficial linear mapping—it could take the researchers a century to understand it. The permutations run into millions."

He gave an exaggerated sigh. "You make me feel better. Fancy all those no-good scum in the slums being able to live forever! Or should we more deserving types make sure they don't get even a smell of it?"

It was a solid statement of the intolerable politics of a gift no society could sustain. I said, "We should make sure that nobody gets a smell of it, ever."

The wolf grinned. "Not even David?"

"Not even. I'd like a long life but eternity could be a nightmare."

"Good boy. But Bernard Shaw said that nobody could attain a useful maturity in less than three hundred years."

"Who's he?"

He snorted at my ignorance. "He's dead. The point is that a little goes a long way but the whole lot could—would—destroy us. Which makes one more reason for keeping you under my eye. One piece of information too much in your investigative head and you aren't young

David Chance anymore; you are a bomb primed to blow humanity's common sense sky high in its greed for life. You need me, lad. Never forget it."

I said, and I think I said it very nastily, "I won't, just as I won't ever forget that you warned me not to trust you in the finish. What's your interest in the legacy? Would you like to live forever?"

He drove for a while in a murk of self-disgust. "Serves me right. My big, wagging mouth! So each of us will have to watch the other, won't he?"

There are times when you trust instinct because the complexities have become too great for logical decision. I trusted Jonesey because it was simpler than not trusting him. What's more, he knew it, but I couldn't resist a perky shot in the dark: "What you really want is to be in the box seat at the prize giving."

He was, as too often, way ahead of me. "You're waking up, young David. Who gets the apple of discord, eh? Not Armstrong, anyway, and I don't favour your green-eyed monster of a father, either."

"Your Department?"

"Why them? They're human and open to corruption and this could be the biggest corrupter in history."

"Who, then?"

"As idiots keep on saying, 'That's a good question.' The trouble could start when a couple of pretty ordinary blokes like you and me find we have to answer it. How does that grab you?"

It horrified me.

I have never gone back to Gunnamatta; there has been no reason why I should. The Farnhams must, surely, be dead and the city will have spread to trample its bush and farmland; another of the last resorts of space and quiet will have vanished under factories, pollution and people.

That saddens me now but at the time I was a city type to whom countryside meant little; too much of it would bore me into yearning for crowds and clangour; perversely, I liked solitary fishing trips but there, too, a couple of days would set me itching for streets and noise. I said as much to Jonesey who told me, disgustedly, to take a look at the past because there wasn't much of it left.

We were by then on the southern beach of the peninsula, heading southeast with the open sea of Bass Strait on our right. We could not see much of it through the narrow strip of natural park that protected the coast from Rye to Cape Schanck, with Gunnamatta halfway between. What glimpses of the sea I had were forbidding—huge, grey, white-crested waves rolling in to crash on the shore, the sound of them travelling in a subdued roar. Some of the lower ground was still under water and the Greenhouse Effect swelling of the ocean would keep it so for years to come. The wind was cold, blowing in from the South Pole through most of the day; who liked this brand of rural solitude was welcome to it.

Gunnamatta was a retirement village, a place for pensioned-off public servants to see out their old age as cheaply as a chronically bankrupt State could manage without callously abandoning them. The houses were mostly 5B Standard, four rooms of poured walls with reinforced glass windows and weathercreep insulation to save on light and power, all stamped out in the factories and erected by a single workman with an all-purpose autostructor. There were such places on the outskirts of the city proper, but none with the large front garden plots of these houses. Gardens were not a luxury to appeal to me then; I estimated their planting areas as seven metres by three— almost profligate then and damned near impossible now except among the fenced-off rich—and most of them seemed neatly looked after. The dwellers would have had little to do but look after them. That, to me, would have been the edge of death; I liked a garden for looking at while someone else weeded.

Jonesey had a scale map of the area with the Farnham house pencilled on it, a longish walk outside the village. It was hard to imagine living like this by choice, half a kilometre from the nearest neighbour with only trees, sky and a freezing wind for company.

As we pulled up I saw a dappled cow at the back of the house, untethered, munching grass. We saw so few animals outside the zoos that my attention was held by its contented chewing, but I did not make the connection between milk and cream and usefulness until Jonesey remarked on it. There was a time when such things were taken for granted. History often sounds like a compendium of unlikely things once taken for granted.

Because he was so still, I had at first missed the grossly fat man seated on the middle one of three steps leading up to the tiny porch. He sat bolt upright, eyes closed, face to the sun, liver-blotched hands flat on his oversized thighs, jowls hanging down to the folds of the tyred neck. I judged him about eighty years old, senile and ready for a heart attack. The fat brother.

With his stiff, controlled attitude he looked like a blind man hearkening to a hushed, elusive world. If he heard the small crunch of our feet on the gravel path between the two miniature strips of lawn, he gave no sign.

I stopped only a touch from him, with Jonesey half a pace behind me, and said, softly as seemed proper to his involution, "Mr. Farnham?" He did not move. "Do you hear me, Mr. Farnham?"

Behind him and over his head a voice said, "He hears you but it doesn't register; he won't answer."

Shadowed by the porch and the wire screen door a tall, slender man surveyed us. I said, "You'd be Derek Farnham?"

"No, I'm Evan. That's Derek."

That lump had been the most beautiful thing Adelaide Cormick had ever seen. Evan's neutral tone suggested that it was just a lump. The reversal of names and descriptions caught me off balance; I said uncomfortably, "But Miss Cormick told me—"

"That I was the fat one? That stupid bitch has been talking, has she? After all this time!"

Jonesey had been staring hard at the fat man. "He's too old to be Derek."

"He's sixty-one; his life has not been the sort that preserves youth. Now, what do you want? You with that thing round your neck, are you a reporter?"

"A freelance journalist."

"There's a difference? There's nothing here for you."

"We think there is."

Evan Farnham opened the door and stepped onto the porch. He was what I had imagined Derek would have become, carrying little useless weight, still physically strong and preserving the hard, professional voice of the policeman.

"Do you, now? Memories of a broken-down sportsman? Heroes of the past?" He took a step down and laid a hand on his brother's shoulder; it was a protective gesture at odds with his unloving bluntness, but Derek did not appear to feel it. Evan asked in his flinty voice, "Is there money in it?"

That was ugly but promising; immediate venality suggested that he had, despite denial, something to tell. I said cautiously, "There could be. Depends what you have."

"Money we can use. Come inside."

I edged up the steps, careful not to touch the blubbery wreckage of Derek, and eased past him.

Evan said, "If you fell on him he wouldn't notice. Or, on a bad day, he might."

This was a tougher man than the one who had

watched at his brother's bedside, grieving; the lives of Derek's guardians could well have been as cruel as the man's own.

Like the others in the village, it was 5B Standard—lounge, two bedrooms and kitchen with a tiny shower-toilet—furnished in a mixture of the 5B models, though not much more than colours and curtains and carpetboard flooring permitted individual taste. The whole village would have been much the same to the eye, kept spotless by the grime-resistant finishes on walls and ceilings, even-temperatured thanks to weathercreep, almost identical room for room as there are only so many ways to arrange a minimal choice of template-cut furniture. The construction was a product of research and factory design and would be as flawless and monotonous half a century after as on the day it was delivered and erected, but I would have preferred Anne Blaikie's cluttered, stained, leaking, crackwalled semislum as a place to live in.

Perhaps it suited the ageing Farnhams—garden to potter in and cow to tend . . . I wouldn't have called it a life.

Evan sat us on a couch under the wide front window and himself on a straight-backed chair by the standard two-metre vidscreen (I counted the terminal outlets; they must have been folk of limited interests) where he could watch us and the door and Derek, Buddha-still on the second step.

"Go on," he said.

I began my prepared speech. "I'm David Chance—and this is my partner, Mr. Jones."

"Jack Jones," said my partner smoothly. "Sunrise Interviews."

I had never heard of the firm and doubted that anyone else had; he was having his meed of private amusement.

Farnham told him, not joking, "You look more like a retired pug than a writer."

"Could be. What does a writer look like?" With a ghostly smile Farnham absorbed the hit and Jonesey followed up blandly, "Actually I'm an editorial consultant." That could have meant anything senior to the newest office boy and I hoped he would not go on calling up playful fictions. "You don't look like what Miss Cormick described, either."

Evan's face tightened to a slight wariness. "You've been getting around, haven't you? Yes, I was heavier then; now I'm older and I've had my own illnesses and a breakdown. Caring for him"—the jerk of the head was more resigned than loving—"is work, bloody heavy work sometimes. Go on, Mr. Chance."

I had got no further than that we were researching a new book to update the history of Project IQ when a woman came quietly into the room.

She would have been much the same age as the brothers but the years had treated her little better than they had Evan. She was not lined or stooped but her expression carried dreary age; too much suffering and anger and despair haunted her eyes. I was reflecting that the young Derek had led her a fine dance of faithlessness before he bequeathed himself to her as a rotting hulk, and that her life must have been as close to hellish as humans can devise for each other, when Jonesey got to his feet, reminding me of good manners and the necessity of staying on the friendly side of these people.

Evan said, "This is my wife. She should hear what you have to say."

He told her who we were and I asked, "What about Mrs. Derek? Surely she should be present."

The woman took a chair by her husband and smiled a purely social smile. "I was Derek's wife." She gave her explanation coolly, asking nothing of us, simply making the situation plain. "I was Mrs. Derek until I divorced him under the Non-Supporting Spouse provision and married Evan. Then we took Derek in adoption since it entitled us to make the maximum claim in supportive allowances. It was a purely financial manipulation. As you see, he is quite mad." She used the word with the simplicity of one who has faced truth and outfaced it. "Gentle and harmless," she added, "or they would not have made us keep him."

The "new psychology" incarcerated only the dangerous and the deranged kinless, not the merely helpless. The State was saved much expense while the relatives had no choice but to assume the ruinous burden.

Jonesey said, "He should be a total State charge; he suffered grievous mental assault in line of duty."

It was a little too sudden. Evan took her hand as she turned shocked eyes to him, and he told her, "They know about Conrad. They're reporters on a Nursery story and they've seen Adelaide Cormick."

She recovered quickly. "We can produce no evidence of assault. Enquire of official blank walls and you will find that the Nursery might never have existed. Could you prove assault?"

"I think so, ma'am." (Jonesey could be old-fashioned in manners and address sometimes; they say that a slum upbringing is very conservative.) "We do know about Conrad. So do plenty of others—nurses, gardeners, cleaners and more we haven't located yet."

"Are you crusading?" She was unimpressed. "You will discover all mouths shut by the Secrecy provisions."

"Maybe not by the time we've done with them. Miss Cormick was present at a damning meeting and she talked to us."

She said with quiet dislike, "One of his bitches."

Jonesey met that head-on. "But she loved him."

"To her distress, I hope."

"Yes. I think it changed her life, not necessarily for the worse in the long run."

"Trial by ordeal? Evan and I know all about that. What do you want of us?"

I explained what we knew of Young Feller's movements. "What we need now is anything you can tell us, anything at all, no matter how small or apparently meaningless, that may give us a line on where he lived and who looked after him during his year and a half out of the Nursery."

She was not much impressed. "Do you imagine you would be allowed to publish what has been hidden so long? It would mean opening up the whole disastrous Nursery story."

I said, "Knowledge forces issues. The story is in the public interest."

"That ancient press cynicism! It may well be not in the public interest."

"Then we will, no doubt, be stopped."

"But still knowing enough to make blackmail demands to assist your careers of public enlightenment."

Jonesey said roughly, "You play' em as they lie, ma'am."

Evan said to her, "There's money in it."

She frowned and stood up. "I want none of this. Aside from personal feeling, these are muckrakers."

He persisted, pushing sulkily, "There's things we could do with."

If we had not been present there would have been a blazing quarrel. She stiffened with anger, then relaxed with the deliberate surrender of long acquaintance with the inevitable. He wanted the money, so . . . "You talk to them. I'd rather not hear it."

She went quickly through the passage to the back of the house.

"She hasn't had it easy," Evan said, "and you've upset

her." He leaned forward, hands on knees. "You've upset my wife quite a bit. A month's money at our pension rate would be some compensation."

It was not as big a demand as he probably thought it was; your idea of wealth depends on the base of need you work from. I said nothing; if you wait and let them talk, some will talk themselves right out of a demand they feel ashamed of having made. Not so Evan, who knew what he wanted.

"Doesn't the sneak industry keep a slush fund for this sort of thing?"

I would have held out but Jonesey was too impatient for haggling. "All right, a month. How will you have it? A note of demand on your general store?"

"That'll do."

Jonesey arranged it through the Credit Allocation terminal; neither Evan nor I saw what ID and Charge he used but I had no doubt Armstrong would foot the bill.

I told him most of what we knew, though nothing of the legacy or our informants. When I came to the delicate references to Derek and tried to hedge the facts, he said, "You don't have to tiptoe. He was the boy's dog." When I was done he asked, "How did you get on to the Cormick woman?"

"My business; I'm buying, not selling."

"What you call protecting your sources? All right, she was a looker. Very nice. I got most of her story from Derek and you've only told me that she didn't know the half of it. She saw just the surface. That Young Feller was a magician."

Jonesey said, "No, he wasn't and as a psychiatric nurse you don't think so. How did he do it?"

"We don't know. Nobody knows."

"The other Groups thought he simply knew more about the operation of the mind than we do."

"The other Groups? You *are* in deep. I'll tell you what

I think though Petra, his wife then, insists it was hypnotism. She won't have my explanation because it reflects on her pride as a woman. I think Young Feller displayed himself as a sex object—very subtly, in the way a young boy can get away with it, pretending to be all innocent and unintentional, just having a puppy crush—and Derek fell for it. I'm not talking about the way a teenage boy can seem sexless and a badly balanced man can go overboard for him; that may have been the basic thing Young Feller worked from but he had extra weapons Derek had no chance against. Those C Group kids always got their way when they wanted it; they could have run the place but that wasn't their plan. They wanted to learn how ordinary people tick, so they carried on testing and working us out. It can't have been easy for them; they didn't think the way we do. Don't ask me what their way was because I wouldn't have a clue; they had a different kind of intelligence and that I can say but can't explain. Nor could you. Could you, now? The result was that finally they were able to understand us and use us, and the one that got fully used up was Derek. He was their key to contact with the world outside, so Young Feller made him his slave. Exactly that: slave. He did it by projecting himself as a desirable thing, and when one of them decided to project personality it was as near to fascination as you could get without losing control of yourself.

"The way I see it, the kid found Derek's two weak points and used them both—his sexuality and his vanity about his body. He played at being delighted by the man's virility and physical beauty so that Derek thought he was the senior partner—the grown man teaching the lovely boy, like the old Greek ideal before it got out of hand—while all the time the boy was ensnaring him, heart and mind."

I had to interrupt there. "If what Miss Cormick said was right, it wasn't a physical thing."

"I'm sure it wasn't. I wasn't long in the Nursery, but

long enough to know what everybody there knew, that the C kids rated us with the higher animals. For them, sex with one of us would have been like having it off with a monkey. Derek never could see that side of them; that's why I think there was at bottom a sexual tease, never to be fulfilled, and the boy was cunning enough not to let Derek see what the real relationship was. So there was Derek, laying every woman in sight, including la belle Cormick, thinking himself the great lover when in fact he was sublimating the urges Young Feller stirred in him. He was a puppet, kept ready for use when the time came."

It seemed to me that this was not quite good enough. "The approach sounds valid but there was a more difficult obstacle than virility to be overcome: the Police Intelligence indoctrination of absolute loyalty. That is achieved by psychological pressures built up over years by experts. It comes close to imprinting. It should have been a barrier to ultimate surrender."

Evan paid resentful attention, having no answer ready; he said snappishly, "Well, it wasn't. Those kids had *power*." He gazed at me so long that I began to suspect some hidden significance in my objection, but in the end he said, "There was something about you when you came to the door that puzzled me. Now I see you're a bit like him."

"Like who? The young Derek?"

"The Young Feller. He wasn't as pale and you're older now and changed, but as a teenager I'll bet you could have been, say, his cousin, except that they didn't have any cousins."

Given my parentage, it was likely that some points of resemblance existed but I did not want to flounder into trying to explain it away.

"Accidental. Likenesses are common; there must be plenty of others."

Evan stood up. "Not all that many. They were distinctive. I've some pictures."

He went out of the room and down the passage. Jonesey muttered to me, "How many people do you know that ever saw Young Feller?"

"My father, Armstrong, Blaikie, Miss Cormick."

"Any of them mention the likeness?"

"No."

"Not even your father?"

"No. He would have mentioned it."

"Would he? Well, it's there. I spotted it our first day together." He gnawed savagely at a thick knuckle. "The disgusting bastards!"

"Who?"

He did not answer because Evan was back with an album of holograms open at a picture of a man and a boy stripped to jockey shorts on a brilliantly green lawn, smiling at the camera, arms around each other's waists. "We weren't supposed to take pictures but Derek had a few squirrelled away."

Derek Farnham had certainly been everything that Anne Blaikie and Adelaide Cormick had said of him, a spectacular breeding stud, but the boy was ordinary. He was well enough made but there was a faint sickliness about the pale skin that did not seem to have taken a tan like the man's. His face could have belonged to any nondescript schoolboy; whatever intelligence lurked there was not on display. I could see no likeness to myself, but they say you rarely can see your own resemblances.

I said, "Just like any boy."

"While it suited him. And when it didn't suit him or his sibs, they could *burn* with genius. They were terrifying."

Jonesey looked from the hologram to me and back. "As you say, a cousinly likeness."

Evan had other pictures. The prize was a montage of the three Groups, three pictures mounted side by side. "The Groups despised each other and wouldn't pose together but these were all taken on the same day, when they were seventeen, just before A and B were sent into public life. The thin ones are A Group; the middle lot is B group, they turned out to be artists and they were always a bit plump. You can see that C Group had normal build but were paler and looked younger."

The names were written under the pictures. I studied Arthur, tall and thin then as now, and then the others. Save for the variations in height and plumpness they were very like, not identical from Group to Group but obviously six brothers with six sisters. I said, "I'm thin like A Group, but that's all."

"More than that," Evan said. "It's noticeable."

"I'm no relative. They didn't breed."

"Don't be too sure. I think A had their bit of nookey when they got loose in the world but if there were any kids nobody acknowledged them. They weren't as contemptuously superior as C but they wouldn't have made public admission of sexual slumming."

That did not amuse me and probably coloured my tone as I said, "I know who my parents were."

Evan backed off. "No offence meant, but the resemblance is close."

Jonesey had the gall to chuckle. I changed the subject deliberately. "What have you to tell that's worth a price?"

Evan tried unsuccessfully to look sly. "How do I know what's worth how much?"

Jonesey stopped chuckling. "Shit or get off the pot. What have you got that we couldn't find out for ourselves?"

Inexperienced in gutter bargaining, Evan gave in. "This for a start: Young Feller didn't take advantage of a grass fire to break out of the Nursery; he *started* the fire. It was planned. When he and his sibs thought it was time to begin a proper check on the real world they simply got one of them out—Young Feller because he had his stooge under control."

Jonesey interrupted sharply, "You weren't there then. Who's your source?"

"Derek. Now I tell it my way, eh?"

"Sorry. Yes, your way."

I thought that little burst of interest would cost money before we were done. Evan's not-quite-suppressed grin showed that he thought so, too, but he carried on willingly. "They had patience; they planned it a couple of years ahead. They planned it for when they were physically capable of dealing with an adult population on its own terms and in the meantime played games that put the staff off the scent. The two girls began acting up when they were sixteen, when their menstrual periods started, a bit late like the rest of their development. They looked about thirteen and put on a show of distress through menstrual tension, and part of their emotional act was a few silly escape attempts. They were bound to fail, designed to fail and look like outbreaks of rebellious temper; after a while they calmed down and the Psychs decided that a troublesome phase was over. What the girls had done was test all the security points until they knew as much about them as the designers. Then they sat quiet while Young Feller worked with Derek to put on muscle and reaction speed.

"He was waiting for hot weather and what he got was the first year of the Long Drought. You'd remember it, Mr. Jones, when the northern half of the country drowned in tropical rain and the southern states baked in ten years of dry hell. That first year there had been a short winter rain, enough to raise the grass twelve or fifteen centimetres, so that the Nursery sat in the middle of hectares of tinder, dried and brittled by west winds.

"And one day Young Feller went for a walk in the grounds with a piece of curved glass from a broken bottle and a couple of ounces of cleaning fluid filched from the nurses' pantry. The rest was sunlight and a stiff breeze. He started it on the west side of the complex, far enough back to be sure it would sweep right round the buildings. They were safe, protected by sprinklers, fireproof construction and wide surrounding driveways; all they suffered was some smoke damage. The whole staff turned out to fight the fire with improvised beaters because they had nothing else, and Country Fire took too long to get to them on a day of more district calls than it could handle.

"The kids weren't allowed to do any fire fighting and in fact they went into hysterics of fright, as if their cute little razor-blade minds couldn't cope with shock and danger. Or so everybody thought until afterwards, when they remembered how the brats had hindered and hampered during the first ten minutes until a couple of small outbreaks had become walls of flame rushing over the grass. It went round the Nursery in two blazing wings, just as they had planned it, and tore across to the eastern perimeter hedge, moving so fast that one of the gardeners who was coming on duty and shortcutting across the lawns from the dormitory wing was caught as he ran.

"It hit the eucalypts round the guardhouse and they exploded the way they do when the sap and oil catch; the guardhouse went up and the whole perimeter hedge on that side. The power from the concealed fence failed as the copper melted from the ceramic insulators—all according to plan—and the whole security system was exposed. An off-duty soldier was sleeping in the guardhouse; he burned alive. The fire leapt the road and licked up the Cormick home paddocks, burning a small herd of cattle caught between fences. Young Feller strolled to freedom through the western perimeter, behind the fire and the fire fighters, at his leisure.

"The three left in the Nursery went into transports of horror. Oh, the poor men roasted! And the poor cattle! And where was Conrad? What had happened to Conrad? But by this time the Psychs had begun to put two and two

205 ı Brain Child

together and see that they had been led right up the garden path, not by a display of superior thinking but by
schoolboy-level simplicity. The kids had divined their fear
of incomprehensible intelligence and played right under-
neath it, on people's own brute level. Great joke!

"To them it was just that, a huge gag based on misdirection. Once they saw that the Psychs were on to them
they stopped pretending; their attitude became mockery—
that is, when they bothered to take notice of the staff at all.
They had what they wanted—one of their number out in
the world as a vanguard observer of the savages in habitat,
and they knew their value. They loved their joke, knowing
nothing could be done to them.

"They were wrong about that. The staff had long ago
ceased to love their charges and now they hated the cold
bastards who pretended remorse but were callous when
their pretence ran out of steam. The Psychs tried to be
objective, protesting that the kids were the products of a
pragmatism designed into them, however unwittingly, and
that they could no more identify with 'normal' humanity
than humanity could feel fellowship with them, but at bottom they wanted their blood as hotly as the nonspecialist
staff. They showed willing enough when they finally got
permission for an all out assault on the superhuman
minds, and they went at them with drugs and sensory
probes and tests that didn't stop short of physical and psychological torture. They meant to discover what the bio-
surgeons had made, if it had to be tested to destruction.

"That's one of the true reasons why Young Feller's escape was never revealed; the State did not want the public's
interest turned on the Nursery and what was going on there.

"And the kids beat them. That was effectively the end
of Project IQ. It couldn't handle or assess its own results."

He stopped as if that were the end of his account.
Perhaps he expected a further offer. Instead, I prodded,
"What did the other Groups think about all this?"

"They didn't know. They'd been out in the world for half a year and were said to be adjusting very well."

Indeed, indeed! If Arthur and Andrew represented adjustment it had been mainly pretence to gain freedom of action. And what of B Group, the fabulous artists who now lived in retirement and whom nobody ever saw? Did they fit somewhere into the story with perhaps a third variety of pretence?

While I pondered, Jonesey was asking whether or not Evan had seen any of the brutality for himself, and it was now that the man betrayed some human depth.

His face changed, his voice changed, his eyes flitted between us with haunted nervousness. His cool listing of facts had been the rendering of a report at secondhand, uncontaminated by contact, but now personal memory was powerfully stirred.

He said with difficulty, "I saw," and balked there, making a wide gesture of his hands, expressing utter uselessness. "You won't be let print any of this, no matter how good you think you are."

"Our money, our business," Jonesey said. "Go on."

"I was one of the extra staff brought in after the fire. We didn't have anything useful to do; we were really only additional gaolers, watchers in a twenty-four-hour round of never letting them out of sight because they knew how to play tricks with the electronic monitoring. We saw what was done to them. They were the horrible outcome of an unready science but what happened to them was worse.

"Hypnosis could not touch them and truth drugs they threw off with a toss of the mind; nobody knows how much functional control they had, but no drugs of any kind could touch their minds. Sensory deprivation chambers did a little better but not much; they produced autohypnotic states where stimuli evoked an occasional free association that wasn't revealing, only puzzling. They didn't *think* in our sense of the word. We made the guess that they used the subconscious mind directly, like a map of mental territory they could survey from above and eliminate whole areas of reasoning at a glance, go from problem to solution without the rationalising stages and arrive at answers that seemed meaningless to us. That was our attempt to think of their minds in a way that reduced them to a familiar level. Actually we stood at the edge of an unknown we couldn't enter without drowning.

"The next stage was direct probing, electrodes in the brain, psychotape recordings of response-types and intensities and regions of stimulus. On the stupid horrorvid plays they call these things mindreading machines but they never read a useful synaptic spark from those kids. Probing could advance mental therapy when it was used on criminals and lunatics but the C Group readings made no sense; the Psychs didn't know enough to know how to interpret them. Or perhaps the kids fooled them.

"The kids resisted; they had a repertoire of mental routines for relieving the pressure from their minds and when the Psychs lost their nerve and their common humanity and used physical torture the kids used some form of nervous control just as they controlled their autonomic systems. They suffered appalling mistreatment and laughed and talked through it. They sent their pain away somewhere and the Psychs were half out of their own minds with frustration and the knowledge of what they were making of themselves by what they did.

"They were frightened of their own actions and of what they saw in the kids and much more frightened of all the things hidden. They were right to fear. Those kids could concentrate physical strength to a degree that made them tigers in the flesh as well as in the mind. They were kept under by remote-control stunners supplied by the police. Even the kids couldn't shed a high-voltage jolt."

He paused for a couple of long breaths, looking down at his hands as they shook.

"It sounds to me," Jonesey said, "as if with all their advantages they could have thought their way out of the Nursery at any time."

"They didn't want to leave." Evan's face reflected his bafflement before the irrational. "That was the worst of it, that they put up with whatever was done to them. They had to live until their scout returned. We could think of no other explanation. And none of us wanted to think of what would happen when that day came. They gathered all their forces to live until they had Young Feller's report. And then we would see and feel what they could do. That is how we read them.

"Imagine them as castaways, desperate to live in a world of howling, biting mongrels, who stopped short of killing because they needed their aliens alive.

"I couldn't take it. I stood two months of it and then resigned with the Secrecy Acts pointed at me like a gun. I wasn't the only one. It gives me nightmares still to remember what the human animal can do when it is afraid. When I think of the Project I am afraid of God."

The religious revival was then still in the future and it was strange to hear the name of God uttered seriously and with submission. My unattuned ears heard echoes of old mysteries, concepts as far removed from our lives as the minds of Young Feller's suffering sibs.

Jonesey may have remembered religion from his youth and was in any case less impressionable. "Derek! What about Derek? Where does he fit in?"

Evan, with his moment of purgatory eased, straightened on his chair to become a canny pensioner questing for a handout.

"This is where he starts to fit in." He eyed Jonesey with the nervous determination of a man in unfamiliar country. "How's your pocket? I reckon Derek is three months' worth."

That was not as outrageous as he probably thought

but he was well out of his depth, an averagely honest poor devil unable to extort with the flair of the man who means it. I said at once, "Too much."

Jonesey surprised me by patting my arm, meaning, *Pipe down, Junior*, and asking, "What could you do with it? Too much for a bender, not enough for a holiday and maybe too much for what you can give for it."

Evan jerked his head at the outer door and Derek entranced on the step. "He doesn't come cheap; the State covers only essentials. But he's my brother." He ground to a stop, having more to say but no willingness to beg.

"Little extras," Jonesey suggested. "For affection's sake but hard to come by."

"You could put it that way. Then there's her. A woman likes a few clothes that aren't off the State coupon rack."

All things considered, he wasn't greedy.

Jonesey said, "You should have asked for more but now you're stuck with it."

"And I've only your word that you won't cancel the transfer anyway."

"It's a hard world, chummie! But I'll tell you what we'll do: I'll plug the transfer irreversible so you get it even if what you give us wouldn't sell for horse shit. In return you'll tell us everything, all the bits you would have left out because they're too self-revealing, too private, too hurtful—even if it means bad-mouthing Mrs. Farnham and showing Derek up as a brat's lapdog. And if what we get is good, we may be generous."

My thought was, Tell Armstrong that!

He sat awhile watching our faces but it was not money that was on his mind. He was wondering how far we could be trusted; the kind of reporters he thought we were don't command much public confidence.

"You blokes protect your sources, don't you?"

Jonesey was virtuous. "Some of us have gone to gaol for it."

"You can't say I told you any of this. Under the Acts they could put me away for life."

"You're safe, man. It isn't worth our reputations to turn a source in."

He could be a convincingly pious bastard.

This was what Evan told us:

2.

What happened after Young Feller left the Nursery was horrible and you can see the end of it sitting there on the steps. Derek was left in the Nursery when Young Feller came to town, shocked but ready to carry on his job, believing his lovely boy would come back.

He told me all this after the final breakdown, unreeling his mind like a tape with only one thing on it, the same thing wept out in a hundred different ways. The boy made wreckage of him; he got whatever he wanted from Derek, knowing exactly which psychic buttons to press; it was the most complete response conditioning ever achieved. Scientists would call it an elegant procedure, their phrase for neat and faultless. I don't think he meant to wreck Derek but when the end came he was too much involved with his Group to think of the pawn. Derek was minor—prepared, used and forgotten. He was only human, you see. He didn't matter.

So there was Derek in Westerton and Young Feller in Melbourne. He'd acted at the first sign of good burning weather but now he needed Derek in the city with him, so he went to his home. Derek had a place in Malvern then, a six-room 3A Special since he was pretty senior, and that's where Petra was with the two boys. I was seconded up-country at the time, so I only know this part from Petra, and you'll soon see why she doesn't want to listen to it or talk about it.

The boys were at school; she was alone in the house when Young Feller knocked at the door. With him looking younger than his true age, what she saw was a schoolboy dressed in summer shorts and shirt and long socks, with the badge of a private school on his shirt pocket, looking nervous and apologetic while he twisted his cap in his hands. This was the morning after he ran from the Nursery; I know that because later on, when I knew more about the things he did, I checked news files and found out that a boy from that school had been attacked and stripped that same morning and left in a back lane with a workingman's clothes thrown over him and his own taken away. The man's clothes had a letter in the pocket with a Westerton address on it, and that man had reported being mugged and stripped in Westerton the night before. You can see that the kid was mighty efficient, getting to Melbourne as fast as that.

He spun Petra a yarn about Derek training him for sports and telling him to look him up when the holidays were over. For all she knew, this could be true, since she didn't know much of what Derek did away from home. She had a fair idea of his bed hopping but not how much of it and he used Departmental secrecy to keep her in the dark about where he was and when. She didn't even know he was at the Nursery, but she had an unlisted vid number for calling him if she needed him urgently. Derek was a raw bastard. Still, he didn't deserve the payout he got.

Petra said Derek wasn't home and the kid persisted that he needed him. She wasn't going to hand over the unlisted number to some strange boy but he kept at her, trying to talk her into putting him in touch. And talk her into it he did. That's why she has to insist it was hypnotism; there's her pride to be saved.

She says he kept changing his stance while he talked. He began nervously but there was nothing nervous about his growing confidence as he held her attention, though she didn't notice that at once. What she noticed was that an ordinary-looking boy began to look like a pretty attractive boy, especially as his face took on different expressions until she found herself liking him, and then a bit more than just liking him. Petra was no cradlesnatcher, but he got right to her until she found herself asking him inside with her doing the talking to prevent him leaving. I don't contradict her when she says she was hypnotised but I think it was not like that at all. Young Feller knew all about sexual attraction from Derek and from watching the nurses and maybe leading them on a bit to test his ideas and get them right, and you can bet they wouldn't tell about a kid giving them the hots. So he adjusted his posture and his expression until he hit on the male type that would arouse her. I suppose there was also some sort of psychic and physical magnetism; some people seem to have it, though we don't know how it works. Anyway, he had her stretched on the lounge-room floor, promising him anything if he'd give it to her, make love to her—anything at all. The unlisted number was his for the raping. Except that there wasn't any rape. He got the number without so much as unzipping his fly, then got up and left her there on the floor. All he said was "You wouldn't want Derek to know how I got this number," and walked out.

Bastardy, you reckon? I've had years to think him over and I don't think he had a cruel mind; he was a boy alone in a jungle and he had to use everything he knew. If you were after a big prize—your whole future life—would you think twice about kicking a randy cat out of the way? He didn't think of people as human. He was human. We were just *Homo sapiens sapiens*—there's a double-barrelled joke if you like—but he was *Homo mirabilis*, a million years in the future. Nobody could be happy about what he was, but once you try to understand, it's hard to blame him.

So let Petra say she was hypnotised and dumped if it helps her hide from herself that her deep need was broached and used by a young monster. I'll never say it to her face but deep down she knows it. That's why she's sitting in the kitchen.

Once he had the vid number, Young Feller had Derek in Melbourne in two days on a faked-up special leave to look after his kids while his wife was supposed to be ill.

I wouldn't have dreamed of interrupting Evan—I was enthralled by this rough picture of the mutated mind at work—but Jonesey had the bloodhound's nose for sniffing before trusting a doubtful scent. "Then why did he lay Derek cold at The Willows? Derek said he would have helped him anyway."

I can only tell you what I think about that, making a guess at how Young Feller's mind worked. In spite of his violence he would have killed only if there was no way to avoid it. Two men died in the fire but their deaths were accidents—he couldn't have foreseen that a gardener would take a shortcut right into the path of a galloping front and it's a fact, so Derek said, that the sleeping soldier had wangled a sickie from the MO and shouldn't have been in the guardhouse. The boy saw them as unnecessary deaths, and regrettable, but he didn't waste tears on them. You can argue that starting the fire was dangerous and irresponsible, but he had to have all attention directed away from what he was doing and perhaps he overestimated the staff's ability to control it. It isn't possible to follow every quirk of his mind but in eighteen months of mugging he never killed or seriously injured anyone.

But, about The Willows: The thing there was that he didn't want the Cormick girl running around the district telling everyone that Derek helped his escape; he wanted Derek loose, not in gaol, so he staged the attack to keep Derek innocent. Perhaps he reckoned, too, that she would never tell the story through sheer shame about her secret lover turning out to be a sexual rat and a boy's lapdog. I hold no brief for the way Derek treated her but I think Young Feller judged her correctly and pushed the right buttons. Then he came to Melbourne, suckered Petra and had Derek running to the city to see his beloved boy. It'd make you sick if you didn't know that he was playing everyone like pieces in a game and had no feeling for them. Or maybe he did. How can you tell?

He never went near the house again. He didn't have the deep control over Petra that he had spent years perfecting with Derek; he didn't want to drive her to do something desperate because, naturally, she hated him. Eventually she realised who he must be but she had to keep her mouth shut for Derek's sake. He used to meet Derek on a park bench or somewhere of that sort and we never knew where he lived.

That was a body blow, the denial of the essential fact we needed. I heard Jonesey curse softly while I thought uneasily of the wasted cash and a smouldering Armstrong.

Derek knew the boy could look after himself and realised that what he didn't know he couldn't reveal under questioning or by accident. He'd have been psycho-probed if anyone had guessed the connection. He was happy to serve his boy, but the boy needed knowledge of a kind that was not in Derek's head. Derek was no second-rater but science was not his field and biology was right out of his reach, while what Young Feller wanted was an education in gene topology and all its ancillary disciplines. That added up to a full twelve years of regular general education followed by a university course in the life sciences and topped off with years of post-graduate work in genetic structure with topology as the last hurdle.

The first part was manageable. Getting hold of elementary texts in sociology, psychology, mathematics, political theory and any useful thing you can think of was easy—the boy stole them. Derek taught him all he needed to know of social mores and behaviour in a couple of days. When he came to tell me about all this he said the boy couldn't believe in some of our social conventions and adopted them like an actor who knew his play was a bad joke but had to con the public. He read a few books on political systems, asked, "Do you believe this rubbish?" and never referred to them again. I suppose the truth is that we don't believe in them. And that makes the joke silly and sour.

Soon a course in reading of thievable textbooks wasn't enough. He swallowed the basics quickly but after that Derek couldn't tell him what to look for next; Young Feller knew what he wanted but not where to find it. At last Derek suggested a tutor, not because he would teach the boy much but because he would know where to take all the next steps. They looked through the advertisements of university crammers and picked out a few. Young Feller took the list and that was the last Derek saw of him until he returned to the Nursery to kill himself.

That was when the crack-up started—

Jonesey cried out, "The tutor! His name!" His voice was hoarse with need; the name would be worth a year of the Farnhams' pensions, but the man did not understand its importance.

I never heard it. I don't think Derek did, either. The boy just went off with the list and never called Derek again.

I thought Jonesey would rage or weep but he only dropped his head and muttered to his private gods, "The bastard doesn't know one useful thing!" He looked up at a resentful Evan and apologised, "I'm sorry," but it sounded like a curse. "Please go on, Mr. Farnham; there may still be something."

And bugger you, too, mister! Still, you're paying for it. Derek went back on duty, but he was changed. He did his best to play the skirt chaser everyone expected him to be but his heart wasn't in it, only his prick. His heart was with Young Feller, waiting for him to come back, like a dumb beast missing its master. Before I resigned I began to get some idea of what was wrong with him from things he said without noticing he had said them, and I was very upset about it. Wouldn't you be? Your own brother reduced to a parody of the games master with a crush on one of the junior boys! But I didn't guess how bad it really was until I heard how Young Feller went back.

He walked into the Nursery one day, bright as brass, straight past the staff as if they didn't exist and into the Group quarters to see his kin. The Super sent for him to go to the office and explain himself and he refused, said no and wouldn't listen to argument. The Super sent a couple of hefty male nurses to frog-march him and he broke the arms of both of them. That was the first time they saw what the kids were really capable of in short-term speed and strength; until then they had realised they were dangerous, now they saw them as murderously competent. Derek was sent to reason with the boy and went back white and shaking. When he had his breakdown he told me what Young Feller had said to him, that when he wanted his dog, he'd call him. I think the boy must have been close to breakdown himself by then.

Nobody knew what to do. The kids had put up with the treatment dealt to them while Young Feller was away but they knew that now there wouldn't be any more putting up with it. Anybody trying it would probably end up dead.

The kids took over their own lives completely, demanded food when they wanted it, allowed one female nurse in their quarters for use as a servant, refused to talk to anyone except to give an order and sat around all day in a square, looking at each other and saying a word now and then. Young Feller demanded Blaikie as their attendant; I don't know why he specified her but there must have been a reason. She'd been his baby nurse but he wasn't sentimental; there must have been something else.

They negated all the indoor surveillance circuits. I say "negated" because it isn't known how they did it. Everything stopped functioning until they died, then started up immediately. It sounds like mental control but that's hardly possible. Or is it? Could the mind influence electron pathways? One of the Psychs seems to have talked about something he called quantum recognition theory but nobody understood him.

So they had all the privacy they wanted and even Blaikie couldn't swear they were doing much communicating with each other, though she knew as well as the rest that the brats could say whole paragraphs with the smallest shimmer of language. She was the only one with them for the three days before they died and she said that when it happened she didn't know until one of them fell over.

Jonesey said harshly, "She lied!"

That doesn't surprise me; she was a bit choosy with truth. But what do you know about her? No use asking, I suppose? Only buying, not giving away.

Well, they died and that was the end of it. No announcement, no warning. Why warn the dumb brutes who had never known how to treat them? Autopsy showed nothing. They simply stopped living when they saw nothing to live for.

All right, all right, I'm guessing, but think it out for yourselves: They send a scout to case the human culture and see what the zoo is like outside their cage, and it is worse than they had guessed, a madhouse where they could never exist. How would you feel, stranded on an alien planet among semi-intelligent animals who know just enough to be barbarians who think themselves civilised and who can't, in your terms, communicate a thought or an idea that isn't twisted or stupid or false?

Perhaps that is what Young Feller told them. Or, perhaps, something happened to him out there that made him see continued existence as impossible, and they sat for three days discussing it, seeking ways to stay alive without risking spiritual and psychological paralysis. When they had seen all round the problem, they bowed out.

That's my view of it.

I had to ask, "Are you sure there was no warning, no final word of any kind?"

I was sure but if you say Blaikie lied, I'm not sure any longer. Someone else thought there should be a message. One of the A Group boys walked in there the day after the deaths, asking questions, swearing the C Group kids wouldn't have phased out—that was the way he described it—without leaving a clue, but he wouldn't say why he was so sure. He got nothing from anyone; they had nothing to give.

But how did he know they were dead? He said he felt them vanish, that all the kids felt them go! Nobody believed him but nobody dared, either, to lay a hand on him for questioning. The place was a hive of lethal secrets and if these kids had some esoteric means of communication that would be the last straw. All they wanted was to see the last of them. I know for a fact that they didn't so much as report his visit.

Young Feller's death was the stone end of Derek. When he heard about it, he collapsed. Literally, I mean, flat on the floor, crying and raving and violent with anyone approaching him. They sent through channels for me and I sat all night with my half-mad brother in my arms while he dribbled out horrors.

His love for Young Feller paid him out for every treachery he had committed against Petra since the day they married. It broke him forever. I hope the boy didn't understand what he did when he called Derek his dog, didn't realise that lesser minds could shatter at a touch. Or perhaps he was making a clean cut of a relationship that was over, and didn't know the full power of his manipulation. I don't want to see him as a monster. It's unbearable without that.

They hospitalised Derek in Melbourne and the prognosis was bad. Then the Nursery was remodelled as a psychiatric hospital and the Department had a ward there, so Derek was transferred to it, but putting him back into remembered surroundings was a mistake. On the second night he cut his throat.

But you know about that.

Since then, Petra and I have looked after him; neither of us could stand the idea of him mentally dead in an institution, without a friend. He was a bastard but he was our bastard and he needed love. You can understand that, can't you?

He never recovered for more than short bouts for whispering when his mind seemed to clear, and over the years I got the story in broken bits that had to be spliced together. Do you know what he's doing out there? He's working out new training routines against the day Young Feller comes back. The death didn't happen; his beautiful boy is away but he will come back and every morning in the sunlight they will work out on the lawn. Think of it—a hundred and forty kilos of him, a great bolster of flesh, teaching the boy grace and agility on our little spit of a lawn!

He started almost at once to eat like a pig. Some sort of compensation, I suppose. He doesn't just eat mechanically; he enjoys it, loves it. So why not let him, though his needs stretch our resources to the limit? He won't do anything for himself. Not can't, won't. If he turns his attention away he might miss the boy coming back to him.

He makes for a full life and a bloody unhappy one but we'll see it out. It's hard, very hard, but we haven't learned to hate him. All the same, I wish he'd die. His heart must give out soon. All that weight . . . There has to be some life left for us to live.

He does no harm, just sits, waiting. Petra can get his attention sometimes, for a minute or two; I, more rarely. We have tried to tell him the boy is dead but he doesn't hear. He sees and hears only what pleases him, like food.

I think that's all I have for you.

3.

Jonesey paid up, more than generously I thought, signing away Armstrong's money for a fine batch of background information without a thing that could lead us a step further. While I was supposing that he was sorry for them he ruined good intentions with nagging, pinpricking questions, returning twice to the unknown tutor Young Feller had sought in the Classified Professional columns, homing in from desperate angles until Evan's temper frayed and he told us angrily to go. "It's bad enough begging handouts from scavengers without being badgered afterwards!"

Jonesey snapped back at him, "Don't blame us. You did the asking and gave us bugger all for the money."

I tried to be fair. "It's good material. Nobody had heard any of this before."

"And we're not a half pace forward!"

Evan started to push us out and Mrs. Farnham appeared in the doorway, in no friendly mood. "Why are you shouting? I won't have it in the house!"

I said, "We're going. Please pardon us," and got quickly out through the screen door. Behind us two pairs of hostile eyes urged us out of their lives. I was only too happy to leave this place of terrible memories and in my clumsy hurry brushed against the motionless Derek. I felt the flesh of his huge shoulder give like a cushion and in a thoughtless, panicky reflex I turned back and muttered the conventional, "Sorry, I didn't—" and shut up as I realised the uselessness of it.

I was bent slightly forward and for a couple of seconds his vacant eyes looked straight into mine—and blinked within their folds of flesh as the glassiness left them. He saw me.

The thick lips opened a little way and the unpractised beginning of speech crackled unintelligibly. The great, soft frame suffered a convulsion that flowed out from his hips to shake the massive thighs and rise up through his body. His arms heaved and strained towards me. He was trying to stand up.

Twice he forced his unused throat before he was able to croak with an awful joy, "Conrad! Young Feller!"

His monstrous face was momentarily radiant as I felt the tips of his fat fingers on the back of my hand.

His voice urged its rackety sounds with the hunger of a lifetime. "Where have you been, boy? Where?"

Jonesey grabbed my arm, hissing, "Come away, man!"

The big head swung to him, peering, asking, "Who is that?" and then back to me. He leaned forward until I feared his weight would topple him down to the path and a frantic, shocking knowledge broke his face into pain. He cried out, "You aren't Conrad! You're old!" His hungry gaze quested right and left. "He was here. I saw him."

He was trying to turn round on the step when the trance descended again on his mind in a wiping off of all expression. He relaxed his tumultuous effort to stand and sank back in a vast, collapsing bundle.

I was struck stiff with helpless pity and horror; I nearly fell as Jonesey dragged me to the gate while behind us Mrs. Farnham's voice screamed at us, "Leave my house! Go away from here! Let us alone!"

From the car I glanced back at Derek and he was as I had first seen him, statuesque, staring. Whatever delusion ruled him had cancelled me; he had returned to waiting.

Jonesey took off at speed. There was no traffic along this backwater and we had a long, empty stretch ahead of us before townlets would appear; we fled from the wreckage of Project IQ.

I said, "I wish I had never got into this. All I've seen has been blighted hopes, twisted minds, megalomania and double-dealing, as though no decent humanity existed."

Jonesey agreed that there weren't too many of us, recovering his spirits at the drop of a phrase.

I was savage and morose. "Us? How many double crosses are you playing at the moment?"

"Haven't counted, but my motives are good."

"That's an excuse?"

" 'Deed it is. You'd better believe it, lad, because the other way the nuthouse lies. And I've had enough of that for one day."

"And a bloody unproductive day."

"I wouldn't say so."

"You said so back there."

"But we're not back there and the mental cylinders are firing in the fresh sea air. There's a chance of finding that tutor."

"How?"

"I'm not sure but the pieces are clicking together. Computer memory is a wonderful thing."

"If you know what you're looking for."

"The trick this time is to make it tell me what I'm looking for."

"You and what genius hacker?"

"Me and Daddy Hazard. He's our brainbox."

And why not? He began this chase; let him further it. "Next stop Westerton?"

"Not so fast. First we think a little. It may be time now to take Piggy out of the game; the board is getting cluttered with people and I can't see that he's any more use to us after he pays today's expenses."

My heart dropped to my stomach. "We can't just dump him. He'd have us killed!"

"Oh, no, he wouldn't once I've flashed my ID and explained how interested the Department is in his activities. My people know enough to do more than stop his age treatments; they know enough of his financial dirty tricks to strip him of his money, and what else would make all those years worth living?"

Putting trust in Jonesey was one thing, gambling my life on his certainty another. I was not in control; I could only mutter that I hoped he knew what he was talking about. But I had to confess that I would feel safer out of Armstrong's reach.

"Safer? David, my rising hackles tell me there's worse than Piggy in store before we're done."

"Jesus!" Dismay was all I was capable of.

"A very present help in time of trouble, I'm told, but I prefer to depend on Jonesey—and even on David when he stops worrying and starts thinking. You might, for instance, start thinking where all those cars came from that are sitting a little way back from our tail. It isn't an area where escorts appear out of the blue."

Two cars, one red and one black, both of them recent, powerful models, matched our speed some fifty metres behind us. A third, older and less sleek, was possibly maintaining pace farther back. As I watched, the third disappeared into a side road. "Two only," I said. "What's suspicious about them?"

"Their existence. We're only coasting, so why don't they pass us?"

"Is it a sin? You're jumpy."

"I'm careful. Get the road map from the glove box. Find the next patch of conservation park land."

It was quite a distance away. "The other side of Mornington. There's a stretch about seven kilometres long from there to Mount Eliza. Straight as a ruler."

"Nice," said Jonesey. "If they make a move, it will be there. No builtup area, no witnesses and a straight run for a fast getaway. Suits me."

"Why the melodrama? Two cars on a highway don't make a holdup plot."

"Who said holdup? Glove box again—the spectacle case."

I fumbled through the papers and oddments of tools and cleaning rags to find a beautiful pair of telelens spectacles that would have cost six months of my income.

"Put 'em on. Look in the red car and see how many are in it and how they are sitting. Don't turn round! Use the driving mirror. Why let them see you looking?"

Feeling as though I had wandered into a bad vidplay, I did as he asked. Normally it is difficult to see through a windscreen even when it is close but the telelenses brought the red car seemingly to touching distance. There were two men in it.

"The driver," I said, "and another man in the back seat."

"That settles it."

"Settles what?"

With the calmness of discussing the weather he talked about murder. "Well, now, if he wants to take a shot at you—" At me! At me! "—and he sits in the front, his driver's head will be in the way as he comes up, so he sits in the back with a better field of fire."

"But who would—" This was preposterous. "Who?"

"Piggy. He knows where you are, where to send his hoodlums."

"But why?"

"I've been thinking about that, wondering why Anne Blaikie, who spent nearly twenty years with those kids, didn't mention your family likeness. Let's say she thought about it and held out on Piggy until she had worked out a way to screw a concession out of him in return for an interesting titbit, and in the last day or so she told him, in return for whatever she could get. He hadn't noticed because he hadn't seen the Group in a quarter of a century. He probably doesn't visit CAG 3. Why should he? His firm doesn't run the place; it only siphons off what the State doesn't want and lends its professional name as a convenient cover. So he pondered your visit to Adelaide Cormick, who lives so handy to the old Nursery block, and wondered did you pay it a visit, to talk with your relatives. Next step would be a search through files—with a little help from old political connections—and up comes the genetic match. Heigh-ho, but Piggy has nestled a serpent in his bosom. So, Piggy will bite before he gets bitten."

It held together all too well. The two cars in the mirror were suddenly wild beasts out for the kill.

"Piggy will have reasoned, quite correctly, that A Group has set him up by putting you on the job to use his resources in order to track down the legacy. What riles is that the possibility of his waking up to it was always plain and I didn't consider it." He shot me one of his side glances, between regret and mockery. "Not much use saying I'm sorry, is it? Not to worry, young David; all is not lost."

We swept into Mornington and I thought sickly of

the conservation stretch coming up too soon. "What can we do?"

"We can play a little game to assess the opposition. And then, luck willing, take action, and I don't mean evasive. I didn't take you under my Departmental wing to lose you so soon. Take your coat off."

"What?"

"Your coat. Take it off and bare all that recording Lurex to photograph the action. That necklet sees only what's in front of it but the shirt covers three hundred and sixty degrees, no?"

"Yes."

"So keep it activated. We want pictures of all concerned. If they're Piggy's boys, that will be the end of Piggy."

I felt more stunned than afraid but my chattering teeth told the truth as I said, "Or us."

"Don't believe it, lad. Coat off!"

I stripped it off, baring the green Lurex, feeling that I was about to photograph my own death. Yet I think I was influenced by Jonesey's indecent calm.

The town ceased abruptly at a clean edge and we moved into the conservation area, an endlessly straight stretch of highway bounded by bush on both sides. Save the two behind us, there was not a vehicle in sight.

Without warning, Jonesey accelerated from a placid hundred to a hundred and fifty and for a short while the pursuit slipped back. We gained perhaps three hundred metres before the two cars closed the gap effortlessly and this time took position no more than two lengths behind us. After that it was not possible to doubt.

Jonesey said gently, "Stop worrying."

I was too nearly petrified for anything so trivial as worry. Helpless, freezing funk takes different forms with different people; with me it manifests as a monstrous calm from which the muscles would not erupt if they could, while the senses are alerted so that each sight and sound registers brilliantly and forever. My eyes were fixed in rabbit fascination on the driving mirror as the cars set themselves in place behind us.

We were about a kilometre into the bush area when the two began to crawl forward, the black car on Jonesey's side, the red on mine. Jonesey pushed up to two hundred and again they matched us, still coming to box us in.

"Silly sods," he said. "That's a city manoeuvre for killing in a crowd. But we haven't got a crowd, have we, lad?"

I heard the words without retaining any meaning. My whole life was fixed on the open rear window of the red car with its new detail of a hand resting there with a gun in it. The world was a tunnelled vision of the gun coming gently up to claim me.

From the corner of my eye I saw Jonesey reach into his armpit holster for a tiny automatic that would have fitted into a lady's handbag, and rest his hand with it against the upper rim of the steering wheel.

"See them and learn, lad! City boys too stupid to recognise the need for fresh tactics."

I saw only the gun closing up behind me as the red car came level with our boot.

Jonesey said quietly, "Head down, lad."

I heard without understanding. He slapped me violently on the side of the jaw, shouting, "Down, down!" and it seemed that an age passed before I saw meaning and forced my fright-bound body into simple movement. But I was already too late.

Jonesey stepped hard on the brakes and as we screeched on the road surface the other cars hurtled up on either side of us, taken by surprise.

I heard two shots, one beside me and one somewhere outside our car, and felt the wind of Jonesey's round as he shot the driver of the red car when it raced helplessly past us. The other was from the gunman, reacting wildly and uselessly to the instantly changed situation.

All I knew at the time was that guns were firing before the deceleration smashed my ducking head into the dash-board and I went out cold.

I came to flat on my back, staring at the sky. My forehead hurt. I was on the side of the road with scrub shading me. Something nearby was burning; brown and white smoke drifted across my sight and in the air was the crackle of burning brush and the smell of eucalypts afire.

Jonesey's voice asked, "All right, lad?" His face swooped down over mine as he knelt beside me.

"All right." I started to sit up, gasped and lay back again. My raised head had become a ball of instant pain, all the headaches of an age in a single onslaught.

Not far away I heard a helicopter and as the ache subsided to a nearly bearable fury there sounded the *thump-thump-thump* of a line of Fire Brigade smother bombs.

"What's burning?"

"The bush. And the red car. I winged the driver and he went over the edge. Turned over and over and his hydrogen tanks went up. Our radio was still working so I called Fires and Ambulance and Road Help. Fires has just got here."

Ambulance was a welcome word; the ache was developing into the sharp chopping of a small axe between my ears. If only to have something other than pain on my mind I asked, "Why shouldn't the radio still work?"

"We went over, too. The black car sideswiped us as he passed. He hit the front bumper hard enough to throw us off the road but I was slowing and had some control. The car's on its side but not damaged much. Road Help may be able to fix it."

"You pulled me out."

"Had to. Couldn't leave you there with a little bushfire blowing up on us. Besides, I need you. Got to be practical."

I plodded round what was operating of my mind. "Where's the black car?"

"Pissed off when he saw the fire start. Reckoned there could be too many questions to answer if he stayed around."

"Am I bleeding?"

"Big gash across the forehead. Lots of blood. I've got no water on board and Ambulance would crucify me if I wiped it with a dirty handkerchief."

I lay still, hoping the pain would recede; it did not. Jonesey kept on talking but I lost track of meaning. I remember that he seemed to be enjoying a fantasy of revenge on Piggy. He was sure Piggy was the prime mover.

Sooner or later—it seemed forever later—Ambulance arrived. Somebody bathed my forehead while somebody else said, "Don't move him yet," and there was a sound of equipment being dragged close. A pad was placed gently but painfully under my head and the portable X-ray generator whined briefly. "Lovely little frontal fracture. Not depressed. He'll be all right."

At last came the welcome prick in the arm. As I waited for darkness I heard Jonesey say, like a disembodied voice in a tunnel, "Here's my ID. I want his shirt. Don't argue with me! Give me the shirt!"

Pain vanished in sleep.

8 • A JONESEY INTERLUDE

My business is to fill in what happened while David was out of action. Must get it right, says David, and since he wasn't on the spot, the job is mine.

Dickens and Tolstoy, move over—here comes Jonesey!

It's a wonder he lets me do it, knowing now what he did not know in those days, that he was asking for accuracy from a man who usually wrote his official reports three times to remove the fancy embellishments of the Jonesey persona who took over from the staid family man behind the nom de guerre. There, you see! Nom de guerre instead of alias, even now, with me well into the sere and yellow.

"Jonesey" was a personality I pulled on like a sweatsuit for track work—cunning, low class, smart with the dialogue, spot on with the action, wise with the nastiness of tough-guy experience. "Jonesey" got me through many a rough ride and blustered his way through more than one encounter when the little man inside was wishing for a hole to crawl into.

Now that I've made sure you won't trust a word I write, here goes:

* * *

David was twenty-five when all this happened, though most of the time I found it hard to believe he was more than sixteen. He was bright, in the way a smart teenager is bright, but he behaved like someone who had grown up insulated from the smarmy facts of human behaviour and couldn't believe that the things he had written about as a newsman could actually happen to him.

Most orphanages bred tough brats who'd kick your teeth in as soon as look at you, but he had been reared in one of those semi-autonomous State-subsidised institutions whose excess income derived from well-off parents in trouble with the Population Control Act and who could afford to put their unacknowledgeable errors out to grass. He had come out ignorant and pilotless and after seven years still needed a nanny.

I was no nanny and it must have been some surplus of the father instinct that made me put out a guiding hand, but when I wasn't feeling fatherly I felt more like shaking him loose from his innocent teeth. And then I had to bloody near kill him when I turned us over on the highway. I blame myself; I should have foreseen an attack of some sort. Just too busy showing what a cunning old master of the game I was.

The Hazard molecular bone-bonding technique was well established by that time and I knew the hairline fracture would not keep him in hospital more than four days, but there was work to be done and no time to waste now that the knives were out.

Once I had the lad's shirt, and Ambulance had carted him away, I had only to wait for Road Help. They arrived complaining about novice drivers who bought grief on an empty road. Glad to be of assistance, however, now that we've told you what a twit you are, and how did it happen? Was that burned-out car in the burned-out conservation area burned out as part of the performance? Why, then, sir, the police will be interested—identification of bodies and so on.

I flashed my ID and told the clowns that my Department would tell the police what it required of them.

Yessir, yessir—very impressed—but for our routine report, how did it happen?

I explained that the burnt ones had tried to pass on the left, which was reprehensible in them, had swayed as though in poor control and ripped off my front bumper (which certainly was missing), then skidded and overturned into the scrub. I, fighting to manage my bucking beast, had gone off the road fifty metres farther on. They had burned—poor, unfortunate drunks—but I had had time and thought to kill my ignition. No hydrogen torch for Jonesey. I said nothing of the black car. Why complicate an issue from which obvious gain could be extracted?

Road Help hauled my car upright, opined that it needed garage overhaul (I played with the idea of soaking Piggy for the repair bill but discarded it as a last straw of impudence that might cause him to do something ill-considered and unexpected) and gave me a lift back to the city.

I was not much concerned about David after the paramedic's verdict, so I concentrated on getting home for a shower, a change of clothes and treatment for my bruises. I had to explain to Elaine, but all she said was "Holy Jesus!" in the suffering voice that meant I shouldn't be allowed out alone. She used to worry too much.

After that, the most urgent job was to get proof of Piggy's involvement (that is, the pictures of his thugs), which meant a call to Westerton. I vidded CAG 3, waved the Lurex shirt at the green-eyed monster and said I needed it run that night.

Nothing seemed to surprise his blandness; he checked the time and suggested that I could be there by ten o'clock.

I explained that my car was not available; could he, perhaps . . . ?

He didn't argue but was definitely testy about agreeing that he could and that he would bring the necessary equipment; he made me feel that he expected a useful result for his trouble.

I didn't want any part of this affair in my home (never take your work over the doorstep) and suggested that we use David's flat.

"Unsuitable," he said, meaning bugged.

"It won't be by the time you get there."

"Is that wise?"

"That's what the shirt is about."

He seemed very faintly disturbed but asked no questions. There was much to be said for a logical mind, if little for the owner of it. At least, he didn't fuss. "Very well; ten o'clock."

I told Elaine, "Late job; see you in the morning."

"Take your first-aid kit," she advised, deadpan.

I took instead a bugging detector and a basic vid-tool kit. My ID got me unwilling cooperation from the apartment house caretaker, who thought David had too many peculiar callers; I had to give the lad a faked-up, hush-hush bill of social health before he let me into the flat, but he went away feeling that he had glimpsed mighty secrets of state.

Locating the listening bugs and removing them took an hour of dismantling and replacing wall fittings. What had been done to the screen was beyond my expertise, so I disconnected the whole thing. Which should have made Piggy jump. He may have watched me do it.

Old Greeneyes arrived dead on ten o'clock. I looked for the little scar and decided that this was Father Hazard. Standing where the screen could not see him, he raised his eyebrows. "Disconnected," I said. "I don't know how to handle those bugs."

"I need it for the shirt."

He looked over my tool wallet, decided it was good enough, and together we unscrewed the terminal knobs and button-plates and lifted off the face panel. That took about five fiddling minutes. Removing the bugs and reconnecting the vid occupied him for fully thirty seconds with no fiddling at all. It was sobering to see a genuine talent at work.

He showed me the bugs—tiny, remote-controlled microchip units. "Do you need these for Armstrong?"

I shook my head, thinking about how this mind worked smartly on a single datum and wondering what sort of mind it ultimately was.

He said, "With screen surveillance nullified, I can only assume you intend a confrontation with Armstrong."

"Smart thinking."

"Obvious, but will he not send men to discover why his bugs are dead?"

"No. He's made one bad mistake today, bad enough to make him suspect a trap here."

"Please explain."

"In a moment." I said sharply, "You don't seem interested in your son's absence."

He didn't hesitate at all. "Should I be? I assume him to be occupied elsewhere. Surely you would have told me if he were hurt or in trouble."

Greeneyes, one; Jonesey, nil.

"He's in hospital. You won't lose him; he'll be about within the week."

"Tell me about it."

I held up the shirt with its metallic stripes. "You'll see."

"Have you the necklet? I cannot connect the Lurex directly to the screen."

I had taken the necklet rather than have an Ambulance man souvenir it, not knowing it was necessary. You can be lucky. "The interesting part is on the shirt. There's nothing much in the interview."

"Interview?"

"The Farnhams."

Without comment he hooked the necklet into the display terminal and switched on.

At the interview's end he sat for a moment in thought, then said, "I trust you paid him well."

"For what?"

"His mention of the tutor. He or she can be found if still alive."

He knew with certainty what my convolutions had wrestled with as a complex possibility. "So I thought, but I paid his poverty and not his wit."

"Dear me, a classicist! You are sometimes unexpected, Mr. Jones."

"Jonesey."

"As you wish. A sentimental classicist with sympathy for the victims of life."

Perhaps he was sneering, perhaps not; the bland delivery gave statements their exact meaning, without overtone, but a man who recognised the less-quoted lines of Shakespeare could not be wholly cold. However, it was not Shakespeare I wanted to talk about.

"How did you know when C Group died?"

Suddenness could not surprise him. He answered with a barest touch of annoyance, "I do not know how. All twelve of us were in some degree conscious of the existence of the others, though unaware of the consciousness. We became aware in the manner of realising that a lifelong background of continuous noise has fallen silent. If it had not ceased, we might never have noticed it. We hypothesise that it is a random genetic effect concerned with synaptic spark gaps, a sensitivity latent in the genes and unintentionally brought to dominance by the surgeons who"—his face twitched in a grimace of deep distaste—"meddled like roadside tinkers with our makeup."

With a waste of cunning (you have to keep trying) I suggested that, given the legacy, he might be able to trace it.

"To what end? It is a useless ability. There seems to be some evidence of sympathetic resonance in quite ordinary persons but the faculty remains rare—recessive."

"So much for the marvels of the mind."

"And so little. The genetic code, when fully cross-indexed by some garbage-sorting computer, will be found to have more possibilities for error than founts of evolutionary improvement. The limited access given by sexual congress produces a quota of monsters, throwbacks and genetically transmitted diseases with only a very limited trial-and-error production of the so-called fittest—that is, those who can thrive in local conditions but would be totally unfit in any others. The legacy will be what common parlance calls a trap for learners."

I couldn't argue against that; it seemed all too likely. Still . . . "There could be rewards also."

He ignored the bait. "The shirt, please."

My position would have to be unassailably strong if I was ever to surprise him in a statement he did not wish to make. Measuring my technique against his intelligence was pitting a barnyard duck against an eagle. And he was a plain-minded man by comparison with the labyrinthine C Group intellects that he admitted he could follow only partially.

I handed over the shirt.

He produced a gadget from his pocket, a short length of flex with at each end a small spring clamp issuing from a box the size of a wristwatch, and with it clipped the necklet to the shirt.

The screen lit up with a dog's breakfast of disconnected form and colour, confused shapes and swatches of superimposed hues. From the speakers a barely human sound that seemed to be a dozen versions of my voice yelled in discord what might have been, "Down, down!"

Hazard said, "This is a full circle view. Was David not wearing a jacket?"

"He took it off to get a visual of what was happening behind us."

Hazard played with a little rod on what I took to be control surfaces on the clamp-boxes. The insane visual froze and the voice stopped. "Recording a full three hundred and sixty degrees raises definition problems but the superimpositions can be sorted." He added an unexpected courtesy: "Please be patient, Mr. Jones. Um—Jonesey."

It was impossible to decide where his humanity began and ended; he lacked consistency.

After several minutes during which I had the impression that he did complex mental mathematics while visualising circuit diagrams, he tapped out a few commands on the clamp-boxes. The visual salad disappeared except for the view directly through the windscreen; this rotated from left to right as if we sat in the middle while the visual circled round us. The definition was poor but the details could be recognised in context; my voice registered as a badly trained male chorus. My fist made an unpleasant smack on David's jaw as I yelled at him; the sounds of gunfire, recorded from too many angles and not sorted as well as the visual, rattled like half a second of hail.

I said, "Turn it back; you've started in the middle."

He tapped once and the view dissolved in blackness, to evolve colour as David removed his coat.

When the sequence had been run through to the point where I removed the necklet, Hazard offered his opinion that my manoeuvre had been neatly executed, but: "It is an action I could devise but might have difficulty coordinating." To my incomprehension he explained, "My brain would be simultaneously aware of the consequences of physical and planning error and of the existence of other possible solutions—a recipe for hesitation. Do you see how it is? Different mental systems, different values, different weaknesses, different advantages. Your mind screens out all but essentials whereas mine recognises and sorts possibilities. Excellent for logical conclusion but retardant to action."

"Self-preservation is reflexive."

"Is it? Perhaps. It is an evolutionary weapon that I do not possess. It would seem to imply a basic, overweening selfishness, yet observable human behaviour contradicts this while simultaneously affirming it. Your psychology exhibits discomfiting paradoxes."

I said he should talk to a Psych about it.

"Be sure that we have done so. Many possibilities but no satisfactory answers. Reactions modulate from individual to individual with resolution dependent on variable and transient factors." As usual when he had completed one of his chatty detours, he changed direction without warning. "One must assume that Armstrong was responsible for this?"

" 'Deed one must. Can you enlarge a section of the picture with that dingus?"

" 'Deed I can."

I don't think that was mockery; he sounded like a connoisseur savouring an odd idiom. "Then let's look at the two men in the red car."

He found and enlarged them until it was possible to recognise them through the distortions of the rumpled shirt and the light streaks on their windscreen. I had seen them often on the back verandah, in camouflage dress. "I've knocked off two of Piggy's private bodyguards. He'll be carpet-biting."

"Piggy is Armstrong? And he will take no immediate action?"

"In his place, would you?"

"I cannot say. I would have to think whereas he might act precipitately, emotionally."

"Not Piggy. He knows now that I also am the enemy; he has misjudged me as badly as he misjudged David. He will be seeking more information on me before acting. And he will be coming up against informational blank walls, making him wonder what sort of double cross lies behind them and who is operating it. David leads directly to you, but who is behind me?" Then, nitwitted as ever, I had to spoil my momentary superiority. "We have mental systems in common, Piggy and I—we both have criminal minds."

That was Jonesey big-noting himself again. The criminal mind is mostly myth, being much the same as yours and mine with the limitation of an overwhelming ego-fixation and a degree of cunning as distinct from brains. Criminals use so much violence because they can't think their way out of problems; real people are outside their understanding, just as Hazard and I hovered round the edges of each other's mental processes, each slightly unreal to the other.

I tried my hand at quick subject-changing. "Why didn't you point out to David that his resemblance to you must soon arouse suspicion?"

For once I caught a fully identifiable expression on his face, a ludicrous, helpless dismay as he said, "I had not noticed it. Now the matter is raised, he does not, to me, seem very like." He became apologetic, halfway human. "You people are family oriented; such concurrences do not occupy me. I do not scrutinise for likenesses."

Stalemate; David's behaviour cried aloud that he hadn't noticed it, either. It is true that few people know how they appear to others; an artist who came to self-portraiture in middle age told me that his face never ceased to surprise him in its variance from his conception of it. Jonesey, weaving and dodging to get under the Hazard guard and discover his real attitude to David, wasn't landing a single punch.

Old Greeneyes said tentatively, "You must deal with Armstrong; I should make errors of ignorance."

For a moment I felt positively in charge of things, the agent with the answers. "I'll pull his teeth in handfuls. Stop him biting."

Hazard showed his outline of a smile. "Metaphors disturb me; I have a literal mind, but I wish you success with his teeth."

"There's a job for you, too."

"The tutor, yes."

"Can you find him?"

"You must do the finding, if he or she lives. It is a matter of collating information and discarding what does not fit until one name remains. The search will necessitate access to data beyond public reach."

"Classy hacking?"

"You know that is out of the question. There must be no protective clearance of data and I cannot actively appear in this business. You must use your Departmental contacts to obtain permission to scan records protected by the privacy code."

"I must?"

"I will tell you how, but you must do it."

"So that you do not appear actively?"

"Quite so."

He unclamped the flex from the shirt and necklet, and the necklet from the vidscreen. The clamps went into his pocket; he held out the necklet to me and I took it. He smiled—openly and genuinely smiled at his thoughts —and I felt that something less than pleasant was coming. It was.

"Jonesey, have you reported to your Department that the legacy definitely exists and that you have unholy suspicions of what it might contain?"

He had me cold; he knew more of common psychology than he pretended and had poked a gamester's hole in the Jonesey facade. I blustered a little. "I haven't discussed my thoughts on that with you, either."

"It was not necessary. You are a signaller of body language, not hard to read. You suspect my intentions and doubt your own. Well, then, we must protect each other's secrets until we see what the legacy in fact contains. Then the decision making will begin in earnest, eh?"

I did not answer; I could not. Common sense said that the thing should be destroyed on sight (but that is not the same thing as a set intention) and a small voice protested against the destruction of knowledge, the ultimate vandalism. We all have our points of cowardice; this was mine. I would wait and see.

"Now," Hazard said, as if the matter had been dealt with and filed away, "I will tell you how to find the tutor."

And he did.

A great deal of it—that is, the early, easier parts—I had already worked out, but he was far ahead of me in seeing what led where and the kind of collation needed. I had hoped to reduce the possibilities to manageable size and then proceed by elimination—meaning the plain, slogging legwork that is most of what I am good for—but he meant to home on the right goal in a single sequence of operations.

Some of the information would be very tricky to obtain because I needed reasons for some of the outlandish requests I would have to make for access to Private Data Storage and Dead Files. Patiently he devised reasons for me, and most of them seemed practicable. I would have to reconsider some of the details and could probably bring it all off, but he did not understand the terror implicit in lying to the Department; he was unable to envision a logical procedure failing.

"There, now, Jonesey; shall we say, three days?"

"I'll try." In fact it sounded like a job for three weeks.

"Don't be awed by the operations involved. Make the computers think for you."

I would have to; my competence in the face of an avalanche of data was minimal.

"Now I must go. The night has not been wasted, but I have work to do."

Leaving, he paused at the door. "Which hospital is my son in?"

"Southeast Public."

"Thank you."

He went.

I had been wondering whether in his role playing he would remember this essential piece of characterisation of the loving father. What hurt was that he had known I wondered and had held me on the string until the last moment. He had a sense of humour of a pawky sort. Or only a sense of mockery?

As I packed up my own tools I felt second-rate and incapable, out of my class but with no means of withdrawal from the contest.

Armstrong could not be left to simmer. I was in Toorak next morning, still a mass of bruised stiffness and bad temper but early enough to have to wait while he got out of bed. I hoped he had had a late, crowded and worried night. In his place I would have made a long production of dressing and breakfasting, forcing me to fume in waiting silence and work myself into a flurry of those second thoughts that generate mistakes, but he was too anxious to discover what had been done to him.

He came in dressing gown and slippers, blank-faced with banked anger because my visit was an impertinence, a flaunting of contempt, an announcement that I had no fear of him.

He led the way to the back verandah and two armed minders came behind, to station themselves at either end, watchful but out of earshot. New faces, I saw. Wondering at their sudden promotion to confidential status? Or did they know about the car and its crew, and step uneasily into those charred shoes?

The creep of Piggy's ageing showed cruelly in the morning light; the limitations of the therapy were apparent. His recent actions had betrayed, also, a thinning round the edges of his mind; he had not yet realised that yesterday's power broker was losing his grip and that today's obsessed man was a fading shadow.

He sat himself down, letting me stand while he stared at me in silence, the usual treatment when you are not sure of your ground but hope to dominate by imperturbable menace. Wasted on Jonesey that morning. Piggy was no A Group game player, able to assume superiority and effortlessly demonstrate it.

Too many preliminaries for my taste. I said, "Wrightson and Caselli burned to death."

"I know it." After a lifetime of dealing with emergencies, control of his voice was second nature.

"Don't ever attempt to wipe off David Chance, or do him any damage, or thwart this investigation."

His unwavering stare counterfeited confidence as he tried to regain the initiative. "You give me orders, little man?"

I laid my Departmental ID in front of him.

All his discipline could not hide shock and the sickness round his mouth. He leaned forward to read the symbols and trace them gently with his fingertips as if to convince his eyes that they did not mock him. With a gesture of defeated spite he pushed it off the table.

"A thousand bent snoops in town and I have to pick the odd one out!"

Simple human bitterness. He was failing badly. I said as I picked up the plaque, "My guess is that you were gently guided into hiring me. Untouchable Files has been accumulating data on you for thirty years, waiting for you to do something foolish and become touchable. Yesterday you did it, but only a couple of expendable thugs got hurt, so you aren't yet worth pursuing to a finish."

I stopped there and played the silence game back to him. He stood it for half a minute. "What do you want?"

"It's too late for offers. Did you think there might be a price I'd snap at?" (Might there be one? Nobody had ever offered it and I had never thought about it.)

He raised one shoulder fractionally, let it drop. In his world every man could be bought; certainly a low-grade op like Jonesey should come cheap.

I said, "You could be right but I'm too young to be written off for treachery. My report went in last night and we have a full visual record of the murder attempt, so you have nothing to gain by wiping me out—except Departmental retribution." All untrue. I had made no report but he was in no position to risk disbelieving me. "From now on your file will swell a little with every move you make. You'll have electronic surveillance from genuine experts, men who could monitor your pulse and temperature if they needed to."

He turned his head to stare across the back lawn at the city skyline fresh with morning; I think he did not trust himself to look at me. "Just go. Get out."

"Glad to. The air smells of an ageing animal and the fear of death." That was cheap, but his kind rouses the venom in me. Besides, he had tried to kill David, who was in my care. I twisted the knife: "The minds in CAG 3 led you to hire David. Have you realised it?" Of course he had; his lips opened a little and twitched and closed again. "Should you feel moved to burn CAG 3 to the ground or blow it up or have its occupants die mysterious deaths— don't! Should they die by accident, though you have nothing to do with it I'll frame you for it. So light candles to their continued good health."

There was no more to be gained. I paused at the door to drive my point home. "The game goes on but you are out of it. For good. Off the board."

He said, still with that control that by now must have had a permanent grip on his unstirring soul, "Don't ever come near me again."

"Not willingly, Piggy."

How wrong you can be about the simplest things.

There's a difficulty here. It is not possible for me to tell all I did in locating the tutor or the nature of the lies I had to tell to obtain access to Dead Records; to do so would indicate precisely which Department (with an unacknowledged Covert Section) was involved. That indiscretion would see my grey hairs falling out behind bars.

The best I can do is to give some indication of the nature of the problems faced and overcome.

You must understand that back in the twenties, when Conrad fled the coop, private coaching was big business; the daily advertising in a big city would run to hundreds of insertions of sucker bait for cram courses. Automation had just about eliminated the "working class"; you either had a specialty or you were on the dole. The day of "learning on the job," starting in late teens and climbing the company rungs, was also past; you came in with a technical background or you didn't come in at all. Kids stayed at school, taking degree or diploma courses to keep them off the streets and from under their parents' feet, but what did that do for them? When everybody had an advanced background, who got the nod? The answer was specialised cramming; the kid picked a promising line of work, sweated it up and then went tooth-and-claw for whatever opening offered.

It was milk-and-honey time for the crammers—for the good ones, that is. My old standby for potted wisdom, George Bernard Shaw, noted that "Those who can, do;

those who can't, teach." He wasn't sneering; he knew that the most capable performers don't make the best teachers—too busy, too impatient, too expectant. The devoted ones who couldn't quite make it become the teachers, the disappointed ones who know it all but haven't the extra spark that ignites success; hundreds of them hit the streets at the end of every curricular year. Their betters scoop the jobs while the losers teach the people who will, in turn, become their betters.

It still goes on. Bitterly learned economic management has improved the situation, but in the year I had to excavate, microbiology was still big business and the crammer lists were immense, dismaying.

First I had to establish the date of Young Feller's escape. A friend in Country Fires was able to locate the date of the Cormick call for help, and I knew that the boy was in Melbourne on the next day, with Derek following two days later. Then they passed a few days in learning the customs of the natives and in assimilating a stew of basic texts. How many days?

I doubted that Evan Farnham had a precise memory, and in any case a tentative call earned me only an insult and a blackout. A call to Arthur Hazard produced a laconic, "Cover a period of two months," and my heart oozed out through my toecaps.

At the time I was covering there were one evening daily, three mornings and five wide-circulation weekly prints in Melbourne. Tracing these through newspaper morgues was no trouble, but getting the printouts occupied half a day and gave me a list of over five hundred hungry crammers. After culling the biology specialists and allowing for a few who might or might not touch the subject, I had eighty-seven contenders. A run through Funeral Notices eliminated eleven of them. Seventy-six to go—and pray God my target had not left the country.

With the next step trouble began. It was necessary to obtain the serial numbers of their Student Access Library Cards, and that is Blocked Data, part of the Personal Information guaranteed against unlawful intrusion by the Data Base Privacy Act. The move with Blocked Data is, of course, to wangle an Authority to View. To this end I created a web of fake investigation concerning matters far removed from Project IQ. And that will have to satisfy you. After all, it satisfied my Superintendent, didn't it? Keep that one in mind.

Next, I needed to know which of my seventy-six possibles had (a) consulted an unusual number of biology texts, files, programmes and references over an eighteen-month period and (b) consulted information for studies far advanced beyond student requirements. The reasoning here was that I could not see how it would have been possible for Young Feller, without an identity, to obtain a Library Card; he would have been forced to "captivate" a tutor and use his access.

This required more lying and fantasising to get my nose into Central Library records, and what it gained me was not one name but three apparently engaged in running neck and neck through the whole field of biology and its ancillary subjects.

Why so many? Could he have used all of them? I consulted Arthur, who asked, "When did the activity cease?"

"After three months."

He was startled and showed it. "Are you sure?"

"Quite sure."

He said bleakly, "I underestimated him. His Group's mental capacity . . ." He shrugged, admitting incomprehension. "That allows no time for laboratory work; biological experiment is not fast. Thought experiments, perhaps? Computer simulations? Perhaps he could have managed with those. You must look for evidence of invasion of the Register of Experimental Data. He must have attempted it."

The RED holds work at the front edge of the art, available only by direct permission of the experimenter concerned; it is both the preservation and the protection of his work.

"Out of the question."

"Violations," he insisted, meaning: *Check records for hacker violations.* Such attempts had been known although stealing knowledge was, then as now, a serious crime with overtones of possible espionage and treason.

Hacker crimes were, broadly speaking, checkable through news files. An outbreak of violations had occurred in the fifth month of Young Feller's freedom—two months after the conclusion of his "regular" studies—by a method that would have been of no use to a student or laboratory thief or to any but a phenomenal mind or a mere voyeur hacking for kicks. The nature of the material scanned was of course not revealed, but such a plunderer could only have been the boy. What he had done was break into the homes of people who were absent and, fully prepared apparently with the codes, used their terminals to lift the wanted information with no attempt to avoid the backtrack. The viewing had in each case lasted no more than a minute, allowing him to escape before the backtrack could set the police stirring; in that time the total content of the file had been viewed but not copied.

Committed to memory! In some cases months of work had been merely looked through with photographic speed, and because the thief had no fear of the backtrack, the information areas had not been destroyed or any effort made to disguise the entry. The ransack had operated at the very pinnacle of advanced theory and practise and had covered eleven countries.

When I told Arthur, he commented, "He would not

destroy," and allowed himself two seconds for thought. "He would have traced the existence of the files through theoretical articles in the science journals. Find the articles and discover whose Access Card was used to consult them."

"There could be ten thousand bloody articles!"

"Not so; only a limited number would have been of use to him."

"I wouldn't know them."

"My sisters would. Call me tomorrow morning."

They must have spent the day in CAG 3 ratting through those old magazines—hundreds of them, which must have made Central Library very curious but not to the point of notifying authority—and sorting the pile for me.

The result was wasted effort. The cards of all three tutors had been used. There was nothing for it but to case the three. Footwork.

And on that, the third day of the search, I was called to my Superintendent's office, where he said, "I have allowed your structure of lies and evasions to stand in the hope that you would fall off when it became high enough. Fall off now, while only I can hear you make an ass of yourself. What are you up to?"

There are times when cornered rats tell truth for lack of a big enough lie to hide behind; this, with the ego deflation that goes with it, was one of them. I should have known that watertight requests and reasons attract as much suspicion in undercover circles as blatantly false ones. Jonesey had revelled in his cleverness once too often.

At the end of the tale, which the Superintendent appreciated as a connoisseur of involution and human nastiness, he gave me his most genial smile—the one that suckers crooks, politicians and chorus girls alike—and asked the million-dollar question: On what ground did I consider myself the only safe repository of the information that might lie concealed in the legacy?

What could I say but, "I don't think anybody could be trusted with it."

"Save only yourself?"

I had no answer to that because in the depths of truth I was not sure how I felt about the bait of immortality.

In the end he said, "We'll have the legacy here, I think. Here. Nowhere else."

He put on the straight-from-the-shoulder, trust-me look that every liar, including Jonesey, can call up at will and said, "If this Department can't keep secrets, who can?" He knew how much credence I would place in that, and returned to immediacies. "You must carry on your paper chase with David Chance, but we will have our eye on you. Several eyes. And we will watch Armstrong; you will hear no more from him."

Now that one more person knew of the possible bomb in the legacy, what would he do with temptation? Who would he tell? My bet was—nobody, save the laboratory man who would be needed to do the interpreting and unscrambling. Some secrets are too big for sharing, even with the most trustworthy of Superintendents.

9 • THE STUDIOUS CROCODILE

1.

I woke with a filthy headache, flat on my back with my skull in a clamp and my gaze fixed on the ceiling. I was in bed in a darkened room, though some light glowed through frosted panels. I must have whimpered or groaned because a nurse hurried in with a "tsk-tsk" and a needle for my forearm.

When I woke again the headache and the clamp were gone. I turned my head gently to ease a stiffened neck and my father's blank voice said, "He is awake," but when I opened my eyes it was Jonesey's that looked into mine with a concern instantly erased.

"Tough bugger, eh? Hard to kill!"

My father glanced at him with the faintly questioning air that was one of his more tumultuous expressions, then turned gravely to me, settled his face into a competent sketch of fatherly interest and asked politely, "You are recovered, I trust?"

" 'Deed he is and ready to get back into action."

A white uniform remarked starchily from the other

side of the bed, "Mr. Chance will be examined for possible discharge tomorrow, not before."

Jonesey asked, "Should I stand in the corner?"

"If you wish," said the uniform and left us alone. I found out later that she had had more than her fill of Jonesey during my three days of sedation.

I felt astonishingly well, clearheaded enough to recall the noisy confusion of the final seconds in the car and to work up an urgent curiosity as to what had happened, but sensible enough to be unsure how much could safely be spoken here.

My father had one of his moments of logical insight and assured me that this was a private ward and that we could speak freely. Nothing like a flash credit rating, I thought, and a father who has one.

Jonesey told me what had happened to Armstrong's thugs but seemed to take little pleasure in his successful violence; he blamed himself that the encounter had happened at all. Then he related his interview with Armstrong and this time displayed a spiteful triumph in his deliberate screwing of the man's hopes and fears. My distaste must have showed because he snapped at me, "He was trying to kill you!"

I was peculiarly unable to feel that in a personal way; it had all become unreal. A simple investigation into a good story had exploded into madness, perversion, greed, paranoia and now into murderous intention against myself; what had begun as a game with a spice of not too urgent danger had turned into an exposure of human rottenness with no player permitted much honour or decency. I felt distanced, an onlooker at unpleasantness.

What an innocent young creep I was in those days.

I said, "Without his dream Armstrong will collapse." Neither of them seemed to think that worth a tear. "What puzzles me is how he became alerted to the idea of life extension in the first place. Would he have had the knowledge to work it out alone?"

My father said, in the grudging tone with which he dispensed the obvious to those who couldn't see it for themselves, "My sister Astrid fed it to him long ago as a side issue, a speculative comment in a workshop progress report on an unrelated subject. It was necessary that his interest in the legacy should not slacken. An additional carrot on the stick."

More and more things seemed to devolve back to my green-eyed progenitor. "You didn't think to mention that to me."

"What need?"

What, indeed? Telling me or not telling me would have made no difference to anything that had happened, but a failure to be wholly logical is one of the necessities of being genially human. There would be nothing gained by explaining this to my father. "If he's off our backs," I said, "that will help. We'll feel freer with nobody looking over our shoulders."

Jonesey's reaction to that was an abrupt sullenness but my father seemed nearly gleeful as he said, "But there is somebody," and to my surprise gave Jonesey a hearty dig in the ribs, surely a gesture of outrageous camaraderie. "Tell him, Jonesey; it is your story."

So I heard about the chase for knowledge through the Blocked Data bases and Jonesey's disastrous encounter with his Superintendent. My father summed up: "Jonesey was holding his Department as a threat over my head, now it hangs over his. Such justice!"

His minimal smile spoke of complacent enjoyment of a situation that filled me with fright. I said, "We've got to stop. We've run out of rope. If we go any further into this we'll finish in more grief than I want to think of."

My father's short bark was almost like laughter. Jonesey said, "We can't stop. I'm under orders to continue." Like a man tasting aloes he added, "So are you."

"Your Department isn't running me!"

He explained to my shocked understanding, "You can be drafted on a temporary basis because of your specialised knowledge of the affair; they can do that under Internal Security Regulations. Do it willingly, lad, and they'll have less legal hold on you. They won't want to pull you in on a special service basis because then they'd have to pay you; that would mean explaining you to the auditors and eventually to the State minister, and covert sections don't want to explain anything, especially to ministers, until they are sure just how much they are prepared to tell. So take advantage of the setup and stay voluntary. That's the word they use to explain temporaries—good people conscious of their obligation to the State. Like you. Then all you have to worry about is the Official Secrets Act. And that's plenty."

This nonsense was all of a piece with the rest of the fantasy. "Does this make me some sort of spy?"

"No. More like some sort of sucker who's run out of choices."

My father remarked placidly that the relationships were growing complex. "The situation is developing an intrinsic interest, regardless of the outcome." He placed a bony hand lightly on my cheek. "But I have work waiting. I'm sure you will continue to do well under the changed conditions."

With that effort of parental tenderness, he left. "Someday," Jonesey said, "I hope to turn him over a slow fire."

That was sufficient to swing me to the defence. "Just because you find him pulling the strings all the time?"

"Partly. Nobody likes being a puppet. And partly because he keeps information to himself."

"On the need-to-know principle. Isn't that routine in your kind of organisation? His reservations haven't hurt us."

"No? If I'd known of his fiddling from the start, I'd have put the whole thing into the hands of my Super and bowed out."

"Just the same, go easy on Dad. I owe him a lot."

He exploded, "And he's calling in his IOUs, isn't he? Oh, isn't he just!"

He was right but I wanted him to be wrong; we stayed quiet, not wishing to be at loggerheads, until he said, "Sorry, but that's my view of him. I don't want you hurt by people who use, abuse and throw away."

I had a knife of my own to twist. "Now that your Super is party to the big secret, how far do you trust him?"

"As far as I trust myself."

Before I could label that an evasion he stood up to leave. "You can quiz the Super yourself; he's waiting to talk to you. I'll look in tomorrow." He went off, leaving me apprehensive and full of questions, only saying over his shoulder, "Don't tell him any lies; he's out of your class."

God knows what my inexperience and dismay expected of the head of a covert section. Someone austerely impressive, subtle, profound, alert with latent menace?

"Call me Super," said the elderly, pudgy part Aboriginal who bustled into the ward, "it's much easier than my name." He bustled himself into the bedside chair, gave me a huge smile full of teeth and surveyed me like a benign uncle prepared to do his best with a dull nephew. "And how do you feel after your adventures with the not so secret service, eh?"

Apprehension faded in immediate resentment of his approach. "I don't feel like being laughed at by a fake-friendly copper."

He raised a finger. "*Not* a copper. Different service altogether. And you mustn't be rude. Don't forget that you are working for me now. I hope that, er, Jonesey told you so."

"Working? Acting, unpaid."

"Precisely. Our budget can't afford unexpected extras."

"So at least you can't send me to bed early for tweaking your nose."

His manner changed abruptly. "Don't bank on it. I can do worse things."

"That's better. The steely-eyed stuff sounds more honest."

He said sharply, "Believe it! Now, to business. I don't imagine that you do in fact credit this idea of genetically determined immortality. Or do you?"

Straight to the heart of it, leaving no doubt as to what really mattered in the damned legacy. He roused in me an angry intention to sidetrack this fascination with an idiot dream that promised to scramble the brains of intelligent men. Jonesey's warning went for nothing.

"Of course not, nor have I ever said that I do. It is a theoretical oddity, no more than that."

The lie slipped out, smooth as silk ribbon. I had a tiny twinge of nervousness at the possible future consequences I might be initiating, then decided I had no reason to be frightened of this fat little civil servant. (I look back on my worldly wisdom, and cringe.)

"Yet," said the fat little civil servant, "you allowed my man to think you believed in it."

"Jonesey? I mentioned it to him to get his reaction; we didn't discuss it. The important thing was that Armstrong believed it."

"And now Armstrong is not important?"

"I'm told not. Is he?"

"No. And what is the root of your disbelief in immortality?"

The answer came directly from notes dictated by my father in that induction period before the search began, when we had roughed out a piece to be called "Fabulous

Dreams and Futile Facts," a crowd pleaser taking the pop out of popular science.

"Continued life on this or any other planet must be based on decay and death so that mutation can continue to replace ineffective life forms and keep pace with the climatic evolution of the environment. Immortality or even a too-extended life span means species stagnation; a type remains forever with all its shortcomings and no means of improvement. Superficially the thing may seem possible but there will be a fundamental blockage somewhere in the genetic interaction."

His cold smile was not at all avuncular. "That sounds more like philosophy than science."

"Are you a scientist?" His annoyance showed that he was not. "Perhaps you find the idea of immortality appealing—like Armstrong. You don't really want a contra argument."

He turned away. I could not see his face as he crossed to the window, a slightly ludicrous figure with short legs, too much belly and on his mind one of the monstrous classic wishes. The view of the city skyline did not seem to inspire him. "Until the thing appears—or fails to appear," he said, "it remains a figment, not a subject for planning. Tell Jonesey what you have told me. I don't want him distracted by dreams."

"He's sharp enough to work it out for himself once he's had time to think about it."

He said abstractedly, still with his back to me, "Don't expect too much of him; he hasn't had your education."

"Shakespeare, Browning and Shaw."

"The idols of a browser, but don't underrate them. Armstrong didn't see through it and he has more avenues to knowledge than a self-taught gumshoe."

"Armstrong will never see through it. He's obsessed."

He came back to stand by the bed. "Just don't feed Jonesey fantasies. I want him dependable."

His assumption of mastery, as mover of pawns, loosened my irritable tongue. "Why should he trust you with the legacy, either?"

The chubby cheeks twitched. "Why, indeed? Nor would he, I imagine."

"Nor does he trust my father." It was as well that he should understand the ramifications of the labyrinth of distrust. I was too angry to think that he might understand them better than I.

His lightness vanished without a flicker. It was the Superintendent of a covert section who said, "Nobody trusts those souped-up intelligences—or that other Group with the chisels and paintbrushes." He stared hard at me, giving orders. "Confide in Jonesey because you are young and unwise. Don't move without his agreement. I won't see you again unless it becomes necessary."

He went away, leaving the mention of B Group hanging heavily. Did they—Belinda and Bernice, Barry and Bert—fit somewhere in the pattern? My father had dismissed my only suggestion of their involvement.

But my father was no superman, merely a *different* man. He could be wrong.

My father would have thought his one visit a sufficient gesture, if gesture it had been (the question of his feelings and attitudes plodded like a vamp accompaniment under all my thinking), but Jonesey turned up quickly to collect me when I vidded him that I had been declared fit for discharge.

Its few days in the service garage had seen his car refurbished with a fresh coat of colour, some panel beating and a contented purr in the engine. "Looks too new, too noticeable," he complained. "Have to knock it about a bit."

Then he wanted to know what the Super and I had talked about. To my debunking of the chance of immortality he was contemptuous: "Did you think I hadn't worked that out for myself?" I knew that he had not and that he was not prepared to admit that the idea had allured him; one of his more endearing honesties was that he never pretended to be truthful. "And did he swallow it, David, or did he point out that an advanced genetic science could thumb its snotty nose at natural law? Cyclic oestrus was a coital determinant until man's emotional drive overrode it and altered his psychology to fit."

I could have pointed out that it also opened the way to gang rape and the million inhumanities of marriage and divorce and brutal moral paradoxes but he would not have been impressed. Each time a basic change is made in a system whose possibilities are close to infinite, like the genetic code, Pandora's box of troubles opens wide. Tinkering, once begun, has to continue forever its attempts to regain disturbed balance. Worse than rapidly mutating viruses, much worse.

"No, he didn't, but he didn't say he was convinced, either." Since Jonesey only snorted at that I needled him with the news that his Super did not trust his double-dealing agent's resistance to temptation. "Why should he?" he asked in a comfortless rerun of the Super's own reaction. "He didn't recruit me for my naive wholesomeness."

Where no comment could be adequate I changed the subject. "I'm running short of cash."

"Isn't Old Greeneyes financing you?"

"Not directly. I need a couple of days to myself to write up a few scripts from his notes. They'll sell."

"Knows just how to keep you in line, doesn't he? Be a good boy and Daddy will fuel your professional career." I let that pass. (But it hurt.) "I was thinking of doing a jokey little number on genetic surgery and extended life. It might draw a reaction from somewhere."

"It might draw a bullet in your brain. Don't do it. At least, not yet. There might come a time when it's worth the risk."

"My risk, you mean."

"Quite so, and the Super won't even pay you for it." Pulling up outside my apartment block, he said, "Stick to your bread-and-butter articles for now. I'll vid you when I've got these crammers lined up."

A pretty terse morning for all concerned.

I had barely time to shape and trim two articles before Jonesey was ready to pounce. "This one first," he said, offering me an ID portrait of John James Cuyper—thin horse face, worry-drawn cheeks of middle age, flap ears and startled eyes, fourth-generation Dutch-Australian, Senior Preparation Tutor in half a dozen sciences (crammer) and family man of blameless life ... no police record, at any rate. "His Library Access Card was the first to be used, two weeks before the others."

"What's our excuse for the interview? How do we know his connection with events?"

"His worry! Forget excuses, lad. I flash my ID and put the fear of prison and truth drugs into him. Record it all for your book—if you think it will ever get written—but from now on we are official. The specimens wriggle on the pin of excuses, not we."

The Cuypers lived in Malvern, a moderately plush suburb on the edge of decline into shabby gentility. Theirs was one of the ancient red-brick dwellings whose tiled porch and frail timber architraves spoke of lavender and lace or whatever the twentieth-century icons may have been. Those houses were ill-designed, difficult to weatherproof and expensive in upkeep, so we could assume that the family had a reasonable income but not quite enough of it to move into a desirably exclusive neighbourhood; the Cuypers belonged to that precarious class who balanced income, appearance and pretension on a knife edge of making-do and jangled family nerves.

We had chosen Sunday morning for what I foresaw as

more raid than interview and we found Cuyper doing the expectedly proper thing as staid householder, pottering in his garden.

He was as thin as his photograph suggested, narrow as a stick and quite small, only a few centimetres over a metre and a half, a wisp of a man. The startled eyes were real, not the effect of studio lighting, as though he found the world a permanently surprising place to inhabit. We were about to prove it to him.

With a fine suburban suspicion of strangers he examined Jonesey's ID, flummoxed at first and then scared into whispering as he asked what we wanted of him. The exhausted voice suited his leaf-in-a-breeze physique.

Jonesey used an official voice that sounded like a policeman reading his notes in court. "My Department thinks you may be in possession of facts relevant to an ongoing investigation."

"How extraordinary!" The thin tone meant, *Oh, God, why me?* and his eyes searched the ID as if it might tell him. "What facts?"

"For instance, the details of your association with Young Feller."

"With whom?" His incomprehension was genuine. "Is that the name of a criminal? A . . . sobriquet?"

"Is it ever!" Jonesey became cheerful. "His name was Conrad Hazard."

"I have never heard of him."

"Oh, but you have! Everybody has. Think back, Mr. Cuyper. Well back."

Cuyper became flustered, actually wringing his hands, an activity more often heard of than seen. "I have never—" But he had, and the thin edge of memory was sudden terror. He asked forlornly, "Wasn't that the name of one of the Project IQ children? One had heard—"

"One surely had, Mr. Cuyper. This one used your Library Access Card back in 2021. Used it very frequently."

I had read of a man's jaw dropping in dismay; now I saw it happen. Cuyper's lean face extended downwards farther than I would have thought possible while his hands rose slowly to cover the large, uneven teeth and his eyes stared over them, stricken. He said something through the barrier of his hands that might have been, "Oh, no . . ."

From the corner of my eye I caught movement on the porch. A woman, thin as Cuyper, stood in the doorway, peering, suspicious.

Cuyper dropped his hands to mutter, "I didn't know. How could I know? Nothing was ever said."

"About the Library Card?"

"About anything. They died, those children. I never saw them."

"You saw one."

"But the Card! I didn't do anything wrong."

"No?"

He shook. "Nothing badly wrong. Not seriously wrong. Not criminal."

From the doorway the woman asked, "What's the matter, John? Who are these men?"

She kept her voice down, almost hissing in her need of secrecy, while her glance darted to the neighbour gardens on either side. She was, for God's sake, as much concerned with her respectability as with her husband. As far as I could see, nobody listened in.

Jonesey crooned, "We should go inside."

The poor devil nodded; in his eyes was the prospect of a lifetime shredded by an error, an ignorance, a weakness a quarter of a century in the past.

Two skinny, half-grown children had joined the woman, wondering from behind her skirt with their father's startled eyes. Cuyper, ushering us in, stopped on the porch and her gaze grew shocked as she saw the fear in him. He made a vague gesture of his long hands, a shooing motion. "Go inside, Laura. Leave us alone. I want to talk to these gentlemen alone."

She bridled, but fearfully. "John, I have a right—"

"Just go. Please. Leave us the sitting room. It's an old matter . . . a shock of remembering. I'll explain it . . . afterwards."

"Who are they? Tell me!"

"Library police." That was quick of him, the picking on a minor body that would frighten her less than the truth. "Now, please leave us alone."

She withdrew backwards, shepherding the children but still looking to see that no neighbour was spying matter for gossip.

Everything in this business, it seemed, brought out the smallness in people; only Adelaide Cormick had come through with something like common honour. The rest, including Jonesey who was the best of them, were selfish, devious or mean in spirit; even the loving hearts of the Farnhams had hardened at the prospect of profit.

And I? I was nothing at all, everybody's cipher to be used or disregarded at will.

The Cuyper sitting room was furnished with an eye to the period of the house—overstuffed lounge suite, small table and buffet in some dark timber like oak, vid framed in the same, and all of it old; the Cuypers had never quite made it to the point of being really able to afford their middle-income appearance.

We chose the big chairs and he perched himself alone in the middle of the sofa like a man abandoned by his kind.

Jonesey prompted, "Conrad."

Cuyper shook a disconsolate head.

"Come on with it, Mr. Cuyper—the man who used your Library Card, piling up a reference bill that must have stretched your resources to pay it."

"He paid it. But his name was Magar. That's what he told me."

He pronounced the name with a light accent on the first syllable, watching expectantly for a reaction from us. Jonesey glanced at me and I spread my hands. It meant nothing that we knew.

Cuyper said, "I think it was a joke of a kind. A nasty kind." He nodded suspiciously at my necklet. "That's a reporter's piece, isn't it?"

"For Departmental record only, not publicity. Please explain the joke."

"Magar is Hindi for the broad-nosed crocodile."

"So?"

"The Raj English pronounced it mugger."

A joke indeed. Jonesey asked, "When did you make the connection between Mr. Magar and muggings?"

"Afterwards. When he had gone away. Finished with me." He was pleading for our belief in him. "I was never sure but it seemed to fit. You know, the newspaper reports? He finished his study and the muggings stopped soon after. No more reference bills to pay, you see." Almost in tears, he said, "He was a terrible, dangerous young man."

Jonesey registered elaborate boredom, unimpressed by drama. "Tell us about him. All about him, from the start."

"But what will happen to me?"

"How should I know? Probably nothing. Unless you killed somebody. Did you?"

"No! Mr., Mr. . . ." He realised that we had given no names and that Jonesey's ID told only of his Departmental authority. He was close to wailing. "I know I made a little dishonest money and I helped with a forgery. That is, I didn't report it."

At last Jonesey unbuttoned the big, expansive smile designed to assure the victim that he was a kindly pussycat at heart. "We aren't much interested in peccadilloes twenty-five years old. The history of Young Feller is what we care about. Right?"

Cuyper nodded unhappily and sat awhile sorting his thoughts. Here is what he told us, with the stumbles, repetitions and false starts edited out:

2.

It didn't weigh on my mind after it was over. I mean, how should it? I didn't know who he really was. I made a little money when I badly needed it, just getting started in my business, and it was underhanded but I didn't know anything that made much sense. And nothing came of it. I was never questioned, so I stopped being nervous about being found out.

I didn't forget Magar, though. I never will forget him. I didn't know who or what he was, only that he was like nobody else I ever met. Or wanted to meet. He came to me out of the blue and when he had what he wanted he disappeared, and nothing ever happened to make me think of him as anything more than an oddity that came and went. Except when I found out accidentally what magar meant and how the times fitted. But I didn't *know*. Yet you people must have known all the time.

I thought Jonesey might correct him but a side glance showed only the impatient restraint calculated to keep the gabbling sinner on his confessional knees.

Well, anyway, here was I, new in the cramming business, not long out of the university—good honours and some post-grad and already a hundred job applications turned down—scraping a crust by coaching kids whose parents thought education would keep them out of the gutter, not knowing that the world is run on opportunism and cunning. Brilliance counts but who you know is as important as what you know.

And this boy came in.

He seemed about fifteen or sixteen, a bit gangly and not quite shaped but pretty big for a teenager. He had those extraordinary eyes. Green! Not the usual greenish hazel but *green*. And there was something peculiar about them, not hypnotic or any nonsense of that sort but old and disillusioned, as if he had seen it all and was prepared to make allowances for everyday nitwits. I felt that I might be some incompetent he would put up with because he knew I would do my floundering best.

Another thing—he was pale. Not as white as the gentleman assisting you here, if you'll pardon me mentioning it, but white enough to be noticeable among a people who make a point of fashionable tan. There was nothing overall wrong with him but he was strange, different, and I disliked him on sight. That world-weary look, I suppose. But if he wanted coaching and could pay for it, then I wanted his money and to the devil with first impressions.

There was no student with me at the time, so he loomed up to my desk and said, "You will require my name for your records. It is Magar."

His expression was quizzical; something was expected of me, some reaction, but I was tasting the name. Hungarian extraction? Slav? Turkish? None of them likely with that skin, those eyes.

"Francis James Max Magar," he said brightly, still quizzing me, and I was so unsettled by his appearance and behaviour that I failed to recognise three of the most famous Christian names in bio-genetics.

You become accustomed to odd approaches from students, particularly the dedicatedly mediocre, but I stopped in the middle of writing down his name when he said, in the suddenly formal voice of a youngster imitating the vidplay version of an intellectual, "I wish to study bio-topology."

Just like that! As if I *could* teach it! Still, I wasn't letting him go until I had put out a few feelers, so I pulled myself together to ask how much biology he had studied and where. He said the most curious thing, that he had studied none at all because there were no biology texts in his school.

That was hardly believable. I asked which school but he ignored the question and said again that he wanted to learn bio-topology.

Me, without lab facilities for even simple biology! I was a crammer, not a prac man. As for bio-top, that was the apex of a whole series of ascending disciplines. I knew it dealt with inter-gene structuring but it was computer-programmed research, not a subject for struggling crammers.

He heard me out and retired behind his eyes for a spell of thought, as if I weren't there. After a while I had to speak for the comfort of hearing a familiar sound to dispel a creeping uncanniness, and I asked him how old he was.

Without coming back from whatever landscape he was contemplating he said, as though a part of his mind made the gesture without interfering with a more pressing activity, "Somewhere between eighteen and eight hundred."

If it was meant to shut me up, it did.

In his good time he said, "No laboratory work, then; experimental records, diagrams, photographs, computer mockups, will serve. First, a syllabus of reading, from elementary texts to the most advanced theoretical papers. Then I will consider what next."

Next! Lunatic or genius? Perhaps a little of both.

The conception was impossible. I mean, the greatest genius of history could not ingest an entire discipline in that fashion and only a ratbag would think of trying. However, I was close to the breadline and there might yet be something in it for me, so I explained that he would need to spend hours each day on expensive terminal time, to have print library as well as data library access and magazine subscriptions. In the later stages he would need data crosslink research programmes and the whole thing would cost a fortune.

"Money is not a consideration," he told me. "Please write it all down, with approximate costings. I will pay for your time."

I'd have copied out fairy tales in Swahili for anyone willing to pay by the hour, so I started on the listing, not hurrying and at least conscientiously preparing an intelligent outline syllabus. I expected him to scan the result—and the costing—glimpse the reality of his dream and fade out of my life.

When I had done I told him what should have occurred to me in the first place: "You will need a Library Access Card."

A fleeting tension, perhaps the shadow of a frown, made me think he had never heard of such a thing. For perhaps a second he retired, thought and returned in a blink. "Can you arrange that?"

"Student Access must be recommended by your sponsoring school."

There was no more hesitation. "But you have such a Card?"

"Naturally."

"I will buy it from you."

That was the moment of revelation when I should have let the whole business drop, but I was intrigued by this peculiar nonstudent without an acknowledgeable background; I wanted to know more. So I said, "Oh, no. My living depends on up-to-date access."

He counted out a thousand dollars from an inner pocket—this was before the universal credit system—and laid the notes on my desk in the most seductive pile of paper my penury had ever seen. "Sufficient?"

It hurt me physically to say, "I can't sell my livelihood."

He nodded, approvingly I thought. "At least you are not stupid with greed. Keep the money."

There was I, staring at the windfall, unable to think of anything more intelligent than, *God send me idiot children with money,* while he glanced at the list of studies and requirements, put it in his pocket—and left.

Without a further word, simply left.

What I did then was stupid and left me open to what came after. Please remember that all my life had been spent as the student son of poor parents, scraping for money, grinding away my waking hours in preparation for jobs that weren't there when my student days were finally over. I knew nothing useful about the real world and what people did to each other when one was gutter-wise and the other wasn't. I had debts, I had needs, I had expenses. I went through most of that thousand dollars in an afternoon on hire purchase and books and clothes.

Magar was mistaken; I *was* stupid with greed.

I was sure he would not show up again, though you never can tell with oddballs, and there was in fact no sign of him until one day I thought I had run against him in the street.

Physically run against him, I mean, rounding a corner as someone came from the opposite direction. We brushed quite sharply, backed off and apologised and pretended that each wasn't offended by the other's clumsiness. I had a moment of recognition, almost used his name before I saw that the soft brown eyes and sunburned skin belonged to a stranger and that this young man was older. I thought no more of it or of him, even when I discovered my loss. Back in the office I decided to mug up on some material on plate tectonics that was being mauled by the science journalists—pressure gradients on contact edges. Geology was my main field, you see, not the bios. I dug for my Library Card and couldn't find it but it didn't occur to me that my pocket might have been picked. I vidded Loss and Replacement and took the usual official wigging for carelessness together with the ninety-dollar replacement demand. I still had enough money to cover it and the three-day wait for manufacture of the personalised duplicate with the new molecular identification pattern was an inconvenience but not a tragedy. I knew the lost one could not be used once the loss had been reported and the ID pattern put on hold.

On the third morning, while I still waited for my new Card, I was tutoring a third-year girl when I saw through the one-way glass to the little waiting room, the young man who had reminded me of Magar. I was sure he was the same one. He sat there with a fixed, bright smile as though he knew I could see him and wished to establish a pleasant rapport.

His presence unsteadied me in the same way that Magar had done, simply by being himself. I tried to ignore him but kept stealing glances through the glass—and saw his smile grow wider as he held up what was clearly a Library Access Card.

Puzzled and uneasy, I finished the hour and got rid of my student.

He didn't wait to be called in; he came with loads of self-assurance and loomed over the desk in the same way that Magar had done, and dropped the Card in front of me.

It was my own, the lost one.

"My thanks for the loan." It was the voice of the boy Magar but this fellow was older and taller. Or was he taller? A slimline suit could trick the eye. But he surely was brown-eyed and darker skinned.

I said, not too brightly, "I must have dropped it."

"Let us say, I picked it up."

"Then you should have returned it to me at once."

"I had need of it."

"You couldn't use it. I reported the loss."

"Of course you did, but I needed to have it copied." I suspected that some sort of con trick was coming because copying was impossible by any agency but the Master Indexing Computer. He went on, smoothly as you like, "Now each of us has one and my instruction can proceed as soon as you report your Card found. The system requires that the new ID pattern be returned to Master Indexing storage and your old pattern reinstated. Then you will receive a Penalty Account for careless custody, for which I will reimburse you."

With a quick, efficient movement of both hands he swept coloured contacts from his eyes and Magar's brilliant green retinas blazed at me. He had spoken with the precision of one who knew with exactness what must be conveyed and his meaning was plain, that he intended to use my ID and Access Account. It was a shock but in its insanely logical way not unexpected.

I maintained sufficient self-control to take up the Card and ask, with a shaky touch of scorn, "Copied?"

He produced a second Card, also in my name. "Copied."

The visual reproduction was exact but any competent amateur could have achieved that. I made the obvious check to dispose of his pretension. I called Loss and Replacement, explained that I had found my lost Card, took a mild dressing down for wasting Departmental time and was assured that my ID was being immediately returned to File. After a couple of minutes I called up Student Access Menu and got it on-screen at once. Then I tried the "copied" Card, knowing it must fail—but both were perfect, both worked.

I believed, as everybody believed, that this was not possible. The individual molecular count in the ink is supposed to be induplicable except by the Indexing Computer, which is isolated from cross-access. For God's sake, each imprint is a random configuration!

Jonesey broke in on him like a maniac. "So how was it done? In the name of unforgiving hell, didn't you try to find out?"

Cuyper cringed back, fearing that Jonesey was about to hit him. Seeing his face, I feared it, too. It must have been an almighty shock to his secret-loving system to realise that identification—which meant identity itself—could be faked. If that were so, the self-contented world of all-knowing Covert Intelligence could fall to pieces overnight. As to what could happen to confidentiality, crime and finance . . .

I broke in before there was violence. "Young Feller wouldn't tell him. The secret was his strength."

Cuyper panted at me like a man whose life has been saved by a passing stranger.

"It's still a secret," I said. "The world would have fallen apart by now if even one crim knew how to do it."

Jonesey nodded blindly. "Go on, Mr. Cuyper, but please don't frighten me like that again."

Cuyper had shocked him with the vision of the underpinnings of his world knocked away.

Yet, it occurred to me, there had been millennia of history before universal identification had been introduced. What sort of world had that been, the one our grandparents lived in?

Of course I asked, still not truly believing what I saw, but he only put a finger to his lips and grinned knowingly, like a playful clown. "What you don't know you can't tell."

He made me feel like a five-year-old. It was almost a

weeping five-year-old who asked—in fear of the answer—
"What have you done that you need a disguise?"

He bent close for a conspiratorial whisper—oh, he was
enjoying himself: "I have picked a pocket, forged a docu-
ment and relieved a few outraged citizens of some of their
money." His tone changed. "I take no pleasure in the spo-
liation of others. My soul suffers for it."

I can't explain to you how, for that last sentence, his
mien altered to something like desolation, an extreme consciousness of sin. I found myself believing and utterly confused by him.

He continued. "Those are not small matters but they
were necessary if I am to do what I must do."

I studied him more closely, wondering what species of
fixation I dealt with here.

With his face so close to mine I could see that the
suntan had been applied in unusually meticulous fashion.
Most users splashed it on reasonably evenly and were satisfied that they looked like God's gift to sexuality, but Magar's makeup had been applied by an artist. It was shaded
to the contours of his face, the underside of his chin a little
lighter than the face and neck, the curves of the ears not
forgotten or skimped, the creases in the eyelids and at the
corners of the mouth not choked with accumulated lotion.
The light tan extended all the way beyond the hairline and
into the area of the skull. His hands, too, were finely tinted,
the palms more lightly than the backs and the creases at
the knuckles carefully attended. The colouring vanished
over his wrists under his shirt cuffs; I was sure that his
body was tinted all over.

It looked real, not like a suntan. If he stripped he
would be taken for a man from the milder tropics.

It struck me that he could not have applied the stuff
himself; the job would have occupied hours of the time of
someone prepared to walk round him, study curves and

shadows and details of movement, prepare a plan of application and follow it exactly.

Which meant that he was not acting alone. Alone in what? And where did bio-topology come into it? My head rattled with apprehension of some criminal gang using my office and my Card as adjuncts to their plans (what plans?) and because I was, in spite of attainments and degrees, still wet behind the ears in my knowledge of depravity, I made some stumbling declaration of my honesty, my civil obligations, my duty to report him and his confessed forgery—

"Report me?" he queried. "Who am I?"

Who, indeed? As forger he could be anyone he liked, and at least one of his carry-cards was in the name of Cuyper.

"Besides," he said, "you have spent my money and cannot afford to return it. Can you? Of course not. How, then, will you explain having accepted a thousand dollars from an innocent student in return for the promise of educating him in a syllabus you cannot teach? I have the syllabus you wrote for me and for which I paid."

His variable smile returned, this time as the plea of a schoolboy loaded with charm and ruthless in exploiting it. I know that I shivered. It is no use trying to explain his ascendency. I know I was not hypnotised; I simply was in the presence of an amoral kid who could twist me in his fingers and treat my shreds of intellect as disposable waste.

Talking to the police would be hopeless; mention of a duplicated Card would brand me a nitwit.

"I will use the Card in your name and pay you the price of the accounts. If your conscience pricks," he said with a sort of solemn gaiety, "you can shoulder the demands yourself and donate my contribution to a charity of your choice. But I think you will make the best of a bad job, as they say. Let your conscience decide, in battle with cupidity, stupidity and fear of the law."

He laid no stress on "stupidity"; he didn't see it as an insult, only as a fact.

"Now you must elaborate this outline syllabus; I can't waste time coming back for alterations and afterthoughts. Write sufficient information for an intelligent man—" You will have read of eyes twinkling with amusement; his twinkled, literally, like green flashes, when he said intelligent. "—to proceed without you."

For the next two hours that is what I did.

After that, I never saw him again.

I didn't want to see him, but there was no shortage of evidence that he was operating. He did not merely use the Card in any normal sense, he made a great splurge of using it. He called up more texts in a day than anyone could possibly study or do more than glance through, and he wasn't simply recording them for later use because that would have shown on the accounts. In madder moments I had a dizzy impression of him absorbing entire pages like a high-speed camera and never needing to see them again because they were indelibly in his brain. That was fantasy but the money wasn't fantasy. It arrived on time, always, and always triple payment. What could I do but take it?

There was one thing in his procedure that puzzled me: He used only part of my syllabus, jumping from subject to subject, leaving large areas untouched.

Jonesey said, "Your fantasy was more or less the fact. Don't try to grasp what Young Feller was; nobody can do that. As for the gaps in the syllabus, he was using two other Library Cards at the same time. At a guess, he was trying to reduce the chance of library staff noticing the excessive use by one person. Nobody seems to have noticed. Why should they? People are always doing things that have simple explanations if you only know what they are; you'd drive yourself silly chasing them all up."

Cuyper plainly didn't believe him; in his mind there had to be some explanation other than the flatly impossible. And, on the whole, his interest was on his own immediate destiny.

Jonesey was welcome to his fantasies.

What will you do to me? I was cornered, you can see that. I had to go along with him once I'd spent his money. Anyway, it was a long time ago. There's a limiting period on old charges, isn't there? I was not much more than a kid, remember, and just starting up and in need of anything I could get.

Have you ever seen the face of a child who knows he should be punished but toughs it out to cover his terror? That was Cuyper, flaunting his small courage in daring our righteousness to call him wrongdoer and threaten the lightning of the law. But his soul shivered.

Jonesey said with insulting boredom, "You don't matter and Young Feller is dead. Nobody today gives a damn about your poor little secret. You may even have been helpful—a little. Pity you didn't ask him who did the paint job. I don't suppose he'd have told you but even a genius may let something slip in an off moment—if his type of genius has off moments. Come on, David; we're finished here."

3.

Jonesey's brusqueness was so insulting that I got him out of there quickly, in sheer embarrassment. Not until I had time to think it over did I begin to see how much the faking of an identity had upset him. It struck at the root of the State system, but I was too annoyed with him to appreciate how staggered he had been. "You were too rough with him, Jonesey. He was just a kid caught up in something he didn't understand."

He swung the gate hard enough to rock the fence. "Listen to who's saying it! Cuyper's still shitting himself twenty-five years later. Bloody little wimp."

I looked back and there they were, the skinny four of them on the porch, huddled together for shelter and comfort and love, watching us with dismay in the parents' eyes and a communicated fear in the children's. I felt guilty. On impulse I went back along the path to say, "You can believe him. Nothing more will happen. For you it's closed."

Cuyper breathed relief but his wife pointed to my necklet, unappeased. "What about that? That's a report to somebody."

"No, Mrs. Cuyper. It's my file for study in case some small detail will help us to the things we still need to know. No one else will hear it."

It was a soothing lie, because in fact the Super would hear it, though my bet was that after him it would vanish into his private file; I did not trust him to see it as shareable information. I trusted him as far as I could throw him—about a finger's length.

By then I was trusting practically nobody, only excepting Jonesey in more or less neutral areas.

When I rejoined him he snorted, "Galahad!" and sulked in silence while he rocked back to normal. When I tired of his tantrum I asked, "Do you want to see the other two today?"

He grunted that one was dying of narcotic-induced cancer and the other was over eighty years old and senile. "They didn't see Young Feller until a couple of weeks after he took Cuyper's Card and realised one wasn't enough. So they wouldn't know about his green eyes and pale skin; he would have modified his manner, too, by then. All they will know is that their Cards were stolen and copied and then all that lovely money started coming in. He'd have found ways to blackmail them into silence."

"Still, there could be something . . ."

I tried to imagine the working of a mind that could deal with such a huge input, absorbing sheets of data with the speed of seeing, long tapes at a single hearing, entire books in a flicker of turning pages—and could not. I could only mutter that just the same we should try the other two.

"Maybe later," he said, "when we've digested what we've got."

"The Card? There must be someone who knows how that was done. If he wasn't got rid of."

"If he's alive he won't tell. That's a secret to upset empires."

"Truth drugs."

"First you have to find him."

"That's all we've got."

"Not so. Who applied the suntan? A first-class art job, from Cuyper's description, so much so that he remembers it in detail. Who've we got on the art side?"

There could be only one answer. "B Group."

"I had a feeling they'd show up sooner or later."

"But my father said—"

"Daddy said whatever he thought would keep Sonny quiet." His mood had turned savage again. "So, let's find out what Daddy says to Jonesey—at gunpoint, if need be."

I put that down to frustration and used the car vid to tell my father that we were on our way with urgent questions. He answered with the long-suffering, "Very well," of endurance with fortitude.

To rouse his interest I said, "B Group is involved."

That, as it turned out, roused more than interest; it signalled the setting up of an operation I could never have dreamed of. But his only answer, without welcome, was, "I shall expect you."

10 • LOVING FATHER AND LOYAL PARTNER

The gun, as it turned out, was not so much unnecessary as preempted, though I think Jonesey would have had more sense than to make a gesture he wouldn't dare follow up.

At CAG 3 my father waited for us on the steps of the porch, wearing one of his vestigial expressions that had to be read by instinct. I suspected, *The retarded children, needing guidance! Can they feed themselves or breathe without assistance?*

I said, "G'day, Dad," sounding and feeling like a ham actor, and his green gaze flickered (sardonic amusement?) as he answered gravely, "Good afternoon, Son." A sense of humour hid there but what did it laugh at? Was a "normal" son a good joke or a sour one?

He turned to Jonesey. "I hope you will be brief. I am busy."

Jonesey grumbled weary disbelief, "You're always busy, aren't you?"

"True."

A stillness fell. In my father's view an exchange had been completed; it was our move. I said, "I have a necklet recording, Dad."

He accepted the inevitable. "Then we must go inside." He led the way.

The sitting room was in a more apparent disorder than I had yet seen it. Floor, tables and chairs supported pieces of electronic equipment and repellent bio-electronic models. One little thing like a tiny battery sat above a jar in which floated what may or may not have been a real human heart; if it had twitched I might well have been sick.

Jonesey said, "You need a housekeeper."

"I do not. Everything is in its correct place."

"You could have fooled me."

"This is part of the laboratory; the living space is incidental. These practical structures represent work in progress. Seated here"—he pointed to the one empty chair—"I can observe each one while I consider appropriate action. Successful laboratory work is ninety percent thought; most experiments are basically thought experiments." He tossed a pile of stapled notes to the floor. "Sit there."

Jonesey sat. "And that way, you just don't think mistakes?"

Irony was wasted. "Procedural errors, very rarely. There is the occasional fault born of imprecise data." From an armchair he removed a large sectional model of a human eye with a slim metal tube hanging loosely from the optic nerve bundle, and placed it gently on the table. "There, David."

I sat and he held out his hand. "The necklet." His patient gaze said, *Please waste no more time; I have eyes, hearts, batteries and tangles of wire to mull over and thoughts to think.*

I handed it over.

As usual he showed no special reaction to the recording. When it was done he sat silently waiting until Jonesey had to ask, "Do you know how the duplication of the random pattern in the ink of the Card was achieved?"

"It's of no importance."

"Wrong, Mr. Hazard; it's of vital importance. If that knowledge is still around, our entire social system is in danger. No one will be able to call his name his own."

My father smiled the brittle smile of wisdom putting youth back in its box. "Then the system will return to the condition of earlier years. I doubt that impersonation was widespread in former centuries."

"Simple impersonation is detectable by simple methods; Card reproduction may not be detectable. Have you no idea at all how it may have been done?"

"There are several obvious approaches, but it is not strictly in my field. It could involve bio-magnetics. My sister Alice might be interested; I am not."

Jonesey's expression said something like, *You bloody well will be if I put the screw on you,* but he knew better than to make the threat.

I suggested, ready for a similar dismissal, "The suntan lotion—"

"Some professional makeup artist, no doubt. Theatres are full of them."

Jonesey, out of temper, asked, "Would he have known theatre people?"

"If he had wished to. You have heard that Conrad was persuasive."

"But why not a real artist, a painter?"

"A waste of talent, but why not? Or why not a beauty parlour attendant?"

"But an artist? As in B Group."

My father smiled on him. "Are you flying a kite, Jonesey?" He turned to me. "Have I the correct idiom, David? Thank you." He settled back and let his gaze linger on the optical model with its metal attachment, finding its possibilities more interesting than ours.

Jonesey insisted, "It's a logical guess."

"Associative, not logical; a possibility among others, not a deduced probability."

Jonesey looked murderous but I was by now getting the hang of the paternal method and could hear the whirring of wheels as decisions were made. I said, "You told me once that B Group could not be implicated. Do you hold to that?"

"I told you that B Group would not of their own will have endured close contact with any other. The rest you inferred."

"So you were directing my attention away from them?"

"Naturally."

So the decision had been made. "Why."

An edge of irascibility told me I should have deduced all this for myself. "I did not want you venturing into situations beyond a fledgling capacity to handle. You have had time to begin to understand that contact with the Groups can be neither straightforward nor ever wholly satisfactory to yourself, and that this is not simply a matter of relative intellectuality. It is a matter of differently oriented mentalities, different ways of thinking, associating, perceiving, understanding—above all, different ethical standpoints and ideas of what takes precedence and why." He leaned towards me, stabbing with a finger, who rarely employed gesture. "Do you realise these things?"

"Yes, Dad."

"You don't! You think you do. You realise them as you realise the existence of ice at the South Pole, though you have never seen it nor can conceive of its huge reality. Nor can you imagine the reality of mutated minds."

He sat back, flint-eyed, leaving me feeling that I had been taken by the scruff and shaken.

Just then, from the edge of vision, I became aware of a fourth presence and turned my head slightly to see my uncle Andrew leaning against the doorpost, listening with a sort of pale amusement. He winked sympathetically at me. Jonesey, at a greater angle, could not see him.

My father continued to flatten my self-esteem. "Conrad would have brushed you aside like a beetle, not worth crushing. B Group—well, I don't pretend to altogether follow their reasonings or their activities. They are wholly themselves, deriding all others. They weave webs of ideas, words, fancies and they trip listeners on their own misunderstandings. They take and they never give. They despise me and my sibs. They despised C Group. Or perhaps affected to. The fact is that they no more comprehend the materially logical mind than we are able to trace the workings of what we see as metaphysical imaginings. There is a gulf of rationality between us and we do not know if either logic is finally viable."

Jonesey said unexpectedly, "Both."

My father gave him the pleased smile you offer a bright child. "Two viable logics in one universe? Expound."

"Different pathways of mental evolution. You go one way, they another. Maybe see different aspects of one reality. A thing works or it doesn't. Lizards developed their forelegs into wings, mammals developed theirs to make thumbs. Wings are right for birds, thumbs are right for us."

"Jonesey, the reading man, picker-up of uncoordinated wisdoms!" It was actually a compliment of a kind, but a jab followed it. "Are you, then, ready to confront B Group?"

"Not without your assistance."

"Wise! David?"

I said, with no assurance at all, "I've no choice; I have to go on to the end. The Super's calling the shots now."

My father gave his rare cackle of a laugh. "So? Not even he should count on a continued upper hand."

I expected him to enlarge on that encouragement, but instead he stretched a long arm to pick up the optical model from the floor and turned it in his hands, grinning at me in a fashion I could not read. He said quite loudly, "You will need preparation."

The suddenly raised voice sounded like a decision taken and a signal for action.

And so it was.

Jonesey had barely time to ask, "What sort of preparation?" before Andrew said from behind us, "All you will need and more than you expect."

He came swiftly into the room carrying a small, bulbous instrument with a slender metal nozzle, like a schoolboy's water pistol, and squeezed it directly into the hapless face Jonesey turned towards him. Jonesey cursed in useless surprise, tried to get out of his chair and collapsed before his knees could straighten.

My mouth was still shocked open when the fine spray brushed the mucous linings of my nose and mouth and I knew a momentary strange euphoria before the darkness fell.

I woke in the same darkness and turned my head, seeking light. My neck was unwilling, like a rusty thing. Near me someone moved with a whispery rustle of clothing. I said, "My neck aches."

A woman's voice answered, "That will pass," matter-of-factly, as my father might have spoken with his baritone softened to contralto. She would be tall and bony, red-haired and green-eyed—one of my heretofore invisible aunts. "You have lain too long in one position; an analgesic will help."

Her voice was just a little indistinct, as if she spoke through gauze. Darkness, ache and the mention of analgesic roused a disturbing picture: Did she speak through a surgical mask? What was happening—or had happened?

I heard her fumbling near my head and something clinked against glass as she stirred it. "Can you sit up?"

I tried, and could have done it in spite of protesting

joints, but she put a surprisingly strong arm under my shoulders and lifted me to hold the glass to my lips. I swallowed something cold and mildly sour. "That will do until you can exercise."

With tension whimpering a little in my throat, I asked, "Why is it dark?"

"It is not. Your eyes are bandaged."

Frightened fingers found that they were indeed, and so was most of my head. "What have you done to me?"

She said without emphasis or sympathy, "You have undergone an operation."

"I haven't been ill! There was nothing wrong with me!" Memory filled in the immediate past. "Andrew gassed me. Why? I didn't need any . . ." I ran my fingers again over the bandages, feeling for a pad, a tenderness that might be a clue. Nothing. I squalled with the rage of the helpless, "What the hell happened to me?"

She began, equably, to say, "I told you—" but I shouted her down. "I was not ill! There was nothing wrong with me!"

"You could not see well enough." Her tone suggested a private joke. "Now you will be able to."

"That's bloody nonsense!" My mind scuttled for cover. "Where is Jonesey?"

"Your associate? Surely his name should be Jones."

"It isn't. Where is he?"

"In Melbourne, I believe. I understand that he had to inform his Superintendent of the course of events. He said he would return."

No Jonesey. The darkness deepened in loneliness. "I want to see."

"Not yet. Soon." She had the animation of a vidivox construct.

"Who did this? My father?"

"He designed; I operated."

Frustration and fright erupted then in a bout of shouting and threatening until she said in her even tone, "If you don't stop that noise I shall sedate you. You are in no danger. You know that your father would not have you harmed."

Jonesey's doubts and my own indecisions rose like bile in the throat. "I know nothing of the sort! I don't know what he would do or let others do. I don't know anything!"

She did not answer. There was no sound at all. She had gone.

I wanted light but my hands plucking at the bandages found them fastened too securely. They found also that there were plugs in my ears, explaining the blurring of the woman's voice.

So I lay still in darkness, patting at my ears and making no sense of the statement that I could not see well enough. Well enough for what? I needed Jonesey badly, just to hear him swear and chide, soothe and sneer, all in one sentence, though I knew he played other games under the shell of friendship. Everything was a shell game to him, thimble and pea.

Time stretched unbearably but in fact it may not have been long before my father padded in, saying, "Astrid tells me you are disturbed."

"Wouldn't you be, not knowing what has been done to you?"

He answered the question rather than the rhetoric of anger. "Perhaps, though I am by nature sanguine."

It was too much. I screamed at him, "You're a bloody monster!"

His disembodied hand patted my shoulder. "No, no, I want your welfare only. I have permitted nothing that your friend Jonesey did not approve of."

"Approved? By force? Trickery?"

"He considered and agreed. That should comfort you;

he seems to love you very well." He corrected himself. "To like you very well. These terms of affection have fine shades, not always logical in application."

"Oh, for Christ's sake! What is going on?"

"Your search is, we think, approaching resolution." He took my hand between his two, held it a moment and dropped it, in a momentary intimacy he did not know how to continue. "For the next step we need a less vulnerable instrument and therefore you have been provided with— um, how should I phrase it? With protective colouring, a colouring of innocence to conceal your capacities."

"This makes no sense."

He snapped with the irritation that rose quickly at interruption, "It will! Well, now—it has been plain from the first that Conrad may have claimed shelter from his B Group relatives. May have. There could be no certainty and much to argue against it, but the possibility existed. You wish to comment?"

"I'll grant it was sensible to keep me away from them. I've learned enough along the track to see that I don't understand anything about you . . . you people."

"We freaks?"

"I didn't say that."

"Why not? From your standpoint it is a just word. Always see clearly what you mean; do not let good manners confuse thought. Likewise, beware emotion."

That was, if you like, a warning from the horse's mouth. "Please go on."

"We planned from the beginning against the chance that you, our instrument—irreplaceable instrument— might have eventually to confront B Group as researcher. That one of them was implicated became clear when you uncovered the duplication of the Library Access Card. A connection between one of them and Conrad was at once apparent to us, though not to yourself; your own suspicion was simple flailing in the dark, not a deduction, while for us the matter of the random patterning of the ink pointed definitely to Belinda. More of her later."

He was silent so long that I risked a question. "Wasn't her distaste of Conrad great enough for her to refuse him? I know something of what he could do, but could he operate on his own kind?"

"Not his own kind. Three Groups, three kinds. Belinda is as different from Conrad as he from you or I from him. Against his empirical psychology, which appears to have been a thuggish application of manipulative strength on detected weakness, her aesthetic reactions would have had no defence." His voice dropped to a dry speculation: "What he could have done against me or mine I cannot tell. My Group is colder, less easily destabilised, but perhaps that could have made for him a weapon against us. Such domination would be traumatic for the dominated. Witness Farnham. I have called Conrad a thug, but he was only eighteen, his intellect not fully developed and his observation of humanity limited to the narrow and specialised orbit of the Nursery. Nor had he developed self-knowledge to the point of full control of his half understood abilities. So, quick psychological violence was all the implement he had; I feel that, given time and study, he would have been less aggressive. Fine minds are not unreasoningly cruel. The unfortunate Farnham might have been caressed and protected if Conrad had had the time and the knowledge to avoid the sacrifice.

"But these are things we cannot know. What matters is that he could have had his way with Belinda if he needed her, and it seems that he did need her. Therefore Belinda becomes a link in the informational chain and you, the scanning instrument throughout this search, must approach her. With great caution. You will be taught how to do that."

Scanning instrument prompted my demand, "Just what have you done to my eyes and ears?"

"Given them powers. You will not need that clumsy necklet again except as occupational camouflage; you are wired for sound and vision as no man ever has been before you. You are my finest accomplishment in bio-electronic design." His voice actually rang, in a small way, with pride.

I, the experimental animal, with a memory of the plastic eyeball turning in his hands, asked uncertainly, "Are you saying that you have made direct connection to the optic nerve?"

"What else? Sight and hearing have been equipped with bypasses that will record their signals directly on a molecular layer imprinted on the bones of your skull. What you see and hear will be stored for recovery in minute detail."

All I could think of was, "I don't feel any different."

"Why should you? The incisions are healed; no pain-carrying pathways are involved; the intention is that you be physically unaware of the recording process. That is part of the surface innocence disguising your function."

"Like a bloody robot—mindless."

His bony fingers crept over my hand again and his voice dropped to a level of intimacy, of confidence sharing. "Like a secret self."

Despite the ham phoniness, it worked, appealing to vanity and an awareness of myself as something more than a young man indistinguishable among millions. It soothed and pleased. Conrad was not the only button-pusher in the family.

"Astrid tells me she will remove the bandages this afternoon."

He had said all he had come to say and I heard him leaving without unnecessary farewell. The abruptness rankled and I called after him one of those futile shafts with which we bolster pride after the event: "You should have asked me before you operated!"

"Why?" His voice came from where I had decided the door must be. "You would have argued and been unduly troublesome and Jonesey would have been tempted to threaten with his silly gun. A fait accompli always has a calming effect."

I should have known better.

Aunt Astrid was an efficient woman and no lady. She had the hard hands of a workingman and the unsentimental deftness of a garage mechanic; she ripped off my bandages with a no-nonsense competence that rocked the brain in my skull. Surgeon she was, nurse she was not.

She unwound a couple of layers of blindfold, hooked the plugs out of my ears and asked, "Can you see anything? Light?"

"Faint light."

Another yard or two were unwound. "Now?"

"Lighter. I see a shadow—your hand?"

"Yes." More unwinding. "Now?"

"Much brighter."

"Does the brightness distress you?"

"No."

"Close your eyes."

The last of the blindfold came away and she slipped what felt like a pair of spectacles over my nose and ears. "Open!"

I saw clearly in a light that seemed curiously soft although the glasses were not tinted. "Clear. It must be early morning."

"It is midafternoon; the lenses are protective, not corrective. I will switch on the lights; do not look directly at them."

At once articles stood out sharp-edged, but the lenses were in some fashion glare-reducing. "No trouble."

"No pain? No glare?"

"None."

"Wear the glasses for twenty-four hours as a precautionary measure. You can have him, Arthur."

I saw my aunt Astrid for a moment before she turned her back—green-eyed, tomato-haired, rawboned—a transvestite version of him and nearly as tall. She nodded to herself in the satisfaction of a job well done and went off with the stride of one with urgencies elsewhere, I and my rearrangement done with.

The bed creaked as my father came into view to sit on the edge. "You see that no harm has come to you."

"I should have been consulted."

"Stop sulking! The thing is done. Accept it."

I said nothing to that; what could I have said? He groped for my hand in that repeated gesture that he must surely have copied from familyvid soap opera. It was not embarrassing, merely empty; I had to remind myself that he was doing his best with unfamiliar feelings in a belated relationship.

What he had to say, however, was practical. "David, I want you to tweak the lobe of your right ear."

"What? Why?"

"To, so to speak, switch yourself on."

I felt the lobe; there seemed to be nothing unusual about it. I gave it an experimental tweak. Nothing happened.

He smiled with his usual difficulty. "You are now recording sight and sound."

There should have been some sign, an inner buzz, a flush of warmth, a sudden sharpening of vision. Nothing. "I don't know. I think you've got it wrong."

"If you were aware of the switching process, there surely would be something wrong." He stood and moved to the foot of the bed, facing me, outlined against the full-width wall screen opposite. "Watch my left hand. Now the right. Up. Down. Now—tweak the left lobe. So, you are switched off. Now we shall see what you have seen."

He produced a small, flexible metal disk padded with rubber to make a suction cup and placed it on my forehead. It clung tightly and I felt a sensation not easy to describe, like that shadow of a tingle that comes when you approach a pencil or even your finger to that point an inch or two above the bridge of the nose, as though the pineal gland had stirred and reacted.

My father said, "There is a very low current passing, about equivalent to a synaptic link."

He pulled out a long lead from one of the terminals, attached it to the disk and switched on the screen, which filled immediately with his face bent forward, wearing its difficult smile and saying, "You are now recording sight and sound."

My voice answered him pettishly, "I don't know. I think you've got it wrong."

The little scene continued to play itself out. I saw the vidscreen framed within the real screen as my father stepped in front of it and spread his arms and directed my attention here and there and told me to tweak the left earlobe, when the picture vanished.

Beside me now, he said, "That should have been a complete reproduction of what you saw. Was it?"

It had not been quite that. The sense of personal replay, as though I had actually repeated a section of my life, was strangely daunting, both real and unreal in a confusion that might in an earlier age have raised a cry of witchcraft. Unable to pin down the strangeness, I asked, "Can you run it again?"

"As often as need be."

Watching carefully I saw what had registered only peripherally on the first run, that the picture did not quite fill the screen but faded to a blur at the edges, and that within the blurred area objects flickered in and out of clarity. Also, the reproduction did peculiar things with light; some points were clear and others hazy in varying degrees, advancing into and withdrawing from prominence.

"Reality," my father said. "Your eyes are not simply undiscriminating camera lenses; they are operated by a brain that decides and selects. The recording surface picks up what your brain selects from what your eyes see; it retains what your attention lights on or falls away from; it reproduces peripherals if you consciously notice them, fades them if you do not. The picture we get is of what your brain considers immediately relevant, though everything else is there in more or less noticed fashion. You would obtain similar effects in sound reproduction if you were making conversation in a crowded room with music playing. Minor glimpses and sounds are stored as minor items, but they can be observed in replay, and what seemed of little significance at the time of recording can be reconsidered in later observation. Nothing is lost; what might be forgotten is retained."

It struck me, like a small, friendly thunderbolt that I was in my cybernetic way one of the most unusual people alive.

My father may have been clumsy with his gestures but he was no slouch at reading faces. He said, "I thought you would come to appreciate the experience."

So much for his plaintive difficulty in understanding "normal" human beings.

Next morning I was out of bed and on the front lawn when Jonesey's car came down the drive, its new colour already so scruffy as to defy reason; the ageing must have taken time and effort.

He got out and came across the lawn to stop a couple of arm's lengths from me, sounding my mood and wearing a sort of hangdog defensiveness. I tugged my earlobe, registering his self-satisfied cockiness in disrepair, to take a vidprint of it later for production when his superiorities became insufferable.

He said, cautiously for him, "I couldn't stop it, David."

"No, you were out cold."

"They kept me sedated until the operation was over."

"Just as well."

"What?"

"Just as well. How could they have worked with you around the place, yelling and waving a gun?"

For an instant he was blindly furious; I had taunted his ego a degree too far. Then he decided to laugh it off and made not too bad a show of it. "You cheeky young bastard."

I agreed, "Young and a bastard, and interested in your expressed approval of the internal wiring."

"Well, when I thought it over—"

He hesitated long enough for me to finish for him. "—you saw it as a bloody good idea. Admittedly, by then you couldn't do much else."

He loosed a little of his irritation. "For Christ's sake, boy, I'm a professional! I have to approve of a setup like this. It's ideal."

"You don't give a bugger what I get shoved into so long as it gets a result. My minder!"

He had the grace not to pretend shame. "I care, but just the same I have to welcome a gimmick that will see the job through. They'll tell you agents can't afford friends, and that's true, but they still have them. But the job gets in the way of other feelings and the job comes first. So you're being used up and I'm agreeing instead of being outraged. But, Jesus, boy, we'll both get over it."

"You can stop suffering," I told him. "I've thought it over and I agree, too, since objecting wouldn't get me debugged, or even sympathy."

"All right, you've made your point: I couldn't look after you when the unexpected happened."

"Be comforted. They reckoned you dangerous enough to knock you out first."

"Nuisance enough! What hurts is being manipulated and second-guessed. The Group had this planned from the start; it was for them only a matter of waiting for the right time to do it, when you were sufficiently blooded to be able to handle a touchy assignment. They're the real prime movers in the machinery."

"Yet they didn't foresee your Super's intrusion."

"I wouldn't bet on it. Anyway, he's as bucked as a rutting rabbit over this development; he loves it. He's talking about setting up a squad of wired agents."

Behind us my father's voice remarked in its dry, unemotional way of delivering emotional judgments, "That is unthinkable. Such a squad would represent a wholly unjustifiable invasion of privacy in a State already dangerously overexposed to random scrutiny."

Jonesey turned to face him. "Who'd have thought you cared! If the Super wants a new technology, he'll get it."

"Not so."

"He can bring pressure to bear—more than you'll believe."

"Pressure? He?" My father's voice rose a fraction. "The State created the Groups and the State cherishes us in its secretive way. Your little man will learn that it is we who bring pressure to get what we want. Tell him, if you like, that I said it."

He turned to lead the way inside.

I was never a great hand at hiding my feelings, and Jonesey muttered in my ear, not pleasantly, "Real class, you Hazards, aren't you?"

And in fact I was contemplating the advantages of belonging to a family that mattered.

In the cluttered sitting room my father said, "Jonesey's watchdog role will be difficult because you will have to see

Belinda alone. Your biographical research story will suffice to gain an interview—when we have examined and
streamlined it—but she is no fool to be taken in by an
unnecessary assistant. She is no fool to be easily taken in at
all. She will realise who you are soon enough, depend on
it, and your good impression must be sufficiently ingrati-
ated by then. Your task will be to prevent her throwing
you out in contempt or anger or plain boredom, and to
that end we will devise verbal strategies, but you will have
to face her without immediate support. Jonesey will protect your comings and goings—"

"Against whom and what?"

He said dismissively, with his usual attitude of all dangers being secondary to his planning, "We will come to
that. You will be alone with Belinda, playing the respectful
young A-Group get, openmouthed and earnest and prepared to swallow whatever nonsense she feeds you. Believe
me, it will be nonsense."

"Then what do you expect to gain?"

"Information. Even nonsense has to operate from a
factual reference point, and we will examine every word
and intonation recorded by you. The critical techniques of
structuralism may be of use in the scrutiny."

"And you think you will deduce the location of the
legacy from that?"

I had broken the train of thought again. "The legacy?
Oh, that. Perhaps, perhaps, but first things first."

"I don't follow."

His sombre regard belonged to a father doubting his
son's intelligent fitness for the job. He said, "You must
look further ahead. Jonesey's more suspicious view of reality may suggest to him what the first things are."

And so it did, shaming me. "Two things," he said
slowly. "One: Why did there have to be a legacy? If Young
Feller had something to give, why didn't he just give it? I
get the feeling there's something hidden here—like,

maybe, the sort of nasty joke that a despairing man might play on his tormentors."

"In the fashion," my father suggested, "of a time bomb set to destroy the finder if he is stupid enough to leap on the treasure without due care? I agree. I cannot predict the nature of it but there are several possibilities, and that is why it must fall into no hands but ours. Otherwise this whole search could have been conducted openly."

Jonesey jeered mildly, "You, of course, will understand and not be destroyed?"

Jibes were wasted on my father. "I may well be hoodwinked but our Group is better prepared than others to recognise a trap. It may cost one of our lives, or two, but not, I think, all four. Your second thought?"

Jonesey told me later that this was the point at which he began to respect the Group, the point at which he saw that they were not simply sitting back and allowing their troops to take the flack while they relaxed in a comfortable headquarters. Being Jonesey, he made no parade of his change of heart but carried on with his analysis.

"We need to know why C Group killed themselves. It's hard to accept that it was because of anything he found out from this Belinda. What would she know? From what I can gather of her Group, their interests are purely aesthetic, not easily expressed in common terms, very spiritual and way out."

My father muttered, "They can be down to earth enough."

"Maybe so, but what could she say to Young Feller to make him throw the game in, him with an intellect beyond anything we can imagine? There was somebody else beyond her, somebody who knew facts or ideas or what-have-you that poor little raised-in-a-nursery Young Feller could not. Somebody who broke him. Maybe by accident."

My father said with plain approval, "That is more or less how we see it."

Jonesey rattled on triumphantly, "It could have been a simple fact, obvious to David or me but not to him because even his mind couldn't plumb the whole human culture in a few months of living like a rat in a hole. It could have been something too basic to be obvious to the complicated mind."

"Excellent, Jonesey. But beware. Between you, find the person, but approach him with caution. If he is the one on whom the joke is to be sprung, you should avoid being caught in its teeth."

For preparation they gave us a grudging two days that aside from one disturbing demonstration, told us little more about B Group than was available in the media morgues and the essays of art critics.

Jonesey asked at once, "Why Belinda rather than Bert or Barry or the other one? What's her connection?"

"Paint," Andrew said. The word seemed to him sufficient. He sighed for our un-Grouplike incomprehension. "Leave it until we have filled in the background."

So, the background:

B Group were taken from the Nursery when they turned seventeen, and had already created their first major impact on the local art scene by the time Conrad ran for freedom. At the time of his escape they had also survived their first aesthetic scandal and become famous, fairly wealthy—and reclusive. That is to say that they refused all but essential public roles and statements and got away with the insolence because they were too precious to be interfered with. The point of their existence, to those who had created them, was observation of what they did, a strictly hands-off operation.

These wary, talented teenagers accepted the conditions of the outside world with a pointedly controlled enthusiasm, offering little comment but working in their studios in a creative frenzy, like young animals skipping in their first freedom. The art world, which had been allowed only glimpses of the progress of their juvenilia in early years, held its breath.

The crash came quickly. Within three months they held their first exhibition for critics, dealers and psychologists, and it was a total disaster. The juvenilia were history and the present was outrage. The material has never been put on public exhibition by request—more like decree—of the icily furious artists.

What they had created pleased nobody but themselves. Criticism and expertise made little of it but were either too cautious to declare it meaningless and worthless or uneasily aware of meaning hovering just beyond their conceptual reach. Only a few were incautiously downright; one exasperated woman dealer said of Belinda's paintings that they bore the same relation—allowing that they meant anything at all—to the day's avant-garde as Picassan cubism had in its day borne to the scribblings of children and were similarly indecipherable. To which a smouldering Belinda replied that her work rationalised that relationship, a gnomic throwaway that endeared her to no one. Asked to enlarge on it, she pointed out the impossibility of enlarging on a complete statement, cleared the dealer out of the studio, slammed the door and refused to communicate for a month.

In hindsight, something of the sort should have been expected, especially by the psychologists, who said nothing at all.

The other three—sculptor, photographer and self-styled "manipulator"—offered no more concessions to understanding than Belinda and made no secret of their contempt for critical opinion. The critics—most of them, to give their due, honest and knowledgeable—professed themselves open-minded but unconvinced, while the general public yawned its vast lack of interest in yet another ratbag art hoax. A few speculators offered for odd items that mocked with a misty promise of comprehensibility and were refused, bluntly. Art, meaning unfettered creativity, was not for sale, particularly not to auction-room money-grubbers who were told with venomous coolness, *Fuck off!*

As my father had noted, they could be down to earth enough.

That they were teenagers, albeit very special teenagers, did not bolster any disinterestedness in the evaluations of people who had spent their lives in the pursuit and explication of excellence; they would cheerfully have seen the four juvenile throats cut. It was the general public, suddenly alerted to the ongoing but half-forgotten Nursery story, that applied a decisive thrust—for the love of money, not of art.

The State that had created the Groups at vast expense to the taxpayer found itself expected to return something more for the money than an art that most regarded as nose-thumbing fakery. The State applied to the psychologists, who suggested the obvious way in which it might tame its aesthetic tigers and extort a return on the public outlay. It was, simply, to withdraw all financial support—make the green-eyed brutes produce comprehensible work, or starve. So much for the hands-off policy when votes were under fire.

The plan succeeded, in its fashion. Or, in B Group's fashion. The four retired into their studio complex, refused to talk to anyone at all and, presumably, worked like furies. After three months they held the historic exhibition that added a debatable novelty to human aesthetic experience.

Put plainly, what each did in his/her medium was to examine the various modern schools and exhibit, in each mode, a group of works recognisably generic but critically, philosophically and technically advanced beyond anything done before. They included, with undisguised condescension, an attribute that simultaneously mocked critical appraisal and tamed public opinion into a purring pussy:

They made the works accessible to the understanding of the uninstructed majority for whom modernist art hovered between a hoax and an insult. Beyond the strangeness of these paintings and sculptures and photographs could be descried the nearly familiar and the evasively beautiful. And something else.

"Hypnotic!" was the appreciative word of the moment. You looked and you continued looking until your mind could hold no more. "Hypnotic! Absolutely hypnotic!"

The psychologists pointed out that the word was illusory in itself, that what gripped the eye was the use of a subtle technique that led the attention inexorably from point to point until the entire work was assimilated. Then you could start again. Nothing hypnotic about it, just a superb technique.

Exactly, the public agreed, *absolutely hypnotic!*

Bert's "live manipulation" proved the point to the public mind. He put two hundred gymnasts in the middle of a football field and trained them in patterns of movement executed to the spasmodic rhythm of bells struck at what seemed random intervals. His gymnasts moved ceaselessly, forming patterns that dissolved tantalisingly in the moment of completion while the only sound heard by thirty thousand rapt spectators was the resonance of small, quiet bells that needed fine tuning but whose mild dissonance piqued rather than distracted. Watchers agreed that the attraction did not lie in the not-quite-forming patterns but in the endless flow. You couldn't stop watching; your eyes wouldn't look away. Hypnotic!

B Group laughed all the way to the bank. And all the way home. And far into the night behind their slammed studio doors. Why not, when they had pulled off the most successful stunt in the history of art? Told to earn their keep, they had done exactly that with an exhibition of what they publicly and loudly described as rubbish, toys, the kind of thing they could turn out by the gallery-filling tonne—and thereafter did so in the name of gullible money.

When their artistic integrity was challenged, they mocked: "You wanted saleable knickknacks and we made them. What's your complaint? They are product; they have nothing to do with art."

By the time Conrad fled the Nursery they were becoming rich beyond the common dream, reclusive and contemptuous of the humanity that cordially detested them while finding their "product" irresistible. "You have to have the stuff," said those who could afford it. "It's hypnotic!"

All this tells you only what it told Jonesey and me, that B Group was difficult, self-regarding, contemptuous and impossible to like. And, of course, vastly talented. But in what? Art, process work, practical joking or barefaced effrontery?

"Jokers," I decided, "giving art the gold-plated raspberry."

Andrew's agreement was conditional. "Their jokes are deeply serious, not at all amusing, telling humanity what it showed them of itself. Art of any kind means little to me or to my Group but their technical skills frighten me and have frightened others. Look at these."

He projected some magazine illustrations onto the vidscreen, and there was nothing at all hypnotic in the two-dimensional views. To my admittedly untutored eye they showed little logic in any naturalistic sense though there seemed to be some preoccupation with form. I don't mean form in the sense of symmetry or associative recognition. All the pieces Andrew showed, whether painted or sculpted, were peculiarly, almost randomly shaped but were bafflingly allusive, like the word on the tip of the tongue that the mouth cannot pronounce while the brain scratches for recall. Their form was immanent but lurking, unwilling to emerge.

"Look closely," Andrew said and showed a picture of something like a crystal tube whose ends folded in on themselves like a Klein bottle and emerged at points along the barrel, to fold in again at the freshly exposed ends and emerge and again fold in until a bowellike maze coiled shimmering on the screen. All the irregular, purposeless buddings formed—or so it seemed—a single continuous surface.

"Ingenious," was the best I could do; it meant nothing at all to me. Jonesey merely looked uncomfortable; he knew more about art than I but his appreciation stopped short somewhere about Renoir.

Andrew nodded at empty air in the middle of the room. "Now see a holographic reproduction."

A figure of brilliant clarity sprang into three-dimensional suspension, the crystal glittering with a light that seemed to flow inside it and beat at the surface as though seeking escape. It was the same exhibit as the last, imbued with life. Faint, very faint indications of colour moved slowly from the centre of the main tube into the daughter buds, splitting and splitting. I saw that the Klein bottle appearance was superficial only, that the conveyed depiction was of connections within the mind and within and within and within . . . and that at the core was a profound understanding that study would reveal . . . reveal . . .

I was distantly aware that Andrew spoke and that my mind refused him. My enthralled eye had been led out of one branch into another already traversed, but that in itself had a meaning to be grasped . . . the essential repetition of fundamental ideas seeking each other in covalent truths . . .

The hologram vanished.

I came to in an instant fury of deprivation and heard Jonesey cry out, "Get it back! I was seeing, catching the idea of it!"

Andrew was unwontedly grim. "There is no idea, only

fascination. Conscious thought is subverted, held to a circular discovery of nothing. You stared at it for six minutes."

How long? A few seconds, surely. Yet the recollection was elusively timeless, an act of concentration without duration.

Jonesey sounded mutinous as he complained that he had never seen anything like that although plenty of the B Group work was on public view.

"Nor will you. There are only a few such pieces and they were withdrawn as soon as their potential was realised. Nasty teenage jokes? It's hard to say. Bert's manipulations are less wholesale, mere cynicisms designed to wheedle money from an audience that feels it has been meaningfully entertained for an hour or two. A vaudeville trick."

That required digesting. Jonesey said, "Six minutes!" but his disgust did not query the figure any more than I had. "That thing's dangerous. It could hold a person rapt while his home was plundered around him."

"That actually happened and led to confiscation of the more potent items. They were stored for expert study but I doubt that the enraptured experts arrived at useful conclusions. Most of the work holds the eye until it has absorbed an overload of meaningless detail and the attention span falters—some two minutes for the average person—but the withdrawn items are more viciously powerful."

Jonesey snorted for talent misused. "Demonstrating what they could do when pushed."

"Maybe so. I have heard that the armed services' camouflage people are interested in the techniques but quite unable to reproduce them."

"Hypnotic camouflage! Mesmerise the enemy with big ground displays and then manipulate him!"

Andrew asked, "Manipulate, how? The condition is self-induced, almost equivalent to sensual deprivation;

outside influences are noted but not reacted to. It is a static condition. A questioned subject disregards the question; he cannot be distracted from tracing the pattern."

"So it's just trick stuff, useless."

"You think it just a spiteful joke against the idiots who pay fortunes for what the makers deride as factory trash? The auto-hypnotic effect has not been deeply probed because investigators have not been able to reproduce it and the artists stand on their right to protect trade secrets, but I think uses will be found. Nothing is totally useless."

Jonesey suggested, "The appendix?"

"*Homo sapiens sapiens* is in process of discarding that by an evolutionary practice that will reverse itself if a need for the organ arises. Meanwhile—"

He eyed me with his familiar avuncular curiosity as it deciding whether or not his promising young nephew deserved tipping and how much.

"Meanwhile," I said, "I am expected to screw secrets out of this witch in her own studio, which could be full of these snappy little distractions. She may know how to penetrate the trance."

"Indeed she may, but she will scarcely decorate her home with the product she publicly despises. In any case you can be protected with slightly distorting spectacles. They are a commercial product obtainable from any art supply dealer, developed for the clear viewing of Hazard artworks. They nullify effectively. The fact that they do so suggests that the hypnotic effect is mathematically calculable and lies in the use of colour and design to delude and deflect, but until now there has been no compelling reason to test this. However, David, you will be able to examine pictures, if necessary, quite safely. Some aesthetically obtuse people are almost immune to the effect of the paintings, so wear the spectacles and be obtuse."

End of subject. Short silence.

Jonesey returned to his first query. "Again, why Belinda? Where does she fit into the tale of faked Library Cards?"

Andrew frowned minutely, gazed out of the window and said stiffly, "We must hypothesise. This is not satisfactory but it is all we can do when test procedures are lacking." He was mildly plaintive, confessing a sin before examiners, conscience-stricken by a departure from linear logic. He brightened a little to suggest, "David, of course, will be our test probe."

I had become hardened to this kind of effrontery. Neither he nor my father was capable of realising another's objections to the good sense of their planning.

"There's some reason to think that the ultimate hypnotic technique was taught her by Conrad. B Group's earlier modes of leading the eye were an extension and development of twentieth-century methods popularised by painters such as Escher and Vasarely. Or so I understand; it is not my field; I am artistically illiterate. The more dangerous attention-capturing modes did not appear until the year 2022 after Conrad had returned to the Nursery. The connection is plain but there is no factual evidence."

Jonesey agreed patiently. "Sounds right enough, but why Belinda rather than one of the other three?"

"He needed a depictive artist who could make an exact copy of a Card. C Group tended to be a little clumsy in respect of such activities; it is refreshing to think of something they could not do well. It may be that any competent technician would have sufficed, but why cast about when Belinda is available? He can trust his unique persuasive powers and have the thing done without complication. Keep it, as you might say, in the family. Yet it is here he meets a check. Belinda, who surely would have possessed a research Access Card, tells him of the induplicable ink. He at once sets out to discover how this effect is accomplished."

A shadow, despondent in what I could assess only as

an unwilling humility, settled on his eyes. "I wonder how long the discovery took him? Your father and I, working together, with excellent analytical tools, spent the six days of David's hospitalisation under Astrid divining the State method. Conrad, working with his mind alone—using Belinda's Card to gather basic information—may have done it in a single protracted, driving session. In hours. It is not possible to comprehend such an intelligence in concentrated effort. It is as well they all died. They were young and untutorable and alone on a lunatic asylum of a planet; they could have developed only as a destructive force."

Jonesey, on the trail, was no audience for obsequies. "You know how to duplicate Personal Cards?" His voice was towering resentment.

"No. We know how it can be done but we cannot do it. It is not a process we or anyone can use without a billionaire's ransom in special machinery. A Personal ID or Access Card is five centimetres by three, cut from a common commercial plastic, and the face is layered with a thickened black ink, again a commercial product, under the white-printed data. The ink crystallises as it dries to a layer approximately point one of a millimetre deep. How many millions of molecules does that represent? No matter. More than enough for the purpose. For all its thinness, the layer is three-dimensional, so that the number of possible molecule sites within it is immense. Into this black matrix are inserted twelve crystals of a magnetically susceptible metallic compound. Iron, cobalt, it does not matter. These are inserted while the ink is still semiliquid and guided into predetermined positions by magnets set at the three axes. Each magnet is separately powered at a strength determined by a computer that provides a new power pattern every time a new Card is presented for individualising. These patterns are not random as is commonly thought, but follow a mathematical progress of slightly differing magnetic influences, so that each metallic cluster forms a uniquely shaped grouping. The ink dries, the magnets are automatically reset to the next pattern of dispersal. That dispersal pattern is what the Access Terminal recognises and checks against recognition data at Central Accounts."

Simple, really—if you can find the pattern sequence—and the entire Australian population could live and die and procreate generations before the number of possible variations approached an end.

Jonesey was not wonderstruck, only bent on information. "So, without a billionaire's ransom, how did he do it?"

"He plotted the positions of the magneto-sensitive molecules in the Cards he needed copied—not difficult once he knew what to look for—and inserted them singly in the correct positions in the duplicate Cards."

"Balls!"

Andrew remained courteous. "I understand your objection but it must have been so."

"How? With a bloody eyedropper?"

"I don't know. Yet it was done, three times that we know of. It was done in a primitive workplace without the requisite equipment. You do not begin to understand what Conrad was."

"I don't understand a physical impossibility, either."

Andrew showed a rare glimmer of impatience. "You have a better suggestion?"

Jonesey shrugged into silence, suspicious of knowledge withheld, his intelligence baffled and insulted by the impenetrable.

I cut through to the real question. "In return for her help, Young Feller taught Belinda the more effective hypno technique. Is that it?"

"It is possible, even probable. He appears to have paid his debts where he could."

His placidity touched off my anger. "To Farnham, for instance?"

"I said, 'Where he could.'"

Perhaps, perhaps, but I would never forget Derek's faraway eyes rising to meet mine as he called me Conrad.

Jonesey had stopped listening to us. I caught his ferocious, self-lacerating mutter, "There has to be some other way."

So there had—some simple way.

During the rest of the time we did not see Astrid again or Alice at all; it seemed they had no curiosity about us or, apparently, about the search for the legacy. The boys were attending to it, so why dither with social niceties while urgent personal projects stagnated on the workbench? Nor were my father and Andrew much more forthcoming; they made spasmodic appearances to ascertain that we understood this point or that but for the most part left us alone to make what we could of the publicly available material.

We were disturbed by how little they actually knew about their B Group sibs. Their ignorance threw into high relief the mental wall separating the Groups. It did not seem to involve dislike in the sense of anger or revulsion (though an irritated contempt was surely present) but a disinterest that barely recognised each other's existences. At some stage of their development each Group had recognised in itself a mental singularity that made it impossible to convey its world view in terms intelligible to the other two. There had been a cool closing of doors and no reopening, and now my father and Andrew worked hopelessly to elucidate models that would explain Belinda to me. They failed. How could it have been otherwise?

When at last they stopped trying and dispatched us back to Melbourne my father said, as a sort of parting comfort, "She may give you bad moments, even some humiliation, but you will come to no real harm from her." I thought of that infinity-seeking proliferation of Klein bottles but held my peace. He added with typical complacency, "A fine intellect takes no pleasure in mere viciousness."

I might have replied that the *Homo sapiens* experience with its own versions of genius suggested the occasional exception, but that would only have provoked a spate of rational argument to tangle my doubts.

As we drove off, Jonesey was savagely silent. We were halfway home before he complained out of his surly depths, "It couldn't be done. Not at a workbench."

He seemed to have a mental picture of Young Feller on a high stool, hunched over an ersatz Card in some garage laboratory, implanting metallic recognition molecules like an old-time biologist fertilising frogs' eggs with a needle. For all his out-of-the-way knowledge and range of interests, Jonesey's mind was a wasteland of gaps and fog patches; his lack of scientific information was astonishing in a man who lived his life among the webs of electronic surveillance. There were times when I glimpsed a basically simple soul joyously at play with the complexities of his job, like a small boy with his first box of paints.

My own preoccupation just then was personal, a stage fright feeling that I was to make my foray against expertise and cynical self-possession with, as my only weapons, a pair of subtle spectacles and no useful knowledge of the enemy forces.

It struck me that I had almost forgotten my internal recording equipment. There was nothing to remind me of it; I could not feel it inside my head, haunting my ears and eyes, waiting at rest on the bone of my skull to begin its work. They had wanted me effectively unaware, and I was.

But those secret circuits could only record what happened, not guard against the happening. Sour humour foresaw the opportunity for dauntless last words: *Tell 'em I died game, pal!*

11 • A PAINTERLY TECHNIQUE

I sat in the flat for two days, summoning nerve while nerve refused the summons. There had been an adventuresome, cocksure ignorance in the first weeks of the chase, then near-death and a deepening immersion in muddy waters. And now only a nasty bewilderment. I was afraid, not so much of unknown Belinda as of unknowns beyond her.

A and B Groups had one trait in common, their insistence on privacy. They lived and worked in protected country retreats whose locations were known but whose constantly changed vid numbers were "silent," and when of necessity they visited townships or the city they did so in any number of incognito personae. Both Groups had succeeded so well in their withdrawals that public interest centered on their work and scarcely at all on their personalities.

They had shut themselves off so effectively that I could discover little idea of what the mature Belinda looked like, nor could any of my snooping media contacts provide me with her vid number.

I complained to a disgusted Jonesey, who asked,"Why didn't you say right away? No trouble!"

He knew damned well that I had wanted to show off, to demonstrate that on my own I could obtain the unobtainable, but he was kind enough not to point it out. He thought that learning the hard way was best.

Within the hour he told me, "No photographs, not even in Department files. How's that for clout! Only some candid camera junk in wigs and dark glasses and what have you. Useless. But I have the vid number; no clout can keep that from privileged computer search. Don't write it down; memorise it."

"She'll want to know how I got it."

"So tell her."

"That your Department gave it to me?"

"That the Superintendent approved you having it."

"Will that impress her or start her into a raving temper?"

"It will impress her."

"I'm not so sure of that. Your Super doesn't impress my father or Andrew."

He poked me hard in the chest. "Use the brain, lad! It's a standoff situation, where the Groups depend on the Department for protection and privacy but can swing enough moral blackmail with politicos to make my Super duck for cover if they have a legitimate complaint of their treatment. The ongoing study depends on their cooperation. The lady's no fool, so she won't fly off the handle. She'll ask questions, like, Who the hell are you? and, What's the Super's interest?"

"And what is his interest?"

"That his Department is sponsoring your history of the Nursery brats and will be responsible for censorship angles."

"Will she swallow a yarn like that?"

"Of course not. She'll check it—and find that it's true. As of today, David, you have Departmental sponsorship. Your literary troubles are over."

The bland insolence of a Department that made free will a laughingstock was beyond acceptance. I bawled at him, "You stupid bastard! They'll grab the lot and never let me publish a word!"

"Calm it, lad. You never did expect to publish once you got on to Young Feller's high jinks. Now, did you?"

He was right, but always there had been in the back of my mind the chance of some upbeat twist, like the surprise ending of a thriller, that would allow me to startle vid and print with the undercover story of the century. Common sense said that this and the faery gold of the legacy were political dynamite, but the fever of the hunt kept hope alive.

There may have been small conviction in my muttering that ways could be found, but I was full of resentment. He heard me out, then talked sense. "Do you know that what is called 'criminal flouting' of the Official Secrets Act can get you shot?"

Every media man knows that; capital punishment is not quite the dead letter popular morality applauds. I had no answer.

He gave me one of the bear hugs he imagines are a universal cure for surliness. "That's life, David. You never get what you go after but you often get more than you expected. In this case it could be the Super offering you an open-ended agreement for future undercover work. Could be!"

He had done a deal and was proud of it. In that moment I could have killed him.

Belinda was the stuff of legend, and dangerous. It did no good telling myself that my father and Andrew had created this witch-woman persona between them by their inability to map her mental attitudes; their trying and failing had succeeded only in creating a mystery figure to trouble my uncertainties.

I said something of this to Jonesey, who listened

grimly, went away and returned later in the day with the records of the IQ and other tests and associated reports from the Nursery since the Groups were tots. He seemed to think they might comfort me.

"C Group first," he said. "You'll see why."

All the various modes of testing had been used and on the whole they correlated pretty well—except with C Group. With them, different test methods produced not only different scores but unpredictably different scores. From the beginning their tests bore no complementary relationship to each other.

The higher the IQ measured, the greater will be the margin of assessment error, plus or minus, because the measurer is probing in an increasingly misty area when he sets tests for an intelligence whose parameters are uncertain. The psychometrists stopped trying to test C Group at age twelve, when they no longer knew what they were testing or whether their test sequences told them anything at all. They did know that they were incapable of devising any means of assessing the four intelligences. They could and did make estimates, but if you offer an estimate of IQ 400, does the figure really tell you anything of what the transcendent brain can do?

I think many a long-held breath was released when the quartet died. A thanksgiving wake would have been in order for all those shattered egos.

The figures for the other two Groups held some surprises. They were high, with my father's Group slightly ahead of B, but not staggeringly high. All of them were, at eighteen, members of the superior one thousandth of one percent of the population, but that alone did not set them into any bizarre personal bracket. It meant only that there were among the planet's ten billions, unlikely as it may seem until you work it out, something in the region of a hundred thousand people who were their intellectual equals or better.

"Both Groups are human," Jonesey said. "Not homo superior, just different. The gene-mixing sent brain power through the roof with Young Feller's lot, but the mixes used for A and B gave twists in unexpected directions, created people thinking along specialised paths. So your Belinda's a mighty clever little bitch with a big opinion of herself and a low one of the people who bred her, but she isn't superhuman; she just works from different basic principles. You could say the same for any brilliant paranoid schizophrenic."

I said, "Those are dangerous, too."

But he had hit the right note. I lost the vision of a Belinda whose dark mind might open like a trap to engulf me alive and whole. I was not wholly reassured but at least I gathered courage to call her silent number while Jonesey sat in the kitchenette where the screen could not see him. My feeling was, *Now God help me if I put a foot, a grimace, a word wrong;* but at least I would make the play.

I sat dead centre before the screen, trying to look like an urgent and expectant investigative journo. I daresay I managed to look uncomfortable.

The tariff timer started up as the call was accepted and I stopped thinking of appearances. The umbral flicker of the screen told me I was being inspected.

Time dragged while I resisted the temptation to be the first to break silence; she would talk or she would not. My hands washed themselves nervously until my scattering wits remembered what I was about and I used the nervousness to tweak distractedly at my right earlobe.

What could she be doing? Tracing the call?

More likely she was studying the resemblance patent to others but only slightly perceptible to myself.

When she spoke . . . Can you see an expression of amusement behind a disembodied voice? I saw it clearly as she asked, "Whose by-blow are you?"

The coarse unexpectedness of it provoked an unprepared reaction in me. "Conrad's," I said to the black flicker of the screen.

I felt rather than heard Jonesey's start of surprise but dared not glance sideways to reassure him.

She thought while the timer ticked off fifteen seconds. When she spoke it was with cool dismissal: "That is a lie."

She had not cut off. She was interested, hooked; the first hurdle was past. I said, "You would think so, but Conrad did many things only Conrad knew about."

"But not that particular thing." A ghost of stiff distaste haunted her voice. "He was fastidious. Your father or mother plainly was not. Who sired or dropped you?"

I said at once, "Arthur."

"I can believe it. That lot rut like rabbits. Why did you lie?"

"To take your attention. I want to talk to you about Conrad."

I expected her to stall by denying any knowledge of Conrad that was not on public record; it was what I would have done to gain time for thought. Instead, she asked, "Why?"

I moved into the prepared story. "I want to write the life stories of the Nursery babies."

"A writer?" A politely puzzled enquiry.

My legendary spitfire seemed not unapproachable; I began to take the running more easily. "A journalist, really, but this will not be a newsman's book. A serious biography."

"Pinning us down for the pawing of generations to come? Will you be famous, little man?"

Tension returned; she was not idly chatting. "Maybe so, if I write it well."

"Who gave you my vid number?"

"The Superintendent of the Department that preserves your privacy and personal safety."

"His name?"

"I don't know. He didn't tell me; I didn't ask. He's part Aboriginal. Maybe something like Ebaterinja."

"Ebaterinja was a painter, not a paid busybody. What is his interest?"

"Same as mine—filling in gaps."

"These answers can be checked."

"I trust they will be. If you decide to talk to me, you must trust me."

"Rubbish; I need only be self-interested."

"Only you can know about that."

"There's your problem." She waited through a long hiatus while the timer ticked quietly. Abruptly she ordered, "Interest me!"

I said at once, "Library Access Card."

As if the words had activated it, the screen cleared. I faced a middle-aged, greying woman who could have been a chubbier sister of my aunt Astrid save that she looked more blowsily ordinary. Only the brilliant green eyes spoke of strange beginnings and those were subdued by her nondescript clothes and an air of being unconcerned with her appearance. She was a green-eyed, ageing housewife answering the vid in the middle of a bout of dusting and cleaning.

She spoke now in a tone indicating nothing more urgent than the price of fish, but what she said carried its own impact. "If you run that road you'll have to run it to the end."

It sounded disinterested; it froze my blood. I said, almost in reflex, "I'm halfway down it and there's no place to stop."

She nodded, agreeing with me. No place to stop. "Be here tomorrow morning at ten o'clock. Alone."

"Thank you."

She cut off.

Jonesey said, "I hope you recorded that."

"Yes."

"Let me see."

We hooked the cup-and-lead to the vidscreen and re-played. Jonesey had not seen the replay in action and was furious at the lack of background; I had been so intent on Belinda-of-the-strange-powers (who existed only in my apprehensions) that I had scarcely noticed her surroundings; they appeared only as blurred walls and shapes of furniture without depth or fullness. My father had means of sharpening these incoherent images but we had not. Belinda, however, stood out in near-holographic liveliness.

"Hausfrau!" He had expected some sort of ogress to strop aggressive wits on. When she had spoken her few sentences and cut off he grunted, "Doesn't waste words."

"She found time for a threat."

"A warning."

"There's a difference?"

I don't know what he heard in my voice but he leaned over the back of the chair and gripped my shoulders. He is a strong man and he gripped hard. He asked, "Do you want to pull out?"

"You've already told me I can't."

"You can't refuse but I can show you how to be too sick to carry on."

For a moment I considered it. I was in a sense psyched up to face Belinda, like a runner on the blocks, tensed for the pistol; what worried the less prepared reaches of my mind was the thought of who/what might lie behind Belinda, the shadow that was yet only a suggestion of an entity. The unknown was more disturbing than the known and I felt that my blind luck had held too well, so far. It could run out.

We have never spoken of it but I believe that Jonesey thought my layman's innocence was being pushed too far by people prepared to trample it on the way to their goals. At first he had been one of them; now he offered me a way out and cowardice made me refuse him. Sheer inability to face him or my father after all my brash young-man talk determined me to risk an unknown danger rather than disappoint those who had had no right to manoeuvre me into it in the first place.

I asked, "Can I have a gun?"

His fingers eased. "Can you use one?"

"I've had some target practice." It was a lie and perhaps he knew it. I said, "I'll feel better if I have something to hit back with."

"At Belinda?"

"Not her. At whoever . . . I'll feel better."

That is why he let me have the little short-barrelled pistol and shoulder fitting—easier, more skeletal than a complete holster. He wanted me to feel better. "Fairly accurate up to six metres. Not a real weapon, a frightener."

He showed me how to position it so that it was not outlined under a loose coat and how to snap it directly out of the clip without wasting movement in a drawing action. I practised instant aiming like a flash crim in a vidplay until we both laughed like kids and I said, "I feel safer already."

He shook his head. "Stay a little bit scared. It keeps you careful."

Jonesey dropped me at Ferntree Gully, at the foot of the Dandenongs. "Get a taxi from here. You're on your own."

Point of no return. "Where will you be?"

"Around. Don't know exactly but I'll keep an eye on the house. Just in case."

In case of what? What could he do outside while the action was inside? After all, I had a gun . . . that silly little frightener, useful perhaps for overawing children.

He said, "Don't think of me. Think of yourself and her. She'll keep you busy."

I tried for airiness. "You reckon?"

" 'Deed I do."

He was feeling responsible and fatherly; I was his special apprentice, to be looked after. Or to be thrown to the wolves if the job demanded it.

"Go on," he said. "Piss off."

According to my taxi driver, all the locals knew where Belinda lived, but she was the district's invisible showpiece. None of them had ever been past the gates. Alarms everywhere, it was said. What sort? Well, nobody knew, exactly. Anyway, they weren't all that interested; Belinda was old news.

He was a specialist in the leading gambits of an established gossip, telling in a variety of insinuations how he rarely took anyone to the house, that it was years since he had dropped anyone there and that when he did they never got in. The bloke on the gate chopped them off quick smart.

Had he ever seen the lady?

Well, yes, well, no. "She drives straight through the town, all big dark glasses and scarf round the chin."

From Ferntree Gully the road winds steeply up towards the Sherbrooke Forest area, but our stop was less than halfway up.

"That's it," he said. "Now what?"

I paid him. "Hang around for half a minute and make your day. You'll see me go in."

"More likely see you set back on your arse." He settled down to wait on disaster.

In the Dandenongs the roads are cut from the mountainside, so the houses are either above the way on one side or below it on the other, and those hillsides are steep. Belinda's place was below the road on an incline too harsh for reasonable treading. I stood on the verge and looked down on a curving driveway that dropped from an iron fence (electrified?) and gatehouse to a long, narrow roof under which three floors thrust from the slope to form a single storey at the upper end and three storeys at the lower. The house nestled among trees that soared level with the roof and below them wattle and boronia and broome made a jungle.

I thought she must be a tiger for exercise. You could climb up or down in her bushland garden or stumble sideways on uncleared ground; the thing you could not find was level footing.

I had stood only a moment, taking it in, when the gatehouse spoke. "You want something?"

The speaker watched me incuriously. I said, "I have an appointment with Miss Hazard," and moved closer to look in on him. He was elderly but had the shoulders of a weight lifter—gatekeeper and chucker-out, if required, with at-his-command electronic defences better left unprobed.

He asked, with the insulting politeness of the bored who are sure of themselves, "Do my good looks take your fancy?"

Behind me the taxi driver snickered. I said, "No, and I apologise. My name is David Chance."

He did not react to the name or consult a list. "Ten o'clock's yours. It'll be near enough to it by the time you walk down."

He waved a hand over a circuit breaker and the iron gates slid apart.

My aggrieved taxi driver said, "Well, stuff me!"

I had a journalist's eye then rather than a literary curiosity; my mind homed on the story and the words spoken; I did little descriptive writing because that was what was processed out by the waspish impatience of an editor demanding "human interest," i.e., who got hurt and how badly. I tended in those days to see only what I needed to see. That is what had caused Jonesey to complain of my auto-recordings that I saw everything and observed nothing.

This day on Belinda's winding driveway was for ob-

servation. I went slowly, telling myself that I was saving
every detail of the Witch's Castle for later study. I did a
few turns, heel and toe, to let the necklet pan a full circle.
That tool did not depend on me for its intake.

What I saw, only an easy leap below me, was less a roof
than a seamless bubble, some ten metres wide and thirty
long, with heavily opaque patches over most of its surface
and a few semiclear capes and islands. There was one
small, totally clear space but I was at the wrong angle to
discern what was lit below it. The effect was of a great
dappled animal at rest. The roof was not glass but one of
the pseudo-silicates whose translucency could be electronically controlled to a desired pattern, fabulously expensive
to install and run and speaking aloud of the fatness of the
Hazard income. It had to be Belinda's studio, occupying
the entire top floor—working space, viewing spaces, lightless and lighted and shaded spaces. In some local power
station needles would jump when Belinda set her studio
lighting for the day.

Trees on the higher slope had been removed in favour of shrubs so that nothing obstructed the sunlight. It
was noticeable that only on the verges of the cement driveway was there any attempt at decorative gardening, and
there the border was of mutated pansies, floral monsters
in purple and black, blue and velvet brown, watching with
wicked pixie faces who came and went.

The rest of the block—a good hectare of it—gave the
appearance of bushland dropping steeply down to a distant back fence, until a second look showed it to be bushland speckled with exotica—orchids, rock roses, tropical
cacti and creepers and rushes that did not belong in this
southern climate, telling of husbandry with special soil
foods and expert tending. To me it looked a mess, even
though a dramatically effective mess, but out of keeping
with the familiar growths of the mountainside. Above all it
was a deliberate mess that probably seemed orderly in its

owner's eyes. I had to allow that Belinda's taste would extend to subtleties unapparent to mine. To me it was a colourful rubbish heap.

I moved slowly down to a point level with the middle storey, where an open balcony circled the whole building under the spreading bulk of the studio. Doors and windows suggested living quarters.

The ramp took me finally to the ground floor, which seemed to consist of no more than an entrance hall with a staircase plainly visible inside the open door and, opening from the side, glassed-in lounge.

From above, Belinda's voice startled me. "You're late. Fred will show you up."

I was late by just the two minutes wasted in dawdling my way down, delaying the inevitable. I could not see her. The place was probably salted with expensive gadgets designed to save her the trouble of everything but painting and breathing.

Fred waited at the door. He was another big man, taller than I and broad and plug-ugly and despite his years could have settled my hash with one hand.

The square, white entrance hall was just large enough to hold the staircase that wound out of sight in a narrow curve, and was absolutely bare of decoration. Only a door to the glassed-in lounge broke the starkness; it seemed Belinda was not one to adorn her house with her own creations. Yet a glance into the lounge caught quite a number of paintings in the massive gilt frames of earlier centuries; I had the rapid impression that these were very old pictures, relics of the centuries before the development of perspective.

I would have stepped inside to gain a better idea of a collection ill fitting my conception of an arrogant B Group artist but Fred grabbed my arm with no beg-pardon and swung me to face the stairs. "Up 'ere. She's waitin' for yer."

As a butler he was a dead loss. Aside from his manner,

his hair was uncombed and his face unshaven, his work shirt torn and none too clean and his hands grained with old dirt; I placed his real work as restraining the lower jungle from engulfing the place and his odd job as no-nonsense steering committee. As I climbed he spread himself across the bottom stair to leave me no option but upward and onward.

The total environment registered as a blunt means of throwing visitors off balance and keeping them so.

A single vertical window-strip lit the staircase, which made an unbroken progress from hall to studio with no landing or door to the middle floor. A sort of tradesmen's entrance.

Nor was there a landing at the top; I stepped straight from the last tread into the studio and stopped to take in the huge room.

Belinda was at the far end in a pool of daylight, her back to me while she worked at a canvas. Without turning she said, "There's nothing to gawk at. Come down here."

There was surely nothing to gawk at. Three hundred square metres or so is a large stretch of flooring—many houses are only a sixth of the size—and only the manipulation of light from the pseudo-silicate ceiling gave some sense of pattern. The end where I stood had an air of dereliction; it was almost lightless. About halfway down the interminable floor a patch of filtered daylight fell on three easels supporting what I took to be canvases, turned to the wall. At the far end Belinda worked at the focus of two beams of sunlight that printed her on the air like an intaglio burning against a dark ground.

That was all. Not a single picture hung in that matt-white expanse.

My steps were loud though I tried not to hurry, not to be minimised by size and emptiness. I had covered a third of the demeaning distance when she asked, still with her back to me, "What do you want?"

"To talk to you, of course. You know that."

"So, begin talking."

It was a commonplace technique of rudeness but I was unready for it and further put out by realising that I had forgotten my first imperative—to record. Between fumbling at my earlobe and scrambling for a sensible opening I fell into beginner's banality, gaping tyro with his first celebrity. "I expected to see your pictures here."

The words dropped dead in the vast space.

"Why?"

Indeed, why? "Traditional impression, I suppose. The conventional expectation."

"*Vie de boheme?*" Still she did not face me. "Canvases stacked against the wall, studio light facing north, smell of turps, scraggy model on greasy couch?"

"Not really. Just some pictures."

"A thing finished is finished with. Why should I have last week's work cluttering my eye today?"

She wore trousers and a long smock. The hair that I remembered as straggling was caught in a black scarf; perhaps she was working in some thin medium that splashed. "Why not? Are they dead as soon as you've completed them? The place has the personality of a tomb."

That was insulting but she only sighed, "Oh, hell!" and stretched her arm to fiddle with something behind the easel. "There! Feel at home."

In two seconds the walls came alive with paintings, exposed in a blaze as panels slid aside and the ceiling adjusted itself to flood them with filtered light.

I turned slowly, recording the treasure of four walls with the necklet as well as the deeper vision, not seeing in detail or attempting to see, simply photographing the presence of upward of a hundred paintings, large and small, bright and dark, complex and simple, in the knowledge that my father would, if it mattered, process each glimpse into a detailed reproduction. Asked to describe the collection I could only have muttered about abstraction and surrealism without much idea of what I meant and a certainty that the terms were inappropriate; there was nothing so familiar as a portrait or recognisable as a landscape in the whole display. Painting is not a consuming interest with me; I was and am one of the sturdy philistines who know what they like and like very little.

However, I was not there to discuss art and had no need to pretend more than casual interest. "This is your private collection?"

"Yes. Who else would want them?"

So this was the inspirational work, not the commercial product. "Posterity, perhaps."

"Bugger posterity. Art is communication; if it doesn't communicate, it's wasted. I'm left talking to myself."

I tried a mild irritant. "I'm told that all the really great artists were appreciated in their own time."

"Van Gogh, for instance? Sold one picture in his lifetime. But he was great."

Clever David, bowled first ball, but still trying. "Maybe, but I thought you people despised all art but your own."

"We despise critical ignorance. Van Gogh was great in his day, Rembrandt in his and others before them." That accounted for the pictures downstairs. "What do you know about art?"

"Virtually nothing."

"Then stop scratching for an opening."

She laid down her brushes and turned round at last. The ill-fitting trousers and smock made a bag of her; she looked like one of the women dressmakers despair of; she wore no makeup and the scarf round her hair inflated the line of her cheeks until she seemed a chubby cherub whose innocence vanished in a glitter of green eyes. At close quarters she was only a scrubbier version of the woman of the vidscreen—with a difference. It worried me until I located the thing wrong. "You were wearing glasses when I vidded you."

"So were you."

Carelessness. I had worn the glasses because that was how I wanted her to be accustomed to me, and had forgotten them when I entered the house. I affected nervous vagueness. "Was I? I wear them only for close viewing. Do I look different?"

"Should you? Is this our topic for the morning?"

"I'm sorry. I'm nervous. I don't know where to start with you."

"You have a right to be nervous. Is that why you carry a gun?"

The question startled me; I had forgotten I had the thing and echoed vaguely, "Gun?"

She pointed to my left armpit. "There." I made an attempt at good-humoured dismissiveness: "You shouldn't be able to detect it."

"What use would be an artist's eye that could not observe minute variations of shape and balance? Why do you need it? For notions of personal drama?"

Contempt could only be shrugged off. "Self-defence."

"Against whom? Masked enemies? Spies in the night? Have you ever shot anyone?"

"No."

"So you need target practice. Why not begin with your father?"

She was not smiling. "Are you serious?"

"Why not? Who would miss him?"

"I would."

She mocked, "Are you serious? Perhaps the time has passed; it is too old a story. We really need to know each other better."

She reached behind the easel to a dim bulk of objects in shadow and tossed me a folded canvas chair. "Sit down."

She opened another chair for herself and plumped down on it like a sack of potatoes, knees spread, elbow on knee and chin on elbow, eyeing me without enthusiasm or encouragement. "Start with yourself. Details."

The trouble with even a roughly prepared script begins when the other party attacks on an unexpected front. "Where do I start?"

"Beginnings. Your mother. Who was she?"

"No idea. I never knew her."

She laughed. "You're your father's son, aren't you? His psychic image, fish cold."

It was unfair but she gave me guilt like a stab in the dark. The ghostly identity had not seemed to matter when my father spoke of her. She had not mattered to him; he had spoken always as though I was the central figure in his stumbling affection. And I, grappling with my fairy-tale translation into son of a momentous man, had not questioned his priorities.

I became doggedly defensive, my shame with its back to the wall. "He didn't want to talk about her and I didn't try to force him."

"Poor, bereaved Daddy!"

Her mockery gave truth its day. "Not that. He didn't care." Having blamed him, I had now to justify myself. "I said I never saw her. She died in childbirth."

Her eyebrows shot up and for a moment she rocked, side to side, an image of silent laughter. "Did he tell you that?"

"Yes."

"And you believe everything Daddy tells you?"

No point in lying; she knew more about him than I ever would. "Not everything."

"That's in your favour."

"Is my mother still alive?"

She took her hand from under her chin and leaned

even farther forward. "No. He killed her. Or had her killed."

Rejection of that was automatic, a simple denial of such violence. "That can't be true."

She straightened up and became still again with the faintest of smiles, saying nothing.

With the denial done and silence in which to think, I *could* imagine him methodically ridding himself of a nuisance. He was capable of much that I was not. But to kill, undetected, is not easy now and was not easy then. Unpremeditated murder, followed by instant flight, may baffle the law hounds but any planned murder leaves a trace of some kind. "He would have been caught."

"He was."

On every day of this search reality shifted wickedly around me. I felt like a thwarted child as I tried to ward off the indefensible. "That would be on the Department file."

"Which you have seen?"

"No; I haven't that sort of privilege." But Jonesey had seen it when he checked my genetic match, and his dislike of my father had always seemed unreasonably beyond his spoken suspicions.

She sighed. "It's a corrupt world, little pilgrim. Someday the facts of life will overwhelm your cloistered Orphanage upbringing."

"You have checked me out?"

"Did you expect that I would not? Sam told me all I needed to know."

"Who's he?"

She told me, with a bright beam for my dismay, "Sammy Armstrong; who else?"

My shock was all she could have desired. I had thought that robot of greed and menace removed from the play, and here he was in unguessed alliance. "What's he to you?"

"Very little. Forget him—for the moment. Let us look

at you, the product of a specialised, rich man's Orphanage upbringing, old-time public-schoolish in its images of Uprightness and righteousness. You didn't learn much about realities."

"What's that to do—"

"Shut up!" She had the Nursery talent to dominate without effort when it suited her. "Running ragged in the gutters would have taught you about corruption but Arthur could not have used a streetwise brute. You would never have met him. That might have been best for you. As it is, you were the lucky accident he had been forced to acknowledge when he was arrested. He escaped punishment because he was and is the property of the State, just as I am and my sibs also, parts of an ongoing observation that will end only with our deaths. His ability to kill became an observed fact, neither punished nor psychologically corrected lest interference cloud the results. Nor should the public discover that a bold experiment in fostering genius had created a murderer. The public is too snugly sunk in stopgap moralities to realise that every living thing is a potential murderer. So, corruption and cover-up and the manufacture of lies! The valuable specimen was immune to punishment—and now he knew it. He had killed for fear of the population laws and now he knew that he was effectively above them. With reasonable care he could do as he pleased. Do you begin to understand your father?"

Such subversion does not penetrate fully at once; my main feeling was a wry satisfaction that all this was secretly printed on my skull for him to see and hear and answer.

I said, "No, nor you. I understand only that all you Nursery folk live in a world of lies."

"Aspects of truth," she said, making it a correction. "Sammy could have told you all this; he was the political godfather of the Nursery. I suppose he saw no reason to inform you. He is economical with data."

But he had not known my identity in time.

—while Jonesey would have considered silence better for my peace of mind

—and my father, busy with his role playing, sought only my good opinion

—and the Super, no doubt, felt that it did not count as "need to know."

All of them had a use for my ignorance. But what of this one, this Belinda? "Why do you tell me? What do you gain?"

She made a tiny clapping motion. "Better! Your brain is working. You want information about me, so I give some about you—an earnest of our collaboration." She leaned over to pat my knee, like an approving aunt. "You use me, I use you. Fair's fair."

"Is it? What am I to do for you?"

She stood, folded her chair and put it away behind the easel. "Give me your chair."

"You haven't answered me."

"The chair! I'll tell you when I think you're ready to do it."

I folded the thing and gave it to her. "That's not good enough."

"Don't be so urgent. I will prove my goodwill by giving you what you want."

"The full story of your association with Conrad?"

She stood pensively, the chair in her hand, ageing and dowdy, anybody's harmless charwoman—with a head full of secrets and steel-hard decision. "Do you really need all of that? For your book? Is the book real? Do you actually intend to write it?"

"I hope so. What else would I need?"

"The grail. Sammy's dream and Arthur's desire, the legacy that may or may not exist."

She brought it out as casually as every other revelation, laughing at me. "Surely you know Sammy told me that! He tells me everything."

"What's he to you?"

"Nothing at all—but he loves me. At any rate, he wants me. That's the same thing with him." With ugly waggishness she cupped hands under her breasts and swivelled her fat hips at me. "How do you see me as femme fatale?"

She meant to disgust me, and did. "So my father's Group aren't alone in rutting like rabbits."

"Oh, but they are! There's a gap of sophistication between rutting for relief and seduction for value received. My price to Sammy was high. Am I to blame if his foolish heart stayed in my uncaring little hand?"

Her blood ran with the same ice as that of everyone else in this degrading search.

I said, "I think you would be," and risked a remark no man in his right mind would make to a woman: "But you were a generation younger then and in better shape."

"By God, you are your father's son!" She was highly diverted, not at all put out. "Do you think he wouldn't fall for today's desiccated harridan? Don't believe it! I can get what I want now as easily as then."

Another who could "persuade"? I tried to put the thought away from me. "And what did you get?"

"Think!"

That was easy. "The distribution code for the recognition implants on the John Cuyper Library Access Card."

"Good, good! The reasoning?"

"Conrad had need and Armstrong could supply it. He was no longer in politics but he had the connections forged over three decades in unions, government, business and crime. Force, bribery, blackmail, he could call on all of it. He could have obtained the code from the operators themselves. He was aware of you and you knew it because you had had eighteen years to study him in his Nursery visits. So you marked him down."

The last was guesswork though not unlikely but she

shook her head. "I paid him no attention in the Nursery."

The obvious took its time rising to mind. "Conrad! He was the one who saw into people to play on their weaknesses. Conrad fingered him and you laid him."

"There, now! When you use your head you don't need me at all."

With so much new information to absorb and so many directions to follow as she led me by the nose, I could only say what came to mind.

I said, "Don't be so bitchy silly," releasing irritation, sure that she cared not a damn while she pursued her own ends. "And you're probably lying. Why should you have done it for him? Why should you have forged the Card for him or taken any interest?"

I doubted that she would let herself be provoked but trying anything once was better than not trying at all.

She clutched her breasts in infuriating parody and squeaked, "Infatuation! First love!"

She was too awful for laughter. "A and B Groups detested each other and the Cs hadn't a thought to waste on either of you. So why did you help him?"

She turned away. It was for only a moment but I felt that, briefly, she had not wanted me to see her face. Then, for a while, it seemed that she had changed the subject.

"Sam was here last night. I whistled and he came. He told me all he knows about you and your threadbare project. I did not tell him that the Card forgery had been detected." She smiled with the love of cool mischief. "That would have frightened the rest of his secondhand life out of him. Love or no love, he might have tried to kill the evidence—me. With fool's luck he might even have succeeded. As it is, he told me that you have spoken with the woman at Westerton and with the Farnhams. And you have yourself given me Cuyper's name." Her face grew sombre and she hesitated over words in a difficulty of expression, perhaps a rawness of feeling, saying with great unwillingness, "So you must know that Conrad could get what he wanted of people."

"He winkled out your sexual soft spot and stroked it." She did not answer and I pushed a little harder, "Like the rest of you he could drop his sexual fastidiousness when he wanted something badly enough."

She looked me up and down—literally—from toes to head and down again, without a twitch of expression before she said, "Your idiot book, if it is ever written, will have empty spaces at its heart. You see the minds of the Nursery Children through the distorting lens of your own. You have little idea of my needs and motives, even of Arthur's, and no conception of Conrad's. Conrad had no regard for me, none at all, and he never lowered his standard, for me or any other, for so much as a minute, a second. He did not consort with brutes. Conrad seduced me into love and never laid a hand on me. He made himself the sexual ideal he detected in me and he led me like a bitch on a leash, adoring and at call. He needed my services, not my worship, but he also needed to overcome my sibling dislike quickly. He was not ruthless. His need was great."

Through all this her voice held an arctic cold.

I could not hold the jeer out of my own. "How you all forgive him, the virgin stud!"

She said quietly, "You are disgusting but you cannot help that. He told me: Trap Armstrong into lechery, for his assistance—and I did."

"Conrad used everybody, loved nobody."

"What manner of thing are you to criticize him? He belonged to a humanity a million years distant. I think he had a special affection for Farnham but the man became a burden and was abandoned. I know that Conrad never degraded his body. Nor, for that matter, did I. Sammy never laid me, as you put it. He thinks he did. Conrad taught me that illusion. Among others."

There was a warning here but I was committed and could not order events. It was a small comfort that the truth of whatever might fool and trick my senses could be recovered later from the deep record.

"And, having taught you a little and taken what he wanted—the Card—he dropped you as he dropped all the rest."

"Think as you please." She returned to the easel. "Enough of Conrad. We must assess the other vast void in your foredoomed book, your total ignorance of aesthetics. Take off that necklet."

"Why?"

"I doubt you'll understand much of what I tell you, but I do not record my private techniques for the public domain."

"A pity but fair enough." I laid the necklet on the floor for lack of any other place. It had fulfilled its diversionary purpose.

"Now, look at this."

She indicated the painting on which she had been working. With most of my attention fixed on her I had gained only an edge-of-vision impression of white on an uneven surface and pale yellow circles expanding from the centre like an archery target. Now I saw that the canvas surface was not merely uneven but pushed out and in, haphazardly it seemed, so that the whole was a maze of ridges perhaps a centimetre high or deep over which the paint was spread like a pattern pasted on to follow the highs and lows.

I realize that this description is meaningless but the reality was meaningless to me, too, and so uninteresting that I had to fumble for comment and fall back on truth. "I don't react to it at all."

"I'm not concerned with your reaction. I want to show you some elements of technique so that in your writing you will at least know what the technical terms mean. And you can't inspect a canvas from that distance."

I moved closer. As naturally as I could, trying to make it appear an habitual action, I slipped the spectacle case from my pocket and put on the glasses.

"Now, look closely—just there."

She placed a finger on the centre of the painting where I could now see a small red spot. As I bent forward she whipped the glasses from my nose and on to her own, and faced me with the look of a disapproving schoolmistress. "I thought you might arm yourself with distorting lenses."

I mumbled about not wanting to fall into trance in the middle of a discussion.

"Your father bequeathed you no brains. Do you think I waste tricks on my personal work? The distorting techniques are very difficult but not to be wasted on serious painting. They are for fools who wouldn't know art from their elbows. For that work the shapes and colours have to be blocked in first in neutral tones that can be painted over. I wear glasses myself to apply the final colour. It requires an exact application to paint what the eyes *will* see as well as what they *should* see; I practised for nearly a year before I obtained saleable effects. Stupid stuff but it buys champagne and caviare." She added with something like irritation, "The early work was easily arrived at, but Conrad taught me greater illusions. That was his money-making gift for my assistance. Now, your lesson."

I bent forward again to her pointing finger, hesitated, then put the glasses on again.

She mocked, "Better sure than sorry!" I fixed my attention on the red spot. "The central position is simply a designer's signal that all the relationships in the picture are centrifugal or centripetal." Her finger moved, running

down a ridge zigzagging to a lower corner. "The uneven-
ness acts like a second theme in a musical composition. Do
you follow the analogy?" She continued, "You must learn
to interpret painting as you interpret music, holding con-
trapuntal concepts . . . But first the scumble technique. Do
you know what that is?"

"No."

"It is the application of a thin layer of a light colour
over a darker one, to modify the dark colour—soften it,
shade it, even sharpen it against contrasts. So, here is a
pure white background—or is it?"

On inspection, it was not. There were areas of white
on white, matt on gloss and streaks of an in-between white.

"See? You must practically stick your nose to the canvas to see the variations, but they affect the eye subtly at a
normal viewing distance. See how it deepens the effect of
the ridges, making them recede or project more than in
fact they do? Light is refracted in various directions
through the thicknesses of the scumble, giving different
effects at different angles of vision. If you sweep your eye
across the canvas you can receive a momentary effect of
billowing motion; that is one way of implying restlessness
on a still surface. Now you know why some artists' work
breathes life and in others it is static."

I tried moving my eyes across and back, then up and
down and there was indeed a mild impression of ripple
across the canvas.

"You see?"

"A little. A sort of latent movement."

"Good; I'm not wasting my time. Now observe the
yellow circles for a different use of scumble. Notice the
first—and at once it leads the eye from rim to rim and
upward to the next. And to the next. And at the outermost
there is a complex use of coats of varying thicknesses and
shades to somersault the eye back down to the red spot at
the centre. And that, you can see, has edges that disappear

under the white ground so that it spreads and spreads, growing larger and fainter."

And so it did. As simply as that, the trap was sprung. The technique was reversible. She had spent the whole night designing this picture to grip through protective glasses.

What follows here is reconstruction, not memory but an amalgam of vague recollection and deduction and later information. Call it a dream, if you like.

The red spot, I saw, had no defined edges. Under the white layers pale tendrils undulated gently, sweeping out from the centre to rise like tiny swimmers at the yellow edges of the first circle. Vision crossed the circle, leapt to the next and on and on until at the boundary of the canvas it fell back down the yellow cascade to the centre. Up and down and around, in fascination . . . Again and again . . .

I felt Belinda's hand and tried to shake it away, but she turned my head slightly, and suddenly the spot blazed. Its tendrils rose through the white ice; it was a primitive life form from a deep ocean, a crimson eye considering me without passion.

The canvas swooped forward and around me until I was enfolded almost at its surface, a consciousness moving like a gliding bird along its curves and crossings. The ridges and grooves were terrain, hillsides up whose gradients I glided to their summits, to plummet down the great gorges of their farther slopes.

I heard Belinda murmuring incomprehensibly but all my attention was held by the intricate, endless white landscape that beckoned and lured and never satisfied but swung into new vistas and fresh, untravelled directions.

She placed her palm, I think, across my eyes and I cursed her. She placed her finger on the red central spot as if to guide me, but my eyes were voyaging through white and yellow fields of ice, finding new signposts and decoys in tints so pale I could not name them.

I think that then she stood behind me with her hands flat to my skull and pushed my head forward with determined strength until my nose nearly touched the crimson eye that stirred in its dark depths and swelled and burned as I spiralled down into it. I floated at its heart.

All the time she muttered and murmured and it may be that some of the words penetrated my concentration because in my mind stirred an instinct of smouldering desire, of a love literally the colour of blood.

It was a strange idea and my body stirred to it although for me the colour of love had always been the deep blue-black of the night sky.

But there were more loves than one and more passions than tenderness and simple joining. A crimson love was an older love, humid and cloying. Excited, I felt erection rise against its confinement of cloth.

I sensed meaning beyond the competence of words, violence and possession beyond restraint. My limbs grew warm and tight with blood. And death rose up to tempt me—the ultimate explosion of the male mantis, the spasm of ecstasy as the female severed his driven head. My body gathered itself to spring to the act of love.

Awareness now was split between action and feeling but it seemed that Belinda came between me and the canvas, her head at the centre, her face towards me while the blood blazed all round her. I was not sure what I did or what time passed but I knew that I had taken off my clothes, that I was naked and burning.

Her wordless murmurings assumed the quality of spells, forcing me to look at and into her, down the years and their changes to the aching girl who had left the Nursery so long ago.

She had been lovely then. Nothing was lost. She was lovely still.

Imperatives entered my mind, piercing the tide of need. I tried to reject them, not seeing them clearly but experiencing glimpses of thought about death and loyalty and affection. I know that I spoke. My mouth said, "No, he did not do that," while my mind knew that he might well have done it. Done what? It slipped away from me. "He is my father." What that illuminated or justified was beyond me but it came up out of the darkness to be said.

I put out a hand to caress her lips but she smiled and withdrew and there followed a time of torture while I ached and she refused. Then she demanded and it was I who protested.

Something feather-fine touched and touched and touched the glans of my penis and I came close to choking in the effort to cry out, "Now! Now!"

At once I saw her entire and naked. My sight slid down from smooth shoulders over rounded breasts to a tender swell of stomach and the invitation of thighs. She touched me again and my body convulsed; I could not bear such touching. I stretched my arms.

Again the refusal and the aching and the demanding and the weakening resistance. She was beyond withstanding. Whatever she wanted, I would give it.

I cannot describe what I felt then or what my reaching limbs encountered but my body exploded in monstrous orgasm, endless paroxysm in the heart of red violence until a voice cried out in the exultation of stress overcome and ended, and I tumbled down a well of deep exhaustion.

I woke lying on a couch in the clutter of gear and fittings behind the easel. Below the edge of the canvas Belinda's solid legs were firmly planted; I heard the faintest *whish* of her brush making broad quick strokes. I sat up. She heard me and peered round the side of the canvas.

"Are you recovered?" The tone was perfunctory, the voice of one wanting to be rid of a nuisance.

"From what?"

"You fainted. You slept for three hours. Have you some disability?"

"Not that I know of." Does a fainting person remember the onset of the faint? I did not, but the thing had never happened to me before. Some physical projection of the stresses of the past weeks choosing its moment to manifest? She had been explaining the scumble technique. I had bent forward to examine a point on the canvas. It was possible to faint, I recalled, as a consequence of sudden bending . . . granted some prior imbalance in heart or head. But I considered myself healthy.

I said, "I'm sorry if I frightened you."

"Frightened? How? You fainted. People faint and the planet continues to spin." She returned to her work.

"Sorry, anyway, for doing the unexpected. And thanks for putting me on the couch."

"I didn't touch you. I called Fred; he is the household muscle. I—we—don't care for contact. You must know that."

Didn't touch? Something like a memory—or like a conviction of a thing heard or read—said that this was not so. She had touched—somebody—recently.

The thought flickered and went out as she said, on another tack, "Your father vidded me while you slept." She was not pleased about it.

"He did?" How could that be?

"He wants you to visit him—urgently."

Behind my mind a shutter opened and closed too quickly for me to recognise what lay there. It was lost. "I'll vid him."

"He said *visit* and he said *urgently*."

I grumbled to myself, "How could he have known I am here?"

"Didn't you tell him?" She put her head round the canvas again to say venomously, "I want to know who gave him my silent vid number. You?"

"No." Could Jonesey have been in contact and told him where I was?

"Then who?"

I guessed wildly, "The Super?"

"Unlikely but never fear, I'll ask him. He'll have to arrange a change of number. At once." She was working herself into a virago's temper. "And you can take this thing out of my home."

She handed me Jonesey's little gun. "It sprung from its clip when you collapsed. Why do you carry it?"

"It makes me feel—" There I groped for a word.

"Grown-up?"

That was too close for comfort. "This business has had its nasty moments and I like to feel capable of hitting back."

"At whom?" She was contemptuous. "Who carries a gun eventually finds a use for it."

"That doesn't have to be true."

"But it is. Who's your target?"

I snapped at her, "There's nobody I want to shoot." But there was. The shutter opened and closed on knowledge instantly covered up.

"Not even someone who has done you only harm?"

"There's nobody like that."

"Oh, lucky you! Fred tells me that the special brace you wear is called a slipster. Criminals use it for fast firing at close range. Are you someone's hired assassin?"

"You know who employs me—and it isn't murderous big-shot Sammy."

"Are you leaving now? You have the confirmation you came for."

I fitted the little gun back into its carrier clip and moved out from behind the easel. Doing so, I trod on my spectacles where they had fallen when I fainted, I supposed. "Damn!" One lens was shattered.

Belinda laughed. "You didn't need them, did you?"

No? A wisp of recollection was instantly denied. It was disturbing. I put the glasses in my pocket. "I still don't know why C Group committed suicide."

"Ask Sammy." Before I could protest she said, "Go away. You've had your interview."

"One more thing."

"For God's sake! What now?"

"Does the legacy exist?"

She laid down her brush, turned to me and appeared to come to a decision. "It exists. It is here. I'll show it to you if that will get rid of you. Little good it will do you or anybody."

There should have been a surge of triumph but the careless suddenness of the offer robbed it of drama, demoting it to a side issue. Perhaps in her view it was.

We crossed the studio floor to the three easels that stood alone facing the wall. One at a time she turned them about, explaining with sulky rapidity, "I painted these to Conrad's minute instructions. He sketched the designs and laid out the colour combinations and spatial relationships. I painted them like a child at one of those picture games where numbers must be connected to reveal the form. I had no idea what I had achieved or what the designs meant. I have little now."

As had I. The three canvases were roughly similar in that each featured something like a parallel-stemmed vine that moved diagonally across the picture ground; there were black and red and blue areas that the vine wound over and under, and sometimes there were gaps in the covering areas through which sections of the creeper-stems were exposed. After a while I perceived a shadowy second vine reflecting the twistings of the first.

I bent forward to see more closely and with the change

in the angle of vision the whole surface shifted into a new pattern wherein the bright and dim vines reversed their relationships, and ripples in the background proposed exchanges between them.

I stood straight and looked down and the colour values altered again. This was trick stuff on the grand scale but without any of the hypnotic effect of Belinda's commercial paintings.

I said, "Genetic relationships. The double helices and the messenger system. No—systems, plural. Seen from different—what? Points of view?"

"Even my ignorance divined as much. Or as little. Are you done?"

"Give me a moment."

The others seemed much the same save that one had a three-dimensional effect when viewed from the right and the other from the left. All modes of communication and contact covered in three dimensions? That would be for others to determine. I had the recordings; the rest would be up to my father.

Vague trouble stirred my mind at the thought of him.

"Are you wise now? A partner in the secrets of life?"

"Not my line. Somebody else may work it out someday."

"Conrad thought not. He said that a little child might follow it but no expert ever would."

One could reasonably trust Conrad, I supposed, to sow mines and booby traps. "Thanks for the interview."

"Make it last; there will be no other." I felt her eyes on me as I set out across the empty floor. As I reached the door at the head of the staircase she called, "Remember your promise."

I turned back. "I haven't promised anything." But I felt uneasily that something had passed between us and been forgotten.

She stood in midafternoon sunlight, framed by the

easel, middle-aged and dowdy, stocky and foursquare and not hiding contempt. "You will remember when the time comes."

"What are you talking about?"

For a fraction of a second I knew but could not grasp anything so fleeting. She turned back to her painting—not the same picture, something grey and pallid—and would not answer.

At the foot of the stairs Fred opened the door and farewelled me in his fashion. "I don't like people wearing slipsters. They make killing too easy."

Confidence returned with the sight of open air and daylight. I said, "They're meant to, aren't they?" and started on the long climb to the gatehouse while beside the path the pixie faces of the pansies made snide pretence of knowing all that had passed.

Jonesey was a problem requiring consideration—for reasons as hazy as they were obscurely urgent—but he started on me at once as the car ran downhill. "You had a hell of a long session. What were you getting, her life story?"

There was to be no time for consideration. "Most of it, and a lot of interesting stuff about Conrad."

I had three things uppermost in mind. One: I had three hours to account for, in detail. Two: The hours of sleep could not be disclosed to a Jonesey whose hair-trigger suspicions would assume foul play and give no credence to a simple faint. Three, and most importantly: I must get to the Nursery without delay.

Accounting for the three hours required only invention; I rehearsed events to myself, time spent in explaining pictures, being shown over the house . . .

"Aren't I to be told what happened?"

I said quickly, because it was a stress in my mind, "The necessary thing is that I have to get to the Nursery right away."

"Why?"

"My father wants me there immediately."

He was incredulous. "How do you know that?"

"He vidded Belinda while I was there."

The improbabilities crowded in as soon as I had spoken and Jonesey saw all of them at once. "*He* vidded *her?* The Groups haven't spoken to each other in years, don't recognise each other's existence. What the hell's going on?"

"He wanted me, not her."

"So how did he know you were there? And how did he have her number?"

One mistake after another. "He tried to get me at home and when I wasn't there thought I might have gone after Belinda. It shows how urgently he wants me." I thought that last touch was clever.

Jonesey ignored it. "The number! How?"

"She asked that, too—pretty annoyed about it—but he wouldn't say." I grasped at the only possibility in my reference, "He must have got it from the Super," and realised at once that Jonesey could check that by the car vid. More as diversion than information I returned to my father's urgency. "He wants me out there as fast as I can made it."

"Why?"

"He didn't tell me; you know what he's like. He wouldn't talk in front of her."

"What was their attitude to each other?"

"Cold. Polite."

He asked again, to himself, "What the hell goes on?"

"Will you take me to the Nursery?"

He laughed. "I surely will, lad. I wouldn't miss a bar of this. The further you go, the worse it tangles."

"In any case, I have something for him, too."

"Such as?"

"The legacy."

He drove for a while in silence; then his comment was, "So it's real."

"You always believed in it."

"Did I? I had to tell myself to believe in it or all this would have been pointless nonsense. Have you got it with you? What is it? A notebook?"

I tapped my skull. "It's here—a complete record from all possible angles."

"Angles?"

"It's a triptych of paintings. Conrad told her what he wanted and Belinda painted them."

He crowed like a rutting rooster. "The game's over!"

"Don't bet on it. The paintings are riddles and hidden meanings. And it's possible that Armstrong's still a player; she says he knows why C Group killed themselves."

"Round and round in bloody circles!"

"He's her boyfriend, after a fashion."

He flung me a disbelieving glance, chewed the idea over like something rancid and asked, "What does after a fashion mean?"

"I don't quite know. There's trickery involved. He thinks he beds her but in fact doesn't. Something Conrad taught her, she says."

"What now? Witchcraft? You'd better start from the beginning."

At least he was not checking the vid number with the Super. I gave him a long invention, stretching every little incident and exchange, introducing a meal we had not eaten, making much of examining paintings and learning technical details. I hesitated at the incident of the gun, was on the verge of mentioning it when one of those flashes of recollection or understanding or whatever they were put a wary clamp on my tongue. The gun seemed best not brought to notice.

Then I found that Jonesey forgot nothing, least of all unanswered questions. When he was sure he had his facts in order he called the Department on the dashboard vid.

Almost indecently, my luck held. The Super was not in his office—and no, he could not be contacted while he was making his weekly report to the Cabinet.

"Shit!" Jonesey left a callback message and told me savagely that only the Super had the decision status to override the information ban on a Group number. I was relieved enough to suggest that my father might have his own sources of proscribed information, as Armstrong had.

"He might be Little Lord Jesus, too, but he isn't." By now we were close to the inner city perimeter and he switched to the outer ring road to skirt the busy areas at speed. "Nursery, here we come, needing answers. A lot of answers."

Something deep inside me said that the answers would come too late, but it was a thought below the level of overt thought, so to speak, and it vanished unexplained.

It had been nearly two o'clock when we left the mountain; the sun was still high as we entered Westerton. We were through the township in moments and alone on the highway when the vid beeped and spoke an identification code in the expressionless tone electronically flattened to defeat speaker identification by band scanners. "I have a callback from you."

"Yes. A-Grade One used a silent number today. Did you give it to him?"

"No. Anything else?"

"We have the bequest the heirs are waiting for."

"Indeed. Very good." The circuit removed any elation the Super may have felt. "Where are you?"

"Crechewards. Close to."

"Understood. Anything else?"

"No."

"Be careful. Keep in touch. Out."

Jonesey sucked in a long, slow breath. "That Daddy of yours will have to talk much and fast."

I didn't dare a word; I had been negotiating mine fields.

We drew up outside the locked gates of CAG 3 and the closed-circuit eye swung onto us. Whatever signal it passed, the laboratory did not at once answer. When finally it did, we were not welcome.

My father's voice bellowed, "What the devil do you want? We're busy here! Work can't stop for every—"

He broke off as I stepped out of the car, placing myself between Jonesey and the eye. "I'm here because you bloody well sent for me!" I gave the eye a large, slow wink. I could depend on him to be quick on the uptake.

He was. "There was no urgency. Still, now you are here..."

"I have the legacy."

He did not reply. The gates slid apart.

We pulled up by the steps of the porch as the tall form in a laboratory overall came to meet me. For once an emotion could be identified in him, something close to excitement.

The shutter behind my mind opened—and stayed open. I knew why I had come to the Nursery. I had remembered when the time came.

I went lightly up the porch steps as he said in his stolid fashion, "This is excellent news."

Oh, the orgasm and the promise! Remembered now.

I told him, "But not for you, Father," and saw his sudden puzzlement turn to shock as I slipped the little gun from the fast-draw clip and at a distance of a single pace shot him through the head.

Jonesey must have reacted without thought. His kick broke my elbow before I could fire again and the gun flew somewhere out of sight and out of mind.

My father turned slowly as he crumpled and I screamed with frustration and despair as the left cheek exposed the little scar that identified him as Andrew.

I dropped to my knees, howling because I had failed the woman who had given me the supreme experience of my life. There Jonesey held me with all his weight and strength until people came, though I fought, one-armed and yelling, until the needle jabbed without kindness into my neck.

There is a moment between sleeping and waking when dream and consciousness mingle and are confused, when the fine strand of dream dissolves as reality intrudes and the dream returns to the darkness.

Most often these waking dreams fade quickly from memory; life takes over and the day begins.

Not always. Some wake up sweating or shaking or weeping. I woke up howling, a lunatic sound, they told me; my aunt Astrid said that if she believed in Hell she would have thought I was tumbling into it, wailing the loss of a soul all the long way down.

The dream came out of darkness into its own reality of desires and perfections. I stood naked and looked down on her shoulders and breasts and the last entry of blood-red need, and relived the moment ecstatic and anguished and triumphant beyond human achievement.

The sheer physical tension of the reliving woke me and in the moment between the mind and the world the other reality appeared. Her lovely young face crumbled to middle age and plump flesh and greying hair as she laughed at me with the malignance of an illusionist whose deceptions are complicated and cruel. Inexplicably, she was fully dressed in smock and baggy trousers while I stood naked and stupid and degraded on the skewer of her enmity and contempt.

Memory supervened—Andrew's scar and the terror of failure and myself flailing and yelling in the horror of error and the betrayal of trust.

I was fully awake then and struggling, in flight from

both reality and dream, with Jonesey scarcely able to hold me down, panting and forcing and bringing his knees up to pin my straining arms.

Then there was Astrid with a needle and a swift stab into a vein.

I heard Jonesey say as his voice receded down an infinite tunnel, "If his mind's damaged I'll kill that murderous bitch."

It was the same each time I woke until at last the hypnotherapist came. He had to work, at first with great difficulty, through and over the sedative drugs that calmed my hysteria and terror; it took him four days to bring me to the point where I could face the real world without lapsing into manic despair.

12 • INTERVAL—WITH JONESEY

David knows almost nothing of the four days except by hearsay. Most of what happened to his body and mind was shunted into the mental dark by those automatic censors that deny access to things intolerable to the sanity. I don't doubt that a lot of that shunting away was urged on by Santiago (we'll come to him) but there were other things happening in CAG 3 that he could not know about until he was ready to return to our rotten, demeaning game.

I had to realise that all my cocksure handling of human beings, all my knowledge of them, counted for nothing against the reality of a man grovelling in the pit of his own consciousness. The broken arm was the least of it; the broken mind was bad but could be cobbled together, set back in order; the broken life was the sickening thing, flayed of all its protections and crying out every anguish of its twenty-five years . . . the mother whose absence had lain smothered in the cellars of consciousness . . . the father who came like a gift of God only to recede into an enigma . . . Belinda, who offered paradise—and in a limited, momentary sense delivered—but exacted a lifelong price . . .

the Orphanage that had seemed to be the real world but was too soon recognised as no more than a refuge from the hard eyes outside . . . the world itself, where he crouched in corners, wearing his camouflage of adult confidence while he looked out, ignorant and disoriented, on masks and lies.

By night and day the body slept—without rest—while mind and dreams howled aloud at both darkness and light.

I stayed beside him through the worst of it, miserably unhelpful, because the total self-absorption of the others had to be denied, if only by my clumsy manning of the post.

The Super arrived on the first night, savage at what the Group machinations had led to, but saying little because they operated beyond his brief to punish effectively. He saw that David's case was desperate but he banned outside help. Astrid, he said, would have to nurse him, though her activities as a surgeon covered only a theoretical knowledge of nursing. In any case she was useless and after a day of ill temper and badgering I persuaded him to bring my wife up from Melbourne to take over. Elaine had had nursing experience and was, after all, an occasional employee of the Department. Until then I had to deal ineptly and squeamishly with the excremental problems that afflict the helpless. Astrid refused, flatly, to assist there.

A frustrating experience began when Arthur put the transfer cup to his sedated but moaning son's forehead and ran a long lead out to the vidscreen three rooms away, where closed doors shut out fits of raving and weeping.

I went along to discover what had caused this collapse but didn't learn much. What we saw was more or less what you have read in David's account of what passed in the studio and it showed more puzzles than clues. The record was clouded and distorted by a ghostly simultaneous action, impossible to discern accurately, hovering behind and through the visual like a spectral double exposure. It began when he leaned forward to the white picture with yellow circles and persisted, like a washed-out remnant, until he lost consciousness. This coloured background doppelganger had its complement in sound, an almost subaural mutter erupting only now and then into speech.

I guessed, and Arthur confirmed, that the background stuff was the true record of what had occurred but that a controlled mind had been able to see and hear only as wispy peripherals. Reality had impinged at deeper levels.

"The factual record can be recovered," said Old Greeneyes in his flat way. "Technically, not difficult."

He became practically invisible for a couple of days while he worked on the recovery.

David's version of what he saw was curiously unevocative. His vision of a young Belinda should have been really startling to cause the unrestrained sexuality of his gasping and choking response but was in fact very much the picture of an ordinarily pretty girl with her clothes off. But what rouses Bill leaves Bob cold and we did not suffer the urgings that, presumably, lay in the subauditory muttering. Evan Farnham would have spoken of the right psychological buttons being pressed; there's a different console for each of us.

Arthur insisted that the clues were plain, but what they were he kept to himself as he went off to the workshop.

Elaine stood four hours of the upheaval of terror and primeval shock from David's depths before she told the Super that he must bring in a psychiatric hypnotist or risk total disintegration of the patient.

He resisted and argued, and shouted with anger when she told him she would herself brief the news media on the nature of the monsters bred in Departmental secrecy, himself included, and the threat to risk breaching the Secrecy Acts frightened him because no cover-up could be so complete as to prevent some ministerial people getting wind of trouble. That could put his job on the line.

He came raging to me to ask did I think she meant it and I told him that she certainly did and that I (sweating) would back her. His response of blazing silence told me that my future with the Department had just dropped dead. I was too angry to care until later.

That good-humoured, tubby little man was quite capable of leaving an expendable David to rot, until he was convinced that doing so would buy him more trouble than his job's security could risk.

Within twenty-four hours Dr. James Santiago was sworn in, threatened with all the relevant Acts, briefed and in CAG 3.

For half a day he only watched and listened—and, I suppose, planned his attack. Then he demanded to be shown the interview with Belinda. It seemed to rock his self-possession. Finally he wanted David's life history, of which I probably knew as much as anybody.

When I had told him what he needed, he asked me, "Are you prepared to look after him?" and I said, "Yes," not realising what he had in mind.

"Because," he said, as though it explained everything (which I suppose it did), "he has no one else to turn to."

There was something in that; in all his raving David had shown no sign of trust in anyone but myself (and I had worked professionally hard to get it) and even that was a kind of love/hate asking for a response that the careful Jonesey persona had kept dangling, ungiven.

Santiago said, "A surrogate is better than none at all," and I saw where my tongue had landed me.

"You mean a sort of stand-in father?"

"Just so."

"No! I wouldn't know where to start."

He fixed me with pale, patient eyes and pointed out that I had done my share of rearing two children.

"That was different. David's twenty-five."

"Not so different. He is disastrously deficient in worldly experience and an emotional adolescent. He needs guidance."

"You need an expert."

"Yes. A no-nonsense character like yourself."

Elaine, sitting on the edge of the bed while the spasms of speech and crying went on beside her, laughed at the description but said to me, "You have your share of responsibility for what has happened to him."

She wasn't being wifely or unsympathetic; she was being determined, and she is not one to relinquish a point easily. She would have risked execution and taken me with her. So I said nothing to an argument I was bound to lose and Santiago took consent as read. He began to discuss with her the necessity of steering David, as soon as possible, towards a carefully selected girlfriend . . . an experienced woman . . . maybe a little older than he . . . They went at it like a couple of old hens over the teacups, but when she suggested that he seemed sure of a successful treatment he showed himself something less than that.

"What we see here is a manifestation of psychic shock, the equivalent of a paralysing punch to the solar plexus of someone who has never been badly hit before. The result has been, in simple terms, to shatter his psychic defences, which are often more flimsy than people guess. Usually they rebuild themselves, more or less effectively. The mind is astonishingly resilient."

I asked, "And if they don't rebuild?"

"We shan't think of that yet. The dementia of the lost soul is abysmal. My task is to establish a mental equilibrium in order to let healing processes begin. To carry it on will be your business, Mr., er—"

"Jonesey. No mister."

"Just so. Your business will be to provide him with a normal human point of contact and trust by which he can assess and judge others. He believes in nobody save, a little, yourself, so you must become his lifeline."

"You can bring him through?"

"Probably. I think so. Only a fool promises a miracle." He became businesslike: "Now we start by bringing him to full consciousness." He smiled thinly. "I must depend on you to calm him physically."

Three minutes later I had a raging demon on my hands, broken arm and all, screaming and clawing and using its body like sprung steel.

Exhaustion came none too soon, with me close to the end of my ability to hold him. He seemed to recognise me then and put his head on my chest to cry, not quietly but in lunatic hysterics.

"Promising," Santiago said. I'd have had more than mere trouble handling a case that wasn't.

Elaine chose the moment for light comedy. "Percy is useful for this sort of thing. He is very strong."

Santiago surveyed me, red-faced and holding a squalling madman to my unloving chest. "Percy?"

Perce I can stand but Percy suggests unmanly shames.

"It's his name." Santiago offered her a polite smile while I turned my back to let David down on his pillow.

Now that it is all in the past I can confess—a good word for it—that the whole string is Percival Julian Fairley (God forgive my mother's taste in romantic fiction) and I still wish that after forty-odd years of marriage Elaine could get over finding it so happily incongruous. Her standing joke is that it fits me like somebody else's skin.

Now you know why I chose Jonesey as an alias. It

makes me feel human. Percy etc. is a side of me that never quite believed in itself.

Psychiatrists, particularly the technological, electro-probing kind, made me think of torture chambers, while psychiatric hypnotists gave me the crawling feeling that witch doctors were real and at work among us. Then, grudgingly, I had to admit that Santiago was gentle, human, unfussy and efficient.

"In four days, yes or no," he said, and went at it with drugs and a hands-on soothing technique that I had not known was in the hypnotic bag of tricks.

In a matter of hours he broke the hysterics down to a kind of crazy loneliness, a dreadful depression of stillness and empty eyes. It was bad but better than the incessant terror. At least there now seemed room for the man to move back into the shell of his mind.

Through long sessions Santiago sat by the head of the bed, muttering into David's ear with an occasional pause to examine him and nod to himself over minute changes I could not recognise.

When I moved closer to listen in he motioned me away. "Leave us alone. The bed of the mind is blocked with the detritus of a lifetime, sewage that must be cleared away. You don't want to know these things of a friend."

I went, but I did want to know; there's an urge in all of us to uncover the horrible—in somebody else. You tell yourself that you can know the worst of a friend and it won't matter. But it will. To know all about somebody is to be forced to recognise a repellent stranger—and maybe yourself. Santiago was right to warn me off.

On the second day the improvement was remarkable; David's colour was nearly normally white instead of congested and mottled, he was able to smile instead of grimace, he even ate some food, but there were still crying fits between the sessions of hypnosis. During one of these Santiago pushed me to the bedside. "Take his hand. Hold it."

I picked up the slack fingers, not prepared for him to fling himself at me and cling like a drowning man. I tried to break his grip gently but he only clung the tighter. Santiago signalled, *Let him hold on.* What could I do? I'm not one for close physical contacts and emotional displays make me nervous, but I had to let him cling. Quite suddenly he was asleep and I could set him down.

"I hate this."

"You are all he has just yet. He trusts nobody else."

The implications were horrendous. Surrogate fatherhood I could endure as a matter of giving advice, setting the lad straight about the world's realities, but the emotional fixation of a son twenty-five years old was beyond me. "I thought that patients tended to fixate on their analysts."

"I am not analysing; I am bolstering basic psychic strengths and taking great care that he does not fixate on me." He offered a little sugar to my sullenness: "It will be for a while only. Soon he will be normal and feel as embarrassed as you. Meanwhile . . . please be father."

I told Elaine about it when I got her alone and all she said was, "It will do Jonesey good to unblock his feelings a bit."

In all our years I had not known that she felt like that about me. Nor did I easily accept the hint that Jonesey was not an alias but a hiding place.

On the third night, just before he went to sleep, a fairly tranquil David asked after Andrew. "Did I kill him?"

"No."

He shook with relief. "I missed? So close?"

He was urgently guilty about it, wanting me to say yes, but Santiago had told me that while information might be suppressed, direct questions should be answered and no lies told.

"No, you hit him—in the right arm."

"Arm? But I aimed . . ." He was thinking of something like a near miss over the ear. "I couldn't have."

"You could, you did. On a fast draw you couldn't hit a bloody barn door."

He managed a grin, faintly relieved, faintly mortified, and settled down for the night.

People who have never used a handgun watch the shenanigans of vidplays and think that all you have to do is point the thing and count the corpses. That is only half true; the trick lies in pointing it in the right direction, and if you are untrained, hysterical and in a hurry, the right direction is rarely where your arm thinks it is. There are two common methods of aiming a pistol (aside from the two-handed Magnum grip); one is to bring it up to the target at shoulder level, the other to bring it down. With an armpit slipster neither of these is practicable; you have to draw across the body and fire in a single movement without conscious aiming, which is why a slipster can be used only for a small, light gun. Anything with a decent-sized bore would slow you up and possibly kick itself out of your grip. You learn reflex aiming only by hours of practice as against the twenty minutes or so David had played with it, until snapping it on to the target is second nature, the hand doing what it is told without the checking of the eye. Otherwise all you get is a lesson in how to miss at point-blank range—by as much as a yard.

David hit Andrew by accident as much as design and it is a wonder that the small round knocked the man over. He probably fell down in sheer surprise.

It was a mildly comic outcome of what had been intended as tragedy and the joke was ultimately on Belinda who had taken David's proficiency on trust; it would not have occurred to her ignorance of firearms that a determined murderer could miss. Murder takes planning; you can't just throw it together at a moment's notice while introducing a sucker to trick painting. You need knowledge as well as brains.

Andrew I saw once or twice with his arm in a sling. He did not come near David though his brother and sisters spent an hour or two observing and discussing in a private linguistic shorthand.

By now the Group was making no pretence of friendliness; they regarded all our presences as an insult to their privacy. They tried to behave as though we did not exist but on one of the rare occasions when I was able to attract Arthur's impatient attention I queried him on Andrew's lack of interest in the man who had shot him.

"He feels it best to stay away."

"So as not to upset David?"

"Don't be a fool, Jonesey. Andrew is very angry." He started to leave, then added as though I might not have understood, which indeed I had not. "A bandaged arm might not have prevented him doing violence to that incompetent pawn."

Behind those still faces raged the commonplace and unjustified human furies of resentment and revenge. Interesting. More interesting was the absence of any pretence of affection for David; he had been used up, had found the legacy for them and now was making a damned nuisance of himself. Masks were no longer needed.

Now was the opportunity for another question that had irked me and the Super also: "Why did Belinda wait all those years for revenge? Why the sudden urge?"

"She did not wait, nor was her motive revenge. She is intelligent; she knows that a thing once done is done forever and revenge is waste. But once she linked David with me, she knew what I must want and she set herself to protect the triptych; it was all that was left to her of the most powerful event in her life. She loved Conrad abjectly. Think of Farnham and imagine the nature of the sexual shackles placed upon her. She was—is—in that area, mad. She could not allow her sacred relics to be taken from her."

On his fourth morning Santiago viewed Arthur's "recovered" version of the studio recording. Only he and the Super were present and both were tight-lipped about it afterwards. Santiago conceded that what Belinda had done made child's play of professional hypnotic techniques but would give no details. The Super said only, "It's dangerous stuff that will have to be kept quiet. You'll have a chance to see it later."

"Later" seemed to mean when David was judged strong-minded enough to relive the experience. That sounded to me like aversion therapy run wild but Santiago said it was necessary.

That same afternoon David was wholly rational, out of bed and eating like a horse. The next morning he seemed completely normal. It was miraculous, though I couldn't say so to his satisfied face. I could, however, ask Santiago what he had done, to be told that the case had been much simpler than the violent symptoms had made it appear.

"Catharsis was complete to the point of mental and physical exhaustion, simplifying all approaches. No resistance. All the main elements of trouble were highly visible and audible and attested by the facts of his life history, so it was not like a protracted analysis where details have to be ferreted out in the face of every kind of confusion, self-justification and outright lying. I had a small group of basic hard facts, a clearly attributable trauma and a straightforward course of action. Hypnotic persuasion was the element of acceleration to the healing. And Jonesey, whoever he may really be, was the solid ground in the mental quicksand. All in all, a classic operation."

The final compliment was designed to send me off

with a glow of self-esteem, but like every ignoramus I wanted to think I really understood it all.

Santiago was kind enough not to sigh at the impossibility of the request and it turned out that he had the gift of scaling explanation down to idiot level. "In your business," he said, "you would be aware of the uses of forensic hypnotism."

"We don't trust it. You get answers to your questions but it can't suggest the questions you didn't know should be asked. And those answers can make the ones you do get look unsatisfactory."

"There's truth in that but you shouldn't feel that the hypnotist is only a psychiatric dentist extracting answers from a subconscious jaw." He went on to tell me what he had done with David. I had no hope of remembering all of it but it went something like this:

Analytical techniques had commonly been used to open up a patient's areas of forgetfulness and submerged promptings, but the new breed of analyst recognises that the opening-up procedure can be reversed; selective forgetfulness can be cultivated to distance the impact of guilts and traumas. It isn't a matter of inducing complete forgetfulness, because that would interfere with the essential process of learning from experience; it is more like attenuation, or like storing junk in the attic so that you know where it is when you need it, without having it forever troubling the forefront of your mind.

He had sorted through David's traumatic junk, so to speak, and put some of it where it wouldn't gibber at him every time things went wrong. His present traumas were humiliation over the outcome of the sexual episode with Belinda (which, I can tell you now, was nothing to what was to come) and guilt over the shooting, but these were only exacerbations of the general alienation that all of us had had a hand in bringing to a head.

Santiago's "line," as he expressed it, had been to steer

the lad's preoccupations into productive directions and to prop up his self-confidence. After which, he said, carrying on would be my job.

That brought me down to earth. "It could take years!"

"Perhaps months. No more."

"I'd have to have him in my home."

"Perfect."

"No!"

"Your wife is agreeable."

So he had already been at Elaine. Sly! "She would be! But I can't have him hanging to my coattails indefinitely."

"Not indefinitely, and I doubt that he will snatch at your coattails. My final implants will be encouragements to self-sufficiency. Your role will be as a buffer against occasional doubt and failure. He will learn to trust other people and himself and soon will no longer need you."

I walked headfirst into that trap, grumbling that I wouldn't want to lose touch with the lad altogether.

"You won't," said Santiago and then, with the flattest of deadpans, "sucker."

Elaine and he would have made a good party act.

That night after tea he sprang one of his nastiest surprises. "I want you to sit with David while we run the Belinda tape for him."

I felt queasy about it. Heroic measures can be effective, but this sounded too much like a suicide charge.

"Not so. You don't realise how far he has become emotionally distanced from the events. He should be ready now to see precisely what happened to him and to react to it as an intelligent, balanced man. It will be more of a clinical exercise than you can guess at this stage."

After four days of intensive concentration he was yet patient enough to soothe my uninstructed layman's doubts. What Arthur had done was an extension of classical tape engineering techniques that I make no pretence of understanding. It hinged on the fact that the imprint on David's skull recorded both the urgent and the peripheral. The hypnotised David in the studio had seen what Belinda had bedevilled him into seeing, and this was the major visual element on the tape Arthur had taken from the internal record, but his eyes had also seen the reality of Belinda while his brain was tricked into viewing it as only a spectral presence. So there were two Belindas on the imprint, a radiant and beautiful fake and a dowdy frump reduced to a shadow by misdirection. Arthur had split the recording into two tapes, one showing what David thought he saw, the other what was in fact there. The shadowy "other" he had brought up to strength by computer enhancement. He had done the same with the sound track; the major track was the incoherent mumbling broken by a few words; the minor track, enhanced and magnified, held what the woman had actually been saying.

We were to view the split tracks on screens set side by side, illusion and reality in counterpoint, but Santiago didn't propose to leave it as a simple display. "It could be unwise simply to throw it at him. I will put a clinical gloss over the viewing—stop and start at key points, give psychiatric explanations, real or invented, where reactions are unclear and insert quick lectures to blunt sharp implications. Ideally, he should observe as though his figure in the drama is an exemplary someone else."

All planned to a hair but not wholly convincing to my memory of howling despair. "And if he isn't distanced enough, what then?"

He opened up a big friendly smile to his drafted sucker. "He will have his solid rock sitting beside him, ready to stop the exhibition at a bad reaction. But make sure it is a bad reaction, not just jumpiness."

It still seemed a touchy setup, but at the same time I was itching to see what manner of sorcery Belinda had worked.

13 • THANKS FOR NOTHING

Through the days of delirium I did not know what Santiago was doing to me. I did not know who he was; most of the time I did not know he was there. If what Jonesey has written is a fair description, I must have spent a season in nether Hell, but I came out of it with no memory of suffering; I came out of it like a marathon runner who has reached his limit and gone the impossible distance beyond it, physically exhausted, sore in joints and muscles but knowing that rest and a night's sleep would see all that training bring me back to normal. For training read Santiago. What he did was magical; Jonesey's account details the movements but misses the miracle.

I came to with a complete memory of what had passed in Belinda's studio and on the CAG steps but it was a strangely distant memory, as of heartbreaks long ago that had lost their power to hurt. Yet it had been less than a week . . .

When Santiago told me of the split tapes, told me, too, that there were subliminal visions there that had been computer enhanced to terrible clarity and that I must see and outface them, I was not concerned. From somewhere had appeared an immense self-confidence, a trust in my own strength of mind. Santiago must have accomplished that. The more I think back to him, the more inexhaustible seems his repertoire of cobbling and patching.

He said that the experience of seeing the truth of Belinda, and some truth of myself, might be disturbing, even traumatic, though he had done what he could to buffer me against it.

"Bring on truth," said I, light-headed with confidence. "We could do with some around here."

"I agree, but it will be unpleasant. Still, Jonesey will be with you."

"To hold my hand? I don't need him."

"You have needed him all along. Be less ungrateful."

"I love Jonesey but I don't need him. I don't need anybody."

"There is no such human condition as not needing anybody. Think about it."

I didn't waste time thinking of any such thing; I was looking forward to truth.

Euphoria eventually fell a notch or two and in the end I decided that I did need Jonesey; there was literally nobody else in the world I trusted with my whole heart—well, most of it. I did not need my father. That at least had become clear in my tunnel view of events that seemed so removed from emotion. After what had happened there was little chance of his needing me; he had what he wanted, the triptych, and I would be of no further use. I did not resent him but it was a relief to be free of having to determine an attitude towards him. Like Belinda's studio, he was in the powerless past.

When Jonesey came, in early evening, to see if I was ready for the tape showing, he was full of gossip. "The Super's here with a swag of Special Police escorts."

"Escorts for whom?"

"Belinda for one." He was watching to see if the name made me jump, but why should it? "And that big triple painting from her studio. Arthur and Andrew have been poring over it all the afternoon."

"Two happy conspirators, one slightly damaged. Anybody else?"

"Armstrong. They showed the Super the tapes and he had him roped in right away."

"Great man bites the dust."

"Maybe." He peered suspiciously at me. "You're very bloody chipper for a sick boy."

"On top of the world. Let's go to the movie house and get good seats. But the audience will be the real show, won't it?"

Except for Santiago we were first into the big workroom that had been cleaned up and rearranged as a theatrette with the two smaller screens (about two and a half metres by one and a half) set side by side on the end wall. I imagined my father supervising the destruction of his reference systems in murderous fury.

I counted eighteen chairs. "A gathering. The Super is going to fire scattershot, is he? Or are you the entrepreneur, Doctor?"

Santiago smiled with professional enjoyment. "My role is limited to voice-over; the Superintendent will be master of ceremonies." He went on to discuss the semicircular arrangement of the chairs. "Jonesey, I want you and David on the far wing, where everybody entering will see him from the doorway and from where he will be able to see the whole room; the reactions of others may be useful to his own overview of the proceedings. He should have no serious difficulties, unless . . . ." He seemed momentarily in doubt and asked Jonesey, "Do you think he would attack Belinda?"

I asked, "Why should I?" but Jonesey told him, "David's not the bruiser type but I wouldn't put it past him if push comes to shove. He's on a bit of an up kick right now, so who knows?"

"Keep an eye on him."

I said, "I'm here, too. I can answer questions about me."

Santiago's smile returned, wide and beatific. "So you can, David, but you are a free agent while Jonesey needs some idea of what may be asked of him."

"Like stopping me trying to throttle Belinda?"

"Or Belinda trying to murder you."

"Are you serious?"

He nodded and Jonesey said, "I haven't seen those tapes but I've got a fair idea what's on them." He put on his shark grin for me. "So be a good boy."

Jonesey's diagnosis of my mood must have been near the mark. I *wanted* to see those tapes, to see what nastiness had been hidden from me; I looked forward to them. The adrenaline must have been pumping. We took our seats on the extreme right of the front row and my excited expectation started me babbling. "I haven't a clue what to expect. Not a whisper."

Jonesey murmured, "Santiago says there are some funny bits you mightn't laugh at."

"Stop worrying. This is only a reconstruction of something half forgotten."

I think he was about to deny that but Belinda came through the door and our attention fixed on her.

She was accompanied by two tough-looking escorts ("Department heavies," Jonesey muttered) and she looked seedy and second-rate. Jacket and slacks did nothing for a thickening figure and her hair needed grooming; she wore no makeup and strode like a drill sergeant. The idea of her seducing a David half her age, all those years ago last week, seemed a trick of memory, a nonsense, a never-happening. Yet she was not ridiculous, only unappetising and poorly kempt—and with it cold, disdainful and self-contained in a fashion that suggested something I had not been aware of before, a capacity for violence.

Santiago, standing between the screens, said, "Miss

Hazard, would you please take the second chair from the left in the front row?"

That left seats for one escort on either side of her. She saw me but not a muscle of her face stirred. She turned to her chair and sat down.

Behind them, as if balancing the Department men by some private wardenship of Belinda, came her doorman, Fred, who shifted the chairs on either side of her to make a space between her and her guards. The Group fussiness about contact with "people" was all-inclusive. (Except, memory told me . . . except when we two . . .)

Jonesey said, "I know that bloke. He gave me martial arts lessons when I first started out."

Fred brought his six feet of old brawler ambling across the floor to Jonesey. "Remember you, Percy."

My ears pricked and I didn't dare glance sideways at Jonesey. I wanted to laugh but I could feel his stiff resentment.

"Remember you, Fred."

Fred jerked a thick thumb at me. "You bodyguardin' this rabbit?"

Jonesey (Percy? Percival?) took my part with a degree of heat. "This rabbit has brought down some pretty big game."

"Has he, now?" He frowned severely on me. "I didn't like the looks of you, wearin' that slipster. Only shit carry them."

I gave him my friendliest smile. "Bang, you're dead!"

"Comic bastard! See yer, Percy." He ambled back to Belinda and took post behind her, leaning on the wall.

I said experimentally, "Percy."

Jonesey said with a suppressed rage that wasn't at all funny, "You need permission for that and you haven't got it."

Even euphoria can take a hint; he was the last person

I would want to push too far. He was, in an irrational, unreasonable sense the only solid rock in my existence. Beneath my brash state of mind was the knowledge that I needed him badly and a shadowy idea that Santiago had been urging that on me.

The next under escort was Armstrong, whom I had expected never to see again, stone-faced and making play of being oblivious to his guards—until the sight of Belinda shocked him. He could have been given no briefing and her presence frightened seven devils out of him. She stared blindly through her "lover"—or whatever he was or thought he was—but his face twitched and fell apart and recovered only with the effort of a self-controlled lifetime.

Santiago directed him to the middle of the front row (a starring role, stage centre?) and as he moved to it he saw me. It was not startlement that crumpled him but plain hatred of the instrument of his frustration. He came towards me like a man suddenly stricken with the toll of his borrowed years, joints stiff, loose jowls quivering, head thrust forward like a predator questing for a hold with its jaws. He blazed with the anger of arrogance dragged in the mud by a toy man.

He did not frighten me. Like everything and everyone concerned with Conrad he was far away in false time, all meaning leached out of him. He leaned over me and bent until his eyes were level with mine and I said, "Good evening, Mr. Armstrong."

He spat in my face. His astonished escort did not interfere but Jonesey's clamp of a hand closed over my arm. I said, "I wouldn't hit a hysterical old man."

Santiago answered for him, "Nor should you. He pays you the homage of fear and despair. Win graciously."

Armstrong might not have heard a word of that. He lumbered back to his seat, horribly aged.

A thought struck me. "Jonesey, do you think he knew what was in her studio all the time?"

"No. He still doesn't know. He'd have killed her to get it. He tried to kill you for less."

"So he did. I'd forgotten."

"The memory doesn't rock you?"

"No." He was both relieved and puzzled but I could not help him. I could not account for my mood or condition, only feel that Santiago had engineered them and I had no cause to care.

A stranger came in, a thin, unhappy man whose age I put at about seventy. He also was under escort but I could make no guess about him—but Armstrong knew him and was shocked for the third time. His malevolent eyes followed the poor devil who, after a terrified glance, refused to look at him but let himself be led to a seat in the second row where he hunched with his head in his hands.

"Who's that one, Jonesey?"

"Don't know. A bit of Sammy's dirty past. Looks as if the Super's been playing a game on the side."

I could imagine the Super arranging to trump his agents' leads and claim the kudos, playing Peter against Paul, robbing both and paying neither.

"Do you know what this is, Jonesey? It's an old-time detective story, where they get all the suspects together in the last chapter and play spot-the-killer."

"Which killer, lad? The place is alive with them—real, potential, professional and amateur."

"Which am I? Potential?"

"No; bungler."

"Well, it's all experience," I said, thinking myself airily sophisticated and smart.

The A Group four came in together, so alike despite the gender differences that you might have expected them to walk in lockstep. They marched to places in the back row, deadpan, paying attention to nobody—excepting my father, who halted by Belinda to say without much expression, "Only truth will serve you."

She answered clearly, "That pleases you?"

"You tried to kill me."

That was all. He followed the others to his chair; she stared at the empty screens. I thought, with a snigger, that I had heard the Groups in an intense emotional exchange fraught with meaning. God only knew what went on in their minds; in some subterranean manner of their own they must have raged and hated.

The Super, the entrepreneur, arrived—made an entrance—counted his captive audience and all but took a bow. He said, "Let's get this show on the road," and I couldn't hold back a snort of laughter. What a wonderful clown he was when you were no longer impressed by him. But it didn't pay to laugh too hard and his quick glance told me so.

He sat himself in the rear and Santiago began without preface, "We are to see a record of an interview between Belinda Hazard and David Chance, taken in her studio outside Melbourne."

Belinda was surprised into speech. "Record? The necklet . . ."

Behind her the Super said, "Not the necklet. We, too, have our professional tricks."

My father let loose the loud, contemptuous sound of a braying ass. You could never tell what might stir him but he had plainly had his fill of the Super.

The Super remained equable. "Quite so—*your* trick, Arthur. Carry on, please."

Santiago was precise and bland. "The presentation will not be straightforward. There will be questions, examinations, explanations. Therefore both the Superintendent and I have remote-control units with which to interrupt the screening when necessary." He looked thoughtfully round the room before he said, "This is a fact-finding, not an entertainment; therefore these proceedings are being recorded in toto."

I could not see the cameras; somebody had done a first-class job in a short time. And in toto meant business; what you did or said you were stuck with.

Santiago sat himself in the single vacant chair in the front row, next to myself, and started the twin tapes.

They began in midaction, both screens showing identical pictures, from the moment where in the studio I had remembered to activate my internal recorder, a David's-eye view advancing down a great space towards a figure—Belinda—at a distant canvas. My mouth said, like an echo of the past, "I expected to see your pictures here," and Belinda's turned back asked, "Why?"

Santiago put the screens on hold. "The reason for double screening will soon become apparent. The effect of seeing through David Chance's eyes is not an illusion; the system operates directly from the optic nerve complex and records by signal from the brain after receiving input. The results can be unexpected."

I fancied a tenseness in Belinda; she must have been dismayed. Not that I cared, I told myself, but the hands in my lap shook slightly. I was briefly conscious of a divided mind, part aware and part responding to buried impulses, vaguely sexual. It passed.

Our exchanges proceeded with the exactness of memory to the first mention of the gun. There Santiago used the hold. "This is a significant dialogue, the implanting of a crucial reference to be magnified later. A plan to murder Arthur Hazard was already in Miss Hazard's mind and here was the method, vicarious killing. The lady's very quick brain began the process of indoctrination from, so to speak, a standing start."

Belinda did not react; it was Armstrong who was newly upset. The Super would have given him no chance to confer with Belinda and possible revelations concerning himself must have loomed horrendously. He would have earned whatever came to him, I felt, and I would enjoy watching him writhe. From the depths of my mind a white spitefulness was rising.

The thin mystery man seemed untouched by what transpired on the screens; he remained sunk in his own miseries. Fred I caught frowning at the back of Belinda's head, and I nudged Jonesey. He looked and nodded and whispered that old Fred was no stranger to general wickedness but drew a prudish line at murder.

Prudish? Did he think that was funny? You never knew with Jonesey.

The tapes continued through the crazily offhand talk about killing my father. Came the mention of my mother: "He killed her. Or had her killed." My voice protested that he would have been caught and she answered, "He was."

The screens froze and the Super's voice asked conversationally, "Did you believe her, David?"

I was too unnaturally calm to be taken by surprise; I thought about it. "I'm not sure. It fitted my father's air of cold-bloodedness . . . that is, he often seemed . . . I could imagine him killing someone. I'm not sure what I thought."

I turned to face my father, who nodded placidly, then suddenly laughed at me. His idiot son!

The Super said, "He did not kill her; she died in childbirth. It was spur-of-the-moment thinking on Miss Hazard's part to plant an additional scrap of motive in your mind. As she planned events you would have no time to check the facts. Nor in the upshot, did you. Satisfied, David?"

"I'll believe what I see proved." He was another I would cheerfully see suffer a little. Or a lot.

"Wise. You can be shown the relevant records."

"I wouldn't trust your faked records from one line to the next." I was enjoying the animosity that had sneaked through Santiago's buffers.

The Super only raised his eyebrows. "Well, it's a two-faced world. Continue, Doctor."

Jonesey squeezed my hand, "Good for you," but the Super heard him and growled, "You're no better, Jonesey."

I surprised myself with a muted giggle. The show went on.

At mention of the legacy the Super announced, "We will hear more of that later."

Then Belinda and my screen presence discussed Sammy, and that mean-hearted bastard shrank in his chair. Then he braced himself and stared impassively at the screens. How it must have burned his soul to learn that through the years of fleshly desire he had been tricked into unconsummated ecstasy, had never once had her.

Then came the mention of the Library Access Cards and he knew he was lost.

Behind me the thin man made a soft, mewing sound. So that was where he came in: the plant operator, of course.

The screens froze. "Much mystery here," the Super announced, "with a simple solution. How were Library Access Cards, with their random identification implants, duplicated? Thought to be impossible. David guessed rightly that ex-Minister for Science Armstrong, honoured recipient of extended life treatments, obtained the patterns for Conrad Hazard of C Group. We were so blinded by the genius of that extraordinary youth that we wasted days wondering how, even with the pattern available, he could precisely position the molecular groups. Then we realised the obvious and interrogated the Magnetic Monitors of the time until we found the one who did the job. He simply turned back the progressions until he located

the required old patterns and punched out a new Card.
Right, Mr. Brandt?"

The terrified thin man quavered, "Yes, sir."

"Why did you do it?"

"Mr. Armstrong made me, sir."

"How?"

The victim was so frightened of Armstrong that he
could only stutter. Armstrong said with lazy contempt, "He
was engaged in small fiscal chicanery. I threatened exposure."

One up to Sammy. The implication was that he
thought himself too big to be touched or that the game was
so far down the drain that he might as well go down with
it, jaunty guns firing.

The Super chuckled. "And all for the love of Belinda!"
Armstrong shook through five seconds of torture and recovered. The Super continued, "I have arranged for the
machines to be rejigged so that turning back to previous
configurations will no longer be possible. False identities
are a luxury civilisation cannot afford." Love of probity
dripped from him like melting sugar. "Continue, Doctor."

The scene ran its course until my remark that "Conrad could drop his sexual fastidiousness when he wanted
something badly enough," unwittingly touched Belinda's
most vulnerable spot. The confession of her own illusory
seduction and bondage, spoken with polar cold, fell on the
air like ice splitting into words, frigidly factual as though
the years had rolled mercilessly over the sterile affair until
only the skeleton of memory remained. Her screen presence forced it out as though my jeer had opened a crevice
and all the weight of her shuttered misery had crept
through in icicle sentences.

Of the discomfort I had felt then, nothing remained.
Without pity I sensed the furies at work in her and loosed
a small devil of my own: "That Young Feller was a classy
womaniser for a eunuch who never had a woman."

She refused to hear me. Jonesey said, "Shut up, David. You should be ashamed of yourself."

Jonesey as a shocked old maiden aunt!

"I'm ashamed of nothing!"

Santiago said, "In time you will be."

Maybe, maybe. For the present I was satisfied with a thin, mean malevolence that wanted to draw blood from the helpless.

We moved now through Belinda's lecturette on scumble techniques and the white and yellow picture expanded to fill the screens as the David up there bent forward to examine them at close range—and that was the moment when he delivered himself into her power.

Curiously and quickly the nature of the picture on the right-hand screen changed. It took on the features of a close-up view of canyons and peaks and plains. The point of view moved across and round and down as in the vision of a bird flying over it at low altitude, following a flight path whose direction and necessity were not apparent. The sound was a low torrent of Belinda's incomprehensible murmuring.

That was what recollection told me I had seen and heard.

The other screen, on the left, held only the surface of a white and yellow canvas that moved slowly as that other David's sight slid meaninglessly over it.

That was truth, moved on that day to the periphery of my attention and now recovered. Another truth was on the sound track, not an indecipherable murmuring but Belinda's voice, crystal clear, inciting murder.

The real Belinda at the other end of the row said sharply, "I should not be required to watch this."

Oh, yes, she should!

The screens froze. The Super waited until the silence was unbearable before he said, "I suppose there are limits to mental torture. Take her out. To the next room will be far enough."

She left with unhurried dignity, the escorts following a pace behind. Fred started after them, then relaxed against the wall.

"Not accompanying your employer, Mr. Fellows?"

"Reckon I just tossed the job."

Jonesey breathed in my ear, "Fred would have been a tough operator if he hadn't been born with a queasy conscience."

What came next was ludicrous. It was also shameful and close to unbearable even to my blunted reactions and made plain why Belinda had feared to face the replay that showed her as a posturing, washed-out drama queen and me as a deluded buffoon. It was the stuff of comedy but unendurably unfunny and nobody laughed except, just once, the skinny Monitor who anyway was half out of his mind with terror of Armstrong and the Super and must have needed the relief of hysteria.

At first it was merely strange. The right-hand screen held my illusions and a murmuring; the left displayed the reality of the painting while Belinda's voice spoke directly into my ears, into my mind. Her slow, careful emphasis and choice of simple words were like unrelenting pressure against a membrane that must at last give way. Below my watching calm something rippled like a dreaming snake—peripheral memory returning to consciousness.

"David! Kill your father—for me. And for yourself. He is nothing to you, you are nothing to him. He despises you. To him you are human, of no account. He will throw you away as rubbish. Does he pretend affection? Yes, he does. Do not believe him. He loves only himself."

It was hard, cold stuff in plain, inescapable terms. Jonesey's hand closed on mine, protectively (or in case my conditioning broke?) and I pushed it away though in my mind a drowned dismay stirred and shuddered.

I caught Santiago's eye on me and made an effort to wink at him. He pursued his lips, not fooled.

"He hates you, David. He thinks he soils himself by touching you. Excrement on his fingers! Kill him for that! When you leave me, go straight to him. With your gun. Kill him for sending you here to steal a secret. He wants what I have and he sent you to me to find it. He makes you a thief!"

That was not what had happened but to her it must have seemed the logical deduction.

"I send you back to him with your gun in your hand. For what he has done to you. For the cold heart that murdered your mother. You had no love, no childhood. Take his life for the lives he took from your mother and yourself. For the cold heart that left you alone and belonging to no one. Kill him for that. And for me, for Belinda."

Though I was only attending a vidplay wherein someone else played the role of David Chance, his experience was creating resonances in me. I began to identify.

On the right-hand screen the cruising bird dived into the depth of the painting, into the spot of blood at its centre. The spot swelled to fill the screen, to become a crimson pit. In it swam my enchanted mind, clutched by a half-forgotten rapture while the cool imprinting of commands reached powerfully into deep places.

"Love is the colour of blood, David. Have you ever loved? You think you have but you have not begun yet. Conrad was my love." Her voice gathered warmth and more than warmth, a communicable heat and tremor. "That was enslavement. I will teach you that."

The warmth and tremor were remembered in my crotch; her voice promised and prepared.

"Conrad commanded. He was male beyond imagination. He took me with his mind and I was never free again.

He died but the chains persisted. Shall I show *you* such love, David?"

She was not on screen but the sound of her excited both Davids, the one who wanted and the one who watched. The sound of that other David's breathing broke from the screen in the harsh rhythms of readiness.

"With his mind alone he gave pain and ecstasy, orgasm beyond simple agony and pleasure. I shall teach you that. Now look at me. Look at me, young again and waiting."

I glanced across to Santiago, needing reassurance, and saw that he watched me, not the screens. He smiled encouragement and I attempted a weak grin that could have fooled no one.

On the right-hand screen the situation changed; Belinda stood face-to-face with me, the painting gone. She was the Belinda of Nursery days, seventeen, flowering. "Look down at your body, David. See, you are ready. Your clothes have gone."

And so they had. The scene dipped as he/I glanced down at my screen self naked and aroused. (A lazily working area of my mind saw that she made a statement and at once it was true, but I was too closely involved now to wonder at it.) The other screen showed me fully clothed still but the arousal, the erection, was patent and the Belinda standing eye to eye with me was ageing Belinda in painting smock, relentlessly talking.

"Your father killed the man who gave me love, David."

My voice spoke, strangled and slurred. "No, he did not do that." It must have been an element of reality in me not yet wholly subdued by her and on the screen of truth she frowned in swift impatience. My voice said despairingly, "He is my father," clinging to some basic need the divided mind was no longer capable of formulating.

"He hates you. He is nothing to you. Kill him. For that I will teach you love."

My raised hand came in view, reaching to touch her lips—in one screen the lips of desire retreating to tantalise, in the other the screwed lips of Belinda twitching her head away from contact, revolted. The view tipped as I looked down again to see her hand move to my groin and the picture jerked as I convulsed at the touch.

In fact her hand never touched me. On the other screen the handle of a paintbrush jabbed lightly.

Then I saw her for the first time whole—shoulders and breasts like pale silk in sunlight, the tender swell of stomach and the invitation of thighs. Up there I cried out, "Now! Now!" and down here his heat was replicated through my body.

But I saw also the painter in her streaked smock, mimicking the undulations of serpentine Lilith, grotesque in her concentration on the role, and I heard the sound of her demanding and demanding. "My love for his death; his death for my love. Promise me!"

The noise from the screen was my attempt to say, "Yes, yes!" to pledge anything for the offered gift.

"As soon as you see him you will remember your promise. Swear with your body!"

The jerking of the two pictures as my body ran its gamut of spasms was beyond natural orgasm; the sound of me was an animal in agony, rage and release.

It was no surprise that the enchanted David collapsed and the screens went blank.

I dropped my head because I was crying with the shame of ultimate trickery. And this was distanced, buffered reality! The experience itself must have been a descent into death; I could only hope it would never return in full strength to destroy me.

The rest, after I awoke on the couch, innocent and only vaguely troubled by vanished dreams, was anticlimax.

There was one moment of horror, but it was Armstrong's horror, when she spoke of his swindled years and of animals and the impossibility of soiling herself. He looked like something only half human on the edge of death.

That we were brothers in deception called for no pity from me. He had earned none.

I said shakily, "It's powerful stuff, Jonesey, but it means nothing." I was lying, pretending to myself and to the world that an imagined experience does not count, can not ravage and hurt. "It doesn't hurt as it could." That was true but just the same it hurt, and not trivially. I had been held up in front of an audience as a toy man to be played with.

Santiago said, "Your mind is strong enough; you will deal successfully with it."

I pulled myself together, remembering my audience and reaching for the insouciant line to cover the prat fall. "It must have been a hell of an experience—and all I got was starched pants." I looked for a victim and found Armstrong. "We've got something in common, Sammy—the girl who wasn't there."

Silence told me that was cruelty. He had been stripped of a far longer and deeper illusion than I.

It was Jonesey who did the needed thing and turned attention away from me by asking Santiago how it was done. Santiago said, "I don't know and I don't wish to."

The Super came down to the front to have his say. "It was B Group who developed the hypnotic painting technique early in their careers. Conrad must have showed her how to improve on it, to engage the deepest levels of attention."

Santiago differed. "The painting was a distraction engaging the superficial levels, diverting conscious attention from the real messages. I cannot guess how the visual illusions were commanded and I doubt that the lady could tell us. She probably followed instructions like an operator knowing that pressure on Button A will give suggestion A-plus."

"Ask her."

"No." He stared down the Super's glare. "The technique will be rediscovered when our mental sciences are competent to deal with it. Every new thing is not progress."

The Super, warned off expert turf, dropped the subject and turned to another tack. "Arthur Hazard, were you in fact responsible for Conrad's death and the C Group suicides, as that woman said?"

My father smiled as heads turned to the new focus. "She was guessing."

"But were you responsible?"

"Yes. Of course."

It was a statement, not a confession; he was a man who dealt in necessities, and necessities do not involve guilt. Armstrong growled unintelligibly; nobody else stirred.

"Intentionally?"

"I took a preventive action. The response was their own decision. It had nothing to do with elementary concepts of right and wrong." He bent his head to the Super with the quizzing expression of a benign uncle. "The suicides were a satisfactory result."

The Super did not waste time on hairsplitting and I wondered how much he already knew. He asked only, "Why?"

With his answer my father opened up the whole nest of serpents so that there could be no going back. He had what he wanted—the triptych—he knew he was safe as only a national treasure can be and he wanted the business settled and his workshop cleared of rabble. He said, "Because only a planetful of fools would have given Young Feller what he wanted and even Sam Armstrong wasn't that big a fool. Eh, Sam?"

In that moment Armstrong must have seen all he was

and all he had falling in wreckage, but he had courage to withstand disaster. He took his time answering and his throat pulsed once or twice before he managed a cool, "I took your advice."

My father chuckled, an ominous sound. "Speak up, Sam, and shame the devil. The devious politics of history will preserve your corrupt neck. Superintendent, get that besotted woman back here and we will unravel the matter. There will be no productive work done in this complex until we are rid of the pack of you."

The Super gave the sharp bark of a kelpie at the sheep's legs, not yet ready to nip. "Two men dead, your son driven to the edge of insanity, your own life saved by an accident of incompetence—and your thought is to get back to work."

The brothers and sisters, two sets of split peas, ex-changed glances and in their silent way reached agree-ment. One of the women (I could not distinguish Alice from Astrid) said with lunatic primness, "We have our livings to earn."

One of Armstrong's escorts tried to disguise laughter as a cough and the Super snapped at him, "Behave your-self, Barton! Go and bring Miss Hazard back here."

Nothing more was said until she returned, still-faced. She looked round the assembly as if to gauge attitudes, then sat. I called out, "There's the girlfriend, Sammy—the one who wasn't there."

The Super bellowed, "Shut your brat mouth!" and Jonesey said quietly, "Santiago's changed you and I don't much like what you've become."

"And fuck you too, Percy."

I shouldn't have said that but I wanted to hurt some-one, to extract payment, and I didn't care who paid. An-other reason I shouldn't have said it was Jonesey's open hand across my lips and teeth, rapping at least some sense of self-preservation into me.

Belinda, placidly, spoke the unexpected. "David has reason for anger. I owe him a debt for my use of him. I will have to pay it."

It was an eerie statement of their moral angle, compatible with our own but askew. The difficulty lay in recognising what the Groups' standards were. It was my father who had once said that Conrad would honour his debts. But what would Conrad have considered a debt?

The Super told her, "Probably so, Miss Hazard, but not here or at the whim of an ill-bred lout. I want questions answered, not scores settled. Arthur, you declare yourself the prime mover in this tangle. As I see it, you threw your minimally prepared son at Armstrong in the hope of learning—what? The location of Conrad's hypothetical legacy?"

My father answered in the patient tone of sanity informing a fool. "We hoped that his opportunities for rummaging and interviewing might produce new leads. He did better than hoped. Once the duplication of Library Access Cards came to light, the further inferences were obvious. The query remaining was the precise form of the legacy."

"You were sure it existed?"

"Why else should Conrad have spoken of creating gods from dogs? The listening nurse, Blaikie, told Armstrong, who, when matters became too warm for him, told me. We will come to his involvement in good time. The idea of symbolic paintings did not occur to us and Belinda told nobody, even Armstrong, until she showed them to David. She showed him because she wanted me to die with the useless knowledge just beyond my grasp."

"And David? Surely you didn't have him educated just for this—this escapade?"

"I had maintained some sporadic curiosity in his intellectual development but had concluded that his manipulated genes were recessive, unexpressed. Then he showed aptitude for a profession useful for our purpose at a time when we were sufficiently prepared to undertake the search for the legacy. Aptitude was sufficient where a finely tuned brain might have led to indiscretion. I tried to use filial emotion to ensnare his cooperation and must admit a partial failure there; my affectation of parental interest was arduous and not altogether successful."

I grinned at him with fine carelessness. (But my damned hands shook again; responses deep down were readying agonies for the future.) I needed a wisecrack but could only hold the inane grin.

The Super asked, "Did it take you twenty-five years to become, as you say, sufficiently prepared?"

"Yes."

"It seems a long time."

"A necessary time. We had to know enough of the biological sciences to understand whatever we found, and we do not have C Group intellects. The learning had to be done in what time we could spare from work. We had, as my sister pointed out, livings to earn."

A quarter century of . . . homework. The Groups could not be judged by rational standards. The Super seemed bemused as he said, "Go on, please."

"As you know, we had left the Nursery and so were no more aware of Conrad's flight than any other member of the public. Until he made an error. Consider: Using the skills Conrad taught her, Belinda held Armstrong subject and used him to obtain the Access Cards. Had I known that, instead of having to wait a generation for the information, little of this fuss and scurry would have been required. But Armstrong did not trust me so far even when he was forced to apply to me for help. Why should he, who trusted nobody? But now he found he was to be used again, this time to open to Conrad a conduit to power and authority, and he had the sense to be afraid of what might follow. That was Conrad's error but not, I think, culpable; he lacked essential knowledge of the human mind."

A whining, grunting noise from Armstrong stopped the soulless recital; he hunched forward, clenching his hands on his knees. Belinda said tiredly, "I must pay for him also, in some fashion."

The Super was impatient. "Settling guilts and payments is my affair." Little god Super! "Go on, man."

"Conrad needed access to governmental prerogative and largess; he needed assistants, a laboratory and huge amounts of money. He was, I think, desperate. He was barely twenty years old, intellectually prodigious though not yet at his optimum capacity, but he was suffering pains of physical and emotional development; he had not attained the self-control of maturity and his emotional comprehension was empiric and limited. I read him as half-mad with loneliness and the horror of human surroundings, an intellect striving for balance in a bedlam. He made an error of haste because he had reached the limit of his tolerance of isolation among beasts."

That word too many roused a spasm of resentment in his audience and Santiago had to quiet them. Already used to the idea, I was tempted to laugh and it may have been as well for me that I did not.

My father listened, waited and added serenely, "I use the term advisedly, receive it how you will. To continue: Conrad conceived an offer that seemed to him irresistible and used the only available contact that could reach the top echelons of power—Armstrong, who knew everybody who mattered and had considerable powers of argument and coercion. That error killed him, with my help and Armstrong's. Let him tell it."

He was insufferable in his arrogance, his assumption that the secret-hiding State would visit no consequences on him. But why did he throw Armstrong to the dogs? Contempt? Some private sense of justice deferred? There is so much about them that we will never fathom.

Armstrong said softly, "You animal!" and came out of his chair like an invalid groping for aid. Barton put out a hand to help him and had it slapped away. Armstrong in misery and rage looked something like his true age. He turned to face us all, dredging up a memory of dignity.

"I talk better on my feet. Always did. I made history in my day and now I'll tell you some of it. I'm not on trial here and you'll all thank me for my treatment of Conrad, the cunning Young Feller. Even you, you vanity-stricken, half-Abo keyhole snooper."

The Super murmured with carrying distinctness, "You were born in the gutter and you never got out of it."

"Shut your trap while I'm speaking!"

I could have admired Sammy a little if it hadn't been such a puerile exhibition. His kind can usually find a big gesture when there's nothing left to lose, but this was mere spitting. But that unexpected flash did shut the Super up.

"Conrad told Belinda what he wanted and she told me. He didn't come to me directly because he knew that using his persuasive tricks on me could result in inhibiting my free action and cause mistakes. He wanted money and the talents of others for what he called the donkey work, and he saw that both could be achieved through the good offices of a practical politician who knew the soft flesh of the frightened who could be bruised, and the avarice of those who could be bought with promises—a man who knew the back alleys of politics that Conrad couldn't learn because the textbooks don't exist. If he'd tried to run me he'd have made a hash of it through sheer ignorance."

He looked down at Belinda, who ignored him. A hint of forcing entered his speech.

"I promised her I'd do it because I'd have promised her a palace on the moon if she'd asked for it. She didn't have to play picture games with me; at twenty she really was what Simple Simon over there thought he saw. I know now that she only turned to trickery when it came time to pay a bedtime instalment to keep me snuffling at her skirts. And it took me till tonight to learn that. Twenty-five years!"

He ground it out, suffering alone with no Santiago to buffer him against loss and degradation.

The Super prompted, "The demand!"

"I told you: money, assistance, a laboratory—and total control. Australia had created him and his sibs and left them to rot in an intellectual desert, so it owed them help. His Group was moral about debts; he didn't believe me when I told him that governments equate morality with necessity and opportunity. In his view that sort of thinking would wreck any system overnight. With his straight thinking, it probably would. But we're the products of evolution, aren't we, Superintendent? We adapt as fast as moral niches appear. Yet Conrad thought we would give him what he wanted, particularly if he threw in some goodies as well. Can you guess the bottom line of what he wanted? How about you, Honourless Jonesey?"

An expressionless Jonesey had the answer: "Company, a nurseryful of his kind. He'd spent eighteen months learning how to breed them and now he wanted the cash and the hardware for the job."

"You're a born two-timer, Jonesey; you read dirty minds and serve who frightens you most. Yes, he wanted a colony of C Groupers, an island in the ocean where they could live without ever having to see shit like us again. Perhaps he didn't credit a human mind with savvy to see past the demand; he was contemptuous but the fact is that he understood us about as well as we understand monkeys. There's a joke about brains in that if you can work it out. And there was a sweetener: In return for all he needed he would show us how to make all sorts of subtle adjustments to wipe out genetic malfunctions before birth, to adjust mental shortfalls, to increase learning capacity and grow better bodies, all without the hit-or-miss antics of our kindergarten experts. A supermarket selection.

"I had left active politics but I was still a Nursery consultant and I had the contacts to brace a couple of Cabinet Ministers and enough others to swing the deal. On sight, the deal was practicable. But I had enough nose to smell the rat in it. Like: What will they do when they want something their island can't provide—such as room to expand? Maybe morality was Conrad's bond but his morality wasn't ours; it might contain all sorts of letouts for double-dealing—just as ours does. Like, circumstances alter cases. If so, we could be a finished race, missing from history, in a couple of generations. I went to the only people who knew enough to advise and who would talk to me because of my administrative responsibility for much of their immediate future, A Group. Confiding in Belinda was out of the question; she thought the sun shone out of Conrad's arse. It happened that I picked out Arthur and Arthur said: *'Don't do it; give him nothing.'* Now let the self-satisfied bastard tell you what he told me."

My father pinned him with a dart of placid contempt. "You need not fear her; it was me she tried to kill. You are nothing. I will make your confession for you."

Armstrong tumbled into his seat, this time glad of Barton's arm. And she? She contemplated her hands in her lap, perhaps considering her moral debts and what currency might serve for payment.

My father said, "I gave him three pieces of advice. First, that he confront Conrad directly, because passing the refusal through Belinda would only set her to changing his mind for him. Second, that he have others present at the meeting because no single human being—I use the term for lack of a better—could face Conrad alone. I reasoned that even he could not sway more than one at first contact, that there had to be a period of study, of sizing up.

I was right; we know now that though he could use sex for a crude, poleax attack, depth control such as he used on the luckless Farnham required study and gentle persuasion. Third, the request must be met with point-blank refusal.

"Armstrong had the wit to be frightened; he insisted that I make one of the confronting party. I was uneasy about that but I could not allow him, corrupt and criminal though by then I knew him to be, to face alone a confrontation I had wished upon him. Sensibly, he included also the Chief Psychologist from the Nursery, knowing that the man would concede nothing and would stay quiet afterwards for his own guilty sake. We knew now what had been done in the Nursery. A fourth member, Superintendent, was your predecessor of the year 2022. Search his files and you will find no record of the meeting. Confidential authority breeds its own corruption.

"No comment? Well, we had a guard of Departmental agents because we feared this man. Only your problematical God knows what he might have become in maturity. We met at a small country hotel whose proprietor would not dare to talk. Conrad came alone. He entered the room and, seeing me and the Chief Psychologist, knew that he had failed. I saw the minute change in him as he discarded his plan. He sat down and waited in silence. Perhaps he wondered how the dog pack reasoned in its ragged fashion, or what more he might have offered to tempt it, but he said nothing. He did not open his mouth from beginning to end, then went away without comment or question. We could only let him go. Use of physical force might have meant dead men and shooting him was not to be thought of; if his sibs found out there was no knowing what they might do. In any case, he returned to the Nursery some three weeks later—the time, I presume, needed for the painting of Belinda's triptych. There he conferred with his sibs and joined them in suicide."

He paused on that and when he spoke again his manner, his voice, the entire projection of him had altered. Imagine the grief one feels for the destruction of a perfect artefact and at the same time the recollection of a traumatic event, recollection with a sense of rightness that was not righteousness, and you will be groping towards the reality of the emotional power revealed behind his blandness.

"I recall the moment of their deaths. Half the length of the State distant from them, I heard them go, the psychic sound of them cease. They were the finest creations ever produced by man but this was not their place or their time. It was best that they should go."

There was a hush for the strangeness of it, the regret for a marvel gone from the world but none for his part in their destruction. Yet I think he knew the enormity of the crime better than any of us and also the necessity for it.

The Super was not an impressionable man; harshly and impatiently he broke the spell. "The reasoning, man! The reasoning! You, Armstrong, did you do the talking? Then out with it!"

Armstrong did not stand; he sounded very tired. "We didn't want his genetic gifts. Project IQ had been a stupid error because our experts did not properly know what they fumbled with and the rest of us were urged by dreams. We preferred now to let evolution do its own work. Conrad could too easily steer us in directions he required for purposes we had not the knowledge to guess. We didn't trust him and I told him so. Anything created must be for our good, not his, and we wanted no more of his kind. They were of no use to us; we could not communicate, so where was their value? We needed progress, not entanglements. As for his refuge far from the dirty world, did he imagine we believed a word of that? Give them seclusion and time and they would come bursting out to twist the planet to their needs. Their island would be a plotting base—so there would be no island. Conrad was to return to the Nursery and stay there. And a threat: Another breakout and we would hunt them down and be rid of them forever. That's what I told him."

Not a word about immortality, you notice. That nasty idea was invented by my father, much later, to fuel Sammy's searching.

As to Sammy's answer to Conrad . . . perhaps his claim that we would thank him for it was just. I've had years to mull it over and I feel that between them they did what they must.

And yet the Super said regretfully, almost dreamily, "He should have waited. I would have waited. Thought. Planned."

So even the possibility of power corrupts. *Quis custodiet . . . ?*

My father gave the cackling bark that passed for laughter. "In the knowledge that an overt move would see a planet of ten billions alerted against you? He knew better than to wait on a miracle. The dogs did not want gods and only a lifetime of yapping from the kennels awaited C Group; the mindless noise was to be their hell on earth. They preferred not to be driven insane. They went away."

He hesitated, frowning, and we waited for him. "But how can I know this? I can only guess at how they would have borne life in the dog pound. I only suggest that what has not been easy for us would have been unendurable for them. Or, perhaps, they had reasons beyond the reach of my thinking, transcendental reasons. Be glad they went."

Belinda turned in her chair and they stared at each other, green on green, betraying nothing. Assessing? Threatening? I have no idea. He had been responsible for the death of her life's love—the love that had thought nothing of her, used her and repaid her with the same sterile illusions she had passed on to Armstrong and to me.

It was not the stuff of which great romances are made; the ingredients were finally acid and emetic. And yet . . .

It was he who dropped his eyes. Recognising her right to hatred? Perhaps.

The Super said, "The record of this meeting will be filed and forgotten. History will find it in its own good time. For the present, none of you needs to be reminded of the provisions of the various Secrecy Acts. Observe them. Speak out of turn and they will be invoked—with rigour. Stay quiet; there has been enough suffering. In terms of civil law, David Chance is entitled to file suit against Samuel Armstrong for conspiracy to murder, but I advise against it."

He waited.

My mood was uncaring. "I'm alive. That will do."

"And you, Mr. Armstrong, will do well not to attempt revenge in any form against any person."

Armstrong shot him a moody glance, nodded and looked away.

The Super grinned at him with no kindness. "Now, with old scandals disposed of, we can stop licking our lips and get to the real business of this meeting, the matter of Conrad's legacy, the pictures from Miss Hazard's studio. They are at present in a storeroom of this building, where they will stay for the moment."

My father said, "They are not. I burned them."

I swear to a hiatus wherein time stopped. Those six words were monstrous.

The Super was struck silent, unbelieving.

I may have been the only person present who at once believed. It was so much a part of my growing comprehension of the world that the end of my quest—rite of passage through double faces, double tongues, double deeds—should have been a bonfire of the prize. I might have wept if there had been anything in me but anger. (Deep down some small thing worried, possibly a promise of tears hereafter.)

Belinda stood and faced my father. She whispered, "You could not!" There was desolation in her voice and more than desolation, a draining away of the need for living.

He made the strangest answer, folding his hands under his chin as if for prayer, closing his eyes and saying like a man called to judgment, "It was necessary." He was abject, confessing sin, asking forbearance. "Sooner or later their existence would have become known. Peace would have been ended for you, for us, for mankind." His voice grovelled, pleading a cause. "They could not be allowed to persist, to tempt and betray."

She shrieked on a note that broke downwards into a choked roaring in a constricted throat and started towards him, pride and restraint gone by. He got to his feet, hands outstretched to ward her off while his green eyes begged for understanding. It was not needed. She froze in midstep, breathing animal pantings, and dropped to her knees in a collapse that must have bruised and shaken her, and fell forward onto her face to batter on the floor with hands and head. The sound of her was grief from the pit.

Santiago reached her before the hapless escort could decide whether or not to break the ban on touching. He lifted her head and sharply knocked her unconscious. His inside pocket opened on a travelling arsenal of emergency equipment from which he selected a phial and a small syringe. In seconds she was breathing normally.

"Put her to bed."

There followed a silly comedy of indecision while the escort dithered and A Group watched stonily, refusing to move. Santiago said, "Oh, for God's sake!" gathered her up and carried her out of the room.

The Super, with hell in his eyes, beckoned Barton. "Check the paintings."

The men went out. My father said, "I do not lie. Misdirect, yes, but never lie. *She* knew that."

Barton came back. "Gone, sir." He showed a small scrap of smudged canvas. "Quite a large fire, sir. Bits of frame is mostly all."

The Super swung unsteadily on my father and rested his hand on a chair back, reaching for calm, close to outbreak. "I suppose that now you'll claim to owe the woman some fresh debt for cruelty and outrage!"

My father nodded. "It is not payable. I cannot explain to you the remorselessness of an imprinted love. I destroyed the only thing she had of him. If Conrad had foreseen the end of his meddling with minds, the outcome might have been otherwise."

"That's your burden; you carry it. But why so violent a gesture when we have David's reproduction in fine detail?"

"You have not."

The Super reared, literally, like a horse struck across the muzzle. "The tapes!"

"This evening I set a magnet in the winding core. The tapes cleared as they were exhibited."

"You must be mad!" His mouth fell open and his head shook. Then he roused to point, like a hunting dog, at me. "They can be recovered from his head." But there was uncertainty in his voice.

"Superintendent, I am a bio-electronician, not a house-wiring tradesman. The recording material on David's bones is organic with a minimal dispersion of monomolecular iron. Most of it has been absorbed in the past four days. It is no longer possible to recover the record."

The Super glared like a man demented. My father continued in his toneless way, dealing out his pitiless style of honesty. "The circuits were not designed for permanence; I would not leave you so insidious a surveillance weapon. You may think you could be trusted with it—for your country, right or wrong! I do not think so. Few humans could be trusted with it and your profession ensures that you are not one of them." His lips formed the faint smile that I had learned to recognise as contempt. "Why should you care, man? Are you another with a hankering to live forever?"

Whether or not that struck deep, the Super was a professional. He let go of the chair back and stood straight. "Individual greeds and reasons are not important. It was knowledge. Men died in the search for this thing; at least one went insane in the events that led to it while others have had their lives twisted and ruined. Yet you destroyed it."

"I said once that Conrad might have left behind him a time bomb. I have had several days in which to study the triptych and now I know that he did."

"So *you* know. It's *your* time bomb now."

"No. I do not have total recall. I could no more reproduce the thousands of points of detail of the painting than breathe vacuum. But I have broadly understood them. We four studied for many years in order to be able to understand, and when we saw what was there we agreed that Conrad's work must be destroyed."

The Super was ugly, a brute in need of a victim. "Why? For sweet humanity's sake? Will you tell me it was for love of the lunatic world?"

"Your sweet humanity has a future; we two Groups have none. When we die, Project IQ will be ended. Then you may wipe yourselves off your planet by your own effort if you must but not because we left you the means and the temptation to do it." His mouth assumed the shadowy smile. "You spend your lives evading your elaborate moral systems; it is your good fortune that we practise ours."

The Super sat, suddenly defeated.

I was all at once sick to the gut of my father's posturing, of his assumption of righteousness. The anger that Santiago had left in me (after all, he had to leave something) spilled over. I called out, "Full marks for foolproof vanity! Now let's have some truth about this legacy that a little child might read but your cold-blooded intellect never could. But did. Explain that!"

He did not so much as look at me. "You are a moron and spiteful with it. Conrad meant that an open mind would see what an educated intellect stuffed with certainties would reject. This was, to us, no more than accepting his version of genetic connectivity and suppressing the contra indications we had previously taken for facts. We found his conclusions beyond argument." He was silent through long seconds, with a hand raised asking us to wait for him, until he said with something like an honesty he resented having to face, "I have made the study sound easy. It was not. Ridding the mind of clutter requires an ... unimpeded ... mentality. Humility is not a simple thing. Achieving it was a harsh discipline. Your scientists would have understood eventually but by then their capacity for uninformed experiment might already have meant the end of you."

This was not simple confession; it was laced with puzzlement. It occurred to me only much later that he was admitting to a lack of those feelings that interfere with clear thinking—the passions—and that he was the less thereby, that an untrammelled intellect is not a total blessing. The austerities of a mind embracing only small, balanced, contollable emotions must be formidable. An infinite inner solitude ...

He began again, strongly. "The human genome had been thoroughly mapped early in the century, but that was only a beginning. A map, say of the world, shows only a surface, tells nothing of the third dimension of plate tectonics, lithosphere temperature-variation mechanics, asthenosphere convection flow or even ocean current fluctuations. So with gene topology. What Conrad provided for Belinda's triptych was the underpinning, the set of theorems linking the map with the mechanics and mathematics of organic development. He gave the definitive description of genetic interaction and adaptation—as distinct from evolution, which is a more vagrant process than the word implies.

"He showed that genetic interference by technological means must be in the main counterproductive. There is what you may think of as an ecological system of intelligence. In it, only a mind evolved to fit its surroundings can survive intact; manipulation of the genetic factors governing intelligence risks the production of misfits out of their time and place. Such as C Group. The present human IQ range is culturally manageable; mutual understanding across the range is practicable, even at the lunacy fringe. Breeding super-intellects is possible but useless; there can be no mutual understanding. I cannot speak for B Group but my own Group, only marginally differently organised from the racial norm and without the disadvantage of vastly superior intellects, have considered death and rejected it. That we feel constrained to endure is a moral decision based on self-responsibility. It is complex and it is a measure of the gulf between us. Leave it at that.

"Physical manipulations are equally possible and equally unwise. Too many characteristics are interdependent; one change leads remorselessly to an unintended other, to abnormality of limb structure and muscle leverage, to marrow-deficiency problems, glandular imbalance and undesirable sensory divagations. And to reproductive dead ends. Change is best left to the slow forces that preserve and discard without upsetting the intellectual and physical ecologies."

I don't know what the Department men made of all

this; possibly nothing. Of the others, bully-boy Fred seemed totally bemused while Santiago listened with a sort of courteous approbation, as though any right-thinking man should have reached the same conclusions without the necessity of a lesson in genetics. Jonesey simply listened, a professional gathering data. Only the Super seemed *mutinous*. It is the only word I have to express what looked like a raging rejection of the failure of a need for miracles.

Then my father gave him matter really to rage over—the total death of dreams.

"As for Mr. Armstrong's carrot, immortality, it is a donkey's meal. In a system that depends on death and birth for its operation, immortality is nonsense. Conrad's theorems confirm it. A vastly extended life span is attainable—and that is Conrad's murderous joke, his farewell to the donkeys who would eventually decipher it and take the idiot risk of reaching for the carrot. He built a very human nastiness into the last panel; perhaps your treatment of him shattered all pity. The panel stressed the simplicity of manipulation but most subtly hid the cost. We found it because we suspected something of the kind, but we had to peer closely. Conrad thought that a transparent greed for life, like Mr. Armstrong's, would reach for it without caring for anything but the splendid, blinding fact.

"The methods vary. In most of them the price is sterility or teratological deformity. In some, prenatal cancer is inbuilt, basic to the helix and ineradicable. At this stage in man's career longevity—save by such regular medical props as presently preserve your Honoured few like pickles in a jar—is only a useless flourish. Conrad's legacy was at best a mockery, at worst a deranged joke. He surely did not foresee that it would be preserved as a holy relic by Belinda whom he depended on to exhibit it. The joke has been on Conrad and now it is over. Laugh if you can."

The joke was, in the end, on all of us who had danced

to my father's string pulling, most savagely of all on the woman who had hoarded it in secret and betrayed it for a bungled revenge.

There was one thing more. "It would be well, Superintendent, if your Department used its so subtle lines of international communication to warn those experimental biological teams in Egypt and China what the outcome of uninformed programming may be."

He swept his shining, empty gaze around the whispering room and spoke his farewell: "We wish that you would all go from here now and leave us to our work."

He did not wait for an answer, but followed the other three who were already moving towards the door.

The Super, with his mouth opening on anger, moved to intercept them but Santiago stopped him. "Take time to think, man. You can find them anytime. They'll be here; they have nowhere to go. To them one place is the same cultural desert as any other."

It was an epitaph.

It was also the crux I had waited for. I made myself wait a little longer while the four of them made their way through the room like clockwork figures, not looking to right or left of themselves, business concluded and giving not a damn what any confused humans might think.

As my father reached the door I called out, "Not so fast, Daddy-man!" in a voice that cracked with a whole bent lifetime of malice and brought every eye in the room round to me. They must have thought I was out of my mind. I certainly was not completely in it.

He halted, would have moved on, changed his mind and turned slowly to face me. I fancied that for a second he was apprehensive. He had reason. I panted as I half ran, half stumbled the ten paces or so between us and hard determination must have shown in my face. Reasonably or not, I knew exactly what I was about.

I stopped at just the right distance from him, drew a long breath to take control of my voice and asked, "Is this the finish, Father dear Father? Without farewell?"

I waited deliberately while he contemplated my shaking anger, because I meant to force speech out of him and when he smiled faintly I knew I had succeeded, because I knew by then what his smiles meant.

He nodded slowly. "Without ritual."

I asked, "But are you sure you have done with me? Have you recouped the mean outlay on my upbringing, taken full compensation for the dreary impersonation of parenthood, squeezed the last usefulness out of me?"

Where anyone else would have been brusque and wary, he simply answered, "Yes."

"Then, in the terms of your ethic, you owe me."

"I know it." He was quite serious. "I am more aware of it than you can ever be."

It was my moment. "Well, then," I said, "I'm going to cancel the debt for you," and I hit him with all my strength precisely where I had planned, in the throat, driving that protruding lump of cartilage back into his gullet. It was the most exhilarating instant of my life.

He fell back, choking and clawing at his neck, into the arms of a phlegmatic Fred, while Jonesey grabbed me by the shoulders and shook the sense half out of me while he ground furiously into my ear, "You could kill a man that way if you had enough muscle."

"I meant to kill him."

He turned me around until he could look into my raging eyes, and burst into laughter at some enormous comedy. "Rabbit," he said, "you've botched it again. It takes practice as well as power."

All my ignorance and incompetence and self-doubt came up to my eyes in a flood and like a frustrated brat I cried for my innocence and brashness and stupidity while

Santiago's words came through to me in equable assessment. "Take him home, Jonesey. He's had a bad time but he'll come out of it in a day or two."

And that is just what happened, with all the world ahead of me and a whole life to live.

I never saw my father again.

ENVOI: DEBTS AND PAYMENTS

It was all long ago and now that we have permission to publish, because all those who could be hurt are dead, it hardly seems worthwhile. Still, there is a media man's compulsion to tie off loose ends.

Armstrong died soon after that night at CAG 3. Perce (*never* Percy) says he died of creeping uselessness but I sometimes wonder did the Super exert pressure "through channels" to have his treatments terminated. He had been in a mood to hurt someone and Armstrong was a victim within reach.

My father's warning about inbuilt genetic weaknesses was driven swiftly and unpleasantly home when Belinda and her sibs came down with a virulent, galloping variation of Alzheimer's disease that killed them in months.

They died in sudden senility, legally incompetent and intestate. So the witch woman's debts remained unpaid. Or did they? What she did to Armstrong may have been life's payment to him for being what he was. And I suppose she served a purpose in bringing my inturned self-love to the mirror it needed. She also gave me weeping nightmares for years.

*   *   *

I married Perce's daughter, Janice, so I am now able to call him "Dad," which he resents as a sniggering trick of fate and the eminent Dr. Santiago.

Janice has given me a daughter in whom the most minutely scrutinised genetic scans can find no mischievous fault. "Sport" variations breed out very quickly.

All this is by the way. What marks the real full stop is that my father and his Group all died within a few weeks of each other, he last, just ten days ago. They died suddenly of a multiplicity of simple causes all peaking together. "As if," said one of the examining physicians, "a genetically fixed term had been reached and at the right time they stopped living."

Be that as it may, my father paid his debt.

I am the sole heir to millions that are still in process of being traced and estimated.

He left me a message also, a single sheet of paper addressed simply, "David."

It read: "Violence cannot cancel indebtedness; it can only create a debt for the violent."

He meant that I had not made restitution to him for the final insult.

What should I do about it? Devote his money to Good Works? That I will not; I will spend and enjoy the spending. Whatever he may have thought himself to be, I am human and fallible and not much troubled by the immorality of living on unearned wealth.

Yet I sometimes try to guess what, at the heart of him, drove and justified. Did he finally hold me in contempt or did he, as Perce has suggested, drive me away because he knew himself inadequate to bridge the gap of attitude and intellect, seeing that he would do me more harm than good?

And could I—older now and more clear-sighted and less self-centered—have taught him something of the humanity he could not discover in his bleak, utilitarian mind?

There is no way of knowing.

The questions nag, and always will.